The Dragon King

Book 2

Emma T. Shannon

ISBN: 979-8-9898487-6-8

E-book ISBN: 979-8-9898487-7-5

Description: First edition. | United States, 2025. | Series: The Emerald Sea Saga; Book 2

Text is set in Garamond

Cover designed by Asterielly Designs | asteriellydesigns.com

Map and interior images by Emma T. Shannon

Published by Emma T. Shannon

Created with Atticus

Dedicated to my littlest brother Finn.

Here's a pirate fact for you: Captain Avery's treasure is still missing.

Let's go find it, buddy.

Also by Emma T. Shannon

Song of the Hollow Duology
Song of the Hollow
Storm of the Gods

The Emerald Sea Saga
The Lost Moon

Le Cirque de la Rue
The Dreammonger

CONTENTS

Content Warning	IX
Author's Note	XI
Map	XII
Map	XIII
Glossary	1
Prologue	5
Part One	13
1	15
2	29
3	41
4	59
5	72
6	89
7	98
8	110
9	123

10	138
11	156
12	169
13	183
Part Two	197
Interlude	199
14	203
15	214
16	228
17	246
18	263
19	278
20	293
21	311
22	326
23	339
24	354
25	372
26	384
27	394
Part Three	401

28	403
29	423
30	436
31	449
Epilogue	456
Acknowledgements	461
Chapter	463
About the Author	465

Content Warning

Author's Note

There is a cat in this book. While I cannot guarantee the safety of any human characters, I can promise you the cat (who is named after one of my childhood cats) survives until the end of the series. She might not get her dinner at the exact minute she expects it and will be kicked out of her sleeping spots, but she will remain alive and unscathed (even if she thinks she's starving to death because she hasn't eaten in thirty seconds). All future animal companions are also guaranteed to survive. The humans, though? No promises there.

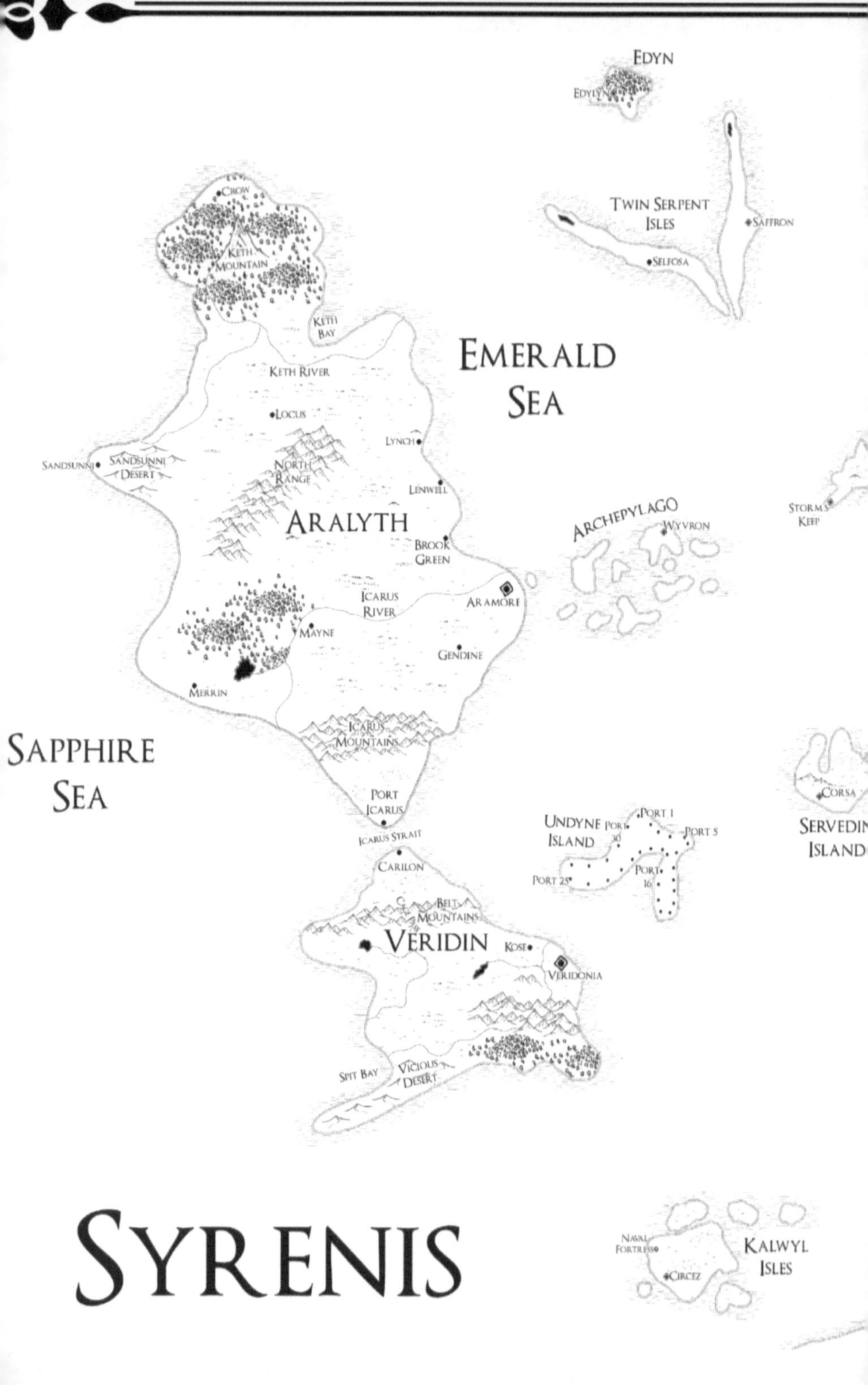

EDYN
EDYLYN
TWIN SERPENT ISLES
SAFFRON
SELFOSA
CROW
KETH MOUNTAIN
KETH BAY
KETH RIVER
EMERALD SEA
LOCUS
LYNCH
SANDSUNNI
SANDSUNNI DESERT
NORTH RANGE
LENWELL
ARALYTH
ARCHEPYLAGO
WYVRON
STORM'S KEEP
BROOK GREEN
ICARUS RIVER
ARAMORE
MAYNE
GENDINE
MERRIN
SAPPHIRE SEA
ICARUS MOUNTAINS
CORSA
PORT ICARUS
UNDYNE ISLAND
PORT 1
PORT 30
PORT 5
SERVEDIN ISLAND
ICARUS STRAIT
PORT 25
PORT 16
CARILON
BELT MOUNTAINS
VERIDIN
KOSE
VERIDONIA
SPIT BAY
VICIOUS DESERT
NAVAL FORTRESS
CIRCEZ
KALWYL ISLES
SYRENIS

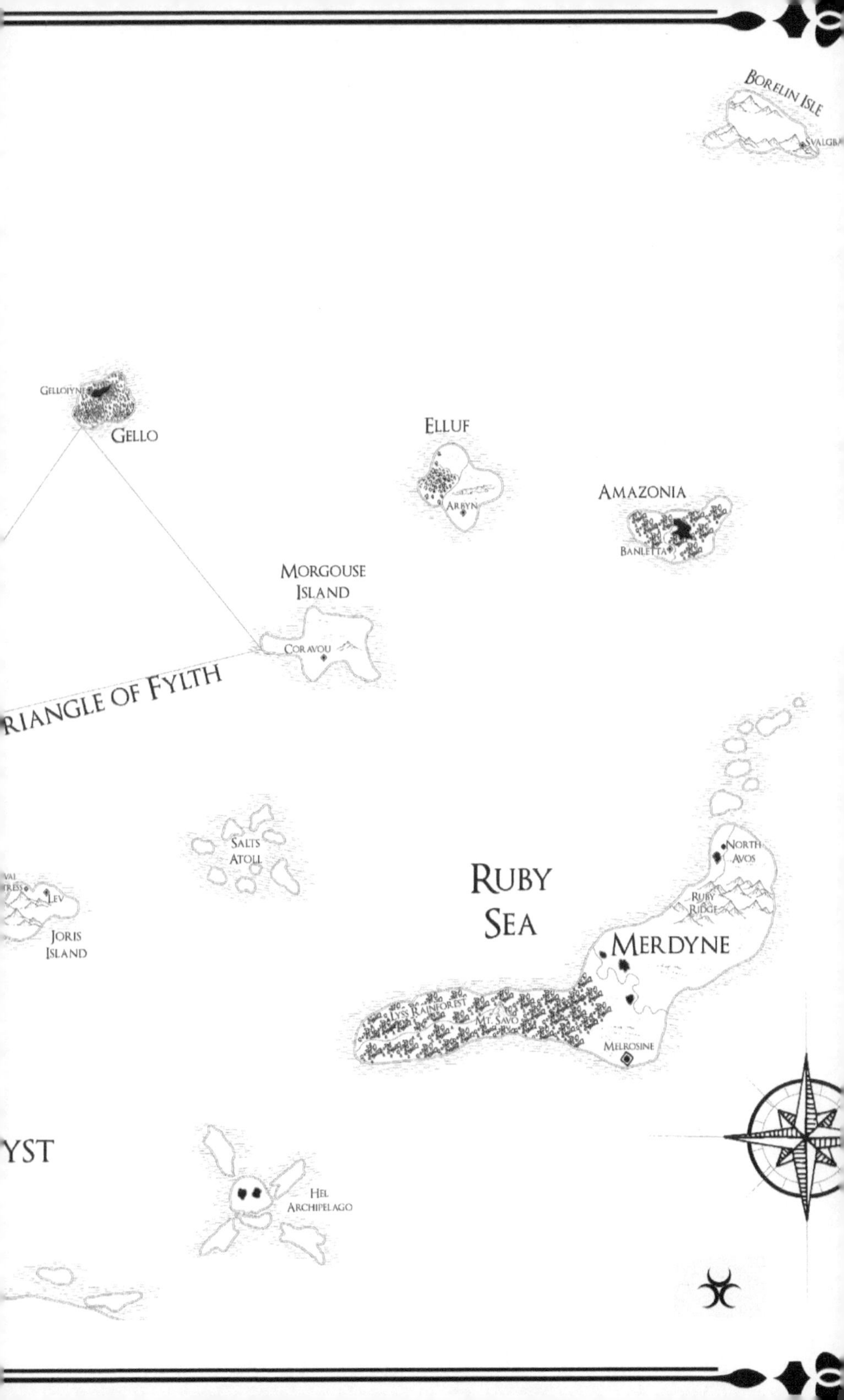

BORELIN ISLE
SVALGB
GELLOIYNE
GELLO
ELLUF
ARBYN
AMAZONIA
BANLETTA
MORGOUSE
ISLAND
CORAVOU
RIANGLE OF FYLTH
SALTS
ATOLL
VAL
RESS
LEV
JORIS
ISLAND
RUBY
SEA
NORTH
AVOS
RUBY
RIDGE
MERDYNE
LYSS RAINFOREST
MT. SAVO
MELROSINE
YST
HEL
ARCHIPELAGO

GLOSSARY

The Four Ruling Powers

The Aralyth Empire

Emperor: Castros Helios

Empress: Mary Jolene Helios

Heir: Anwir Helios

Other Family Members: Iori Helios (second born), Faye Helios (third born)

The Merdyne Empire

Empress: Nefeli Catrione

Heir: Cleo Catrione

Other Family Members: Alis Mila (royal advisor)

Previous Rulers: Moira Catrione (deceased), Ambrosino Catrione (deceased)

The Veridin Kingdom

King: Argos Smythe

Queen: Lydia Smythe

Heir: Elios Smythe

Other Family Members: Connor Smythe (second born), Juno Smythe (third born), Haru and Vivian Smythe (fourth and fifth born)

<u>The Kingdom of Gello</u>
King: Algernon Keats
Queen: Roisin Keats
Heir: Leianora Keats

<u>The Gods</u>
Poet: God of the sand, sea, and sky.
Dreamer: Goddess of the earth, trees, and life.
Lady Lightbringer: Goddess of war, justice, and strength. Patron goddess of the navy.
The Wanderer: Deity of debauchery, indulgence, sin, and adventure. Patron deity of the Wandering Isle.

Pronunciation Guide

<u>People:</u>
Anwir Helios: An-weer Heel-ee-os
Bartholomew Williams: Bar-thall-oh-mew Will-ee-ams
Thol: Thall
Czardas Rossi: Char-dash Ross-ee
Fynch Largos: Finch Lar-gos
Galileo Genovese: Gall-ill-lay-oh Jen-oh-vay-say
Leo: Lay-oh
Illie Valentine: Ill-ee Val-en-tine
Israfel Eliad: Iss-rah-fell Ee-lee-ahd
Jonyth Commodore: Jone-ith Comm-oh-dore

Lonan Ryker: Low-nahn Rye-kerr

Nathalia Divyne: Nah-tall-ee-ah Divine

Natha: Nah-tah

Nox Solveig: Nox Sol-vay

Pleo: Plee-oh

Ryuu Nova: Ree-you Nova

Vesperine Genevieve: Ves-per-een Gen-uh-veev

Places:

Amazonia: Am-ah-zone-ee-ah

Aralyth: Air-ah-lith

Archepylago: Arch-uh-pell-ay-go

Borelin Isle: Bore-uh-lin (Isle)

Edyn: Eden

Elluf: El-loof

Frys: Friss

Gello: Gel-oh

Hel Archipelago: Heel (Archipelago)

Ivenis Justyce Penitentiary: Ee-ven-iss Justice (Penitentiary)

Joris Island: Jor-is (Island)

Kalwyl Isles: Call-will (Isles)

Kelsyn: Kell-sin

Merdyne: Mare-dine

Morgouse Island: Mor-gose (Island)

Salts Atoll: Salts Atoll

Servedin Island: Serve-uh-din (Island)

Syrenis: Seer-en-iss

Triangle of Fylth: (Triangle of) Filth

Twin Serpent Isles: Twin Serpent Isles

Undyne Island: Un-dine (Island)

Veridin: Vair-uh-din

<u>Cities:</u>

Aramore: Air-ah-more

Arbyn: Are-bin

Brook Green: Brook Green

Carilon: Care-ih-lohn

Circez: Sir-keez

Corsa: Core-sah

Edylyn: Ed-uh-lin

Fjarg: F-yarg

Gelloiyne: Gel-oh-een

Lenwell: Lehn-well

Lev: Leev

Melrosine: Mel-rose-een

Saffron: Saff-rohn

Selfosa: Sell-foh-sah

Svalgbärd: S-valg-baerd

Veridonia: Vehr-ih-doh-nee-ah

Wyvron: Why-vron

PROLOGUE

For the second time in his life, the boy was stranded on an island, alone. He was a boy, truly, despite his adamant claims that just because he teetered on the edge of adulthood, that made him a man. He was a boy with no business being alone, surrounded by rubber trees and cocoa trees.

At least this time, he found himself abandoned in a jungle where he could drink the sour juices from lekim fruits and eat soft nuts and sun-warmed berries.

He climbed to the top of the palm tree he'd declared his, finding the makeshift treehouse he'd built out of bamboo and palm fronds. Inside were his meager belongings: a compass, a sword, a paring knife, and a tiny wood carving of a ship. He'd made it himself in those early months of being alone on the island, and while it was lumpy and uneven and, frankly, not ship-like in the slightest, it reminded him of home.

The boy did not truly have a home, not until he found himself on that ship. He lived there for three years, finally finding what he thought was his family, but he'd been booted from it six months ago.

Any day now, he would tell himself as he watched the pink-purple sunrise peek over the emerald canopy, as he watched the golden-orange bleed of sunset drown the jungle in its ichor, *they will be back for me.*

Huffing, he sat on the floor of his treehouse, taking his sword from his belt and sliding his satchel off his shoulder. Inside was the day's bounty: three overripe lekims, a skein of fresh water from a river he discovered two months ago, wild pig meat – that had been a struggle to get, and the wound on his leg from the sarding thing's tusks still wept blood – a few handfuls of loose nuts, and a sliver of moonstone.

Ignoring the rest of his goods, the boy turned all his focus to the moonstone. The scars on his wrists throbbed in tandem with his heart.

You will be loved. You will be a hero. A savior. A martyr. Your family will be safe. It won't hurt.

You are destined for greatness, they said as they left him to die, moonstone pendants hanging around their necks, marking them as the people he would one day kill.

He curled his hand around the rock. It would be easier to throw it, to let it fall to the jungle floor to be forgotten, just like he had been, but sometimes it was better to do the hard thing.

He slipped the stone into his pocket instead, promising himself he would get his revenge one day. As soon as the ship returned to take him home.

Deep down inside, buried under layers of ignorance and refusal and guilt – *so* much guilt – he knew the ship would not be returning.

But he was a boy, a child of fifteen (nearly sixteen), and he relished those layers of ignorance and refusal and guilt. He pretended the ship would return and take him home, that the captain – his not-father father – would apologize for abandoning him, that the captain would agree to teach him everything the boy was supposed to learn on his own amongst the trees.

So far, he'd learned that he hated mosquitoes, that jungle cats were *loud,* and that he really, really, *really* didn't like lekims.

Emptying his satchel, the boy put everything away – making sure his food was secured in case any snakes or cats or devious monkeys decided to ambush him while he slept. His satchel now lightened, he swung it over his shoulder and grabbed his sword, sticking it into the sheath at his hip. There was little to do in the jungle besides train, and he wanted to be the strongest man to ever step foot on the ship when it returned.

If it returned.

(When it returns, he thought, stubborn).

Stepping out of the treehouse, he turned his face to the afternoon sun, basking in its warmth. The jungle floor was nearly ten degrees cooler than the canopy, thanks to the dense branches and leaves creating a living roof that kept the sunlight out and the damp humidity in.

Sighing to himself, he climbed down the tree, feet expertly finding each foothold in the branches. He landed on the mulchy ground with a *thud*.

Breathing in through his nose, he closed his eyes. When he opened them, the world around him was bathed in gold. The hazy, glittery outline of a pocket watch appeared before him, trailing shimmering dust in its wake when he grabbed it.

Inhale.

Exhale.

He pressed his thumb down on the crown.

And around him, time came to a halt.

He started counting in his head as he took off running. Around him, the gold started to bleed, the normal jungle colors of green and brown leeching back in. His breathing shallowed, but he kept running and running.

He got to three and a half seconds before blood erupted from his nose, and he simply couldn't hold onto time anymore. At once, the gilded wonderland vanished. The boy sank to his knees, pinching his nose as he tried to stop the bleeding.

Despite the blood that smeared across his freckled cheeks, he laughed. "Three and a half seconds!" he shouted to the toucans and macaws in the branches above. A few flew off, unamused by his antics but unaffected by the three-and-a-half second pause in their lives. A few tamarins howled like his existence was for their amusement alone.

He wiped his upper lip with the back of his arm and stood, brushing twigs and dried leaves off his filthy trousers.

"You see that, Old Man?" he yelled to the gum trees. "I bet I can get to four seconds if I really, really tried. Just you watch!"

But the old man, his captain, his not-father father, wasn't there. It was just the judgmental tamarins, the flighty toucans and macaws, the bored tree frogs and sneaky tapirs that knew better than to get close to the human boy but were curious as to what he was hollering about.

"Again," he whispered.

He closed his eyes, opened them, grabbed the pocket watch.

Inhale.

Exhale.

Pause.

Go.

Seven months later, a ship arrived. It was not *the* ship, but the boy was on it regardless.

Many years later, he wished he had stayed in the jungle, in his treehouse atop the palm tree, because at least he was safe there.

On the opposite end of the jungle, east of Mount Savo, another child made her home amongst the trees. She had been there longer than the boy – nearing her fifth year – but she lived in a cave, not a treehouse, with a pool of freshwater inside and a door she made herself to keep the unwanted predators – both human and animal – out. Unlike the boy, she wasn't alone, and unlike the boy, she hadn't been abandoned on a sandy beach. She had been sent away for her own protection, and while she hated it at first, she learned to like the solitude and simplicity hermit life had to offer.

And, unlike the boy, she rather enjoyed lekims. Maybe because her governess –nanny, advisor, aunt – grew sugarcane and mixed the juice with sugar syrup and cacao powder, or maybe because she didn't get the citrus fruits at the palace, so the novelty of them was what enticed her.

"Are you excited to go home?" the older woman asked the girl. She combed through the girl's cyan locks, twisting them into a perfect plait that rested against her back.

Even at fifteen, the girl was beautiful. She had an aquiline nose and full lips. Her brown eyes were framed with thick blue lashes that matched her brows and long, wavy hair. Her skin, a deep olive, bore no freckles, and she wore the stretch marks around her full thighs and soft stomach with pride like they were the stripes on a tiger.

"Not really," she said. "I like it here."

She hadn't shared the same sentiment five years ago when she and her aunt-governess-nanny-advisor were dropped in the jungle and left to fend for themselves. Technically, the girl was supposed to stay until she was sixteen, but she wouldn't learn about that detail until many years later.

"Well, what's the first thing you want to do when you get home?"

The girl didn't bother correcting the woman. The jungle was her home, more so than anything else.

She picked up an orange from a basket near her knee and dug her thumb into the peel, prying it away from the juicy flesh. "Take a bath, I suppose," she said absently. "With warm water."

Run back to the jungle, the little voice in her head piped up.

"What do you want to eat?" The woman tied the braid with a strip of leather. "If you could have anything in the world, what would it be?"

Lekims with sugar syrup and cacao powder.

"Meat," she said instead. "And fried bread. And lentil soup. I don't know. I don't want to go back."

"I think you are the only person in Syrenis who would rather stay here than return to the palace."

"I like it here."

"So you said."

The girl halved the orange, handing one to the woman and keeping the rest for herself. She broke off a sliver and stuffed it in her mouth, savoring the sweet juice as it flooded her tongue.

Maybe returning wouldn't be *too* bad. It would be nice to have warm baths again and a working toilet to use. Not having to hunt or forage would be a good change, too. She could sleep in as late as she wanted without worrying about missing the prime window for finding edible goods before the local fauna got to it all.

But she wouldn't have those late nights where she climbed the palm trees to watch Mene and Sin – the two moons – rise in the night sky, dancing amongst the stars with Aster – the red north star – between them.

She wouldn't be able to run outside during a rainstorm and dance barefoot over the mulch, petrichor flooding her senses as she laughed alongside the squawking birds and howling monkeys.

She wouldn't crouch behind a nurse log, watching as a tiger crept silently through the foliage, hunting a wild pig to take home to her cubs.

She would never be as free as she was in the jungle again.

"Chin up, Nef," the woman said with a smile. "You've faced the jungle for five years; you can handle court."

The girl stuffed the rest of her orange in her mouth to avoid answering.

There was absolutely nothing in the world that would make becoming an empress tolerable. She'd rather just stay in the jungle.

PART ONE

1

WOOD SLID BENEATH LEO'S fingernail, the splinter drawing a bead of blood and a string of curses from his lips. Galileo Genovese slammed his hand – the uninjured one – against the wood plank he'd been priming and held up his other hand – the one sporting a splinter right beneath his middle finger's nailbed – to inspect the injury. Truthfully, splinters were the least of his concerns. Of all the injuries he could have gotten as the head shipwright in Undyne Island's shipbuilding city, Port 16, a teeny splinter was the best he could have hoped for. It could have been a steel beam embedded in his skull, but Leo figured that would hurt a hell of a lot less than a jagged piece of wood against his sensitive flesh.

With his blunt nails, he struggled to get a purchase on the tiny thing, which only irritated him further. At least a steel beam to his skull wouldn't need plucking.

Undyne Island, an island under the Veridin Kingdom's reign, was an island built exclusively for the trade business. Each of the thirty port cities along its border specialized in one good or service: Port 1 was agriculture, Port 7 was fishing, Port 13 focused on textiles, Port 19 was livestock, and Port 16 was the shipbuilding district.

And Leo was the *greatest* shipwright Port 16 had ever produced.

Hissing through his teeth, he dug his small pocketknife from his belt and flicked it open, prying the sharp tip against the splinter to wiggle it out. The tiny sliver of wood popped free. He stuck his finger into his mouth, sucking the blood.

"You still suck your thumb?" came a familiar voice. Thickly accented, slightly lisped around the butt of a sugar smoke cigarette, it could only belong to one person. Leo looked up.

Through the green tint of his goggles, he met the gaze of his best friend in the entire world. Lonan Ryker, the only person allowed at the worksite who *wasn't* a shipbuilder, leaned against a stack of wood planks, sucking in a lungful of sugared oxygen before exhaling a cloud of sweet smoke.

For all his faults – namely flirting with anything that looked like it could breathe – Lonan wasn't terrible to look at. He was Leo's antithesis, and while they were as close as brothers, they didn't look the part. Leo's hair was muddied brown and couldn't be tamed no matter what; Lonan's was blond and curled around his ears, sideburns tapering into a neat beard (well, Lonan claimed it was a beard, but *stubble* was probably the closest descriptor for the shadow of hair along his jaw). Lonan had steel blue eyes; Leo's, when they weren't hidden by his goggles, were hazel. Leo's skin was a deep bronze, marred with freckles from all the time he spent outside. Lonan, despite being outside just as much as Leo, had skin so pale it looked like he'd never stepped foot in the sunshine.

"Splinter," Leo explained around his finger, the tang of iron still heavy on his tongue.

"They invented these incredible things called gloves, you know."

Leo flipped his knife closed and chucked it at Lonan's head. Lonan laughed, dodging it easily.

"If you're going to just stand there looking ugly, go be annoying elsewhere." Leo wiped his finger off on his trousers and shoved his goggles off his face, securing his hair back with them. A sharp line around his eyes was clear, the soot and sawdust settling everywhere but the space protected by his goggles.

"I'm quite possibly the most attractive man alive." Lonan flexed as if that would prove a point.

Sometimes, Leo wished he didn't have eyes.

Despite all the heavy lifting and muscle work that went into shipbuilding, Leo remained reed thin, his muscles shy of making an appearance outside of gently toned arms and a stomach that wasn't soft but wasn't exactly flat and defined, either. He'd always been tall and wiry, once again Lonan's foil – Lonan, with his beefy arms and broad shoulders.

"And I'm the king of Veridin," grumbled Leo. He ran his fingers over the wood absently.

"The king of Veridin doesn't suck his thumb."

He also wished he didn't have ears.

For all their squabbles, Leo and Lonan had been the very best of friends for nearly their entire lives. By a stroke of sheer luck – or a bout of unluckiness, considering how annoying Lonan was being today – their parents, who had been friends, both had a son within seventeen days of each other (Leo was older, born on the first of Fortmoon, the fourth month of the year, while Lonan was born on the eighteenth of Fortmoon). They'd met when they were a year old and, twenty-seven years later, they were thicker than thieves. Most days, that is.

"Seriously, Lonan," grumbled Leo. "What do you want? I'm technically working."

"As am I." He took a long drag of his sugar cigarette. When he spoke again, his words were muffled by the butt. "I'm doing my job and reminding you to take a break. Let's go fishing."

Let's go fishing was Lonan speak for *I want to sail around the bay, and I know you'll work yourself to death if you don't take a break, so join me.*

Leo popped his knuckles. "No girls."

Lonan gasped dramatically, splaying his hand out on his chest like he was scandalized at the mere notion of bringing women onto his ship. "I would *never.*"

"And I have two legs."

"You can swim to the boat."

"Wench."

"Jerk."

Leo stuck his tongue out at Lonan. As Lonan walked off to get his sailboat ready, he held his middle finger up over his shoulder, a gesture that was more like a handshake to the two than anything else.

Sighing, he picked up his discarded pocketknife. He shouted to the other workers that he was taking a break and would return in a few hours. Then, after making a stop at his house to grab the fishing poles and tackle box he kept by the door for these spontaneous outings, he hurried to the dock.

Nox Solveig watched helplessly as his bo'sun, second mate, and ex-prison-mate Vesperine Genevieve slid the stack of stone coins towards her, adding them to her growing pile of winnings.

"You're cheating," he said, because there was simply no way she could win round after round of Bleeding Heats, the evasion-type card game that should be called *Bleeding Pockets* after what Ves had done to Solveig's pot.

"Actually, she's not," piped up Nathalia Divyne, the ship's cook. She sat on a crate, a cup of sparkling watermelon limeade in her hands. Solveig had already finished his, the glass sitting off to the side, beads of condensation dripping down it. "She's surprisingly played only legal moves."

"How would you know?" Solveig grumbled.

"What do you think noble ladies do all day?" She cocked one of her dark brows, red eyes peering at him through blonde lashes.

It was Illie Valentine, the ship's navigator, cartographer, and second-best Bleeding Hearts player, who chimed in: "Embroider, gossip, drink tea."

Natha rolled her eyes. "And play cards."

"And take lessons from the navy." That came from Bartholomew Williams, Solveig's first mate, quartermaster, and sworn brother. He was slightly worse at the card game than Solveig, but Solveig knew he was letting him win.

Thol set his hand of cards down and leaned forward, his twisted locks falling over his tattooed shoulders. The smell of lavender and pine assaulted Solveig's senses – Thol's hair oil that he tended to use way too much of.

"Point is," said Natha, "I know cheating when I see it. *Trust* me. Ves isn't cheating. Sorry, Captain, you're just terrible at cards."

"I think it should be against the rules to bully your captain like this," grumbled Solveig.

Illie rose from her spot on the floor, hopping over the game to the helm. She adjusted the wheel and sat back down. Not only was she the navigator, cartographer, and second-best Bleeding Hearts player, but she was blessed by the god of the sand, sea, and sky – Poet – to control the wind.

Three weeks ago, during the attack against the Rabbit Pirates, she had been injured – stabbed through the shoulder and left to bleed out. While the wound was scabbed over and mostly healing now, she still wore a sling to keep her arm from moving too much, lest she risk reopening the injury.

Czardas Rossi – the ship's musician and designated dealer in Bleeding Hearts – shuffled the deck of cards expertly. Having sustained only the most minor of injuries – a nail to the palm that healed up in a matter of days – he was relatively back to normal. When he wasn't playing his violin or singing or checking on Fynch Largos (who was confined to a bed after nearly dying when a bullet entered his lung), he sat with the rest of the crew and dealt cards.

Solveig watched as he tossed several cards to each person, his musician hands moving quickly.

He peered at his cards and decided he was going to leave Czardas at the next port they stopped at because there was simply no way he was dealt the worst hand in the history of Bleeding Hearts by sheer coincidence.

He played a card, regardless. "How close are we to Undyne?"

Illie awkwardly played a card. Her cat, Pleo, batted the dropped card absently, deciding it was more fun to hunt cards than mice. "Two days if we're unlucky. But if the weather keeps up, we should make it there in a day and a half."

Solveig was, unfortunately, the unluckiest person in Syrenis. The fight with Bonny Reed and her crew left the *Serenity* in absolute shambles. Her mainmast was gone, half the railing was somewhere at the bottom of the Emerald Sea, there were more holes in her hull than not, patched up shoddily with broken crates... It was a miracle she was still sailing, and it would take a lot more than a single miracle to get her to Undyne Island to be fixed.

"I want to visit Port 13," Ves said as she played a card that let her win the game instantly. "Natha, Illie, you'll come with me, right?

Someone –" she shot a glare at Czardas "– decided to dump the box of silks I was planning on using to make new outfits with, so I have *nothing."*

"Didn't you ask to borrow some of my wardrobe space –" started Illie.

"Nothing!" interjected Ves dramatically.

All things considered, the crew was getting along surprisingly well. A week after Fynch woke up, Solveig sat down with his crew and explained everything. How his old crew, the Pirates of the Silver Moon, were killed, Prince Anwir Helios's map, the deal that he had to find the body of some ancient dead god and bring it back in exchange for the royal pardon, and how he had sworn to keep it all a secret. Understandably, his crew was still upset with him for keeping such a major secret, but they couldn't stay mad at him forever.

After fixing the *Serenity* at Undyne and getting Fynch proper medical treatment in Servedin, Solveig would bring his crew to the Salts Atoll, where Anwir's map seemed to be leading.

> *Beneath a shadow on the Endless Sea*
> *Where the moon once sat upon the waves*
> *The child who watches with a dead eye*
> *A memory forgotten, a field of graves.*
> *North of refuse and east of swindler*
> *Through caverns of salt and blue glow*
> *The child, and slave to eternal night*
> *Will bring the horizon the moons sink below.*
> *In the chains of the child who once was small*

Then coveted, now lost to the sun and time
By thirteen chimes of the clock of the dead
A city of gold gifted to the maritime.
A kiss from the writer to see through midnight
A song which death can never touch
To find the core go first up then down
The name of the third moon is such.

Somehow, the words along the edge of the map and the lyrics to Ves's favorite sea shanty, *Burn the Ruby,* seemed to line up with the strange riddle Illie had found in one of her books.

One hundred days of darkness will arise
A millennium after the third moon dies.
A tower black and cold as night
A ward against the unknown plight.
A prisoner trapped in eternal dark
A centennial sennight, a lull in the lark.
A chain with a broken link
A chased dream that will not sink.
Through moonstone and haze
At the end of all days
To the north and bound
The dream can be found.

For the two weeks since Fynch woke up there had been little time for Solveig to pore over the three things to figure out a connection outside the mentions of a third moon. If Jonyth Commodore, fleet admiral of the Royal Aralythian Navy, would stop sending troops to sink Solveig, he would have plenty of time to connect the dots when sailing to the Salts Atoll in the south.

"Are you kidding me?!" Solveig watched, distraught, as Ves, once again, won the round. "How are you winning this many times? Did you play cards in Ivenis Justyce?"

"I played with a ball and with myself," she said, grinning like a shark. "It's not *my* fault you're terrible at this game, Cap."

"I'm still convinced you're cheating." He scooped up all the cards and shuffled them before Czardas could, deciding *he* would be in charge of dealing them out this time. "So, until I prove that theory wrong, it *is* your fault I'm awful at this game."

Fynch Largos was not dead, but he wished he was.

Never in his life had he been in as much pain as he was now, lying stiffly on a cot that didn't cushion him as the *Serenity* bobbed with the waves, arms pinned at his sides as he tried to mimic a corpse and not move at all. By some miracle (or, rather, a massive stroke of painful unluckiness), he had survived a bullet to his lung. Sure, he'd been comatose for a week after the Rabbit Pirate *threw* a bullet at him, leaving him to bleed out in the crow's nest, but he was (unfortunately) alive now.

It didn't help that the entire crew was coddling him, either. Ves and Czardas refused to leave his side whenever he slept like they were scared he'd never wake up. Natha cooked soft things for him to eat, going out of her way to cook three separate meals a day just for him since he couldn't seem to stomach anything heavier than soup or mashed korva. Thol did his duty by sitting next to him, checking on the wound – the bullet had entered right above his breast, so the checkups were *extremely* awkward, despite Thol being rather gentlemanly about the entire ordeal – and polishing Fynch's hoard of pilfered guns. Illie would read to him, and she brought her cat Pleo with her, who liked to lay right on Fynch's stomach and purr like she'd swallowed a hive of bees. And Solveig...

He always looked so *guilty* when he came to visit, offering Fynch mugs of cinnamon rum (watered down after he'd learned Fynch was only nineteen) and whatever shiny trinkets he found while digging through the stash of stolen treasure on the *Serenity*.

He didn't blame anyone but himself for what happened, and even then, he didn't really blame himself. He blamed that pirate who threw the bullet at him. And he blamed the navy because they were the ones who sent the Rabbit Pirates after them. He also blamed the goddess of trees, earth, and life, Dreamer, because she was the one who decided humans needed to feel pain, and Fynch felt *all* of it.

He felt it when he tried to breathe. When his heart beat. Whenever he moved even a *sliver* of an inch. When he had to get up to relieve himself, when he swallowed, when he sneezed or hiccupped or reached up to rub his eyes. Every minute of his life was filled with pain, and not even the mugs of watered-down cinnamon rum helped. Sleep helped when he was granted a few minutes of it. Natha started brewing a cup of poppyseed tea after dinner for him to drink. He'd gulp it down, and Ves and Czardas would slip into the room to watch over him when the drug finally knocked him out.

He never dreamed when he was drugged.

With little mobility and no desire to move, lest he make the agonizing pain worse, Fynch was trapped in bed, forced to listen through the open door as his crew laughed. He told them it was fine, that they could go outside and play cards in the sun, but it still hurt – almost as much as his still-healing wound – when they actually did it.

He stared at the ceiling, unblinking.

Would they still be laughing and acting like nothing had happened if I died? He thought.

He was too afraid of the answer to dwell on that.

Sighing (and wincing at the pain that caused), he closed his eyes and pretended to sleep.

"If Castros Helios dropped dead, I wouldn't be upset," Leo said as he cast his line into the open ocean.

For the past hour and a half, Lonan and Leo had been fishing off the side of the slim schooner (built by Leo, registered by the navy, sailed by Lonan) they'd borrowed, and so far, the only thing they'd caught was a single salmon that was hardly big enough for two men to eat.

Lonan glanced away from his line to see Leo's profile. Balancing his pole in one hand, he dug out his pack of sugar cigarettes and popped one in his mouth. "Light?" he asked around the cigarette.

Leo held up his middle finger. A tiny spark sprung to life on his fingertip. Lonan leaned in, pressing the end of his cigarette to the flame. Once his cigarette started smoking, Leo shook his hand out to extinguish the flame.

"Why're you even thinking about Helios?" Lonan asked. He tugged on his pole, trying to lure any curious fish into biting. "You have the hots for him?"

"I will push you overboard."

"I was just asking!"

Leo reeled his line back in and recast further from Lonan's. "There are new tariffs in place for imports. Buying wood is too expensive, and it comes from *Port 3!* How in the Wanderer's name are we being taxed for something *our own country makes?!* It isn't even an *import* at that point, but Helios decided to *triple the taxes.* And you just *know* all that money is going right to his own personal bank account."

Lonan pulled the cigarette from his teeth. "Or into Jonyth's pockets."

Hearing that name seemed to set Leo off. He groaned loudly and smacked his pole against the ship's railing. *"Jonyth Commodore!* He can go sard himself up the ass with a cutlass for all I care."

"Would Jonyth having...relations...with a sword make wood cheaper for you to buy?"

Leo let out a frustrated scream.

Suddenly, there was a tug on Lonan's pole. He bit down on his cigarette and stepped back, reeling in slowly. Whatever was hooked was putting up a fight, yanking back on the line.

"Easy, now," murmured Lonan. He gave the line a bit of slack before reeling it in more. A glint of silver streaked beneath the surface.

He knew it was a fish, but his stomach still tumbled at the sight. The scar slicing through his upper lip, reaching toward the curve of his nose, throbbed.

Quickly regaining his composure, Lonan reeled the fish in, letting it fall to the deck. It flopped helplessly, tangled up in the fishing line.

"Looks like salmon for dinner," he mused. He worked quickly, then tossed the dead fish into the ice bucket with the other.

"Just wait. Soon, Helios will be taxing us on our own personal catches," grumbled Leo. "And we aren't even under his rule yet."

Undyne Island was still Veridinian territory, but with the navy occupation there and Helios's scheme to marry his daughter off to the crown prince of Veridin, the people of Undyne were Castros Helios's – and Jonyth Commodore's – dogs.

Lonan took a long drag of his cigarette, letting the sugar turn to oxygen in his lungs before exhaling a plume of white smoke. "Glory to Aralyth, eh? Long live the sarding emperor."

2

ILLIE HAD MANAGED TO determine two things about the ancient map Solveig had reluctantly shown her.

The first: it was at *least* a thousand years old, and it was missing five major islands: Servedin Island, Morgouse Island, the Wandering Isle, Undyne Island, and Kelsyn.

The second: it shared the same signature in the bottom corner as the moonstone lithograph that tracked the precise movements of the Wandering Isle – three crescent moons, faded with age but unmistakably *there*.

She sat at the desk in Solveig's quarters, the map in front of her and the lithograph above it. Her own notebook with all her notes from her travels around the world was splayed open, her messy scrawl taking up every inch of blank space, and atop everything was the torn-out page from one of her books with the riddle she'd discovered by accident.

Somehow, whoever drew the map a thousand years ago also managed to carve the lithograph that only appeared *months* ago.

She shoved her glasses atop her head and pinched the bridge of her nose, trying to alleviate the tension building behind her eyes.

"Snacks to cheer you up?" came Natha's accented voice. Illie looked up from her mess of papers to see Natha standing in the doorway, a tray balanced perfectly on the tips of her fingers.

"Please." Illie carefully stacked everything out of the way, allowing Natha to set her offerings down – a cup of tea, a pot of sugar, a tray of tiny sandwiches full of salmon cut so thin it looked like paper and cucumbers, and a plate of still-warm cookies.

Illie scooted over, leaving some room on the chair, and plunked three sugars in her tea. "Sit with me," she said. "I could use an extra set of eyes."

Natha did so, grabbing a cookie and stuffing it in her mouth in one bite. She chewed before saying, "Any progress?"

Illie shook her head. She'd already shared her revelations with the crew; she hadn't discovered anything new since then. "I wish we'd gotten that relic from Veridonia. Curse the navy for giving us a fake."

There had been a compass of sorts at the Royal Veridin Museum of History that supposedly had links to the third moon. When she and Ves had gone to steal it, they ended up with a fake that led the navy – led by Natha's ex-brother-in-law – right to them. While they'd gotten Natha out of the ordeal, Illie still wished she hadn't given up the artifact that might have connected all the dots.

Oh, well. She had an ancient map, a moving lithograph, and a strange riddle to work with. It would have to do.

She sipped her tea, the sugar overwhelmingly sweet, and picked up the torn page.

"The first two lines make the most sense," she said. "'One hundred days of darkness will arise a millennium after the third moon dies.' It...seems literal. Four months of darkness – whatever that means – a thousand years after the third moon vanished. The earliest mentions of the third moon I've found are from eight or nine hundred years ago. If that's when the moon fell, there will be a hundred days of darkness in a hundred years. It could be based on the seasons – in Borelin and Frys during the winter, there is no sun. Maybe something like that?"

Natha picked up a sandwich and bit into it. "Maybe."

"That's it," Illie grumbled. "The rest of it doesn't make sense. It just sounds like some silly poem, like someone wanted to write a prophecy and threw a bunch of rhyming words together."

"What about those last lines?" Natha licked crumbs off her fingers and pointed to the page. "'To the north and bound the dream can be found.' Doesn't that sound like what's on the map?"

Illie set the paper down and grabbed the map, turning it until she found the line that seemed to match. "'North of refuse and east of swindler?' Or... 'In the chains of the child who once was small?' Ugh! None of it makes any sense! Sol seems to think the moon is in the Salts Atoll, which makes sense because..." she scanned the wall until she found a world map tacked above the desk. She pointed to the ring of islands. "Look, see? The lagoon in the center is nearly a perfect circle, like a *sarding moon fell there.*"

"But...?"

"But it doesn't make any sense!" Illie cried. "I've been to the Salts Atoll! I think if there was really a missing moon there, I would have realized it!"

Natha drummed her nails against the table. "How?"

Illie looked up, brow knit. "What?"

"How would you have realized it?"

She...she wouldn't have. She'd gone to the Salts Atoll to get measurements and drink pineapple juice on the beach, not to search for a third moon that had been missing for hundreds of years. She didn't find the lost moon because she *hadn't been looking for it.*

She stood up suddenly, nearly knocking Natha over in the process. "I need a bathymetric map," she breathed. "Natha, I need a *bathymetric map.* If the lost moon really is at the bottom of the Salts Atoll, it would show up on a bathymetric chart – a chart showing the depth of the ocean."

"And if it doesn't...?"

"Then the lost moon isn't there, and we will know where to look." Illie grinned. "Somewhere out there is a map that already shows where the third moon is. All we need to do is find it."

Ves sat on a stiff wooden chair by Fynch's bed, eyes glued to his chest as she watched each gentle rise and fall it made.

Hours ago, Illie had marched out onto the deck, announcing that she could find the moon with a bath-something map. She then promptly took to the helm, manning it with one hand, sailing the *Serenity* straight to Undyne. Then, after Natha made dinner, she brought a cup of poppyseed tea to Fynch, who drank it greedily.

And now, she and Czardas sat by his bed, watching him to make sure his breathing didn't stop. He had been too close to death, his body cold, his soul barely even there. She watched him constantly with her second sight, making sure the golden gleam that was his lifeforce hadn't flickered or dimmed again.

"You've known him a long time, hm?" Ves's voice was a whisper.

"Since we were boys," Czardas whispered back. "He tried to steal a rine coin from me, but I caught him. He and I have been together since. He...had a rough upbringing. His ma had too many children and not nearly enough stability to take care of them all. She died a few years ago, and F blames himself. Doesn't help that his siblings shoved the blame onto him. He was in jail, and they said he stressed her out so much she just..." he trailed off as if suddenly worried Fynch could hear them in his sleep.

"I get it," she said, picking at one of her nails with the tip of her knife. She kept no less than six strapped to her body at all times. "My childhood was rough, too. My parents died when I was ten, and instead of going to an orphanage like a good little girl, I joined the Ruby Pirates. Fifteen when I became the Witch of the Sea. Never had any siblings; my parents were lost at sea before they could give me any."

Czardas cringed inwardly. She, like everyone else, knew he had a cushy life before turning to piracy. The only child of Duchess and Duke Rossi – a thoroughbred lady and a famous musician – he'd been raised with only the finest of tutors and governesses, primed as a prodigy since the moment he was born with a silver spoon in his mouth.

But that was *before.* He was a pirate now, one with an expensive bounty on his head. His past didn't matter anymore. Only the present did because the present paved the way for the inevitable future.

A future where they were *all* rich and famous and protected by the shiny stamp that would brand them not as pirates, but as privateers.

He toyed with his fingers absently. "Miss Ves, you were in jail, right?"

"Prison," she corrected. *Jail* was for petty thieves and common crooks. *Prison* was for the worst of the worst. And she hadn't just been to *any* prison; she'd spent four years locked up in Seven-B, the lowest level of the island fortress that was Ivenis Justyce Penitentiary.

"What...what was it like?" he shot a glance at Fynch.

"It was hell," she said honestly. Because it *had* been. "They forgot to feed me or give me water sometimes. I was chained up and left in the dark. I slept on dirt and had a bucket to do all my business in. I spent four years there. I would have died in there if Cap hadn't come to my rescue."

Even though she was still mad at Solveig for lying to her, he was, unfortunately, her savior.

"F went to jail a few times," Czardas said. "He always refused to talk about it..."

"Jail, prison, gallows, loveless marriage..." she just shrugged. "We've all been through it. But that doesn't matter anymore. What matters now is that we're all pirates, and we are getting that sarding moon one way or another."

"You know," Solveig said as he shuffled the cards and dealt them out evenly, half the deck going to Thol and half the deck staying in his hands, "I'm curious. Why did you marry Meadow if she was so against piracy? Why marry a pirate – ex-pirate, I guess – if she didn't like that?"

Thol picked up his cards, organizing them so they fit in his hands just right. The rules of the game were simple: take cards from the other person, match pairs, and don't get the joker card. He held his hand out, letting Solveig take one.

"She was born in a sanctuary city. Her parents weren't pirates, but they worked for them. When she escaped to Wyvron, I guess she just didn't want to be around that anymore. I don't think she *really* cared about my past, but since we planned on having a family, she wanted our child to have a different upbringing than what she was around." He took a card from Solveig and matched it with one of the ones he already had. He dropped them on the deck.

"I can't believe you were a father..." murmured Solveig. He took another card from Thol, cursing when it was the inevitable joker card. Thol just grinned.

"Hardly," he said. "But for a few minutes, I *was* a father, which means you were Uncle Nox."

Solveig made a gagging noise. "Could you imagine me around children? I don't even know how to hold a baby. If it's too young to drink rum, I want nothing to do with it."

Thol took another of Solveig's cards, smiling to himself when it wasn't the joker, and paired it with one of his. "The first time you had rum, you spent the next day throwing up. I'm surprised nobody started calling you *Puke Boy.*"

"They were too busy calling me *Piss Boy.*"

"And whose fault is that?"

"Yours! I didn't piss the bed!"

"Mm. Sure."

Thol took a card. "Sard you, Nox," he cursed when he added the joker back to his hand. "You'll regret that."

Solveig tossed his head back and laughed. "That's what you get for calling me Piss Boy."

Thol flipped him off and held out his hand of cards, letting Solveig take one.

The game continued in silence for a few minutes, cards exchanging hands and pairs falling to the deck. Solveig ended up with the joker again, only for Thol to grab it again moments later.

"So," Thol said, dropping his final pair of cards on the deck, left with the losing joker card. He added it to the pile and gathered up the cards, shuffling them again. "Anwir Helios, huh? Dozens of pirates get executed every day. How come *you* caught his attention?"

Solveig absently rubbed the branded scar on his arm, a reminder that he was – and always would be – a pirate. Thol had his guesses – Solveig was the second most wanted pirate, he had just been thrown into Ivenis Justyce Penitentiary, Jonyth Commodore had a grudge against him...

Solveig raked his fingers through his hair, turning his head to face the sea. The sun had set ages ago, their only light the lantern on the deck beside them. Thol was supposed to be keeping watch since the *Serenity* had been anchored, floating gently in the waves. According to Illie, they would reach Port 16 soon. All they had to do was avoid getting into another fight until then.

The tips of Solveig's ears burned red.

Odd...

"He said it's because I'm good at finding things," he said. "But I think he wanted someone who had enough to lose that they wouldn't think about betraying him and someone who the world wouldn't miss if they were sent to the gallows. Someone he could manipulate, but someone expendable. I'm not sure he even expects me to succeed. He originally gave me a few months; I had to argue to get eleven."

"Why you, and not the Unnamed God?"

Solveig's green eyes slid to Thol. He lifted his shoulders in a shrug. "Nobody has ever seen the Unnamed God. I doubt his crew even knows what he looks like, much less Anwir."

"First name basis with the prince of Aralyth?" Thol cocked a brow.

Solveig grabbed his empty mug – previously holding cinnamon rum, currently holding not even the dregs – and threw it right at Thol's head.

Thol laughed, a deep, rumbling belly laugh when the mug only grazed his ear. "Sard you, Piss Boy."

Solveig's grin was feral. "You *wish.*"

Lonan invited himself into Leo's room bright and early in the morning. They lived together in a two-bedroom house in the heart of Port 16, and no matter how many lock mechanisms and contraptions Leo invented to keep Lonan out, Lonan *always* found a way in.

He barged in, shirt unbuttoned, towel around his neck to catch the water drips from his damp, slicked-back hair, and a cup of what Leo hoped was coffee (but could very well be beer) in his hand.

"I'm going to the shop to get some cigarettes. Need anything?" He took a long, loud slurp of his drink.

Leo blinked, still half-asleep. His hair no doubt stuck up at every angle, his sleep pants bunched around his hips. He wore no shirt, the sticky humidity of late Ulamoon heat too much, even with the window open and the whirring fan he'd made pointed right at him.

"What *time* is it?" Leo groaned. He rolled onto his stomach, burying his face in his pillow.

"Early enough to get some shopping done." Lonan leaned against the doorframe. The sarding fool *knew* he was being annoying. Leo didn't even have his leg on yet; it was too early for this nonsense. "I'm thinking of making fish for dinner. Too redundant? We had salmon last night... You want anything? A treat? Some rice wine?"

Leo sat up and threw his pillow at Lonan. It hit him square in the face, but he didn't even flinch.

"Go shop," grumbled Leo. "I have to work."

He slid to the edge of his bed and grabbed his prosthetic leg, which he kept propped against the wall. Rolling his pants up past his knee, revealing the long-healed stump, he attached his prosthetic – made by Leo himself, the polished wood shiny and cool – and stood. He'd been wearing a prosthetic every day for twenty-one years after he'd gotten sick enough that he needed it amputated when he was seven years old. Some people would stare at it like missing a leg was the most unusual thing in the world – a world where people were blessed by *gods*. Nobody batted an eye at Leo's fire-manipulation ability, gifted to him by the Wanderer – but he didn't mind. There were more important things to worry about.

And he *liked* his prosthetic. He'd made it himself, and he thought it added to his inventor aesthetic. If he could craft a leg that fit him perfectly, people could surely trust him to build them a ship that would reach all four oceans.

He plucked the mug from Lonan's hands and took a sip, glad it was very bitter coffee and not very bitter beer. "I'll see you at the docks later?"

Lonan flicked Leo's forehead. "Maybe I'll grace the docks with my presence. The ladies won't be able to focus on their work, though." He winked.

"Gross," grumbled Leo. He took another drink of coffee before handing it back. "The ladies don't like looking at you. Why do you think they all put on their goggles when they hear your ugly voice?"

"You *wound* me!" Lonan cried dramatically.

"You wound yourself, falling from your ego back to reality."

He stepped into the hallway but paused, adding: "Get me some rice wine. *Someone* drank the last of mine."

3

The pirate ship arrived early in the morning.

Well, *ship* was a generous term.

Lonan wasn't a shipwright like Leo. He could hardly patch a hole, even if his life depended on it. But while Leo made the ships, Lonan could command them; he could bend them to his very will. Ships were like ladies, and he understood both *very* well. And when he saw the red ship lumber into the marina, mainmast missing and shoddy patch jobs littering her hull, even he knew it wasn't supposed to look like that.

Uncrossing his legs, Lonan stuck his sugar cigarette between his teeth and stood up, abandoning his lounge spot against a few barrels. He scanned the yard for Leo, spotting his chestnut hair and freckled face almost instantly. Goggles covered his eyes, his hands slathered in grease as he worked.

Well. Port 16 had guests. Lonan might as well greet them.

He walked over to the ship, catching the line the pirates tossed down with one hand. He wasn't a dockhand by any means, but being polite would make a good impression. He tied the line and shoved his hands in his pockets, cigarette hanging lazily over his bottom lip.

The gangplank was lowered moments later, and seven pirates paraded down. Lonan's gaze went to the three women first. One was slim and willowy, wraithlike with pale skin, almond-shaped honey-colored eyes, and a pink braid down her back. The second was *tall* – taller than Lonan – with a crown of curls and more curves than Lonan knew what to do with, all thick thighs and massive bust. And the third...

He sidled up to the third woman – the toned one with blonde hair and narrow red eyes – and slipped his arm around her shoulders. "Well, well, well!" he drawled. "What've we here? Do my eyes deceive me, or is the most beautiful woman in the world gracing Port 16 with her presence? Lonan Ryker, at your service. And you are...? Single, I'm hoping."

The woman shrugged his arm off, nose scrunched up in displeasure. She took a step closer to the tall and curvy woman. "Not interested," she said, her accent thick.

Lonan grinned. "That's a strange name. And you are...?" he turned his focus to Tall-and-Curvy.

"Ew," she said, shooing him away like a stray dog. "I'm not interested in men, and rats disgust me."

Well, then. He stepped closer to the pink-haired woman, holding his hand out for her to shake. "Might I get your name, fair lady?"

"I'm good, thanks," she said flatly.

There was one more, so Lonan approached the short blonde, who was definitely too young for him, and said, "What about you, ma'a –"

He was on his knees before he could finish the word, his cigarette tumbling to the ground. He clutched his manhood, tears blurring his eyes as pain drowned out all his other senses.

"Fynch Largos," the blond said. "And I ain't a girl."

"P-point taken," gasped Lonan.

"F!" someone – the curly-haired kid with vitiligo – scolded. "You're supposed to be resting! Don't pick fights you can't win."

Tall-and-Curvy grabbed the front of Lonan's shirt, yanking him to his feet like he was nothing more than a sad kitten.

"Woah, there," he managed to squeak through the ebb of pain. "Be gentle, I'm still vanilla."

"You're a worm," she said. "Who are you, and why are you bothering us? Are you a shipwright? We need a shipwright."

With shaky hands, Lonan reached into his pocket, pulling out his box of cigarettes and his lighter. Usually, he had Leo light the things for him, but he put the sugar cigarette between his teeth and sparked a flame. Smoke filled his mouth; he swallowed it and exhaled.

"Lonan Ryker," he said again. "I'm no shipwright, but I can point you in the direction of the greatest one Port 16 has to offer. Now, which one of you is the captain?"

A man with red hair and a deep green coat stepped forward. His emerald eyes were colder than stone, his sharp jaw set. Lonan knew that face instantly.

A grin broke out across his own face. "Well! Captain Nox sarding Solveig, isn't it? Come with me; we'll get you fixed up right away."

Nathalia Divyne did not trust Lonan Ryker in the slightest. Maybe it was because her divorce from Adrian Zimmer was so fresh that Lonan's clinginess rubbed her the wrong way. Maybe it was because, after just a few weeks of being away from her incompetent chef staff and her sleazy ex-husband and his family, her standards for men had been raised.

Well, the bar had been on the ground in the first place, but her crew – Solveig, who was a liar but was doing his best to rectify that, who protected his crew no matter what; Thol, who was as gentlemanly as they got; Czardas, who was innocent and sweet, who liked music and often sang while Natha cooked; and...even Fynch, who was annoying and would lose both his hands if he tried to steal from her kitchen again, but who was loyal and brave and...well, he was growing on her – her crew had picked that bar up and raised it.

"Your ship is in shambles," Lonan said, thankfully talking to Solveig. Natha pressed herself closer to Ves, using her massive stature as a shield. Lonan continued: "No idea how you managed to sail anywhere without a mainmast. It'll take Leo a few days at least to build a new one and get it situated. Her name's the *Serenity?* Beautiful ship."

Lonan led them through the heart of town. Snug houses sat close together, various shops dispersed throughout – all related to shipbuilding, she realized. Places to buy boats, rent them, specialty shops to get materials and upgrades...

There was a temple, too. Lady Lightbringer's. Bushes of flowers decorated the front of the temple, looking equal parts intentional and wild.

Lady Lightbringer...? She frowned. Usually, in coastal towns, the temples were dedicated to Poet, god of the sand, sea, and sky. The only places where temples to the goddess of war, justice, and strength could be found were by navy strongholds.

She watched the temple as she passed it, eyeing the two women dressed in white as they crossed the threshold and entered Lady Lightbringer's territory.

Lady Lightbringer didn't care about justice. If she did, she wouldn't have abandoned Natha in her *many* times of need. She wouldn't have left Natha alone, crying in the darkness of her flat, wondering where she'd gone wrong and if she should have even ever been born, while showering Adrian Zimmer with her blessings and divine support. No, she didn't care about justice. She just cared about the navy.

Sard the navy.

You tried that, piped up an unhelpful voice in the back of her head. *And how did* that *work out, again?*

"Pretty small crew you've got," Lonan drawled, bringing Natha back to the present. "Seven? Let me guess the roles…"

He turned around, walking backward. He had a lazy grin that would have looked nice on anyone else's face.

He pointed at Solveig. "You're the captain. Tattoos over there is your first mate, no? Miss Tall-Curvy-and-Not-Interested is your left-hand woman. Bo'sun? Second mate? Both?"

He took a drag of his cigarette, ignoring Thol, who grumbled something about how Solveig's idea of officer ranks was messed up.

"Blonde hair – the lady, that is – is your chef." Natha's brows raised at that. He grinned and said, "What? You've got flour smeared on your shirt. It's obvious. Miss Pink Braid is the navigator – ink on the fingers, gave it away instantly."

He tapped his chin. Then, pointing to Fynch and Czardas, in that order, he said, "Sharpshooter and musician. How'd I do, Cap'n?"

"How?" blurted Ves.

Lonan exhaled a plume of sweet smoke. "Tattoos is standing slightly behind your captain. A protective vantage point; he can attack from the front and keep anyone from stabbing Cap'n here in the back. Tall-and-Curvy, you're standing toward the middle of the pack. Everyone is in your sight. Lady Blonde has flour. Miss Pink has ink on her fingers. *Mister* Blond has two guns tucked into his belt – oh, they're hidden, don't worry. I can see your hand drifting there every now and then. And while *I'm* not the biggest fan of classical music, you'd have to be blind to not recognize Czardas Rossi."

Natha wasn't sure if she should be impressed or scared.

He tucked his hands in his pockets. "Anyways, it'll probably take Leo a while to fix your ship. If you gentlemen want to stay with your captain while he talks to Leo, I can take you ladies to see the town –"

Thol interrupted, "That's an idea. Ves, you take the others to find lodging. I'll stay with Nox and Lonan."

Lonan's ego deflated. Natha couldn't help but smirk.

Czardas Rossi had never been to Undyne Island before. His violin was from Undyne – Port 23, the music city, made some of the best instruments in the world. But this was his first time visiting, and as he followed Ves, one arm slung around Fynch's shoulders to keep him upright, his gaze darted in every direction, soaking in the sights.

Ulamoon was the hottest month of the year, and this close to the Midline, Czardas was met with the full force of it. The air was thick and humid, the salt almost overwhelming but overpowered by the acrid smell of burning wood and ship polish. His curls clung to his forehead and the nape of his neck, damp with sweat. Fynch's pale skin had taken on a feverish sheen – Czardas hoped it was from the heat and not because he was relapsing.

"Don't worry, F," he whispered. "Mister Thol said he knows a doctor who can fix you up. You're going to be fine."

"F-feel," gasped Fynch, "feel *awful.*"

Czardas tugged him closer. Fynch's lips had a blue tint to them. His breathing was quick and shallow, raspy like he was breathing through a broken straw.

"I know, F," he murmured. "I know. But you're stubborn and stupid, and you're not going to let this kill you. We'll find a place to rest and get you something to eat, and you are going to *bathe* because you smell awful."

Fynch cracked a weak smile. "Just trying to smell like you."

The oddest part of Fynch being injured was that he wasn't nearly as talkative as usual. His soft voice, his lack of interrupting to ramble at any given moment, was...*uncanny.*

The sooner the *Serenity* got fixed, and the sooner Fynch got medical treatment, the better.

Before long, they had found an inn. It wasn't the greatest place Czardas had ever seen, and he doubted it would rate above two stars, but a sign in the window said *VACANCIES*, and that was good enough.

"We should try to get a minimum of two rooms," said Ves, her hands on her hips. "It's likely news of who we are has reached Undyne. I don't *want* to get in a fight right now, but if we have to, so be it. Strings, you got Birdie? Good."

She threw open the door and marched into the inn like she owned the place. Natha and Illie followed. Czardas tugged Fynch close and carefully led him over the threshold.

The lobby had a coziness to it that Czardas hadn't been expecting. Dark curtains had been pulled over all the windows, making it look uninviting from the outside, but on the inside, it kept the open room cool. There was a hearth against one wall, unlit, with a chaise and two chairs around it. On the mantle were several framed pictures. A low chandelier provided enough light in the lobby that having the windows open wasn't necessary.

On the wall opposite the concierge's desk was a display of nautical memorabilia – an old wheel, a sextant, a framed piece of a sail... There were more framed pictures and a few framed newspaper clippings.

Czardas led Fynch to the chaise and helped him sit. His head lolled back, and he stared at the ceiling. Czardas went to the hearth first, looking at the pictures there.

He recognized one as Empress Nefeli Catrione, the sovereign of the Merdyne Empire. It was hard not to, with her bright blue hair and elaborate red crown. She looked younger than he was – maybe Fynch's age – but she was standing in front of the very hearth her picture was now framed above.

On the wall, he spotted a picture of two men shaking hands, standing in front of a massive ship. He recognized one immediately as Lonan Ryker – the scar through his lip and the sugar smoke cigarette between his teeth was a dead giveaway. But the other man was unfamiliar. He had darker skin and a smattering of freckles.

His messy hair was held back by a pair of goggles. Beneath the photograph was a plaque.

LONAN RYKER AND GALILEO GENOVESE

COMPLETION OF THE *VIRGINIA MARY*, 1150

The picture might have been three years old, but Lonan looked exactly the same.

"Well!" Ves announced, startling Czardas with her loud voice. "I managed to snag two rooms. Breakfast and dinner are served daily. Blondie, Pinkie, and I will go get our things from the *Serenity*. Strings, you keep an eye on Birdie."

She tossed him a key. He fumbled with it, nearly dropping it twice before he could hold it to his chest.

He glanced at the number – 202 – and said to Fynch: "Come on, F. I'll help you up. Let's go claim the bed and make Captain Solveig and Mister Thol sleep on the floor."

Fynch managed a weak smile. He stood with Czardas's help and leaned heavily against him. Together, they slowly made their way upstairs and down the hall to the room marked 202.

The room was smaller than any inn Czardas had ever stayed at – though, technically, this was his first time at an *inn*. When traveling, he usually stayed at one of the other Rossi properties or, on rare occasions, hotels that rivaled palaces. Those hotels had entire floors for suites, elevators with liftmen to operate the hydraulic pulleys, in-room five-star dining, and reservation lists that went out six months at least. Those rooms had king-sized beds, closets the size of a small bedroom, massive washrooms...

This room... Well, it had a bed, though it looked more like a stiff cot, with two pillows and a thin blanket. There was a hearth, the ashes long cold, a typewriter desk sans typewriter, a wide open window shielded by thick curtains and a gauzy mosquito net, a slim armoire, and a door that, presumably, led to the washroom.

He was *not* looking forward to sleeping on the floor.

"Come on, F. Let's lie you down," he murmured, walking to the bed. Fynch sat down, wincing the entire time, his face pale and waxy.

Czardas frowned. "Are you --?"

"I'm fine," grumbled Fynch, his voice wheezy. "It just hurts a bit. I have a high pain tolerance."

Fynch did not have a high pain tolerance, but Czardas said nothing. How would he know how the cramps Fynch dealt with each month compared to being shot in the lung?

"I d-don't wanna bathe," Fynch whispered.

"You have to. And I'm *not* giving you a sponge bath."

"Because you hate me?"

"Because that's *weird!*"

"Help me lie down."

Czardas sighed through his nose. One day, he would die, and it would be because of Fynch Largos annoying him to an early grave. Still, he fluffed up the pillows and placed his hand on Fynch's lower back, coaxing him into a supine position.

"We're pirates, Czar," he breathed. "Can you believe it?"

He couldn't, truthfully. Sometimes, he would be up at night, staring at the ceiling, his cot rocking gently with the *Serenity,* and the weight of everything would come crashing down. He was a pirate. A wanted man. A criminal worth eight hundred thousand lune.

He didn't regret it, per se. He would follow Fynch anywhere. But it was strange, going from being *famous* for his musical talent to *infamous* for joining a ship's crew.

As if reading his mind Fynch said, "Do you regret it? Throwing away your life to run away with me, I mean. You could be sleeping in your bed instead of having to sleep on the floor."

He *was* homesick. That longing pang struck his core more often than not. He wondered how his parents were, how they reacted to seeing his face in the newspaper above the words *Wanted! Dead or Alive.*

But he wouldn't have given up on Fynch. Homesickness could be quelled. The deep regret of leaving his best friend behind could not.

He looked at his palm, the bandage that had been wrapped around it for days gone now, the dry scab from where he'd slammed a nail through his flesh irritating.

"The only thing I regret," he said, "is not running away sooner."

Pleo wound around Illie's legs, purring loudly and proving to be a rather cute tripping hazard.

"You little monster," grumbled Illie as she shooed the cat away with her boot. She picked up a chest and groaned under the weight. "Why can't the men do this? My hands *hurt.*"

She hadn't had frostbite in a few weeks, but her palms were still blistered and raw from a grueling wind-wrangling session the day before.

"My back hurts," said Ves as she picked up a stack of crates with ease. "But if we do this, we can prove to Cap and the others that we are stronger than them."

"You just didn't want to be alone with that Ryker man, didn't you?" asked Natha.

Ves held up one of her middle fingers. "Can you blame me? Would *you* want to be left alone with him?"

Natha shuddered. "Absolutely *not.* I am done with men for the rest of my life."

Illie walked the chest down the gangplank and set it loudly on the dock. Most of their belongings had already been piled up. Natha took care of the galley and dining room and the men's quarters – she'd drawn the short stick. Illie was in charge of the women's quarters and Solveig's quarters. She was the most trusted with all the maps, after all. That left Ves to clear out the belly of the ship, lugging all the heavy storage and stolen goods with ease.

She scraped her hair off her face, tying it in a loose knot at the nape of her neck. Heat drew sweat from every pore on her body, running down her cheeks like tears and sticking her hair to her neck and shoulders. Hopefully there was plumbing at the inn. Or, if there were no showers, at least tubs she could fill and soak in.

Maybe a dip in the Emerald Sea wouldn't be too bad. She'd have to find a bathing suit, but she doubted Ves and Natha would say no to an impromptu shopping trip.

As she walked up the gangplank, Illie wondered if grabbing a wind and catapulting it into her face would be a bad idea. Her hands were raw, and she didn't know when she might need her full power, but…

Poet, it was *hot*.

"How long do you think Sol and Thol will be?" she asked, grabbing another crate and balancing it on her hip. Pleo chirruped, weaving around her legs dangerously.

"Well, knowing Cap, he's probably sidetracked and off on some side adventure right now," grumbled Ves. "So, probably *several* hours."

Illie believed it. Nox Solveig was *excellent* at going anywhere *but* where he needed to go.

He needed to go to Lenwell for Thol. He ended up stealing a map from the navy. He needed to get supplies from Carilon, and he ended up liberating it from the Redcoat Pirates' rule and making it *his* territory. He ended up making a stop in Veridonia to steal an artifact – and while he didn't get it, he got another crew member.

If Solveig was in Port 17 with Thol and Lonan, Illie wouldn't even be surprised. Disappointed, yes. But surprised? Not in a million years.

She set the crate down and sat atop it, her stick-thin arms aching all over. She reached out and grabbed a small wind – a tiny gale, no more than a summer breeze – and wrapped it around her body, instantly cooling herself down.

"This is the last of everything," Ves said, dropping three crates near the pile. "Give me ten minutes, and I'll be back with a cart."

As she walked off, Illie let the wind go, allowing it to wash over Ves and Natha.

The shipyard was organized chaos. At least, Solveig *hoped* it was organized. Half-built hulls reached toward the sky, surrounded by discarded wood planks and boxes of nails that were one breeze from falling over. Workers bustled about. Lonan ignored them as he wove through the site, Solveig and Thol following closely behind. Solveig eyed each person they passed, wondering if they were this *Leo* Lonan mentioned.

"Leo!" Lonan shouted. "Laaaaaayyyyyyy-ohhhhhh!"

A head popped up from behind a stack of wood. Messy brown hair, darker skin covered in freckles, eyes hidden by circular goggles... *That* must be Leo.

"Why is your ugly face back here?" Leo asked. He climbed over the wood and hopped down. Shoving his goggles off his face to reveal hazel eyes, Leo took in Solveig and Thol and grinned.

"Cap'n and first mate, here," Lonan introduced. "They need their ship repaired. Ugly as you are, you're the only decent shipwright around here."

Leo thrust out a hand. Then, as an afterthought, he shucked off his thick gloves and held out his hand again. "Galileo Genovese, greatest damn shipwright in Syrenis. Call me Leo."

"Captain Nox Solveig," Solveig said as he shook Leo's hand. "And this is Bartholomew Williams, my right hand."

"You really *do* wear green!" Leo exclaimed. "I always thought that was an exaggeration or something made up, so the saying nearly rhymed. *Captain Nox Solveig cloaked in blue* doesn't sound right."

He pulled his gloves back on and rubbed his palms together, creating a cloud of dust.

"I'll show you to the ship," Solveig said.

"Then why don't *I* give you the grand tour of Port 16?" Lonan slapped Thol on the back. Solveig winced, half-expecting to watch Lonan get disemboweled right then and there, but Thol just frowned and shrugged him away.

"We'll meet up with the others later," Solveig said. Then, waving Thol off, he began towards the harbor where the *Serenity* was docked.

When they arrived, a small crowd had gathered, surrounding the *Serenity.* Most of them wore grease stains and gloves and goggles like Leo – shipwrights. *Embarrassing.*

"Wanderer's *teeth,* your ship looks *awful!*" Leo grinned widely. "How in the gods' names did you even *get here* without a *mast?*"

Luck, mostly, and Illie's control over the winds, but he bit his tongue, not saying anything and just watching as Leo scrambled up the gangplank, eyes wide and hands moving over every surface of the ship.

"Oh, but she's a beauty," Leo continued. "She looks fast, too. Is she? And her *color*. You don't see red ships typically. Well, most people don't *paint* their ships, but this one... Oh, she's lovely. I have a green ship that I made myself. I normally make navy ships, and they don't want those painted."

A chill ran down Solveig's spine. The temples to Lady Lightbringer, Leo making navy ships...

He didn't recall Port 16 being affiliated with the navy at all. Undyne Island was part of Veridin's territory, but with Emperor Castros Helios pushing for his daughter, Iori, to marry the eldest son of the Veridin royal family, anything that was Veridinian was Aralythian.

Solveig climbed the gangplank to join Leo on the deck. He asked slowly, "Navy ships...?"

Leo looked up from the railing. "You're from Aralyth, right? But you're a pirate, so clearly, you don't care about politics. Sard Castros Helios, sard the navy, sard all of it."

He opened the door leading below deck and slipped through. Solveig followed.

"Castros Helios decided to put his navy here," Leo explained once they were out of the public's earshot. "He also decided to raise tariffs on *everything*. Making a ship is so unreasonably expensive now. Which I think is part of his plan. Make materials too expensive, so ships are too expensive so only the navy can buy them, and pirates can't buy new ships."

Solveig's stomach sank. He had funds, but they were supposed to last him until he brought the third moon back to Anwir.

"I can fix this for you," Leo finally said. "It'll take me a few days, but you'll be back to sailing soon."

4

THERE WAS ONLY ONE inn in all of Port 16, so Thol went there after following Lonan around the city. He'd learned, very quickly, that Lonan Ryker was incapable of shutting up.

He also learned where the best tavern was (Shelley's, on the water. Booze was a bit pricier, but the barmaids were busty enough to make it worth it. Lonan's words, not Thol's – he decided he would *not* be going there), where to get a good plate of greasy fish and chips (Rue's, which was two blocks from Shelley's, and while Thol's mouth watered at the idea of crispy fried fish, he couldn't help but feel like that would be cheating on Natha, and gods knew she'd had enough of that), where the inn was (Albatross Inn, no doubt where his crew was), and where the train station leading to the other ports was (useful information. It ran twenty-four hours in a continual loop, hitting each city twice a day).

"So," Lonan said when they returned to Albatross Inn. He lit another sugar cigarette – the fifth one in the past two hours – and stuck it between his teeth. "Blonde cook. What's her status? I wouldn't mind taking her out for drinks –"

"She's not interested," Thol said sternly, channeling every drop of his fatherly overprotective behavior. "She's divorced."

"Are *you* interested in her?" Lonan raised an eyebrow.

"I'm married." He looped his forefinger under the chain he wore around his neck, tugging the two rings free from under his shirt to flash at Lonan.

"Who's the lucky lass? She on the crew?"

He dropped the rings. "She's dead."

That wiped the smug grin off Lonan's face instantly. "Oh," he stammered. "I... Condolences, then. May you meet again in the next life."

Thol thought, then, of the oath every member of the crew swore – *I will pledge my final breath to your name and my first to find you again.* Silly words drawn up by a nine-year-old to make a game of pretend seem more real.

"I ought to find Leo," Lonan announced. "Tell your cook that if she wants to dip her toes in the courting pool –"

Thol simply walked inside the inn, not giving Lonan a chance to finish.

The weary woman behind the counter looked up. "How can I help you?"

"There should be a group here," he said. "Six people. I'm with them."

She rubbed her face. "They're in the dining room. *Please* tell them to quiet it down."

Great. Groaning internally, he followed where she pointed, pushing open a pair of double doors to a small and somewhat shabby – though cozy – dining room. Mismatched rugs covered the wood floors, and several tables were scattered about. Three had been pushed together to create a long enough table for seven people. At the head sat Solveig, his red hair messy and his face flushed.

The woman was right. They were *loud.*

Everyone – except Fynch – talked loudly, laughing, shouting, clinking plates and cups and silverware as they ate and passed dishes around.

"Whoever made these potatoes deserves time in Ivenis Justyce!" exclaimed Natha, who, despite her qualms, shoveled a forkful in her mouth.

"Gimme that. Stop hogging it." Ves grabbed a decanter of deep golden liquid – cinnamon rum. She filled her chalice to the brim and gulped it down. Solveig yanked the decanter back.

"Says you!" he scolded, filling up his own chalice.

"Oh, you're *right.*" Illie scrunched up her face as she chewed a mouthful of potatoes. "Why is it so hot in here?"

"Because I'm here," said Ves.

"Can I –" Czardas reached for the cinnamon rum.

"*No!*" everyone chorused.

Thol pulled out the chair on the other end of the table and sat down. Wordlessly, plates were passed around, followed by the quarter-full decanter of cinnamon rum. He piled some of the food onto his plate – a crispy chicken cutlet, creamy mashed potatoes, roasted vegetables. His expectations were low. After all, he'd gotten used to Natha's cooking.

He scooped up a bite and stuck it in his mouth.

There was no way he could go back to eating anything that wasn't Natha's.

"How was town?" Solveig asked from across the table.

"Did Lonan annoy you to death?" muttered Natha from over the rim of her chalice. "I'm annoyed to death just thinking about him."

"How many sugar cigarettes did he smoke?" asked Ves. "Twenty? Thirty?"

"Did you find any bookstores? I want to go shopping," piped up Illie.

"Did Captain Solveig tell you what Mister Leo said about my patch jobs?" Czardas puffed out his chest. "He said they were good."

"Considering the situation, the materials at hand, and your lack of experience," added Solveig.

Fynch said nothing.

Thol ate another bite, chewing thoughtfully before answering all the questions in order. "It was fine. I know where to find busty women, expensive booze, and fish and chips. I'm still here, so he didn't annoy me to death. I grew up with Nox, so it takes a lot to annoy me. He smoked five. I did find a bookstore – it's attached to the navigation supply shop. It's about two blocks from here. He did not tell me, but I know now. If you didn't make those patches, the *Serenity* would've sunk before we made it here."

He watched Fynch after he finished speaking. His lips were tinged blue, his skin clammy.

It was only a matter of time until the *Serenity* would be fixed. It had been many years since Thol went to Servedin, bleeding and on the brink of death. He could only hope the Blood Doctor remembered the favor he owed.

Only *slightly* tipsy, Illie decided to visit the bookstore after dinner. She put on her boots – she'd forgone them during dinner. Why wear them if she didn't need to? – and grabbed her bag. Ves, Natha, Thol, and Solveig were all in the room Illie shared with the other women, a bottle of cinnamon rum in front of them and cards in their hands. They hardly even said goodbye as she slipped out of the room and out of the inn.

The sun was still high in the sky despite the hour. The streets were crowded, too. Everyone must have just finished work and were headed home or to get drinks.

It didn't take long to find the bookstore Thol had found. Painted bright yellow, it stood out regardless. The blue letters on the window spelling the shop's name – *Pike's Books and Navigation Supply* – confirmed it was the place. She pushed open the door, a bell jingling to alert the old man behind the counter of her presence.

"Welcome in," he said, only barely glancing up from his book. "Anything I can help you find?"

"Could you show me where your oldest books are?" she asked, eyeing a sextant on a shelf with delight. She didn't *need* a new sextant, but her fingers itched to pick it up.

This time, the man did look up. His wrinkled face and long beard reminded Illie of Henry Quill, the man she'd practically been raised by after she ran away from home to become a cartographer. Her heart ached, squeezing painfully behind her ribs. Even though Henry had told her to go, to have the adventure her soul longed for – the one Carilon was far too small for – she wondered if he was doing fine without her. If she made the right decision to run away and take up a life of piracy.

"If you want books from before the Aralythian Conquest, those will be in the very back corner, over there. Look through the contents because the covers won't match." He nodded to the far right corner before going back to his book.

Her heart skipped a beat. Those books would be nearly three hundred years old – since the Aralythian Conquest was two-hundred-dred-some years ago. Just what she needed.

She thanked the man and skipped over to the small shelf in the corner, grabbing the first book she saw. As soon as she opened it, she knew what the man meant by *the covers won't match.*

Someone had torn the body of the book out and glued it to the fabric-bound cover of a *different* book. The title on the cover read *Poems from the Twin Serpent Isles,* but the title on the first page said *Legends from the Fylth Triad.*

She tucked it under her arm without looking through the rest of the book. Anything that *might* mention the third moon went into her growing stack. Soon, there were more books in her arms than there were on the shelf. Struggling under their weight, she shuffled back to the counter and set everything down.

As the man worked on counting the books, Illie spotted a map on the wall. It was a map of Undyne, all thirty port cities labeled, the coast of Veridin barely visible in the corner. She didn't even need to look at the *I. V.* in the corner to recognize it.

"I made that map," she blurted.

The man looked up, then turned to see the map she was pointing at. "Did you, now?"

She nodded quickly, then faltered. What if he was like the Redcoat Pirates? What if he didn't believe her because she was a woman?

"Well, isn't that something!" the old man beamed. "It's a good map. Excellent quality. Perfectly accurate. I get many compliments on it. I bought it in Carilon – in Veridin – a few years ago. From a little shop called –"

"The Ink and Rose!" Illie grinned. "I bet it was Elgar Quill who sold it to you. I was out sailing the world."

"Wiry lad with glasses?" when Illie nodded excitedly, the man smiled widely. "Then *you* must be Miss Valentine."

Nobody had ever recognized *her* before.

Unless... Her wanted poster...

The man pushed the books toward her. "For the greatest map-maker in the Veridin Kingdom. I can't charge you for these. Come back when you have another map for sale, and I'll consider it a fair trade." He opened his book again before she could argue. "I have family in Carilon. My son and his wife live there, and I have a granddaughter. Tia. They don't visit this old man much anymore, but word travels fast these days."

He looked up and winked. "Your secret is safe with me, Miss Valentine."

Fynch stared at the wall, trying to breathe.

Trying and failing.

He'd stomached a glass of water and three sips of broth at dinner before the pain became too much, and swallowing was a chore he didn't have the energy to complete. Everyone was too drunk – on rum, on life, on laughter – to even notice that Fynch Largos, notorious kitchen thief and biggest eater on the ship, hardly touched his plate.

And now, as his crew sat on the floor playing cards and laughing loudly, he stared at the wall, each breath he took painful enough to feel like his last. Every inhale sent iron-thick pain throughout his body, coating his tongue, reaching his toes. Every exhale made his skin crackle like dry paper being crumpled into a ball.

It was only a matter of time, really, until he died.

"How *big* is a moon?" Ves asked after she won another round of whatever game they were playing. Fynch's gaze slid over to her. She was pretty, he thought, with her dark curls pulled back off her face, her jade eyes bright and rum-drunk, her golden lip ring glinting in the light.

"I don't know. Like..." Solveig made a vague gesture with his hands, paused, then laughed when he realized he wouldn't be able to convey the size of a celestial body with just his hands. He held up a fist. "If this is Syrenis, then... Like this?" Next to his fist, he held out his thumb.

"Thumb sized?" Thol arched a brow.

"I don't know!" Solveig shot back.

Inhale. Wheezing, bloody pain.

Exhale. Crackling skin, tightness in his chest.

Inhale. His fingertips felt numb.

Exhale.

I'm going to die.

He closed his eyes.

When Fynch opened his eyes again, he knew he was not dead. The plate of breakfast next to the bed helped, but the fact that he was in agony only proved it. He must have fallen asleep. He wasn't getting much of that nowadays.

There was a note next to the plate. As delicious as the buttered bread and fluffy eggs smelled, he ignored them, grabbing the folded paper instead.

Bird,

I, T, N, and I are running errands. C and S are staying behind.

Back soon.

V.

Fynch was a street rat with the rare ability to read, but Ves's awful handwriting made him doubt his literacy. He had to read it three times to understand what it meant.

"You're up!" Czardas exclaimed, startling Fynch enough that he jumped. Pain throbbed from his lung.

"I'm up," he murmured, too tired to say anything else.

"You should eat something," Czardas said, gesturing to the plate. He should. He wasn't going to. The sound of his skin crackling, the excruciating pain, all of it filled his stomach with nausea. He just wanted to go back to sleep and wake up when the pain was gone for good.

He lay back down, slowly, stiffly, hand pressed against his side just beneath the tender line of stitches. When he was too tired to get up, Ves would clean them, making sure they didn't get infected. Because the last thing Fynch needed on top of a punctured – likely collapsed – lung was sarding *sepsis*.

Fynch always knew he would die young. Urchins didn't live very long. His mother hadn't. His brother had climbed from the gutter and made a name for himself, shaking away the coat of poverty in exchange for something grander. But Fynch...

It was a miracle – or sheer luck – that he made it to nineteen. He just wished this lethal injury would stop dragging out and merc him already, if only to put him out of his misery.

Czardas grabbed a mug of something and held it to Fynch's lips. A few drops fell into his mouth. *Water.*

"Take a few sips," Czardas instructed, tipping the mug so he had no choice but to swallow. Each bob of his throat hurt more than the last like he was swallowing daggers. After three gulps, he pushed the cup away and covered his mouth with his hand.

He could not die fast enough.

Solveig had a reputation. *Captain Nox Solveig, cloaked in green... Second most wanted pirate in the world, Jonyth Commodore's arch nemesis, Anwir Helios's personal errand boy... Yet here he was, stuck on governess duty.*

Captain Nox Solveig? As if anyone treated him like that. No, they acted like he was *Nanny* Nox Solveig.

It didn't help that Czardas and Fynch were both grown adults, Czardas being only four years younger than Solveig was. But to him, they were just kids.

And because *he* was left to watch after them (*"You're just going to go off on a tangent and accidentally liberate Undyne and get us into more trouble than we need right now, so you stay here, Cap,"* Ves had scolded him), Solveig felt like a glorified babysitter.

Of his crew, Solveig knew the least about Czardas and Fynch. He knew they were close friends, and he knew that Czardas came from *old* money. He knew Czardas could play nearly fifty instruments and that Fynch could shoot a fly from midair, clear across the room with his eyes closed.

But that was it.

He sat lazily in the chair propped by the rickety desk in the small room. His back ached in places he didn't know it could ache after sleeping on the floor. Surprisingly, Seven-B – the lowest level of Ivenis Justyce Penitentiary – was more comfortable than the inn's uneven hardwood. The blankets Thol, Czardas, and he used were still strewn about haphazardly.

"What's your story?" he asked, not directing the question to one specific boy.

Fynch didn't answer. Solveig hardly expected him to. But Czardas spoke up like he was used to it. "My mother is a duchess, and my father is a musician – and a duke by marriage. F is my best friend. He wanted to run away, so I followed him."

Solveig resisted the urge to smack his face against the desk repeatedly. Either Czardas was withholding information on purpose, or he had no idea how to hold a conversation.

Solveig leaned toward the latter.

He and Czardas had grown up on opposite ends of the food chain. Czardas, with his blue blood and wealthy, prestigious background, sat at the top, a silver spoon in his mouth and the world in his palms. Meanwhile, Solveig was the lowest of the low, born to a wench of a mother with a belly that wasn't ever full until he became a pirate. And yet... There they were, crewing together as pirates on the high seas.

Babysitting the boys was going to be torture.

Sighing, he finger-combed his red hair off his forehead and pivoted in his seat to look at the newspaper left on the table. Habit had him flipping to the most wanted section, where a grin tugged on his lips at the sight of his name above the five-hundred-million-lune bounty. It still put him in the second most wanted position, but with Bonny Reed gone – locked away in Ivenis Justyce, if the newspaper was to be trusted – a *new* fifth most wanted had appeared.

Worth four hundred fifteen million lune was Bartholomew *sarding* Williams.

He flipped back to the front page to skim the article there.

He read it twice before the silence became too much. Groaning, he stood. "Czardas, you take care of Fynch." He slung his coat over his shoulders and trudged over to the door.

"Where are you going?" Czardas asked.

"To the harbor," he said. "I want to check on the *Serenity*."

The two could handle themselves without Governess Solveig, right?

5

VES KEPT HER FACE tilted toward the sun as she walked, Thol matching her stride with ease. At breakfast that morning, the crew split up: Natha and Illie caught the train bright and early to shop for food supply, Czardas and Solveig stayed behind at the inn to keep an eye on Fynch, and Ves and Thol were left to get local supplies, and to see if they could find any more clues on the lost moon.

Dressed for the heat in baggy pants and a buttoned shirt that she tied around her ribs, Ves basked in the warmth. Four years of being trapped underground in the musty dark had taken its toll on her. She would never get enough sunshine in her life. Her orange leather ledger was stuffed in one of her pockets, along with her pen. It would be easier to take inventory as they made purchases – with the money tucked in her bosom. Ves wanted as much time outside in the summer sun as she could get, and being stuck inside working would eat into her freedom.

"You ever been to the Salts Atoll?" she asked, peering over at Thol. He was nearly seven feet tall, yet only a few inches taller than her at most.

"If you're asking if I've seen something that could possibly resemble a missing *moon*, no. I haven't," he said flatly.

She'd learned, rather quickly, that most of his emotion was reserved for Solveig only.

"I'm *asking*," she stressed, "if you've had a tropical vacation to the Ruby Sea. A honeymoon, maybe? Where *did* you go for your honeymoon? Isn't it custom for newlyweds to spend a full month alone away from home?"

Ves had never been married – nor had she ever entertained the idea – but she was fairly certain that was the norm in all four major countries – the Aralyth Empire, the Merdyne Empire, the Veridin Kingdom, and the Kingdom of Gello.

"I didn't take an extended honeymoon."

She huffed quietly. How she ended up on a crew with a bunch of non-talkers was beyond her.

Still, before she could pester Thol with more questions, he said, "Meadow and I didn't have a lot of money lying around to fund a honeymoon. In instances like ours, the groom's party pays for the wedding, and the bride's party pays for the honeymoon. Solveig is my only family, and he was off on a high seas adventure at the time, and Meadow had no living relatives."

Well, now she felt guilty for asking.

She kicked a rock with the toe of her boot, watching as it skittered across the cobblestone street only to tumble into a storm drain.

"Do you have a list of things we need?" Thol redirected the conversation, taking Ves's guilt with it.

She did, scribbled on a scrap piece of paper tucked away in her orange ledger. With Natha and Illie dealing with the brunt of the supplies needed, Ves's list was short – short enough that she had it memorized.

"Barrels – three of them, at least – and gunpowder. Lamp oil, thread, soap – for everyone else, not for me. I only buy *luxury* soap – and needles – all types. Pinkie said she'd handle getting the rum, so I'm trusting her." She tapped her fingers with each item. Until the *Serenity* was repaired, Solveig had instructed her not to get any rigging supplies. They wouldn't know what was needed until after she was fixed.

"We could split up," Thol suggested. "Meet back here in an hour or so."

She twisted her face up as she thought. It *would* be faster, and the sooner she got her work done, the sooner she could check out that tavern Thol mentioned the day before. But the thought of walking around Port 16 with a wild Lonan on the loose kicked her fight-or-flight instincts into overdrive.

I could take him, she thought. *In a fight, that is.*

"If you get the barrels and gunpowder, I'll get everything else," she conceded. "But send everything to the inn. I want you to show me that tavern after this."

He arched a brow. "The one with the busty barmaids?"

She grinned. "The very same."

Natha stared out the window, watching the shimmering blur of the ocean race by. After being on a ship for so many weeks, sitting on a train felt...wrong. It was too stationary. She itched to get up and walk the length of the car, to march into the kitchen and ask why a pot of coffee and a pot of tea took so long to make, to do *anything* but sit and stare.

It wasn't uncommon for ladies to wear trousers and boots, but Illie and Natha needed to blend in. So, instead of wearing her usual tunic and pants, Natha wore one of Illie's day dresses. It was too tight along her bust and around her hips, and she felt particularly naked without her gloves, but it would have to do.

She rubbed her wrist absently, the mottled, milky scars smooth beneath her fingertips.

"I don't want to pry," Illie began, drawing Natha's attention. *Then don't,* she thought, but Illie continued: "And you don't have to answer this, but those scars... Did your ex-husband do that to you?"

She folded her hands on her lap, trying to hide them. "No. I...had an accident when I was younger. I'll cover them up if they bother you."

"No!" she rushed to say. "No, no, no. They don't! I just wanted to make sure that sarding son of a wench wasn't let off easy. I have some scars, too. The one on my shoulder will scar." She gestured to her arm, which was no longer in a sling now that Thol wasn't around. "I injured my eyebrow when we fought against the Redcoat Pirates in Carilon, but it didn't scar. Sol said all the best pirates have scars."

Something fluttered in Natha's chest. A smile tugged on the corner of her lips, barely there but...there all the same.

"To make a long story short," she said, tracing the outline of the scar along her thumb, "I accidentally set myself on fire."

"*What?!*"

Natha just smiled. Moments later, a cart came by, and a young girl set a tray on the table between the benches – two pots, two cups and saucers, two spoons, a dish of sugar, and a dish of cream. Natha got to work out of habit, making Illie's tea the way she liked it – no cream and three sugars. Then, she poured her own coffee – six sugars, a splash of coffee.

She took a long drink of her liquid sugar, once again looking out the window.

"Oh, you'll like this," Illie said suddenly. Natha glanced over to see Illie's face buried in a newspaper. "People suspect Prince Anwir is going to be visiting either Merdyne or Gello soon. He's been buying a lot of things for travel – maps, too. They'd better be mine – and is rarely home. There's a poll, too. Apparently, the general public wants him to marry Empress Nefeli. I mean, *I* would. Have you seen pictures of her? She's known for being the most beautiful woman in Syrenis for a reason. But a lot of people think he'll go for the princess of Gello. What do you think?"

Illie and Natha had that in common: they loved to read. While Illie preferred history books and texts on myths and legends, Natha devoured the gossip columns and the occasional romance novel. If there was one thing she loved almost as much as cooking, it was *royal* gossip.

She scooted to the edge of her seat. "What are the numbers?"

"Seventy-two percent says he'll go for Merdyne," Illie said. "Twenty-eight says Gello."

She twisted her mouth. "Clear favor for Merdyne. Empress Nefeli might be a bit too ambitious, but Anwir *is* a Helios."

"I don't want him to marry Empress Nefeli," Illie grumbled. "She's too much for him. And their babies wouldn't be cute."

Natha snorted. She tried to imagine Catrione-Helios babies – darker skin, black eyes, hair *some* shade of blue – and lost it. She laughed, her coffee spilling over the edge of her cup and onto her scarred hands.

"You're right," she said through her laughter. "I agree with the poll, but what if he has a *secret lover* he's going to meet?"

Illie's honeyed eyes went wide. "A secret lover? Do tell me more."

"It makes sense, doesn't it?" She set her cup down. "He's refused all marriage proposals; he hasn't made a move on Empress Nefeli or the Gello princess. He could have *anyone* in the kingdom, but he remains a bachelor. He's not a playboy, either."

If anyone knew who warmed Anwir Helios's bed, it would be Natha. In those two years she spent married to her ex-husband, Adrian Zimmer, the only things that kept her sane were cooking and gossip (and even the former did little for her). She'd spent plenty of time around the royal family of Veridin, and she grew up on the upper end of middle class, so it was easy for her to stick her nose where it didn't belong.

Illie nodded intently. "A secret lover makes sense, then. Do you think they're a noble?"

Natha shook her head. "If he's being this secretive about it, they have to be a commoner. Someone at the *very* bottom of the social ladder."

Ironically, where she was now.

She grabbed her cup and took a deep drink of her sugary coffee. "Romance is too tiring," she said with a groan. "I don't recommend it to anyone."

Illie raised her cup of tea in a toast. "I'll drink to that."

Leo pushed his goggles atop his head and wiped his brow with the back of his gloved hand. The heat made his heavy work pants cling to his legs – well, to his flesh leg. His prosthetic didn't sweat – and his hair stick to the back of his neck. Thanks to the Wanderer's blessing, Leo's body temperature always ran hot. It was awfully convenient in the colder months – even Lonan would sleep in Leo's room because of the body heat he radiated – but in the summer?

He was a human puddle of sweat.

If Lonan was working, he'd surely have no shirt on, a glass of something cold in one hand, and a lady in the other. It was *good* he was off running the shop front.

Several years ago, Lonan and Leo opened up a shipbuilding business together. Leo built the ships, Lonan dealt with the books and sales. He had the charm for it; he could talk anyone into buying *anything*. The storefront was a small building by the docks they'd bought. Inside were dozens of photographs and newspaper clippings from their various feats – Lonan showed up to look pretty, while Leo was behind everything. It was also about ten degrees cooler inside than it was under the sweltering sun.

His first cursory inspection of the pirate ship the *Serenity* was that she was beautiful, but in rough shape. But after taking a closer look, he came to the conclusion that she wasn't just in rough shape.

She was in shambles. Shredded apart, ready to die.

He sighed heavily and leaned against an unbroken bit of her railing. "You must have some incredible stories," he murmured to the ship as if she were sentient. "I'm sorry you bear the brunt of the scars."

Leo pulled his goggles back down, the tinted lenses protecting his eyes from the glare of the sun bouncing off the waves below. As he stood upright, a flash of green caught his gaze.

"Oh!" he shouted. "Hey! Up here!"

Captain Nox Solveig craned his head back to look at Leo. He hurried up the gangplank and crossed the deck to where Leo stood.

"How's it looking?" Solveig asked.

Leo faltered. Lying to a pirate would be dangerous, and he – unlike Lonan – didn't have a death wish. He pushed his goggles back again and looked away.

Truthfully, the *Serenity* was beyond repair. Her hull was damaged badly enough that only a complete replacement would fix her, and her keel... Somehow it had cracked, a hairline fissure fracturing the center of it. An entire mast was gone, along with most of the railing. The deck was littered with more holes and scuff marks than Leo knew what to do with, the sails were torn, and the helm had seen better days. The figurehead – a pretty lass at the front of the ship, Serenity herself – looked desperate, like the wood carving wanted to be put out of her misery.

Leo rubbed his face. "I'm going to be completely honest," he said slowly. "It doesn't look good. I'm going to do everything I can – I'm the best sarding shipwright in Syrenis, after all – but... She's broken, Captain. She's been through hell and back."

To Leo's surprise, Captain Solveig *didn't* gut him right there.

Instead, the captain said: "Thol told me to take care of her. I should've listened..."

"Yes, you should have," Leo scolded before he could stop himself. He shook his head, sighing from his nose. "It...happens. I won't say the *Serenity* is the best-case-scenario ship I've ever seen, but she isn't the worst, either. I'm going to do my best, Captain. But right now, I can't make any promises."

Leo shifted his gaze to the mast where the black flag would have been, had the pirates not taken it down when they brought all their belongings with them to the inn. Undyne was under navy control. Nearly every ship Leo had worked on since becoming a shipwright belonged to the navy. Fleet Admiral Jonyth Commodore's *Mary Jolene* was built in Port 16 – not by Leo, but by the (second) greatest shipwright Undyne ever produced. She'd been constructed in that very shipyard alongside some of the most famous ships in history – the *Eldwode's Revenge*, the *Dragon King*... Almost all the ships from the previous generation had been built there, too.

The navy's *Anna Moore*. The *Starless*, the *Sea Lady*, the *Lilac Dream*, the *Blazing Sun*. Only one hadn't been built in Port 16, but Leo still thought Undyne deserved bragging rights.

He thought of the ship tucked away safely in a bunker. Of her green hull, her black sails, the gold painted name, the unbreakable keel sourced from wood that simply should not exist...

If any ship deserved to be a pirate ship, it was that one.

Leo adjusted his goggles. "Don't worry, Captain. One way or another, you'll be back to sailing the four seas soon."

Ves had a new ribbon in her hair when she joined Thol an hour later.

"We're basically on vacation, aren't we, Flowers?" She knocked her hip against his. Thol bit the inside of his cheek to keep from smiling.

"If you count *being stranded in Undyne because our ship is ruined* as a vacation, then sure." He stuffed his hands in his pockets and started walking, following the route he and Lonan had taken the day before.

Shelley's was a single-story tavern right on the water, situated on a boardwalk that stretched out over the sea, high enough to protect it from the tides. The lights inside were dim, the windows covered to keep the heat out, and the smell of booze and something savory hit Thol's senses the moment he and Ves stepped through the door.

A woman behind the counter – *Poet,* Lonan had not been lying – looked up from the spot she was polishing. "Have a seat wherever," she called. "I'll be by in just a minute."

Ves strode through the tavern, going to a small table in the back. She slid into one of the seas, head turned to face the bar, leaving Thol to sit in the other chair.

Meadow, forgive me, he begged the spirit of his wife.

The same barmaid waltzed over. She was short – about Fynch's height – and curvy, with green hair and a stained apron. She said, "Special today is soup. You with the Lady?"

A phrase Thol hadn't heard in *years.*

There were two ways to interpret the words, but they both meant the same thing. *The Lady,* meaning all the navy's ships being named after women, or *the Lady,* meaning Lady Lightbringer, the goddess of war, justice, and strength.

"Would the prices go up or down if we were?" Thol asked, quickly interjecting before Ves could. He wasn't sure how much slang she'd remembered locked away in Ivenis Justyce Penitentiary for four years, and he didn't want to risk getting kicked out.

"Up." The barmaid crossed her arms over her chest. "You on that red piece of sard that came in yesterday?"

"And if we were...?" He cocked a brow.

The barmaid shook her head. The movement reminded him so much of Meadow whenever Thol did something to annoy her – like forgetting that she was craving fried octopus despite her never telling him or hanging the laundry out to dry when he should have predicted that the weather would suddenly turn and drench all the clean linens.

"Boy," the barmaid scolded. Thol flinched. "I'm trying to see if I need to charge you."

She pulled up her sleeve then, revealing a raised scar, the pale flesh curved into a *P*. The brand of a pirate who'd been caught by the navy. Solveig had the same scar.

"Stop turning down free booze," Ves said. "We're pirates. I'm sure you know us. Look at the paper and Flowers here and our captain'll be there."

"Two rums and two specials, then?" the barmaid asked.

Ves grinned. "Yes, ma'am."

As the barmaid walked off, the door swung open, and a group walked in. Thol's eyes narrowed. They all wore uniforms, but they were too far away for Thol to make out any ranks.

But one of them...

He had blond hair and a jawline that was *so* familiar.

The navy men sat at a large table, their loud chatter already grating Thol's nerves. When the barmaid returned with two bowls and two mugs overflowing with cinnamon rum, one of the navy men whistled, calling her over.

And they were supposed to be the sailors who protected the world.

He picked up his spoon and absently pushed the noodles and shredded meat around his bowl, appetite gone. To the barmaid's credit, she didn't seem bothered, not even as she leaned close to the man who whistled at her.

His wife Meadow used to work at a tavern. The thought of anyone objectifying her like that made him sarding sick.

The blond man turned his head, and Thol got a glimpse at his face.

His stomach sank. Even with a full set of pearly white teeth, even with a nose that hadn't been broken more than once, even with hair cropped short at the sides, even with the pristine uniform, Thol recognized that face.

Because it was *Fynch's* face.

Thol frowned. "Do you know if Fynch has any living family?" He whispered.

Ves looked up from her drink. "Besides Strings? No clue. Why?"

He pointed out the navy man. She cursed under her breath.

"Why is everyone suddenly related to someone in the navy?" She hissed. "Are you? Is Cap?"

Thol wasn't. He knew that for a fact. But Solveig...? He'd overheard his mother, Mistress Solveig, speaking with someone in town once, many years ago.

"The training paid off," she had boasted, oblivious of Thol, who was hiding behind a crate of apples – ones he planned to steal. *"Because he had nothing but muscles beneath that uniform."*

He hadn't told Solveig about it. Even if Mistress Solveig *had* slept with a navy sailor, there was no guarantee he was Solveig's father.

Mistress Solveig wasn't the village whore for no reason.

"Well, we know Strings is related to a musician," Ves said as she gulped down the rest of her rum. "And Blondie only had that ex-husband of hers. She's from a noble bloodline, you know. Same with Pinkie. Well, she's not *technically* nobility. Just...from a very wealthy family. Wealthy, nobility, same difference, really."

"We need to go," Thol said. "Talk to Fynch. See if he has any family in the navy."

She took Thol's rum and drank it, too. "Sard the navy and their schemes to keep me from having it off with anyone. Fine, Flowers. Let's go."

By the time the train stopped in Port 30, the shopping district, Illie was ready to go back to her bed on the *Serenity*.

Scraping her hair back to tie in a messy bun, she stepped off the train and onto the platform, Natha close behind.

"I've been to Undyne," Illie said, looking at the city beyond the train station, "but never to Port 30."

Natha, who usually had no energy, grabbed Illie's wrist and started dragging her to the city square. On all sides were stores, outdoor market stalls, even peddlers pushing carts along the cobblestone advertising their wares. Natha's eyes were as wide as the moons Mene and Sin as she drank everything in.

Illie chuckled. Undyne didn't have a mapmaking district – all their maps were imported from Aralyth and Veridin. During one of her voyages with Henry Quill, they had stopped at Port 25 to sell some of their maps. Since Undyne mainly relied on exports, there was no need for a proper sailing district. Undyne was made up of farmers and craftsmen, not people who needed seafaring maps. If there was a mapmaking district, Illie would be just as ecstatic as Natha was now.

Natha dragged Illie into a grocer's. She picked up a wire basket from a stack by the door and shoved it into Illie's arms. "Hold this," she instructed. "I need both hands."

"You're acting like you just uncovered the third moon itself."

"This is a close second." She targeted a wooden stand overflowing with fruit. Her scarred hands danced over the fruits, expertly grabbing only the most perfect ones. She set everything – apples, lekims, pears, grapes, and some that Illie didn't even recognize – in the wire basket.

"Fruits don't last long," Natha muttered to herself. "I could make jam with the grapes, use the pears for dessert... Korva and salted meat will last a long time. Rice has a long shelf life. I could make pasta with shrimp..."

She grabbed some tomatoes and put them in the basket before moving to another stand.

"Did you know that Empress Nefeli's favorite drink is something with lekim juice, cacao beans, and sugar syrup?" she asked, grabbing a cacao pod that Illie simply couldn't believe was the first step to tasty chocolate. "I want to make it, but only two people in all of Syrenis know the recipe. If I'm ever in Merdyne, I plan to become the third."

Illie went over to a shelf full of loose teas. She recognized most of them, but she scanned the labels for a specific blend.

"Lightbringer's Kiss...?" she murmured, pausing at a jar full of dried flower buds. "Natha, have you ever heard of a tea called *Lightbringer's Kiss?*"

Natha, carrying an armful of vegetables and dried goods in jars, hurried over. She dumped everything into the basket.

"No," she said, looking at the tea. "Not as a tea. Lightbringer's Kiss is a type of flower. It's sacred to the navy. Adrian insisted I use them in my wedding bouquet."

The navy.

Illie swallowed back the unease that had built up in her chest. "We should hurry," she said, tightening her grip on the wire basket. There were no winds inside to grab in case something went wrong.

"You go get the dried goods and the alcohol. I'll get everything else," Natha said.

As Illie turned down an aisle, she caught a glimpse of a sign in the window – one she'd overlooked before. Reading it backward and without her glasses took a few tries, but when she got it, her stomach sank.

LONG LIVE THE EMPEROR!

GLORY TO THE NAVY!

DEATH TO ALL PIRATES!

6

"How's the ship looking?" Lonan waltzed up the *Serenity*'s gangplank like he owned it. She *was* a beautiful ship beneath all the damage. His fingers itched to take the wheel and sail her to the end of the world and back. She was *fast,* built for speed and maneuverability. And other things, likely, but that was Leo's thing. Lonan only cared about *sailing* the ships.

"Like your face," Leo quipped without looking up from his toolbox.

"Absolutely, breathtakingly beautiful?" Lonan stuck a cigarette between his teeth. "You flatter me, you flirt. Light this?"

Leo held up his middle finger, a spark dancing there. Lonan leaned close, letting the flame ignite his sugar cigarette. Taking a deep breath of the sweet air, he sauntered up the stairs to the helm. He wrapped his fingers around the pegs of the wheel, giving it an experimental turn.

"Knock it off," Leo called. "No touching. Don't you have other things to do? Like, manning the front of our shop? Taking orders? Annoying literally anyone else in Port 16?"

"Ooh, touchy." He puffed out a cloud of smoke. "Relax, Leo. I came here to see if you needed help. Ah, ah, ah. Before you tell me to sard off, I brought an enticement."

"That's a big word. You sure you know what it means?"

"It means I brought booze."

"I'm working."

"You're rummaging through your toolbox. If you're looking for the jerry iron, it's in your belt."

Leo reached for his toolbelt. Even with his back to him, Lonan could feel the irritation sliding over Leo's face like a mask. He took another drag of his cigarette and lazed his way down the steps, pulling a flask of whiskey from his pocket.

"Still on the clock," Leo grumbled. He took the flask, opening it with his teeth and taking a deep drink. He wordlessly handed it back and got to work, scraping his jerry iron along the seam where the railing met the deck.

Lonan knew, in theory, the *names* of all the tools. He could pick them out from a lineup if he had to. He knew a jerry iron was the metal tool that looked like an inverted triangle on a stick, used for extracting old oakum from seams. He *also* knew that if he was in a life-or-death situation where he had to use a jerry iron *correctly* or die, he would simply perish.

He drank from the flask, savoring the whiskey's burn as it slithered down his throat and settled like lava in his belly. Lips still slick with booze, he brought his sugar cigarette to his mouth, letting the rich, sweet oxygen fill his lungs.

His physician had warned him more than once not to mix drinking and sugar cigarettes. In fact, he technically wasn't supposed to be drinking at all, but Leo didn't know that. If Leo knew...

Well, that would add a whole other layer of stress to Leo's shoulders – stress he didn't need.

Together, Lonan and Leo had four arms, three legs, and one working heart. For as long as he could remember, Lonan had a weak heart. He'd nearly died more than once – one time falling off a ship, the only permanent injury he sustained being the scar that sliced through his upper lip – because his fragile heart simply couldn't keep up.

Leo reached his hand back. Lonan returned the flask to him before leaning against the intact railing, head tipped back to gaze at the sky.

"Are you seriously just going to stand there looking like the lovestruck hero in some bodice-ripper novel?" Leo set the flask down and went right back to scraping out oakum. It piled on the deck in gross strings.

"You admit if I was in a novel, I'd be the lovestruck hero? *And* I'd be in a bodice ripper?" Lonan grinned widely. "How do *you* know about bodice rippers?"

Leo, who knew Lonan better than Lonan knew himself sometimes, grabbed a handful of oakum and threw it at him.

Lonan gagged, furiously wiping his hands over himself to get rid of the tarred hemp.

"Make yourself useful," Leo instructed, tossing the jerry iron at Lonan, who quickly grabbed it before the inverted triangle bit could embed itself in his perfect face.

"I *am* being useful," drawled Lonan. He sat down regardless and began scraping at the oakum. As much as he wanted to go out and test how fast the *Serenity* could sail, once Leo gave him an order, Lonan simply could not refuse.

They had two moods when working: total silence or nonstop bickering. They'd been friends longer than Lonan could remember – Leo was family now, more so than his eight siblings who had all moved along with his parents when one of his sisters got married were. Bickering was normal.

But sometimes, on rare occasions, they had civilized conversations – ones that would eventually lead to bickering but started out calm, nonetheless.

"I can't believe I'm fixing *Nox Solveig's* ship," said Leo. He grabbed a flathead screwdriver, using it to pry out a few crooked nails. "Do you think he'll kill me if I tell him I can't actually fix it?"

"Probably," said Lonan, unserious. "But, hey, at least you'll be famous. Isn't Solveig the most wanted?"

"Second-most. The Unnamed God is number one. I *wish* I could see his ship."

The *Nameless* was a phantom ship, its sightings so rare it made krakens seem common. Lonan wanted to see that ship, too. Not just see it – *sail it.* It had to be fast. Stealthy, too, built for speed and maneuverability and silence. His mouth practically watered at the thought of being at the *Nameless*'s helm. In the history of piracy, it was among the most famous. Lonan could only think of one pirate ship *more* famous than the *Nameless.*

"Shipwright dies after refusing to fix second most wanted's ship," teased Lonan. "It doesn't sound as grand."

"I'm not *refusing,*" grumbled Leo. "I *want* to fix her. I really do. And I *am* the world's greatest shipwright, so don't you dare start with that. I just... She's in awful shape. Wanderer knows how she managed to get here without sinking. She has more holes than you've seen in your lifetime, and you're the town wench."

"That's a lot of sarding holes, then," he mused.

Leo continued as if he didn't hear Lonan – a common occurrence: "Materials aren't even an issue. I don't care how expensive lumber is – well, I do, but not in this situation – because Captain Solveig said he could pay no matter what. And, frankly, I'm terrified to charge him anything, but that's not the point. The *point* is that no matter how much wood, no matter how talented I am, no matter if the Wanderer themselves come to fix this ship, the *Serenity* is right on the cusp of no return."

Lonan used the edge of the jerry iron to pick at the oakum lodged beneath his nails. His heart skipped a dangerous beat. He needed to take a break, and soon, but he lowered the jerry iron and said, "What's the main problem?"

Leo tugged his goggles off and rubbed the edge of his shirt along the glass. "The keel. It's cracked."

Lonan set the jerry iron down, exchanging it for his case of sugar cigarettes. He put one between his teeth – Leo snapped a spark without having to be asked – and said, "Fine. I'll be the bearer of bad news. But *you* will owe me. Big time."

His entire life, Fynch had fought tooth and nail to stay alive. He'd been given the worst odds, a hand so bad he should have folded from the start, but he bluffed his way through, managing to scrape himself not quite to the top but to a landing spot decent enough he didn't want to give it up.

He wanted to give up now, though.

There was something about being stuck in bed, unable to move, wet pain radiating from his lung, his chest, his back, that made life not really worth it. If he could close his eyes and never open them again, he would be content, if only it meant the pain would go away.

The door opened, footsteps shuffled in, the door shut. Fynch didn't look away from the ceiling. Czardas was in the room with him, and Solveig had returned fifteen minutes ago. According to Solveig, Natha and Illie had gone to Port 30 for shopping and wouldn't be back for another few hours at least.

"Birdie," Ves said, her loud voice louder than usual. Or, perhaps his ears were just more sensitive than normal. He shifted his eyes toward her, unable to move much more.

His movements had not been this limited only hours ago.

She perched herself right on the edge of the bed. "Do you have siblings?"

He had Czardas. Czar was the only brother Fynch needed. Still, he managed a slow blink, hoping she would translate that as a *yes*.

"He does," Czardas spoke up. Because, of *course*, he knew. He knew everything there was to know about Fynch. "Five of them."

"Tell me about them," Ves demanded.

Czardas hesitated. Fynch slow blinked again.

"He has three sisters – Starling, Robin, and Wren – and two brothers – Sparrow and Dove. His mother liked birds. Dove and Wren are twins – they're younger. How old are they now?"

Fynch blinked seventeen times. He hadn't seen them since he was their age.

"Robin, Starling, and Sparrow are older," Czardas continued."

"Tell me about Sparrow," Ves pressed. "How old is he? What does he look like? What does he do for a job?"

Fynch sucked in a single painful breath and croaked, "Row is twenty-four. We all took after our mother, except for Robin. I haven't seen him in six years. He was in the navy."

Ves cursed. Loudly.

"Blond hair, green eyes?" Thol, who had come in with Ves, asked. "I'm not sure if you want a family reunion after six years, but you might be getting one. It seems like your brother is here."

The last time Fynch had seen his brother Sparrow was when he was thirteen years old, sitting on the pavement outside the local navy branch, teeth digging into his lip as he tried not to cry.

"It doesn't matter if you can shoot Emperor Castros Helios's crown right off his sarding head," the navy woman he'd talked to had said. *"You have a history of ending up in jail. You're lucky I'm not having you arrested for good right now."*

When Row found out later that day that Fynch had tried to join the navy like he'd done six months earlier, he beat Fynch black and blue.

"You're a thief, Fynch," he'd snapped. *"If people find out we're related, you will ruin* everything *for me, just like you always do."*

That had been the last time Fynch ever saw Row. He'd left the next morning, all his belongings stuffed into a single rucksack, and went north to Aramore, Aralyth, to begin his training. A year later Fynch was arrested for armed robbery, and a year after that his mother died. If Row had gone to the potter's funeral, Fynch didn't know. He'd been long gone by then.

But if Row was here in Port 16...

He squeezed his eyes shut, wishing he would hurry up and die so he wouldn't have to see his brother. Of his siblings, Fynch only ever got along with Dove and Wren. They were the only ones who didn't blame him for their mother's death. They were the only ones who stayed up late, sitting by the door until he got home, no matter how long it took.

Between picking pockets for money, he would steal things for them, too. He stole teddy bears meant for the newborn princesses Vivian and Haru; he stole a pink bracelet for Wren; he stole books about insects for Dove – he risked his life over and over just to bring smiles to their faces.

And then Row left. And then Fynch got arrested again and again and again. And then their mother died. And then Star kicked him out of their house, screaming, *"It's all your sarding fault, Fynch! It's your fault Ma is gone! Don't even think about ever coming back! You're dead to us!"* And then he lived in Czardas's hidden library. And then he stole a compass from the Royal Veridian Museum of History. And then he became a pirate.

And *now,* six years later, lives on the complete opposite ends of the legal spectrum, Fynch was about to reunite with Sparrow – his older brother whom he'd once idolized and wanted to be *just* like. His older brother, who, without hesitation, would put a bullet between Fynch's eyes.

I'd rather have a bullet in my brain than the remains of one in my lung, he thought grimly.

Maybe he could convince someone to kill him later. Natha would probably do it. Or even –

He coughed. Iron flooded his tongue, his lips, as he spat out globs of thick, dark blood. Before he could catch his breath to cough again, his stomach tightened.

Fynch rolled onto his side just in time to vomit all over the floor. In the low light, it looked black, like the remains of coffee, like damp sand. His chest heaved, lungs struggling to take in air, to drown out the acrid tang of blood that simply would not go away, to keep up with the racing of his heart. Each raspy gasp led to another cough – another mouthful of blood spat onto the floor.

"I... I don't feel good," he whispered.

Then, everything went dark.

7

"WE CAN'T JUST SIT around and wait for the *Serenity* to be fixed," said Ves as she paced the length of the room enough times Solveig felt dizzy.

"I'll talk to Lonan and Leo," Thol said. He brushed his fingers against the scar cutting across his chest. "There's a doctor in Servedin who owes me."

"How do you know that doctor is still there?" Ves snapped.

It had been ten minutes since Fynch vomited up blood and passed out. Five since Illie and Natha returned, disheveled and panting and muttering about never riding horses again.

"Then we come up with a plan B," Thol shot back. "Nox, with your permission, I want to take him to Corsa."

Solveig pressed his fingers against Fynch's throat. His pulse beat rapidly, too fast, and too shallow. But it was beating, and that was all Solveig cared about.

The last thing Solveig wanted was to split up. With the navy in Undyne, the *Serenity* unusable, and the crew still injured and fatigued from their fight with the Rabbit Pirates a few weeks ago, splitting up would only make them more vulnerable. But if Fynch didn't get treatment – and *soon* – he would die.

And Solveig would do *anything* to keep his crew alive.

"Thol, you go get Lonan and Leo. Tell them we need to borrow a ship. I'll pay the fee." When Thol didn't move, Solveig shoved a hand through his hair and pointed at the door. *"Now!"*

Thol darted out the door without a word.

Solveig closed his eyes. *Kesh, Trudeau, Zayn, Prokofiev, Gael, Vern, Scorpion. Captain Hardy. Them...* The people he had loved and lost over the years built up – an amount too high for his liking. Yet he didn't want to add to that number. He didn't want to lose Fynch.

He *wouldn't* lose Fynch.

Illie spoke up, pulling Solveig from his thoughts. "I'll go to Corsa with him. With my abilities, we'd make it there twice as fast. I... Permission to go, Captain?"

There was still tension between Solveig and his crew. He *had* lied to them – kept the map leading them to the third moon and the body of a dead god from them. Thol and Illie asking for his permission sent a thorny spike of dread down his spine.

"Granted," he said through his teeth. "Illie and Thol will go with Fynch to Corsa. Czardas, Ves, Natha, you will stay here with me."

"No!" Ves snapped. "You can't force me to stay here. I want to go with them."

"I want to go, too," said Czardas, though his voice wobbled – he was less sure about standing up to his captain than Ves. "Wherever F goes, I go."

"I need you both here," Solveig said, voice taut. "That is not up for discussion."

Ves marched across the room and grabbed Solveig by the collar of his green coat, hauling him to his feet with ease.

"You. Cannot. Force. Me. To. Stay," she growled.

"I am your captain," he shot back. "If you disobey me, I will kick you off my sarding crew. Don't think I won't. I *need* you to stay here."

She shoved him. Solveig stumbled, hardly catching himself before he could fall against the bed – against Fynch. Ves raised a hand – Solveig caught a flash of silver. He dove to the side before Ves could slash him.

"The navy is *here*, Ves!" he shouted. "They're just going to take Fynch to get treatment. I need you *here*, where it isn't safe. If I was planning on fighting the people of Corsa, I'd have *you* go! We don't have a ship. We won't have Thol or Illie. So, *you* need to stay here because you're one of my best fighters."

She lowered her knife slowly.

"That's great and all," Czardas piped up, speaking so reluctantly Solveig almost missed it completely. "But why do *I* have to stay?"

Solveig swallowed the real reason. He wanted to keep as much of his crew with him as possible. Because he couldn't protect Thol and Illie and Fynch when they went to Servedin. Because if he lost one more person he cared about, he wasn't sure he could keep going. Forget about Anwir's treasure; Solveig would turn himself in if he lost anyone else. And Czardas... He was hardly the best fighter on the crew.

He shoved his hand through his tangled red hair. "If you stay, we'll teach you how to fight. I'll teach you how to use a sword."

Czardas's shoulders deflated, but he nodded. "Just...make sure he comes back to me. I can't lose him."

Neither can I, Solveig thought grimly.

Thol found the shipwright duo on the *Serenity.*

"I need a ship," he said without preamble the moment he boarded his ship. "A fast one – the fastest you've got. And I need it *now.*"

"Slow down," said Lonan around the butt of his sugar cigarette. He puffed out a cloud of sweet smoke. "Back up three steps. What's going on?"

"Are you sarding dense?" Thol snapped.

All he could see when Fynch vomited up blood was Meadow, pale and sweating and covered in her own blood, crying silently as she held her daughter for the first and last time. Thol had enough little brothers, but...damn it, he'd gone and adopted Fynch as the sixth.

"He's got nothing but sugar smoke up there." Leo jumped in quickly before Thol could give Lonan a taste of *PUNISHMENT.*

Leo wiped his hands off on his heavy pants, standing slowly from the crouched position he'd been in. He said, "You need a ship? The *Serenity* –"

"The *Serenity* isn't going to be fixed in time, and I need a ship that will get me to Servedin *now,* " Thol said harshly. He flexed his tattooed fingers, reminding the two that he was in the navy's most wanted. Two years of retirement wouldn't take away years of fear.

"Okay, okay." Lonan chewed on the butt of his cigarette. "You want something fast. Don't we still have that tea clipper, Leo?"

"Use your eyes, Lo," grumbled Leo as he pointed to a ship bobbing in the marina. "She's a schooner. The *Harper. Someone* hasn't gotten around to selling her yet. You need to get to Corsa and back?"

When Thol nodded, Lonan took over: "Even with the speed of the *Harper,* it'll take you about two weeks round trip, weather permitting."

Weather won't be a problem so long as we have Illie, he thought.

Lonan continued, "Fourteen days, discount because we're working on your ship... Are any of your lady companions going to be sailing?" Thol glared. Lonan counted on his fingers. "Fifty thousand lune sound about right?"

If Fynch wasn't bleeding out and on the very brink of death, Thol would just steal the ship. But Fynch was dying, and Solveig already agreed to pay the fee, so Thol clenched his jaw hard and said, "Put in on our tab. Prepare the ship for sailing. I'll be leaving on it in an hour."

Exactly an hour later, as promised, Thol stood at the helm of the tea clipper, the *Harper*. Below, in the captain's quarters, Illie sat with Fynch. Should the weather turn, she would come out to coax the *Harper* along. A course had already been set – she'd drawn out the quickest route, going south then northwest to reach Corsa.

Dreamer, he thought, invoking the goddess of life. *Please let him survive the trip to Corsa. Please let the Blood Doctor be there. Please let them remember their debt. Please let Fynch survive. He's too young to die.*

Meadow had been too young, too. So had Evangeline. So had his brothers.

He gripped the pegs of the wheel tightly, knuckles turning white beneath his tattoos.

"You had better remember our deal, Isra," he hissed under his breath, hoping that, somehow, his words would carry across the waves and strike the Blood Doctor right in the chest.

The scar cutting from Thol's right shoulder to his left hip throbbed. It had been nearly ten years since he'd gotten it, but it was deep enough – the scar tissue stretched taut across his chiseled torso – that, occasionally, it would feel just as sharp and throbbing as the day he'd been slashed.

If the Blood Doctor could heal *that* wound, they would have to be able to heal Fynch. Thol knew they were blessed by Dreamer, but the details of that divine ability were a secret only the Doctor knew.

As the sun started to sink beneath the horizon, Illie climbed up the stairs, a plate and cup balanced in one hand, a map in the other.

"Time to switch," she said, holding out the plate and cup. "It's not Natha's cooking, but it's food. He woke up for a few minutes before going back to sleep."

Thol took the dishes wordlessly.

She tucked the map into her pocket, exchanging it for three bundled-up pairs of socks. She put three on each hand, creating thick makeshift mittens. She planned on using her ability, then.

"I'll come get you if you're not up by dawn," she said. "Check on him every few hours. He seems stable – stable-ish, at least. No more puking or coughing."

She grabbed the pegs of the wheel, hands barely bending under the constriction of three socks.

"Don't hurt yourself," he said. "The Blood Doctor only owes me *two* debts."

"When we get back to Undyne, I'm going to buy two things: a bathymetric map and a pair of the *thickest* winter mittens in Syrenis."

He hesitated. "A bathymetric map...?"

"If I can see a picture of the ocean floor, I can pinpoint where Sol's missing moon is." She lifted her shoulders in a nonchalant shrug. "But the lost moon isn't important right now. Fynch's life is, so go eat and get some rest so we can hurry up and get to Servedin."

Illie and Meadow, Thol's late wife, would have been the best of friends, he decided.

"See you at dawn," he said before hopping down the stairs and slipping into the captain's quarters.

Two gas lamps were lit, swathing the room in a gentle orange glow. Fynch lay stretched out on the bed, blankets to his chin. Thol sat on the chair next to the bed and quickly ate his dinner. There were a few books on the bed – Illie's, no doubt. Curious, Thol picked one up and flipped to one of the dogeared pages.

13 Zylfmoon, 920

The warlords from Aralyth arrived in Edyn today. They are burning the homes of anyone who doesn't speak their language. I'm lucky I know it. If I was caught writing this in my native tongue, I would no doubt be executed on the spot. Emperor Farrian Helios is trying, successfully, mind you, to eradicate all cultures. We have to use his money, we have to speak his language, we have to abide by his rules even if we aren't a part of his country. I tried telling the townsfolk not to fight back. It isn't worth it. But nobody listens to me. It's winter, and the winters up north are harsh. Harsher than anything I'm used to. The Aralythians will take everything – our food stores, our furs, our homes. I just want to return home. I don't know how.

-J. C.

15 Zylfmoon, 920

The entire island nation of Edyn is now under Aralyth's rule. Long live Emperor Farrian Helios.

-J. C.

Thol frowned. The writing was slim and precise, the ink so long dried it appeared printed. But this... This was a diary. It had to be – the diary of this *J. C.* individual. And he'd lived through the Aralythian Conquests. He'd lived through the two-day annexation of Edyn. He went to flip the page, but Fynch stirred.

Dropping the book, Thol was on his feet in a heartbeat, reaching out to check Fynch's pulse, to make sure he was breathing, to put his hands on his shoulders to move him onto his side in case he threw up again.

Fynch opened his eyes, his jade irises bloodshot and glassy.

"Thirsty," he croaked.

Thol grabbed the cup that had been sitting on the bedside table. He pressed the rim against Fynch's lips, tilting it back gently to let him take small sips.

He weakly pushed Thol's hand away. "Illie said we're going to Corsa," he whispered, his voice like paper.

"I know a doctor," Thol explained. "They will help you. They owe me."

Fynch didn't respond. He'd closed his eyes, his chest resuming its steady, wheezy pattern as he slipped back into sleep.

Syrenis had two moons, and so it had, naturally, four tides: high tide and low tide twice a day – caused by Mene and Sin separately – and Two Moon high and low tides when Mene and Sin came together. Two Moon low tide was the best time to careen ships to work on their keels since the ocean receded so far out the beach looked more like the Vicious Desert in Veridin than the coastline it usually represented. When those tides happened, no matter the hour, Leo would grab his toolbox and get to work.

Two Moon low tide just so happened to fall in the early hours of one in the morning.

Surrounded by lanterns lit with his own divine ability, Leo – wearing only thin trousers and a linen shirt. Even though it was just past midnight and freezing out, his body never ran cold – knelt in the wet sand to examine the *Serenity*'s keel.

He had six hours until high tide and little more than one hour until the Emerald Sea came racing back.

Rubbing his forehead with the back of his gloved hand, Leo stared at the fissure snaking across the *Serenity*'s keel. It was a hairline fracture at most, likely caused by rough waters or crashing into something. He'd read the newspapers – Solveig and his crew had fought the Rabbit Pirates and the navy on the sea. Either one of those battles could have cracked the *Serenity*'s keel.

The problem, though, was that the keel was the ship's foundation. If it was broken, the whole ship was broken. If it was replaced, the ship wouldn't be the same. The crack was small enough that Leo could, in theory, stuff it full of oakum and caulk and pray to the Wanderer that it would hold. But if it didn't, the crack would get worse. The *Serenity* would sink, and that would be Leo's fault.

He glanced over his shoulder, peering at the dark horizon where the Emerald lurked just out of view. The Two Moon tides were harder to chart than the regular high and low tides. Typically, they occurred between the regular tides – a high, a low, a Two Moon high, a Two Moon low – but during the summer and winter, they were less predictable. Leo would have to consult a chart – there was one in his shop. Somewhere. Probably. Unless Lonan decided to use it as an ashtray – and he simply didn't have the time to play with those lunar odds. If he didn't fix the keel *tonight*, he wasn't sure when he'd get another proper chance to do it. He'd only *just* woken up in time to race down to the marina with all his tools. If he was a few minutes late, that was a few minutes of precious time gone.

"Why couldn't you have blessed me with something better?" he grumbled to himself, lighting his finger aflame to illuminate the patch of wood he was inspecting. "Bless me to control the tides. Bless me to pause time. Bless me to fix ships with a single wave of my hand."

But no. The Wanderer had given Leo the ability to create fire. He could only manipulate the flames he created, and only those flames wouldn't burn him. His body temperature always ran hot – well past the feverish temperature that would kill a normal person. But it sapped his energy, sucking it up like a siphon. One tiny flame was equivalent to running three miles at top speed. He lived on caffeine, rice wine, and Lonan talking to him to keep him awake.

He wouldn't be able to make it to another full Two Moon low tide if it was at one in the morning again.

The best way to fix the crack would be with something solid, like tar. It wouldn't take long to melt it to boiling with his ability – even if it would make him tired enough to sleep for forty-eight hours afterward. But time wasn't on Leo's side.

And the crack was in too vital an area to risk the fix.

Glancing at the horizon again, Leo shook the fire from his hand and gathered up his tools. He extinguished his lanterns, picked them up, too, and began walking back to dry land.

He would have to break the terrible news in the morning.

8

Czardas fell ungracefully onto his backside, hitting the ground hard enough to clatter his teeth together. Groaning, he ignored the hand Natha held out, instead clambering to his feet on his own.

"Your center of gravity is off," she explained once he'd found his balance again. "And you put your entire body into each blow. It leaves you uncoordinated and vulnerable to retaliation. You don't need to use your left foot to throw an uppercut with your right hand. That just makes you unbalanced, which makes it easier for *me* to knock you on your ass."

He brushed himself off, wincing at the soreness in his muscles. He and Natha had been sparring since dawn, using the courtyard behind the inn as a training arena. They'd been alone for the first few hours, but as the sun came up, they'd drawn a crowd.

"Your center of gravity is up here." Natha touched her stomach, right above her navel. "It should be down here." Her hand moved to her pelvis. "Bend your knees – don't ever lock them – and crouch low. You're taller than me, but you'll meet opponents twice your size. You have to use your size to your advantage – you can reach places I can't, but your limbs will hinder you."

Czardas scrubbed his hand over his face. It wasn't even noon, and the sun was scalding. He'd abandoned his waistcoat and rolled the sleeves of his shirt past his elbows, revealing the map of pale splotches across his dark forearms. The thick, humid air pulled his hair into a frizzy mess, the only strands not standing on end being the ones glued to his neck with sweat. He wanted, desperately, to take a break, but if he took a break, he'd think about Fynch, and if he thought about Fynch, he would spiral.

And the moment he stopped training with Natha, Ves would step in, and he just *knew* she would work him to the bone.

"Show me," he said.

Natha crouched low, knees bent, feet just past her hips. Her back was pin straight, tilted at an angle, her hands balled into fists – thumbs on the outside, not tucked in. He watched her closely before copying her pose.

Then, she charged.

She went low, aiming for Czardas's legs.

Think of it as a song, he told himself. *Move with her, not against her.*

He stepped to the side just before she could tackle him to the ground. In her moment of pause where she gathered the momentum to swing on him, he swept his leg out, shin hitting her in the calves.

Not enough to knock her down, but enough to draw her attention. Enough to give her pause.

His mind was always racing. It took speed to read notes, to translate them to his fingers, to keep up with the zipping pace of the music.

He thought of Natha as a song – a fast, fiery, angry song, one played on the violin, or perhaps a balalaika. If she was the music, he was the musician, and all he had to do was play her right.

She went low again, the first note before a crescendo, and he was ready. When she dove for his knees, he grabbed her shoulders, using the momentum that was her crescendo to throw her into a rest, shoving her down to leap over her.

Sorry, Miss Natha, he thought as he lifted his foot and planted it right in her stomach. She coughed, stumbling backward and throwing up her arms.

"Surrender!" she cried.

He knew she was only surrendering so he wouldn't feel guilty about kicking her, but Czardas appreciated it all the same.

"Let's take a break," she said, and Czardas nearly sobbed in relief. She turned to the onlookers. "Go on, shoo! Don't make me get my spoon!"

As Czardas followed Natha through the back door of the inn, he spotted the familiar mop of brown hair held back by goggles belonging to Leo. Leo paused at the counter while the woman behind it shuffled toward the stairs.

Natha pulled Czardas into the dining room, where Ves sat by a window, sipping on a cup of lemonade and staring at the sea through the glass.

"Leo just showed up," he said, sliding into one of the seats. "Where's Captain Solveig?"

"In the room," murmured Ves into her cup. "Trying to read that sarding map.""Didn't we decide this missing moon is in the Salts Atoll?" Natha sat down, grabbing the decanter of lemonade and pouring cups for herself and Czardas. She took a sip and frowned. "Too much sugar, not enough lemon. This is awful."

It was no secret that Natha had a sweet tooth, so Czardas just raised a brow when she finished the cup and poured herself another.

"That's what I thought," Ves said. "But who knows what goes on in that little head of his."

"I hope F is okay," Czardas whispered, mostly to himself.

Wind slipped through Illie's fingers, evading her grasp like she was trying to catch a handful of eels. She cursed loudly when another wrapped around her wrist, only to fly off before she could grab it. Planting her feet on the deck, she thrust both hands out, gripping a gale before it could flee.

"Got you, you wench," she growled.

Then, she threw the gale into the *Harper*'s sails. The tea clipper lurched forward, bouncing over waves with little precision. She slipped, nearly losing her footing. Yanking on the gale, she repositioned herself, then let go. The wind filled the sail completely, driving the schooner to go faster than it could unaided.

It had been less than a day since she and Thol boarded the *Harper* with Fynch, and they were already coasting along Undyne Island's southernmost border, near Port 13 – the textiles district. The fabric of Illie's clothes and the canvas of the *Harper*'s sails were most likely both woven there.

Once she got the *Harper* around Undyne's lower peninsula, it would be a straight shot northeast to Corsa, Servedin.

"Oh, you *wench!*" she shouted as the wind slithered from the sail, dissipating into the sky. Beneath her sock-mittens, Illie's palms were raw and numb, the first stages of frostbite settling in.

Gritting her teeth, she reached for another wind, shoving it into the sails to force the *Harper* faster. Thol was with Fynch – he had been all morning. Last night, apparently, had been rough. Fynch woke up every few hours, shivering and feverish. Since Illie was the only one who could speed the sailing up, she stayed at the helm, commanding the winds to do her bidding.

The sail filled and stayed full for once. Illie slumped over the wheel, exhausted. Wisps of pink hair tickled her cheeks, freed from her braid. She closed her eyes, trying to fend off the exhaustion before she collapsed right there.

I need to check on Thol, she thought, but she didn't so much as lift a finger. She'd check on him once the *Harper* rounded the southern peninsula.

Which, if the winds sarding *cooperated,* would be in just a few hours.

She missed her crew. She missed smelling Natha's cooking from the galley, Czardas's music nearly drowned out by Ves's drunken singing, Thol and Solveig's banter, Fynch's sneaky attempts to steal from Natha... She missed Pleo winding around her legs, too. Her cat stayed behind, most likely fast asleep on one of the beds at the inn.

The *Harper* started to slow. Groaning, she stood up and grabbed another wind, thrusting it into the sails. Her hands were so cold they burned. Still, the wind propelled the clipper faster, so she bit her tongue and ignored the pain. She could pay Thol's doctor to heal her hands if it came to it; she just had to endure for now.

Knock, knock, knock.

In a heartbeat, Solveig had the ancient map folded up and stuffed into the pocket of his green coat. No one in his crew would knock; they'd just walk right in. His heart skipped a beat as he thought of Fynch's apparent brother, Sparrow, who was in the navy. Grabbing his sword and slipping it through his belt, he crept to the door, opening it an inch.

The innkeeper stood on the other side, looking as exhausted as Solveig felt.

"Mister Solveig?" she asked, saying his name the wrong way – *Sol-vig* instead of *Sol-vay.* "You have a guest downstairs."

"Who?" He gripped the pommel of his cutlass.

"Mister Genovese. The shipwright."

Leo. Nodding, Solveig opened the door, thanking the innkeeper with a stone coin he found in his pocket. He hurried downstairs, hoping – *praying* – Leo came with good news. That he would say the *Serenity* was fixed up and ready to chase after Thol and Illie to Servedin.

Leo stood in the foyer, grease covering his face, the clear outline of where his goggles rested on his nose visible by the lack of soot. He looked up, hazel eyes meeting Solveig's face.

"Captain," he said by way of greeting. "Do you mind coming with me to the marina?"

Something sank in Solveig's stomach. Any hope he had of good news flickered out. Something terrible was wrong, and he wasn't sure he could handle it.

Mouth dry, he nodded. Leo pushed himself away from the counter and started walking. Solveig, without any other choice, followed.

The streets of Port 16 were busy; patrons walked in and out of shops, temple doors opened to let the devout in, the train's whistle blew in the distance, people ran toward the station in hopes of catching a ride to Port 17 and beyond. Solveig watched the commotion from the corner of his eye, hand resting on the pommel of his sword as he looked for any navy sailors – for Sparrow Largos in particular.

His tongue felt like lead the entire walk; he couldn't bring himself to say anything to Leo, not until he knew for certain what the fate of the *Serenity* was.

The *Serenity*'s red hull bobbed gently in the calm waters, looking just as miserable as the day she arrived in Port 16. Leo walked the length of the dock, stopping just before her gangplank.

"Captain," Leo began, and Solveig's stomach sank all the way to the bottom of the Emerald.

"Don't sugarcoat it," Solveig said weakly.

Leo nodded once. "There are parts I could fix easily. Building a new mast and a new railing would take me a few days at most. All the holes are easy patches that even Lonan could handle. Sourcing new sails from Port 13 would take a few days, but it would be doable."

Solveig's gaze fell on his ship. He'd only been her captain for a few weeks, yet he was attached to her like it had been longer.

"But...?" he prompted.

Leo rubbed his face. "But the keel is cracked. And usually, I could fix it with some tar and prayers, but it's cracked in such a vital spot that I *can't* fix it, not without removing the whole thing. And the keel is the ship's foundation, so removing it would be destroying the entire ship."

There it was. The inevitable. The truth Solveig didn't want to hear. The *Serenity* was damned. She wasn't even his ship to begin with. She belonged to Thol – the only reason Thol had climbed out of retirement was to lend the *Serenity* to Solveig, after all. And Thol wasn't even *there*.

His stomach flopped, churning with a nauseating dread. He wanted to puke.

"I... I have an offer," Leo said. Sunlight hit his hazel eyes, making them look more gold than green. Beneath the soot and grease splattered across his face was a smattering of freckles.

Solveig inherited his mother's features – her red hair, her green eyes, her pale skin that loathed the sun – but... That wasn't the case for his brother. He rubbed the moonstone gem on his ring absently.

Leo continued: "I built a ship – a brig – that I only just finished. She's stealthy and fast and... Well, I won't get into the details right now because once I start talking about her, I won't shut up. I know the rhyme about you, and that's why I'm offering to give you the ship. She's green – the deepest emerald green, just like your coat. Just... Think about it. I'm not ready to give up on the *Serenity* yet."

Solveig watched the waves lap against the red hull of the ship that had brought him from Aralyth to here. The ship that brought his crew together, the ship that went head-on against the navy, against the Rabbit Pirates, against a tornadic waterspout, and *won*. He couldn't help the sticky sense of betrayal building up inside.

"If you do want to take me up on that offer," Leo added, "You'll have to let Lonan take her on her maiden voyage. He's been the first to sail all my ships; he'd never forgive me if I took this from him."

Solveig took one last look at the *Serenity* before nodding numbly. "I want to see the ship."

Something flickered across Leo's face, settling in his eyes. His spine straightened, his chin lifted, and he gestured for Solveig to follow as he retraced his steps back up the dock.

Instead of leading him to another spot in the marina, Leo brought Solveig to the shipyard – to a warehouse with a rounded top. The large canal leading up to the warehouse led Solveig to believe it was actually a covered drydock.

Leo unlocked a side door and held it open for Solveig. He ducked inside.

"She's made from wood that simply should not exist. I have no idea where it came from. It doesn't match any of the trees in *all* Syrenis. It's strong, too. It's withstood every test Lonan and I threw at it, and it doesn't burn. Trust me, I tried. She's faster than any clipper – she has a sharp-ended hull, not a kettle-bottom. Eighteen cannons – nine on each side – a brig, full galley, two sets of barracks, plenty of other rooms that you can see for yourself, and... Well, the sails I ordered for her came in black for some reason."

Leo turned on the lights and gave a swooping gesture to the ship.

At nearly a hundred feet in length, she was slim and sleek, her hull painted the deepest shade of emerald imaginable. Two masts stretched toward the curved ceiling, black sails tied up neatly. Based on the rows of portholes, there were three floors beneath the deck – likely four if he counted the stores.

Slowly, he walked to the bow, tilting his head back to get a good look at the figurehead. It was a female bust, though she wore no clothing. She had three faces – one on either side of the forward-facing one, each with five eyes. The middle face had branching horns that curved parallel to the bow, carved from white wood instead of black like the rest of the figure.

Nobody knew what the goddess Dreamer looked like, but every drawing, every poem, every mention of her agreed on three things – she had six arms, three heads, and branch-like horns as white as snow.

Heart in his throat, Solveig ran his fingers along the smooth wood of the ship's hull, making his way to the stern. There, beneath the windows of the captain's quarters in gold paint, was her name.

Dreamchaser.

Solveig knew, without a smidge of doubt, that he absolutely had to have that ship.

Leo laid the wood out, hands trembling with sheer excitement. With his regular supplier being on backorder, he'd taken the experimental route, reaching out to the kingdom of Gello for materials. Gello, being ninety-eight percent forest, had no shortage of timber. He received the wood quickly, but it wasn't what he'd been expecting.

He had no idea what trees it came from.

He'd tested a few planks – it was pliable, yet strong, not very porous, and very buoyant – and decided it was perfect for shipbuilding.

It would be the foundation for the greatest ship he would ever build. It was his dream *to build a ship that would go down in history. It had been his dream ever since he was a young boy, a dream he refused to give up on even after he got sick enough that he needed his leg amputated.*

The door to the warehouse creaked open, the smell of sugar smoke flooding the space as Lonan invited himself inside. He sat down next to Leo, legs crossed, and asked, "What trees are these? Oak? Pine? Cedar? Cypress?"

Those were Leo's favored timber. He was especially partial to oak, but he knew the forests of Gello were mostly evergreen.

"I have no idea," he conceded.

"Oh, a mystery, then." Lonan took a long drag of his cigarette. "Wasn't that one ship made of mystery wood, too? The... Oh, what was it called?"

Leo's heart skipped a beat as it often did whenever the greatest – in his mind – ship in history was brought up. It was the only *ship from the previous generation of pirates that hadn't been constructed in Port 16.*

"The Annabel's Tears?" Leo's eyes went wide beneath his tinted goggles. "You're right. Nobody knows what it was made of, and it sank before anyone could figure it out. I didn't think it was Gello made, though."

"Can't you just, I don't know, ask Gello what kind of trees they got over there?"

"I could. But it doesn't seem right." He pulled his goggles off. "There are biology books about all the trees over there. Why would

they keep one *type a secret, and why would they then send a few of the* biggest *trees I've ever seen to me?"*

Lonan snuffed out his cigarette and stood. He brushed his hands off on his work pants then placed them right on his hips. "No idea. Have you seen the princess of Gello, though? Lightbringer, smite me; she is a beauty."

Leo heavily debated taking his leg off and throwing it at Lonan's head, but he decided he'd much rather have it on his person.

"I'm going to build a ship that's better than the Annabel *in every way possible," he vowed. "And I'm going to use this mystery wood to do it."*

"And I *will sail it," Lonan added.*

That night, Leo drew up the plans for the brig. It would be fast, stealthy, and dangerous. It would be perfect.

At the top of the blueprints, in smudgy scrawl, he wrote out a placeholder name, a project title that would eventually be etched onto the hull of his dream ship.

The Dreamchaser.

Six years later, he would finally finish.

9

Fynch dreamed. Or, rather, he remembered. His life flashed before him in muddled strings of half-conscious memories of events that might not have even happened. A birthday celebrated with a chocolate cupcake; a first bleed and his sister laughing at him for being so embarrassed; a rine coin and a forfeited ice cream; a book of creatures that didn't exist; sitting on a father's knee, falling asleep against the warmth of his chest; a mother's face, blonde hair and green eyes and freckles that made her look ten years younger than she actually was.

He liked being unconscious. He wasn't in pain when he was unconscious.

He was in so much unsurmountable, excruciating pain when he was conscious, though.

So, he closed his eyes and dream-remembered.

He was on a boat – he knew that much. The gentle rocking as waves crashed into the hull was familiar. The bed he lay in wasn't – it was bolted to the wall because if it wasn't, it would be rocking with the rest of the ship. But Fynch could sleep anywhere. A stationary bed was a luxury compared to the jailhouse floors he'd spent too many nights on.

The house Fynch grew up in was tiny, hardly the size for six children and two adults. He got used to sleeping on the floor, squished between the twins, Wren and Dove. He got used to fighting Row and Robin for the bigger piece of bread at dinner. He got used to competing with his siblings just to stay alive.

Row. He was in Undyne. Fynch wondered, briefly, what he was up to. Did he get married? Did he have a family, a livelihood that would be absolutely decimated should he realize what Fynch was up to?

Oh well. It didn't even matter anymore. No matter how hard Illie and Thol tried, Fynch didn't expect to live to see this mystery doctor in Servedin. They should just give up, let him die. Stop wasting valuable time and resources on him when they could just forget about him and find the sarding lost moon.

When Fynch's eyelids fluttered open again, thin membranes of flesh doing little to block out the light, he saw pink. Illie. She was sitting – she had to be since she didn't seem to be as tall as normal – and she was talking. No, reading. She was reading out loud.

"'...started in the east, claiming Archepylago first. From there, Aralyth's grip reached across nearly the entire Emerald Sea, from Edyn in the north to Joris Island in the south. As of 959, Aralyth has absorbed the following countries: Archepylago, Kelsyn, the Twin Serpent Isles, Saffron and Selfosa, Edyn, and Joris Island, which was conquered in 958. Covering over half of Syrenis, the Aralyth Empire is the largest, most powerful, and longest-standing, with the first Helios emperor, Egor Helios – 83 to 145 – coming into rule in 102. The –' You're awake!" Illie snapped the history book shut and leaned close, the ends of her pink fringe brushing ticklishly against Fynch's cheeks.

A damn shame that I am, he thought, though, perhaps, hearing about Aralyth's history was somewhat better than thinking about his inevitable demise.

Illie reached out and brushed his hair off his forehead. Cool air kissed his feverish skin, chilling the sweat that had accumulated there. He tried to take a breath but couldn't inflate his lungs enough.

It was like drowning above water. Like someone had wrapped a hand around his throat and squeezed. The acrid tang of blood coated the back of his throat, thickening with each useless swallow.

Gathering up what little strength he had, Fynch reached out and placed his pallid hand on Illie's leg. She scooped it up in an instant, lithe fingers deftly checking his pulse before simply holding it between both her hands.

"Would you like me to keep reading?" she asked.

Fynch, not having enough strength to speak, just blinked.

She held his hand in one of hers, using the other to prop open the book. She continued to read: "'Of all the battles, the only one that was close was the War for Edyn. Aralythian troops outnumbered the Edyn military fifteen to one. It should have been another easy win for Aralyth and the Helios Empire, but the Aralythians underestimated Edyn. Still, the battle only lasted two days, from the thirteenth of Zylfmoon 920 to the fifteenth. The casualties –' I think I'm going to read a different passage."

Fynch closed his eyes, the flipping of pages enough of a melodic white noise to pull him back to sleep.

"Hold it like a *sword,* not like a sarding *rapier,* " said Ves for the millionth time that afternoon.

Czardas stood across the courtyard, gripping a cutlass like he intended to fence with it.

Ves pinched the bridge of her nose. "Look, Strings, you have noodle arms. It won't kill you to hold the sarding thing with two hands, you know. If anything, it'll *save* your life. Blondie, any idea when Cap will be back?"

Natha sat on a wooden bench near the garden of wildflowers and shrubs, a magazine in her hands. She stopped wearing her gloves all the time, but she didn't speak about the waxy burn scars that mottled her fingers and palms, disappearing beneath the cuffs of her shirt.

Without even looking up from her magazine, she said, "No. Maybe teach Czardas to use knives and not a sword. He'd be good at close combat."

She licked her finger and turned the page. Ves's gaze lingered for a heartbeat longer than it should.

"He'd also be good at long-distance combat," mused Natha.

"I'd prefer to not do *any* combat," murmured Czardas.

"Well," said Ves, exasperated, "you're a pirate. Combat is in the job description."

"Technically, I'm a musician," retorted Czardas. "My hands were made to create music, not violence."

"Too much talking, not enough swinging." Ves brandished her cutlass and ran at Czardas before he could think twice.

He threw up his sword to block her blow. Metal crashed against metal. Just as Ves leaned her weight into the attack, someone entered the courtyard.

"There you are," said Solveig. "Can you spare me fifteen minutes? We need to talk."

Uh oh, thought Ves as she swept Czardas's legs out from under him. Those four words were *never* good.

We need to talk. Fynch was dead.

We need to talk. Thol and Illie shipwrecked.

We need to talk. Sparrow Largos and his navy cadre found them.

We need to talk. Solveig was keeping *more* secrets.

Natha lowered her magazine. "There are prying eyes here," she said carefully. "Is this something that requires privacy?"

Five minutes later, the four of them gathered in one of the rented rooms. Solveig paced the length of the room, his green coat abandoned on the bed. That wasn't a good sign. Ves was starting to think he *never* took the dirty thing off. But it was off, and he was pacing the room like a hungry cat, and dread knotted in Ves's belly, a hibernacle of anxiety.

"Is there good news?" prompted Natha, who relieved her pent-up anxiety by folding the pages of her magazine over and over again. Ves knew she was stressed about the navy. If Sparrow Largos recognized them, who's to say he wouldn't call for Adrian Zimmer, Natha's ex-husband?

"There is," Solveig said reluctantly. He raked his fingers through his messy red hair. "The good news is that we can leave this place and catch up with Thol and Illie and Fynch."

"The *Serenity* is fixed?" Czardas's voice filled with eagerness.

Solveig stopped pacing.

"It's not fixed, is it?" Ves whispered.

"The bad news," said Solveig, "is that the *Serenity* is damaged beyond repair. Leo... Leo has another ship. One he is willing to give to us once he speaks with Lonan. I'm going to retire the *Serenity.*"

"You can't!" Ves shouted. "Cap, you *can't!* That's *Thol's* ship, not yours!" Her heart raced hard against her ribs as if they were debating the death of a human and not a ship. "You can't do this, Cap."

Solveig snapped, "I can and I sarding will, Ves. Thol would understand – he *will* understand once we catch up with them and explain it."

"We can't give up the *Serenity!*" Ves's voice rose higher and higher, teetering on the verge of hysteria. The *Serenity* was her home – the first one she'd had in four years. If it was gone, what then? Would her stability vanish, too? The *Serenity* kept her out of the bowels of I. J. Pen. The *Serenity* kept her sarding *safe* when, for *four sarding years,* she'd been locked away in the dark, unsure if each day would be her last.

"Ves, we *have* to."

Solveig's voice cracked. Ves finally met his gaze. His eyes were glassy, wet with tears she *knew* he was fighting to keep from falling.

Because the *Serenity* was his home, too.

In a few months, Ves had gained everything – her freedom, her livelihood, her *life.* But in that same time, Nox Solveig had lost everything. His ship, his crew, his autonomy when he'd been given Sinthoxine, and now that the *Serenity* was irreparable, he was going to lose her, too.

"Did I do something to make the *Serenity* unfixable…?" Czardas spoke hesitantly, softly. Ves was sure there was some sort of musical term to explain the shift between her yelling to his whispering.

"The keel cracked." Solveig turned his head to rub his eyes. "In a spot where fixing it would mean replacing the entire thing, and that… The *Serenity* wouldn't be the same anymore."

"Good thing I learned to pack light," Natha muttered to herself.

"I've made my decision," Solveig said, speaking slowly to keep his voice steady. It was his Captain Voice, Ves realized. The voice that, if she opposed, would label her insubordinate, and moving ships would be the least of her concerns.

So, she forced a smile and said, "Well, Cap. Three ships in less than that many months? This new one better be good."

If Lonan received one more shock, he wasn't sure his heart would keep up. It was one thing to have the second most wanted pirate in the *world* staying just a few blocks from where he lived, but...

Leo had found him in the administration office, smoking two sugar cigarettes at once. He sat behind the desk, feet propped up on the wood, and tipped his head back to stare at the ceiling.

His heart had been acting up all day, fluttery and sporadic in its palpitations.

"I'm giving away the *Dreamchaser*," Leo said without preamble as he shoved open the door and walked right into the office.

Lonan sat up quickly, dropping both cigarettes and snuffing them out before Leo could lecture him. ("One at a time is fine," he would have said. "I can't stop you from smoking. But what would your doctor say if he saw you smoking *two?*")

He laughed, nearly toppling out of his chair. Leo didn't.

"I rarely understand you," Leo said, "but I especially don't understand you right now. I didn't say anything funny."

"No, no, you're right." He reached for his case of cigarettes. "It just sounded like you said you're giving away the *Dreamchaser.*"

Lonan remembered the day Leo decided he was going to build a ship as legendary as the infamous *Annabel's Tears* with the unknown wood six years ago. Between building Navy ships and making repairs for clients, Lonan had poured all his effort into the *Dreamchaser.* The ship's name had been Lonan's idea.

"I'm just chasing a dream," Leo had said one night when the ship wasn't coming together the way he wanted. *"I'll never create a ship like* that *one.*"

"So?" Lonan had asked. *"Your dream is to build the greatest ship in history. My dream is to become the most famous seaman – and to sleep with every beautiful lady, but that's not important right now. That doesn't make you a failure, Leo. That makes you a...a...a dream-chaser. That's what you should name the ship.* Dreamchaser.*"*

For six sarding years, that ship had been Leo's life. His love. His greatest passion. And he was just...just *giving it away?!*

"Because that's what I said," Leo said flatly. "I can't fix the *Serenity,* so I'm giving Captain Solveig the *Dreamchaser.* He needs it more than I do. His gunner is dying."

Something flickered in Lonan's chest. An idea came to him then, piercing like a bullet to his skull. He grabbed a sugar cigarette and put it between his teeth.

"I vowed to man the helm of that ship," he said. "So, Galileo Genovese, I quit. I'm going to be a pirate."

He heard the slap before he felt it. Lonan's head jerked to the side, cheek alight with a stinging burn.

"Are you stupid?" Leo snapped, cradling his hand against his chest. The audacity of that man; he'd been the one to slap Lonan, not the other way around.

"Usually, yes, but –"

Leo slapped him again. "You're giving up everything to just...just become a sarding *pirate?* You don't even know if they'll take you."

"It'll be a caveat; they get the *Dreamchaser*, but they also get me." He flashed a pearly white grin. Leo balled his hand into a fist but dropped it before he could punch that grin off Lonan's face.

"I'll never see you again," he whispered.

They'd been together practically their entire lives. If Lonan joined Solveig's crew, it would be the first time he'd ever truly be separated from Leo. His stomach knotted at the thought, twisting and churning like the organ had been replaced with a writhing snake.

And there was that promise he'd made. A promise he would be shattering the moment he stepped on the *Dreamchaser*.

A promise he'd broken three years after making it, leaving him with a scar on his face and a firm belief in mermaids, but a promise he'd reinforced by never sailing past the bay.

Never step foot on a ship again wouldn't exactly keep his heart from stopping. The heart attack he'd suffered that day when he was twenty-one had been the closest Lonan ever was to death, and he wanted to keep it that way for as long as possible.

Don't sail past the bay was a promise he *could* keep. Unless he joined a pirate crew.

I'll never see you again. Because Lonan would be leaving Undyne for good. Because the arteries around his heart could clot again, leading to a heart attack he might not be revived from. Because he could fall off the ship when his heart stopped pounding, and a mermaid might not rescue him.

There was a knock at the door before either of them could say anything else, the knuckled rap shattering the silence and pulling

Lonan's mind away from mermaids and heart attacks and deaths at sea.

There was a fifty-fifty chance it was a customer or someone Lonan had given the address to in hopes of blowing off some steam. He glanced at Leo before calling, "Come in."

Captain Nox Solveig, green coat draped over his shoulders, stepped into the office. Trailing after him like little ducklings were the musician, the lovely Vesperine, and the *beautiful* Nathalia. The other three must have gone on the rented tea clipper to Servedin Island.

Interesting...

"Leo," Solveig said, ignoring Lonan completely. *Rude.* "You're certain the *Serenity* is unfixable?"

Leo switched into his work mode. If his goggles weren't currently around his neck, Lonan knew he'd push them onto his forehead. "I can show you if you don't believe me. The keel is cracked. She's too far gone."

Solveig glanced at the others as if silently saying *I told you so.*

To Leo, he said, "If the –"

Lonan hopped across the deck and sidled up close to Solveig. He plucked the sugar cigarette from his teeth and offered it to the captain, who just grimaced and shook his head.

"You want the emerald brig, don't you?" he asked with a grin. "The good ole DC. You know, she took six years to build, and even Leo doesn't know what wood made her keel. He thinks it's the same type of wood that the *Annabel's Tears* used."

Something unreadable flickered across Solveig's face. Lonan continued before he could make any hasty decisions. "However, a ship that grand needs a helmsman with equal grandeur. There's only one person in Syrenis who is talented *and* handsome enough to fit the bill."

He winked at Nathalia. She held her middle finger up in return.

"You want the *Dreamchaser,*" Lonan said, "you get me, too."

"Nope," said Ves. "Absolutely not. I changed my mind. I'm not going through with this if that filthy little worm is joining us."

That's when the most unexpected thing happened (aside from a lady insulting Lonan).

Leo said, "There's only one person who knows how to fix her if she gets damaged. I built her completely alone. You'll get me, too."

Ves shoved her elbow into Solveig's ribs. His eyes watered instantly.

Broken ribs, Lonan thought, his brow cocked. *Still not fully healed. Interesting...*

"Fine," muttered Solveig against Ves's very vocal protests. "But don't think you're joining the crew. We just need you to get to Corsa. If any *accidents* happen while at sea, well..."

Lonan's grin widened. "Well, what're you waiting for? I say we load her up and set sail."

Solveig never had a home until the sea. Until the Serpent Pirates and Captain Hardy, until it was just him and Thol – the only brothers left behind, the only brothers who didn't share a drop of blood. The *Sea Wyrm* was his childhood home, where he grew into the man he was now. The *Silver Moon* was the first home he made on his own, scraping together a crew – a family – that helped lift his name into infamy.

The *Serenity*... He'd only captained her for a handful of weeks, but he'd endured a lifetime in those weeks.

Lenwell, sneaking into the naval academy to steal the lithograph of the Wandering Isle.

Carilon and Bowhead Rock, gaining control over the Icarus Strait after defeating the Redcoat Pirates and gaining the Poet-blessed Illie as his navigator.

Veridonia, recruiting Natha and fighting Adam Zimmer, narrowly escaping after stealing a fake compass.

Adrian Zimmer, the *Meredith*, defeating them and gaining a gunner and a musician.

Sailing through a storm, through a tornadic waterspout that should have killed them all but somehow spat them out unscathed.

The Rabbit Pirates, defeating Bonny Reed by the skin of their teeth.

It felt...*wrong* to say goodbye. It felt wrong to replace the *Serenity* with something new. It felt wrong to do it without Thol – without Illie and Fynch – by his side.

Leo had given Solveig three options for the *Serenity*'s decommission: scrap her for parts, beach her and let scavengers take her apart, or sink her to form an artificial reef off the coast of Undyne. Even though the answer was obvious, Solveig still asked his crew.

With Lonan and Leo's help, Solveig and the dregs of his crew hauled the cannons and any last belongings off the *Serenity* and into the warehouse where the *Dreamchaser* rested. Then, he boarded the *Serenity* for the last time.

"I don't like this," said Ves, standing at the railing. "I don't want to say goodbye."

"Neither do I," grumbled Solveig. "But we have to."

"Thol's going to kill you," she said.

How fitting, then, that Solveig's last brother would be the one to end his life. But Solveig knew Thol; he knew he would get punched a few times, but that would be it.

Soon, Undyne Island was little more than a speck behind them. Solveig's stomach knotted over and over again.

At least this time, he would have the chance to say goodbye.

Natha, Ves, and Czardas were silent as they boarded the dinghy hooked up to the *Serenity*'s stern. A captain was supposed to go down with their ship, and Solveig would not miss that chance again. Alone on the ship, he began to walk, inspecting it carefully.

With Lonan and Leo's help, the *Serenity*'s belly had been loaded with explosives.

Solveig checked to make sure the barrels of gunpowder were stacked properly, ready to explode with the smallest spark.

"Well, old girl," he whispered. "Thank you for getting us here. It's time for you to rest, now."

Then, pulling a lighter from the confines of his green coat, Solveig flicked it open and tossed it across the room. Fire caught onto dry wood instantly, eating its way toward the explosives.

"Goodbye, *Serenity,*" Solveig breathed.

He took his time returning to the main deck. By the time he jumped overboard and onto the waiting dinghy, smoke poured from the portholes. Ves grabbed the oars, silently rowing the dinghy away from the ship.

Heat still licked at Solveig's face, drying the tears on his cheeks, when the fire finally caught the gunpowder, and a hole too big to ever be patched blew into the *Serenity*'s hull.

Flames climbed higher, devouring the ship in a starved frenzy of reds and oranges. Wood splintered, cracking and falling into the ocean with splashes that didn't stand a chance against the fire.

Acrid smoke burned Solveig's eyes. That was why tears spilled down his face. Or, at least, that's what he told himself. Natha pressed her fist against her mouth, silencing the sobs that shook her shoulders. Ves stood still, silent, her gaze never once leaving the burning *Serenity*. Czardas cried, too, his tears less graceful.

With a loud groan, the *Serenity* finally split, two halves breaking away and dipping into the sea. Water sprayed the figurehead's wooden face, making it look like she, too, was crying.

And then, at once, she was gone, succumbed to the ocean's hungry waves.

The Emerald Sea was calm now that the *Serenity* was no longer suffering.

10

Natha roamed the galley – *her* galley – in silent awe. The kitchen aboard the *Serenity* had been long but narrow, easy for one or two people, but more than that would be too crowded. But this...

The galley was the size of her old flat in Veridonia, at least, with counter space along the perimeter and an island in the center. Shelves bolted to the walls would be perfect for holding larger jars and barrels and hanging pots and pans. Beneath the counters were rows and rows of drawers and cabinets, providing ample storage space. A double oven and stove took up an entire wall, and a sink – a *sink* with running water – used up a chunk of the island.

She'd already put everything away, and there was *still* space.

And it was all hers.

Lonan, for all his creepy faults, painted a sign on the swinging door – *Nathalia's Kitchen. Do Not Enter.* Of course, that wouldn't stop Fynch from sneaking in, she thought, but...it made it hers.

The crew would be setting sail in the morning, but everyone – not including Lonan and Leo, thank the *gods* – had already settled in.

Like the *Serenity,* the *Dreamchaser* had two separate barracks – one for the women and one for the men. On opposite sides of the ship, there was more than enough space for the entire crew. Hammocks mounted to the walls beneath portholes, wardrobes were plentiful, and each set of barracks had a private bathroom. With Solveig deciding he no longer wanted to use the captain's quarters as his own, it became the medical room – even though there was no doctor on the ship. All the supplies went to the hold at the bottom of the ship, near the brig Natha hoped would never be used. There was a room for Illie, too; all her charts and maps hung on the walls, and her books stacked on the shelves by a desk. Pleo, her cat, was already fast asleep atop one of the shelves.

Natha's galley was on the gunner's deck, near the bow. A floor below the barracks, she'd be able to sneak down the stairs early each morning to make breakfast for the crew.

She paced around the island, plotting where she would put new pots and pans – because, of course, she was going to *politely* beg Solveig to buy her more – when the door swung open, and Ves marched inside.

"Oh," she purred, "this is *nice.*"

Had it been anyone else who marched into *her* galley like they owned it, Natha would have already dragged them out by their ear. But... It was Ves, so she supposed she could stay.

Natha opened a drawer and pulled out a piece of paper and a pencil. While she usually didn't like writing menus, two new people were on the ship, and it was Natha's job to make sure they ate properly. She tapped the pencil against her cheek absently, thinking of all the groceries she and Illie had just bought.

"There's an icebox, so the meat will last longer," she muttered to herself, ignoring Ves as she rummaged through the cabinets. "But the vegetables will start to wilt if they're not used right away. Leo said Lonan can't have a lot of salt, no matter what Lonan says..."

She scribbled down a few simple ideas for dinner.

"I say give that little worm a whole plate of salt," Ves said from across the galley. "Serves Sugar right for being gross. Even *I'm* not that bad, and I spent four years locked in prison."

"Did you not call me over to your table in Veridonia?" Natha didn't look up from her scribbling. "You're a shameless flirt, too."

"Do *not* lump me with Sugar, Blondie."

"I'd rather a woman flirt with me than a man." She tucked the pencil behind her ear. "I'm *done* with men. Does cold soup sound good for dinner?"

"I'd eat rocks if you told me you cooked them."

Heat rushed to Natha's ears. After so many years of working with people who treated her like dirt, people complementing her cooking was...unusual.

"Oh!" Ves suddenly said. "I came here for a reason. Cap wants everyone on deck. Can you spare five minutes?"

Nodding, Natha pushed her paper aside and followed Ves out of the galley and up the stairs to the deck.

Trusting his ship to a stranger he hardly knew should have rubbed Solveig the wrong way, but Lonan manned the helm like he'd been born to. Rather, like the *Dreamchaser* had been built for him to.

"I got Blondie," Ves's voice carried from across the deck. "That's all of us, then. Well, all of us that are here."

It didn't take a scholar to figure out that Ves was still bitter about being left behind. Czardas, too, but his sulking was a lot quieter and less in Solveig's face.

She dragged her feet, joining Solveig and Czardas at the bow. Dreamer's branching antlers stretched over the railing, polish glinting in the light. Ves ran her fingers over the smooth wood, muttering something about how only she had permission to touch the goddess since the goddess touched *her* first.

"A captain is usually elected to their position," Solveig began. He deliberately didn't invite Lonan or Leo to the meeting. They weren't crew, even if he had technically hired them to fulfill positions on his ship. He raked his fingers through his hair and continued: "But I wasn't. I assumed the position and dragged you all in. And since then, I've made some...stupid decisions."

Ves snorted. "That's an understatement."

Choosing to ignore her, Solveig pushed on. "I hid the map from you, I led you into battles we could have avoided, I've put you in danger time and time again. I sent Thol and Illie and Fynch away. I retired the *Serenity* and agreed to let two strangers join us temporarily. I don't want to lose any of you. You're all – Ves, stop glaring at me. I'm not getting sentimental. Look, I'm giving you all a choice. If you want to leave, I won't hold it against you. If you want to usurp my position as captain, I won't stop you. If you want to commit mutiny and throw me overboard right now, go for it. Even if I did make it back to Undyne unscathed, I'd be caught by the navy and executed for real."

For a moment, nothing happened. Nobody moved.

They're going to leave, Solveig thought, his stomach sinking. *They're going to ask to be dropped off in Servedin, and it'll be over. The adventure was fun while it lasted.*

Then a fist met his stomach so hard he stumbled back and vomited on the deck.

As he coughed up bile-thick spit, Ves shook out her hand.

"Well, Cap, I didn't think it was possible for you to get any stupider, so color me sarding impressed," she said. "You're the biggest idiot in the Emerald, huh?"

"What –" Solveig croaked, but another wave of nausea swept over him, silencing him before he could finish. He clutched his stomach, swallowing back bile before he could vomit again.

"If you hadn't come along, I probably would've drowned myself by now," Natha said. "I was miserable, you know. But thanks to you, I got to beat the sard out of my ex-husband. I have a kitchen, and I get to cook for people who enjoy what I make. I'm *free,* and it's because of *you.* Do you think some oath would keep me here if I didn't want to stay? Adrian vowed to never love anyone else, and he cheated on me. Words are just words. I'm here because I *want* to be here."

"I know I was hesitant to join," added Czardas, "but I like being here. And...and I know I would only slow the others down if I went with them to Corsa. We wanted an adventure, Captain. That's why we're here."

Ves looked away, her hair hiding her face. "You're our captain," she said. "Stupid decisions won't change that. I'm your third-in-command; it's my job to call you out when you're being an idiot. You saved my life, Cap. You're not allowed to leave until I pay that back. I'm not sorry I punched you."

"I deserved it," he rasped.

Ves turned around, arms crossed over her chest. "You did. And I won't hesitate to do it again. Now, Cap, did you call us here to lament, or do you have something important to tell us?"He *did* have something else he needed to talk about, but he hadn't expected the first part of his meeting to go as well as it did. Nobody was bleeding or dead, and he was the only one who got hurt.

Raking his hands through his hair, he said, "Illie left most of her books behind. Since Lonan and Leo have the helm covered, we should do more research. We have less than a year to find this...dead god slash missing moon and bring it back to Anwir."

"Still on that first-name basis," said Ves with a waggle of her eyebrows. Solveig debated shoving her off the ship.

"Illie thinks getting a bathymetric map will help," said Natha. "Something about mapping the bottom of the ocean and finding something moon-shaped. I trust her when it comes to maps, so I trust this."

"There's a mapmaker in Melrosine who makes maps of the seafloor," Ves added. "At least, there *was* about five or so years ago. If we sail *past* the Salts Atoll first and head to Melrosine, we could get that map."

"Isn't the Salts Atoll part of the Merdyne Empire?" asked Czardas. Wind blew his curls off his face, exposing a patch of vitiligo over his brow that Solveig hadn't noticed before. "Wouldn't they know about some giant missing *moon* in their territory? If we're going to stop in Melrosine to get a map, we should visit the royal archives."

The last time Solveig visited any archives, it had been just him, Ves, and Thol. A fight against the navy left them victorious and with the moonstone lithograph of the Wandering Isle. *Moonstone.* Solveig rubbed the polished stone of the ring on his littlest finger.

"Actually," piped up Ves. "I wouldn't mind visiting those archives. I want to find records of whoever had my ability before me. There's something I want to figure out."

Divine abilities, the powers granted to people randomly by the gods, weren't hereditary. Instead, when someone who had a certain ability – seeing souls, manipulating the winds – died, their power was given to someone else. Abilities were granted at birth but sometimes took many years to manifest. Each one had its limitations, and even though they were recycled, they sometimes manifested differently. Illie could grab winds and use them like whips, but that might not be the case for whoever had the power before her. If she grabbed too many winds, she got frostbite on her hands. Ves's ability didn't seem to have any real limitations, but she could only *see* life. She couldn't do anything else with it.

Solveig hadn't been blessed by any of the gods, but that was just as well. He didn't need a borrowed godly power to become the pirate he was. He'd done that all on his own.

"Speaking of divine abilities..." Natha turned to look at the two men at the helm. Lonan held the wheel with one hand, the other pulling a sugar cigarette from his teeth to exhale smoke. "Isn't Leo blessed? I've seen him light that rat's cigarettes with just his fingers."

Ves shrugged. "One way to find out. Hey! Goggles! Yes, you. Come here for a minute!"

Leo hopped down the stairs and strode across the deck quickly. Solveig noticed, not for the first time, that he walked with a limp.

"Something wrong?" he asked, hazel eyes darting to each of them.

"Your ability," Ves said. "What is it? You have one, don't you? Who are you blessed by? It's not Dreamer. I'd know another Dreamer-blessed."

Leo blinked, thick lashes brushing his freckled cheeks. "Uh... The Wanderer. I can create fire." He held his hand up, letting a flame spark on his fingertip. "Lonan isn't blessed, so don't ask him."

Fire. Now *that* would be a useful skill to have. He could burn ships down with just a brush of his fingers.

Captain Nox Solveig, cloaked in green, set out to conquer the Emerald Sea. One day he'll go down to the drink. How many navy ships will he sink?

More than he could without a fire ability, that was for sure.

Leo rubbed the lenses of his goggles with his hand, buffing out an invisible smudge. "How many of your crew are blessed?"

"Two," Ves answered for Solveig. "Me – Dreamer – and Pinkie – Poet."

"Poet, huh?" Leo asked. "That's a handy one for a pirate."

"Port!" screamed Illie as she barreled a fistful of wind into the sails.

"I'm turning the sarding ship as fast as I sarding can!" Thol shouted back. He gripped the wheel tightly, knuckles white under the strain of keeping the *Harper* steady.

The ocean and the sky were Poet's domains, and Poet, sard him, was unpredictable. Two hours ago, the sky had been clear and the sea calm. Now... Now, the *Harper* battled massive waves crashing around her and slanted rain that felt like razors against Thol's face.

"Turn it sarding faster!" Illie shouted.

Thol clenched his jaw hard and shoved all his weight into the turn, forcing the tea clipper hard left just before another wave came crashing down, narrowly missing the starboard side.

Servedin was *right* there. Another few hours and they'd be at the harbor. That is if Poet's unpredictable storm hadn't caught them off guard.

Two hours ago, Illie had been with Fynch, reading to him while Thol manned the helm. An hour ago, she raced onto the deck, panic covering her face like a mask. In half an hour, they got the storm sails up, and Fynch strapped to his cot. Just as Illie pulled on her thick makeshift gloves – three pairs of socks over each hand – the rain came down, soaking both of them to the bone in moments. Her dress clung to her body like a second skin, Thol's shirt so transparent that the wildflower tattoos on his chest were visible.

The wheel slipped, sliding out of Thol's grip and spinning helplessly.

"Sard!" he cursed, scrabbling to grab it and get a decent hold.

"THOL!" Illie screeched.

You're almost there, he reminded himself. *You're almost to Corsa. Fynch is almost safe. Just. Get. A. Sarding. Grip!*

He gritted his teeth together and slammed his body against the wheel, rain-slick hands finding enough friction to steady the damn thing.

Lightning whipped across the sky, fleeing from the deafening roar of thunder. Heart in his throat, Thol scanned the horizon for another tornadic waterspout like the one they'd faced only weeks before.

But the horizon was...calm. Still.

Dark and uneven with the outline of Servedin Island.

So. Sarding. Close!

"Illie!" he yelled. "Grab as big of a wind as you can and fill the sails! We're almost out of the storm!"

He saw her hesitate – that tiny beat where she glanced at her hands. Frostbitten, no doubt. Painful, blistered, oozing with fluid and blood that he *knew* had to hurt.

But he also knew – and she knew, too – that Fynch's punctured lung hurt more. Her pain would go away. His wouldn't – not unless he died.

So, she nodded once, then reached out and grabbed a wind, throwing it into the storm sails. Canvas ballooned; the *Harper* shot forward. The wheel slipped in Thol's grip again, but he was prepared this time.

"*More!*" he bellowed.

"*Aye!*" she screamed.

Lightning ripped the sky in two. Above Servedin, the sun peeked through the blackened storm.

"Is it over?" Thol asked. The sight of the blue sky seemed too good to be true, especially with how wet he still was, sprawled out on the soaked deck of the *Harper*.

"I think so," breathed Illie. She lay next to him, chest heaving, socks peeled off her blistered hands. Her fingertips were black, but she curled them into her dress to hide them. "Ha! We did it! We made it!"

She jumped to her feet with far more energy than Thol had and raised her arms to the air, letting out a whoop that sounded more like a seagull's cry than anything else.

Then, just as quickly as she got up, her shoulders dropped, and she whispered, "Sard. Fynch!"

"Check on him." He sat up slowly, wincing at the dull pain in his back. Not from an injury. Loath as he was to admit it, he was getting older. Thirty was hardly *old,* but he sure wasn't as spry as Czardas or Fynch anymore.

"Will you –"

"I'll get the *Harper* docked and registered." *And then to find that sarding quack.*

She nodded and ran off to check on Fynch. Thol scraped his hand over his face, suppressing a groan.

"Well, Corsa," he grumbled. "We meet again."

Only this time, it's not me on the verge of death, he thought grimly, fingers brushing against the deep scar across his chest.

Blood slicked Thol's knuckles – both his and his enemies' – in crimson rivulets that sluiced down his wrists to drip on the deck. As he shook his fists out and pummeled another round of PUNISHMENT *into the jaw of another pirate, all he could think was* thank the *gods* Nox isn't here.

A few weeks ago, Captain Hardy sent Solveig to Archepylago for a job. At fifteen, Solveig was still small enough to slip into places adults couldn't, making him the perfect treasure-hunting candidate for the heist.

And that was fine with Thol because no matter how good Solveig got with a sword, he would always be the little kid he'd sworn to protect.

He swung his fist, knuckles meeting the fleshy underside of another pirate's chin, throwing them back in a slurry of bloodied spit.

"Williams!" a voice – Captain Hardy's – rose over the tumult.

Only...the warning came a second too late.

Blood sprayed in hot geysers, splattering Thol's face and the face of the swordsman opposite him. Fabric and flesh alike tore in shredded ribbons, soaked instantly in red. The pain didn't register at first. For a split second, Thol thought the swordsman was the one who'd been injured.

But then... It set in at once, and Thol was on fire. He'd been split in two, bisected in a cruel diagonal that had him panicked that he'd been eviscerated, too.

He took a stumbling step back, too afraid to look down. Hands grabbed his shoulders, yanking him away before the swordsman could strike again.

"Williams!" Captain Hardy snapped. His voice was warbled. Underwater. Under blood.

He closed his eyes.

"Get...mainland...now..." bits and pieces of Captain Hardy's voice seeped through the pain, but Thol couldn't focus on that.

Panic rose to his throat. His insides were going to fall out. He was going to die. He was going to die, and he'd failed. He'd failed, he'd failed, he'd sarding failed to keep Nox safe.

He tried to move, but his fingertips were held down by the weight of his mortality.

I'm sorry, he thought, *though even he didn't know which brother that apology was directed toward.* I'm sorry I couldn't protect him in the end.

When he peeled his eyes open, half expecting to be dead, Thol was met with blinding lights and the familiar sting of fresh stitches. He sat up only to be shoved back down.

"Idiot," came a monotonous, accented voice. "You pull those stitches, you die. Are you really that suicidal? It would've been nice to know that before I used all my energy to save you."

Later, Thol would learn that that was the most the doctor ever spoke at once.

He blinked, trying to turn the blobby silhouette into something tangible. "What...?"

"Lie down," the voice said flatly. "I was only paid to save you and stitch you once."

A flash of silver caught Thol's eye before he conceded, laying against the stiff cot obediently. He wasn't suicidal, after all. He wanted – needed – to live. To protect Nox. To fulfill his promise.

"Name and age?" the voice droned.

His voice was weak when he spoke, croaky, like he'd swallowed a frog. "Bartholomew Williams. Thol. Twenty."

A pen scratched across paper.

"It's not a pleasure," the doctor said. "Doctor Israfel Eliad. I hope we never meet again."

Doctor Israfel Eliad stared at the bottle of cinnamon rum and debated dumping it into a cup and pretending it was tea. They didn't typically drink in the same way a pirate didn't typically steal, and they never drank while working, except they weren't *legally* a doctor, so they technically weren't ever on the clock.

There weren't any patients in Isra's *clinic* – a series of underground rooms they were so *graciously* allowed to use – so it wouldn't hurt to chug an entire bottle of cinnamon rum.

Well, it *would* hurt. It would go straight to their liver and poison their bloodstream. Their brain would be incapacitated, and if someone *did* show up to the clinic desperate for illegal treatment, Isra simply wouldn't be able to help.

Not that they cared about saving lives. Humans were the least of their concerns, but humans paid, and Isra did like money. Because money bought nice things like shiny new toys – scalpels and bone saws and syringes with needles longer than their fingers – and bottles of cinnamon rum meant for a party of ten people (not one singular doctor).

The pros of drinking: they could get drunk. They wouldn't have to deal with humans. They could shut down the clinic and spend the day sleeping and ignoring responsibilities. They could *feel* something for once.

The cons: their liver and blood and brain and other various internal organs would be shot to sard. They'd have a hangover even *they* couldn't cure in the morning. They'd spend the next day throwing up, and they loathed vomiting. The only thing they'd feel would be misery, and they had enough of that already.

To drink or not to drink, that was the question.

Isra grabbed the bottle and tilted it back and forth, watching the amber liquid slosh inside, glowing gold under the bright light of the clinic.

They didn't even *like* cinnamon rum. If they were to drink, they preferred a dry red wine or absinthe. Cinnamon rum was for peasants – plebians, pirates, poor folk. All the awful p-worded things that Isra was not. But Corsa didn't stock red wine or absinthe. It stocked cinnamon rum, and unless Isra went to a different city to shop, they were stuck with peasant-plebian-pirate-poor-folk alcohol.

Another con: they'd be sinking to the level of *commoners* by drinking an entire bottle of cinnamon rum.

Isra had been born a commoner. Worse, they'd been born *poor* – even spending two years in an orphanage, though that had been nearly two decades ago. Even now, their medical license legally revoked, they were nothing but a quack slightly above the bottom of the ladder. A snake amongst guppies – a snake beneath dragons.

Sometimes, it was best to live in delusion.

Sighing, they set the bottle down and grabbed a pair of cheap gloves – nothing like the leather ones they typically wore. Disposable ones good for cleaning. Despite the clinic being underground, Isra made sure to sanitize everything at least four times a day, not including when they were between patients.

Like they even *had* a steady flow of patients nowadays. With their license revoked and the ban on treating plague victims – despite being just as advanced as the rest of the world, the Alkenio Plague infected Corsa just as badly as it infected Syrenis twenty-four years ago – the only patients Isra tended to were wounded pirates.

Dragon Pirates.

The Dragon Pirate occupation had been in Servedin long enough that some of the youngest children didn't know a Corsa without the tyranny Ryuu Nova brought.

It had been Ryuu Nova who marched into Isra's clinic with his highest-ranking officers a few years ago – Ryuu Nova who put a gun to Isra's head and told them that if they healed another plague victim or someone he did not approve of, their clinic would get a new paint job with their blood and brains.

(Isra had to bite their tongue to keep from making an anatomical remark along the lines of the pistol not being of enough caliber to paint *all* the walls – just a small portion – and there would be bits of skull and hair and muscle as well).

The branded tattoo on their inner wrist burned at the mere thought of Captain Ryuu Nova. With Bonny Reed imprisoned at Ivenis Justyce Penitentiary off the coast of the Aralyth continent, Ryuu Nova stole the place of fourth most wanted. His four hundred fifty million lune bounty hardly reflected his cruelty. Isra always thought they deserved the third place, currently belonging to Captain Ellery Anor. But Anor had more territory, a larger crew, and a streak of violence even Nova couldn't beat.

Isra scraped their dark, silky hair back, pulling it off their face and neck.

"Stupid pirates," they grumbled to themself, the first – and likely only – words they'd spoken out loud since waking up that morning. They should have sworn off pirates ten years ago when they still had a chance – and a sarding medical license.

11

FYNCH'S BREATHING HAD BECOME so shallow Thol's stomach sank every time he didn't see the subtle rise and fall of the boy's chest.

Docking the *Harper* had been easy. The border hardly batted an eye, even though the *Harper* was a registered Veridian ship, not an Aralythian one. Thol had been directed to a port more upscale than he'd been expecting – a merchant port, it seemed. Too glad to be in Corsa – finally – he didn't question it, not as a group of boys rushed out to secure the *Harper* to the dock as Thol dropped the anchor. The ship secured, the boys ran off to deal with the next incoming boat, leaving Thol – and Illie, who'd joined him on the deck moments later – alone.

"He's unconscious," she said softly. "But he has a pulse – a weak one. A *very* weak one. And his breathing is...wet. I can't carry him. My hands..."

Her hands were blistered and raw, fingertips blackened with frostbite, and palms torn apart.

"I got him," he said, and he went to fetch Fynch.

True to Illie's word, Fynch was hardly breathing, his heart hardly beating, and when Thol lifted him, he was limp, the stench of infection so potent he nearly gagged.

Thol cradled him against his chest.

"Where is this doctor?" Illie asked.

Dread knotted in Thol's belly. It had been ten years since he'd last visited Isra. He didn't even know if the doctor was still in Corsa.

Swallowing hard, he said, "Follow me. Their clinic was underground last time I was here. Beneath an apothecary."

Even though it had been ten years, Thol began walking like he'd had drinks with Isra just the day before.

The streets, to his surprise, were mostly empty. Windows had been shuttered closed; signs had been plastered over doors declaring businesses *CLOSED*. A group of street urchins no older than ten or so huddled in an alley, watching Thol and Illie with hungry eyes. They didn't attack, though, likely only because of how wet and disheveled the pirates were. Soaked clothes and a nearly dead body didn't exactly scream *wealth*.

"You said this doctor owes you a favor," Illie said softly, lips hardly moving as she spoke. She kept her shoulders slumped and her head forward, but her eyes darted this way and that, watching the dark corners and back alleys carefully. "What did you do to get that?"

"Two favors, technically," he muttered back. "I saved their sorry ass twice. Once from the navy because they decided to pin a string of murders on them – they were innocent, though. I gave them a solid alibi despite that and beat up anyone who spoke against them. The other was when this group of thieves broke in and robbed the place at gunpoint. Only three people came out of that alive – me, Isra, and the weakest of the thieves so they could tell everyone else not to mess with the doctor."

Illie nodded once in understanding. Thol could only hope ten years hadn't muddled Isra's memory – that they would take those favors and use them to save Fynch's life.

"There," he said suddenly, nodding at a hanging sign. Ten years had weathered the wood, but the carved leaf and shop name were still visible, even if the apothecary itself looked long abandoned.

Thol stepped into the narrow alley next to the apothecary, finding the inconspicuous wooden door against the shop's wall easily. Illie pulled it open, revealing the dimly lit staircase spiraling down.

"After you," she said.

Thol stepped into the darkness, clutching Fynch tightly as he descended the same stairs he'd been taken down ten years ago when he, too, was on the brink of death.

At the bottom of the stairs was a narrow corridor leading to a dead end. Thol knew it was an illusion – that the walls around him hid labs and rooms and the cramped dwelling space Isra slept in. None of that mattered right now, though. The only thing that he cared about was the heavy door tucked against one of the smooth walls – a door Illie pushed open.

The room inside was well-lit, though a bit chaotic, with various chairs and posters and shadow boxes holding macabre paraphernalia – bat skulls and fetal kittens, a human fingerbone, a wet leech specimen. Another door opened up to the clinic room, and yet another led to the labs. Going through the labs led to Isra's tiny apartment.

A flimsy piece of cardstock had been taped to the wall.

No Patients.

No Appointments.

Closed.

Thol kicked the door.

Shuffling sounded from the other side.

"Read the sign," came the monotone droll that was Israfel Eliad's voice.

Thol kicked again, harder this time. Fynch's head rolled limply against Thol's arm. His lips were blue, and his face had taken on a greyish sheen.

"Open this sarding door, Isra, or I'll kick it down," Thol said, struggling to keep the panic from his voice.

Frantic footsteps now. The door swung open.

Doctor Israfel Eliad had hardly changed in ten years. Their hair was longer now, tied in a messy bun. Their dark skin looked pallid – they likely hadn't left the clinic in weeks. Though they were nearly a foot shorter than Thol, they were lanky and slim, all long fingers and skeletal limbs. They had a few scars on their face and shadowed by dark circles that appeared black were grey eyes.

"You," Isra said, their voice so emotionless Thol couldn't tell what they were thinking.

"Me," he said. "You owe me two favors, Isra. I'm here to cash them in. I need you to save his life."

"Agree to sail the ship, Lonan," Lonan muttered in a high-pitched voice. *"It'll be so much fun, Lonan. You won't regret it at all, Lonan. You'll be surrounded by beauties and the sea, Lonan."*

What a load of sard that was.

He slumped over the wheel, the pegs digging into his ribs, and let out the most dramatic sigh he could possibly manage. The pirates – and Leo, that traitor – were in the dining hall. He could smell whatever it was Natha cooked from where he stood, stomach grumbling as he shoved another sugar cigarette between his teeth. There were two reasons why Lonan was at the helm instead of eating with everyone else: someone had to keep the ship sailing smoothly, and Nathalia and Vesperine decided to team up against him and ban him from being in the same room as them until he learned to be *polite*.

Lonan Ryker was nothing if not polite. It wasn't *his* fault he was a romantic.

Sweet, saccharine oxygen filled his lungs; he held the smoke there until the pressure became too much before exhaling through his nose, the scent of molten sugar burning his nostrils.

Polite.

That was fine; he didn't want to eat with them, anyway. He liked sailing, and it was quiet, the sea calm. Wind filled the *Dreamchaser*'s sails, urging her along.

Footsteps ascended the stairs to the quarterdeck. Lonan glanced up through his curtain of blond hair to see Nox Solveig, his green coat billowing in the breeze.

"I can take over if you want to eat," he said. "Natha saved you some. Surprisingly."

Lonan took another drag of his cigarette. "Nah," he said. "Don't really have an appetite right now. I bet Leo told Miss Natha I couldn't have excess salt, so it's probably as bland as sard."

Solveig walked over to the railing behind Lonan and leaned against the polished wood. "When I was a boy, my ma would forget to go shopping sometimes. Once you've eaten moldy bread and korva mash for a week straight, you can complain about the flavor of something."

Lonan glanced at the captain, at the harsh angles of his face shadowed with stubble and red hair. "Mother issues?"

"The only issue I had with her was that she lived as long as she did."

Lonan thought of his own mother – whom he *had* a good relationship with, for most of his life, at least – and cringed. "Ouch. That bad?"

"We used to call her *Mistress Slut-vig,*" the captain said with a chuckle. "Just ask Thol. He once called her *Mistress Whore* to her face."

He couldn't help it; Lonan laughed. "How'd she react to that?"

The captain just grinned. "She was mad, but she couldn't prove him wrong, so she didn't do a thing."

Lonan tried to imagine Thol – massive, muscular, inked Thol with his tattooed knuckles and crooked nose and stature that made Lonan feel very, very small – insulting Solveig's mother like that. They had to have been children because no matter how hard he tried, he couldn't wrap his mind around *current* Thol doing such a thing.

He inhaled another lungful of oxygen before exhaling the smoke, then adjusted the wheel. He wasn't a navigator by any means – far from it, actually. If he was held at gunpoint and told to figure out if a map of Syrenis was upside down or not he'd walk away from that scenario with a bullet in his pretty skull – but he knew ships. He knew the *Dreamchaser*, how she ran, how she liked to be handled. She was, after all, a lady. A very big, very strong, very temperamental lady whom Lonan had to coax into submission. It didn't take a navigator to follow the currents and a compass, but it took an expert helmsman to maneuver a brig with loving precision.

"You and Leo have known each other for a while?" Solveig asked, sliding the conversation from *his* past to Lonan's.

Interesting...

"Since we were in napkins," he said around his sugar cigarette. "Our families were close. Met him when we were about a year old each. Twenty-something years later, and we're still best friends. He's the brains, I'm the beauty."

"Don't lie to the captain, Lo," came Leo's voice.

Leo marched up the steps and shoved a plate into Lonan's chest.

"Eat," he instructed. "Maybe you'll be less ugly with more meat on your bones."

Different body or not, Lonan would still be overconfident. He wasn't all brawn like Thol, but he was sure he could beat Solveig in an arm-wrestling match, even if Lonan had a healthy layer of fat over all his muscles.

"Maybe *you'll* be less ugly with no tongue." Lonan looked down at his plate. Cooked vegetables, a pile of rice, and juicy meat.

Grabbing his fork, he scooped up a bite and shoved it in his mouth. His eyes went wide at once. Despite the lack of salt, everything was seasoned *perfectly* – enough so that he didn't even *miss* the salt. Subtle, smoky spice mingled with an overwhelming savory flavor, balanced to perfection. He devoured the rest of it in just a few mouthfuls.

"Eat Natha's cooking like that," chuckled Solveig, "and you might just win her over. Well, you'll end up on her good side, if nothing else. I'm surprised she didn't poison it."

If Miss Natha had poisoned the meal, Lonan would happily drop dead having tasted the most delicious thing in all four seas.

"How much further until we get to Corsa?" Solveig asked once Lonan finished licking his fingers.

"Not a navigator," Lonan said. "But it isn't much further now."

Even if Isra wanted to save the kid's life, they couldn't. Not without risking their own neck, and they'd gotten too close to death too many times in their thirty years of life. If Captain Nova found out that Isra had used their abilities – both divine and medical – to heal someone *without* his permission...

Well. Isra knew first-hand what those bodies looked like.

They looked at Thol – the friend they hadn't seen in years – then at the boy in his arms. The boy whose lips were blue and caked with blood, whose skin was as grey as Isra's eyes, whose chest was no longer moving.

They *owed* Thol. Those debts didn't just go away because Ryuu Nova strolled in and told Isra who they could and couldn't heal. And if they didn't act *now,* even their ability wouldn't be able to do much.

Gritting their teeth, Isra opened the door wider. "Set him on the table," they said. "And keep watch. No one's allowed in."

They stepped aside, eyes narrowed as they watched Thol place the boy's body on the metal table. The pink-haired girl watched nervously. When Isra turned their gaze to her, she looked away quickly, instead studying an asmyth plant that wound itself around a shelf.

"Out," Isra instructed.

Alone with the boy, they shut the door. Then locked it. Then shoved a chair under the doorknob. Then prayed to Dreamer that nobody would come in and flay them alive for betraying Nova's orders.

From the pocket of their white overcoat, Isra pulled out a pair of gloves, pulling them on in favor of the disposable rubber ones. These ones were leather, soft and buttery, with tiny slits along the fingertips. Flexing their fingers, Isra approached the table. They tore the boy's shirt, then his undergarments off, exposing grey flesh that reeked of infection.

"Hypovolemic shock," Isra said to themselves. "Caused by pneumothorax – traumatic pneumothorax. Entrance wound synonymous with a low-caliber gunshot wound. Insufficient treatment led to infection – sepsis, based on smell alone. Shock from blood loss led to asphyxiation. Patient is approximately eighteen to twenty years old. Born female. About thirty seconds away from brain death."

They flexed one of their hands. From the slits sprouted slim scalpels, tiny blades that flashed in the light. With their teeth, they pulled up their sleeve.

"Perfect conditions for me," they said.

Then they slashed their arm *deep.* Blood rushed to the surface, running in crimson rivulets down their arm, slipping beneath their glove – their glove, which, like the other, had little needles sticking from the fingertips.

Twenty-eight seconds after Isra's diagnoses, they shoved the needles into the boy's chest, forcing their divine-touched blood into his infection-touched bloodstream.

Israfel Eliad, blessed by Dreamer, had blood more coveted than any modern medicine in the world. Though it only worked when the patient was on the extreme cusp of death – milliseconds before their bodies shut down – Isra could heal almost *any* wound or disease.

Including the Alkenio Plague.

Including hypovolemic shock that led to asphyxiation caused by traumatic pneumothorax and sepsis.

Blood poured from the wounds on their arm, trickling into the needles sprouting from their fingertips and pumping into the boy's body.

Ten seconds passed. The boy's color started bleeding back.

Twenty. His lips were no longer blue.

Thirty – forty, fifty, a full minute. His chest began to rise and fall.

One minute was all Isra had needed to pull the boy away from death. With him stable, they could now perform *proper* surgery.

Sliding the needles free, Isra removed their gloves and set them on the counter. Methodically, they bandaged their own arm and tied their hair back. Pulling on rubber gloves, they grabbed all the tools they needed – scalpel, needle, thread, catheter, gauze, tweezers, an antiseptic they'd made with a combination of undiluted alcohol, saline, and their blood.

"Beginning surgery," they murmured, grabbing the leather beaked mask from a hook on the wall and sliding it over their lower face.

Isra grabbed the scalpel and sliced into the boy's chest. Their blood would work as an anesthetic until it had fully consumed the infection, so Isra didn't worry as they cut through layers of flesh and fat and muscle, peeling them back to reveal pristine white ribs and a deflated lung.

"Incision to the lung," they narrated, slicing a tiny hole into the deflated lung. "Inserting the catheter."

Exchanging the scalpel for the tube, they slid the catheter into the incision. As the boy breathed, the catheter pumped oxygen into his lung.

While that worked, Isra got to work cleaning the wound with the antiseptic.

Half an hour later, coat reddened with blood that was both theirs and not, Isra stepped out of the room, mask hanging limply around their neck.

Thol and the pink-haired girl both stopped their pacing.

"Is he...?" the girl started.

"Stable," said Isra. "Alive. Whoever originally treated him should never touch a needle again."

The girl burst into tears and hugged Thol tightly. Isra bit the inside of their cheek to keep from smiling.

"That's one debt paid," Isra said. "Leave as soon as he wakes up."

"I can't thank you enough," said Thol.

Isra rolled their eyes. "Then don't thank me. Just leave."

They turned and disappeared back into the room to hang their mask up and make sure the boy was still unconscious. The cuts on their arm stung.

The day was still young. If Nova brought someone on the brink of death to Isra's office, it would all be over. Their abilities were limited: they could only heal infections and diseases. If Nova brought someone missing a limb or sliced in half or with their brains blown out, Isra couldn't save them. They could only heal a person when they were seconds away from death – and they couldn't use their ability on themselves. Healing them too soon wouldn't work and healing them too late was an act of necromancy, and even Isra couldn't do that. And they could only heal once a day. It took hours for their blood to return to its full potency, so if Nova brought someone in before the twenty-four-hour period was up, Isra wouldn't be able to do a thing.

And Captain Ryuu Nova would realize that Isra healed someone without his permission.

"Your life," they murmured to the sleeping form of the boy, "had better be more significant than mine."

12

THERE WAS A SHIP on the horizon, too small for Solveig to make out any details, and it was headed right for the *Dreamchaser.*

He wished Illie was there, with her spyglass and winds. He wished Thol was there, too, with his unwavering determination and bloodlust.

And he wished Fynch was there, with his guns and his lungs working properly.

"Well, Cap!" Ves pulled two knives from her belt and tossed them in the air. "What's the plan?"

There was no plan. Not a fleshed out one, anyway. If the ship was a merchant vessel, they would raid it. If it belonged to a fisherman or someone else just trying to make ends meet, the *Dreamchaser* would coast by without engaging.

But if it was a navy ship or a pirate ship...

Solveig gritted his teeth together. Together, the only people un-injured enough to fight were Natha and Czardas. Solveig's leg still ached when he put weight on it, the deep cut still scabbed and raw. His shoulder hurt, too, from when he was shot way back at Bowhead Rock off the coast of Carilon. He knew Ves was mostly healed from when she was sliced across the back at that same battle, but the fights against the navy and the Rabbit Pirates had left everyone worse for the wear.

"Um, Captain Solveig?" came Leo's voice. "Not sure what your plan is, but if you could let us know... That ship is navy. Lo could outmaneuver it *easily,* but... I want to see how the *Dreamchaser* fares in a real fight."

Real helpful, those two.

"We can fight," Ves said. "With you, me, and Blondie, we can handle them."

"What about me?" asked Czardas.

"It can't be *that* bad, either," she continued. "It's only one ship. Not Jony Boy or any big shots. Let us fight, Cap. I will scream if you don't let me fight someone. Blondie and I can handle them by ourselves."

Solveig had a feeling that if he didn't let Ves fight, she would fight *him* instead. He was still sore from the last time she attacked him...

He glanced at the black flag waving from the mainmast – a crescent moon stabbed by a sword bleeding five gemstones: sapphire, emerald, ruby, amethyst, moonstone.

"Fine," he said. "We'll fight. Czardas, you can sit this one out if you need to. Ves, how many people are on the ship?"

She got as close to the railing as possible. "Fifteen, Cap. I could take them out *blindfolded.*"

"Lonan! Leo!" Solveig shouted. "Get parallel to them. We'll see how well she holds up against cannon fire. Ves, ready the guns. Natha, you help her. Neither of you are going to engage alone."

"Are we allowed to fight?" called Leo.

"No!" chorused Solveig, Ves, and Natha. Solveig added: "You're not part of my crew. Don't you dare put yourself in danger. I will not save you."

He drew his cutlass, ignoring the dull ache in his shoulder. The wound was old; he could still fight. He *would* still fight.

The navy ship drew closer. Lonan maneuvered the *Dreamchaser,* moving her with ease until she was right next to the navy ship.

"I would recognize that coat anywhere," a voice said, drawing Solveig's attention to the enemy ship. "You must be the captain. Perfect. In that case, I demand parley."

Sparrow Largos jumped from his ship to the *Dreamchaser,* a grin stretched across his face. Fynch's older brother had his same face, his same air of confidence, but where Fynch was skin and bones and bruises and chipped teeth, Sparrow Largos was perfection. A true little sailor blessed by Lady Lightbringer.

"I don't have to grant parley," Solveig growled. "I'm a sarding pirate. Rules don't apply to me."

"No, but you're a sailor, so I'm assuming you'll obey the laws of the sea," Sparrow said with a shrug. "I'm not here for you, regardless. I'm here for your sharpshooter. Don't deny it; I've seen his posters. Where is that rat Fynch?"

If Solveig didn't hate Sparrow Largos before, he did now. Fynch might be annoying. He might have a terrible habit of swiping things from Solveig's pockets or leaving his spare cases of ammo in Solveig's bed. He might be banned from the galley for life. He might be a child Solveig felt a strange sense of responsibility toward.

But Fynch Largos was crew. And *nobody* insulted his crew.

Solveig shifted, sinking into an attack stance. "He's –"

He didn't finish that sentence because Czardas shoved past Natha and Ves and said, "If Fynch had to choose between dying a fiery death or talking with you for five sarding minutes, he would jump into the flames without hesitation. *This* is for all the sard you dragged him through, Row."

Czardas reeled his arm back and punched Sparrow right in the face, whipping his head to the side. Bloodied spit dribbled down his chin. Sparrow stumbled, barely managing to catch himself before he could fall to the deck.

"Czardas Rossi." Sparrow spat a glob of saliva. "Future duke, famous musician, worthless pirate."

"Wait!" Solveig raised his sword, but even he was too slow. Before he could swing, Sparrow swung a punch of his own, crushing his knuckles into Czardas's nose.

Crunch!

"Ves, Natha," Solveig said calmly, watching as Czardas stumbled backward, hands cupping his bleeding nose. "Fire at will."

"Aye, Cap!" Ves grinned.

Solveig turned to Sparrow Largos. "I deny your request for parley. *You* started this fight by boarding *my* sarding ship. I should give Fynch the honors, but he's far from here right now. So, it will be *my* sword you will die by."

Sparrow grinned. He had all his teeth, unlike Fynch. "Bring it on, pirate."

Fynch slowly pried his eyes open, half expecting to see the goddess Dreamer before him. Or...whatever else he was supposed to be greeted with upon death. Instead, when his vision focused, he was met with bright, sterile lights and an empty room. There was pain in his chest, but it was...dull. Like the wound was years old, not weeks old.

He brushed his fingers against his chest, only half surprised to find his shirt cut clean in half. Stitches – fresh ones – snaked along his chest, right above where that ache was located.

Not dead, then. Alive.

Somehow.

Sitting up slowly, he peered around the room, trying to figure out where he was. This wasn't the *Serenity*. It wasn't the ship he'd been on with Illie and Thol, either. He wasn't even *on* a ship.

He rubbed his eyes and silently wondered, *Am I dreaming?*

Then, before he could dwell on things for too long, a door opened, and someone stepped into the room. Fynch reached for his revolver instinctively, fear shooting through his veins.

"Good," said the stranger with a bird's beak. "You're awake. Leave."

Fynch opened his mouth to protest, to complain that he didn't even know where he was, to whine that he wasn't even sure he could walk when two more people burst into the room. Unlike with the first one, Fynch recognized these two instantly. Thol and Illie.

Illie crushed him in a hug so tight, Fynch worried his stitches would break open, and he'd be flung to the precipice of death once more.

"You stupid, sarding idiot!" she cried into his shoulder, her grip tightening when he reluctantly hugged back. She smelled of ink and salt, of home.

"What, didja think I was going to die?" he asked, his voice unfamiliarly scratchy and hoarse. "I'm never going to die. And if I was gonna, I'd go out in a blaze of glory. Not like this."

She choked on a sob and pulled him closer.

The stranger with the bird mask sighed, irritated. "Leave."

Another set of arms wrapped around Fynch's body, forcing all the air from his lungs. His *lungs!* Both of them, working in tandem *without causing him pain.*

"Illie's right," Thol murmured against Fynch's hair. "You are a sarding idiot."

The doctor, again, said, "Leave."

Thol pulled away first. "We're leaving, Isra."

"Good," the doctor – Isra – said. "Before Nova comes."

Nova? Why did that name sound so familiar? *Nova, Nova, Nova...*

"Ryuu Nova?" Illie asked. "The pirate? Why would he be coming here? We can take him. Our captain's bounty is more than his."

Fynch, who had spent more than one night in a jail cell, understood the very basics of bounties. The higher the bounty, the more the pirate was wanted by the navy. Fynch's bounty of sixty-nine million lune was partially because of the navy sailors he killed in Veridonia, partly because of how many crimes he'd committed in his life, and partially because of who his captain was. The higher the bounty, the more dangerous a pirate was, and at five hundred million lune, Solveig stood at second-most-wanted. Ryuu Nova's bounty, four hundred fifty million lune, was only thirty-five million higher than Thol's.

But Bonny Reed's was four hundred eighty million, and fighting *her* nearly destroyed the crew. Fighting her put Fynch in a life-or-death position in the first place. Bounty wasn't everything.

"Ryuu Nova," Isra grumbled. "The warlord."

Where was Natha and her uncanny knowledge of current affairs and popular culture when Fynch needed her?

Isra pointed to the door, wordlessly commanding the pirates to leave. *Again.*

"Come on," Illie whispered, looping her arm under Fynch's arms, taking some of his weight. "Let's go. I bet we can make it back to Port 16 before the *Serenity* is fixed."

"One debt paid," Isra said to Thol. "Don't come for the second one soon."

"Fire!" Ves shouted, clapping her hands over her ears as fire ran down the cannon's fuse.

Boom!

The explosion rocked the ship. Natha lit another two cannons, moving faster than Ves, who watched each blow to make sure it landed.

On the deck above, footsteps and gunshots and clashing swords rang out, reminding Ves that this wasn't a skirmish – it was a battle. One they needed to win if they wanted to see Thol and Illie and Fynch again.

"Can I help?" Czardas. He'd been given a choice – to fight or to hide.

Ves's fingers itched for her knives, to slash the throats out of her enemies. She handed the matches to Czardas and said, "Load the cannons and light the fuses. Cover your ears if you're going to stand close to the cannons. If you run out of cannonballs, start firing...bricks or something. I don't know. Anything that'll sink the sarding ship. I'm going to help Cap."

Czardas blinked helplessly. Oh, well. If he really needed better instructions, Natha was right there.

Slipping her knives from her belt, she dashed upstairs.

Half the crew was downstairs, half was in Corsa, and Lonan and Leo weren't engaged in any fighting, so anyone who *wasn't* her captain was a fair target.

She flipped her knife and stabbed it into the throat of an oncoming navy man. Blood spurted, hot and red, coating her face as she tore the blade free.

She lunged, striking viper fast, slashing the throats of two more enemies in one fell swoop.

"The Witch of the Sea," a helpless fool whispered, their last words before Ves silenced them in a bloody stab. Their body crumpled to the ground, another victim on the Witch of the Sea's list.

In a split second before launching another attack, she turned to see Solveig strike a blond man – one she recognized instantly. Sparrow Largos, Fynch's brother.

Great.

She spun around, the thick scar on her back sending a shock of pain radiating down her spine. She sucked a breath through her teeth and buried a dagger in the throat of an oncoming attacker. Blood that wasn't hers slipped through her lips, settling thickly on her tongue.

Grinning widely, blood staining her teeth, she bared her knives and said, "Well, then! Who's sarding next?"

Fynch's sharpshooting ability did not run in the family, it seemed. Like Solveig, Sparrow Largos fought with a cutlass. He crawled into Solveig's space, striking hard and fast, all finesse and little precision behind each blow. He was built stronger than Fynch, making up what he lacked in gunslinging with muscle. He was shorter than Solveig, but that didn't matter, not as his cutlass crashed against Solveig's.

"When I kill you, Admiral Commodore will be forced to recognize my worth," Sparrow spat.

Jonyth sarding Commodore.

Solveig leaned his weight into the blow, trying to force Sparrow's grip to waver. He growled, "If that sarding idiot thinks you're worthless, you must be the most pathetic of them all."

"Says the man who needed the prince of Aralyth to save him from execution," Sparrow shot back.

Well, Fynch. I hope you weren't planning on your brother continuing your bloodline, he thought.

And then he brought his boot-clad foot right between Sparrow's legs.

The color drained from Sparrow's face, his body going stiff. Solveig acted, smashing his cutlass against Sparrow's to force it from his grip.

Sparrow collapsed to his knees, his sword flying across the deck, abandoned, forgotten as he writhed in pain.

Solveig stabbed his sword into the deck, mere hairs from Sparrow's head.

"You know," he said, "I understand why Fynch wants nothing to do with you. I know a lot about brothers, and I know a terrible one when I see him."

Sparrow, through his agony, spat at Solveig. "You wouldn't know a thing. Fynch killed our mother. He's a no-good piece of sarding scum. You both deserve punishment."

And then Sparrow struck again, slamming his foot against Solveig's thigh, right where his still-tender wound was. Blinding pain seized his vision. Solveig stumbled; his grip on his cutlass faltered.

Sparrow stood on uncertain legs. "I bet he didn't tell you that, huh? If you're such an expert, what would *you* do if your brother killed your mother?"

Five blood brothers, only two with the same father. A woman who should have never become a mother. Two filled graves and two empty.

A little yellow house atop a hill, abandoned after its inhabitants left for good.

He tightened his grip on his cutlass, brandishing it in Sparrow's direction. He said, "It's a damn shame my brothers didn't kill my mother. It would have made life a hell of a lot easier for *everyone.*"

Solveig sliced, his blade arcing across Sparrow's chest in a spray of silver and red.

"Captain!" a voice that did not belong to Ves or Czardas or Natha – or even Lonan or Leo – cried. "Captain, we need to retreat! The ship's going to sink if she receives any more damage!"

Solveig smirked. "A captain should always go down with his ship. Now, get off mine."

"The *Silver Moon* went down without you," spat Sparrow. Still, he did not grab his sword. He did not take his eyes off Solveig, not even as he ran back to his own ship, retreating with his tail tucked between his legs.

Solveig shoved his cutlass into its sheath and raked both hands through his knotted hair.

"Captain!" This time, it was Leo who cried out. "Captain Solveig, that was incredible! I've never seen a pirate fight up close. What are your – Captain...?"

Solveig ignored Leo. It wasn't hard, not with everything sounding distorted. Leo called out again, but Solveig focused on his footsteps, on going to the barracks.

His brothers. His crew. Everything – everyone – he'd ever cared about, gone.

And at the sarding root of it all, beneath his mother's selfishness, beneath the need to appease the gods, was Jonyth Commodore.

Solveig was going to kill him.

Lonan had eight older siblings, though he once had nine.

Hearing Solveig's verbal fight with the navy captain about siblings and terrible parents struck something inside Lonan.

When the decrepit navy ship retreated like a dog with its tail tucked between its legs, Lonan passed the helm to Leo, ignoring his excited ramblings about the fight in favor of going to the barracks. He lit a sugar cigarette and stuck it between his teeth, spotting Solveig on his bunk.

"How many siblings have you got?" he asked around the cigarette. "Or, how many did you have?"

Solveig didn't answer at first. Then, quietly, he said, "By blood? Three older brothers, one younger. Though, who knows how many other half-siblings I share a father with."

"One of five, then?" Lonan leaned against the wall with a *thud*. "I'm number ten. Six sisters, three brothers. You know, for a long, long time, I resented my parents."

"Because of all the kids they had?"

"Well, that, too. Have you shared a bathroom with eleven other people?" He exhaled a plume of smoke. "I don't really remember it well. It's mostly foggy memories and whatever my siblings told me. I was four at the time. Anyway, these people came to our house one day and told my parents they'd been chosen by the gods. They said our family would be blessed, and we'd get a bunch of money, and all we had to do was hand over my sister. Rebecca. She was sixteen. Well, my parents had ten mouths to feed, so they agreed. They sold Rebecca off to the cultists, and we never ever saw her again. My family moved when my oldest sister got married and left me behind."

His memories of Rebecca were sparse. He was sure she had the same blonde hair as him, he was sure she liked to paint her nails every week, he was sure she slept under the window. Did she cry when the cultists came? Did she fight? Did she even want to go? He didn't know if she had friends, lovers, ambitions, dreams. He didn't even know what truly happened to her. Only that she was gone forever, and the money his parents received hardly lasted a month in the Ryker household.

His parents wrote to him occasionally, as did his siblings. He was an uncle to over a dozen nieces and nephews. More than half of his brothers and sisters were married and living happy lives. None of them had heart problems. None of them lived a life like Lonan's. He'd always been the outcast in his family.

But he was also the most successful.

Solveig sat up and turned toward Lonan. He asked, his tone serious, "These...cultists... Did they wear black robes with hoods?"

Lonan blinked, surprised. In all his life, he'd never met anyone who knew about the cultists. As far as he knew, Rebecca had been the only sacrifice they'd ever taken. Foggy as his memories were, he remembered the strangers clearly.

"They did."

Solveig cursed. Loudly.

Then, he said, "My wench of a mother sold two of my brothers to them."

13

ANWIR TOSSED AN APPLE into the air, absently catching it with one hand while he pretended to listen to Jonyth Commodore.

Truthfully, he'd *stopped* listening about fifteen minutes ago, around the time Jonyth made an offhand comment about how Anwir's sister, Iori, should hurry up and marry the crown prince of Veridin so the Aralyth Empire could officially annex it and Jonyth could have better control over Veridin's navy troops. If it involved his sister, Anwir Helios, crown prince and heir to the Aralyth Empire, could not care less. There wasn't a single soul in Syrenis who hated the little brat more than him.

"...reports from Undyne that Nox Solveig was there," continued Jonyth, finally catching Anwir's attention. He tossed the apple up but didn't catch it, letting it fall to the floor with a thud.

He swept his feet off the desk and stood, drawing Jonyth's gaze away from the paper he'd been looking at.

"Solveig was in Undyne?" Anwir asked, struggling to keep his voice flat, void of any emotions.

He'd been the one to save Solveig from being executed. He'd been the one to give Solveig his father's ancient map, the one who set the captain free with the promise of a single letter of amnesty.

He didn't care for the pirate, not one bit. He certainly did not care for Solveig's rugged appearance, his emerald eyes, the way his red hair fell over his face...

He stubbed his toe on the desk and promptly cursed out all four gods, his mother, and Jonyth Commodore.

"The key word there being *was*," growled Jonyth. "He left."

Relief tugged the weight from Anwir's shoulders.

He did not sarding care about the sarding pirate.

He said, "Well, where is he going to go? Our ship is faster than his. We can catch him."

Silently, he prayed to the gods – to Poet and Dreamer, to Lady Lightbringer, to the Wanderer. *Do not let Jonyth catch up with Solveig. Let him find that sarding lost moon so I can pardon him.*

Anwir bent down and scooped up the discarded apple. He wiped it off on his shirt and sank his teeth into the crisp, juicy flesh.

"No," said Jonyth. He rapped his fingers against the paper. "I have a different idea. With your permission, *your Highness.*" He spoke those last words bitterly, making sure Anwir knew just how much it pained him to use his correct title.

Between bites, Anwir said, "Elaborate."

Jonyth's face twisted into a scowl. The fresh scar stretching from his ear across his crooked nose twisted, puckering. Courtesy of

Nox Solveig, though Anwir wished he'd taken Jonyth's eye out completely. Just to irritate him further, Anwir took a loud bite, chewing with his mouth open, little regard for the juice dribbling down his chin.

"We don't go after Solveig," Jonyth said.

Anwir choked. Suddenly, he wished he hadn't been so careless with his eating.

"Instead," he continued, "we strike a different target. Show Solveig that we have the gunpower to take out other pirates. Give him a false sense of security, trick him into thinking we aren't actively tracking him down."

No! screamed the traitor in Anwir, the part that longed to touch the stubble on Solveig's cheeks, the part that turned to jelly when he saw just how sarding tall the pirate was.

"Who?" croaked the prince in Anwir, the part that knew he had a duty to his empire, the part that had to see Nox Solveig as just another filthy pirate who deserved a death at the gallows.

Jonyth set his paper down. "The Unnamed God."

Natha yanked her hair into a tail so tight it pulled her face back. The smell of gunpowder clogged her nostrils, permeating the fabric of her clothing so deep she wasn't sure it would ever leave.

Sending half the crew away had been a mistake. Fighting the navy had been a mistake. Some days, Natha wondered if becoming a pirate was a mistake, too.

She hadn't fought the navy directly, but her body produced adrenaline all the same, pumping it loudly in her ears, drowning out each cannon fire.

"Deep breaths," she murmured to herself, focusing on grabbing the sack of flour from one of the overhead cabinets in her galley. "Deep sarding breaths. Adrian isn't going to find you again. You're *safe.*"

Even though she knew that the fear of her ex-husband was so deeply ingrained in her that every mention of the navy shoved her into a fight-or-flight response that left her shaky and panicked and exhausted afterward.

Propping the sack on her hip, she measured out precise cups and dumped them into a bowl. With each added cup of flour, her anxiety lessened.

"You're safe," she told herself, replacing the flour in favor of cocoa powder. "Solveig will keep you safe. Everyone will. Adrian will never *ever* hurt you again. His family can't touch you anymore. If they try, they'll lose their hands at best."

They'll die at worst.

Natha whisked the dry ingredients together and got to work mixing up the eggs, butter, and sugar. By the time she had the batter poured into a round tin, her hands no longer trembled, and her thoughts of the navy were gone, quashed by thoughts of how she would decorate the cake and if she should spit on Lonan's piece before giving it to him.

She closed the oven with her foot and grabbed a rag, using it to scrub down the counter so she'd have space to work on dinner prep.

"If you're going to stand there, you can at least be helpful," she said, breaking the silence.

She glanced over her shoulder to see Ves leaning against the doorframe, arms crossed, hair piled atop her head in a bun so messy it almost added a foot to her height. Natha didn't know how long she'd been standing there, but she hadn't interfered, so it didn't bother her.

"I'm just here to make sure that cake will turn out," Ves said.

"It will," grumbled Natha. "I made it. Here, peel these potatoes." She nudged a sack of potatoes toward Ves.

"Yes, ma'am." Ves pulled one of her daggers from her belt.

"Use one of *my* knives," Natha warned.

Ves put her dagger back and pulled a slim blade from the block on the counter. Crouching down, she grabbed a potato and got to work skinning it.

Cooking with little salt was more difficult than Natha cared to admit, but she was an excellent chef, and excellent chefs knew how to fulfill *all* the dietary needs of their crew. Pillowy potato dumplings with a basil sauce would pair well with roasted korva – she'd skip the salt in favor of garlic and paprika – and a crusty bread. No salt for Lonan, pasta for Leo, protein for Solveig, a balance of foods for Czardas, and with the cake for dessert, both hers and Ves's sweet tooths would be satisfied.

She sprinkled flour on the counter and began making the dough for the bread.

"Twin moons in the sky for the third has died, aweigh anchor aweigh," came Ves's soft singing. *"The seas are dark, but the spirits are bright, we'll set the Ruby alight. Chart the course for the unknown way, aweigh anchor aweigh. Find the moon and the treasure tonight, we'll set the Ruby alight."*

It was the same shanty Ves always sang, the one from her days as bo'sun of the Ruby Pirates before she was captured and thrown into Ivenis Justyce Penitentiary four years ago. Natha had heard it no less than a hundred times, but... Her hands stilled, fingers sticky with the dough she'd been kneading.

"Do..." she started. "Do you think there really is a missing moon out there? Why would it be wiped from history? Why does nobody else know about it?"

Are we just chasing a fever dream? she thought to herself.

"I've seen a lot of impossible things in my life," said Ves. "I killed a kraken. I rotted in prison for four years. I robbed the empress of Merdyne. Have you seen Pinkie's notes? Every culture in the world mentions a third moon. Mene, Sin, and Moon Number Three. That *has* to mean something, right? Will we find the moon in the Salts Atoll? I don't know. Is it out there? Without a doubt. I just wish I knew what the map meant."

Nobody, not even Illie, could fully decipher the poem of words wrapped around the map's perimeter. Solveig seemed to think it led to the Salts Atoll, but...

But there was no way it would be *that* easy.

She put the dough back in its bowl and covered it with a towel, pushing it aside so it could rise.

"When you're done with the potatoes, put them in the pot over there," she said. "Help me figure out a way to ask Lonan and Leo if they know anything about there being three moons, and I'll give you the biggest piece of cake tonight."

A grin split across Ves's face, wide enough to force her dimples to show. "Deal."

As Natha finished the dinner preparations, Ves, as she reluctantly promised in exchange for two pieces of cake instead of one, set out to find Lonan. Insufferable as he was, all she had to do was flash her cleavage and get whatever she wanted from him. And Natha refused to speak to him. Not that Ves could blame her. She'd have a hard time talking with *any* of the men on the crew if she'd been with Adrian Zimmer.

Just as Ves left the galley, Lonan slipped from the barracks, holding a purring Pleo in his arms. The cat's tail swished happily, thudding against Lonan's chest.

"You," Ves said, already annoyed.

"Me?" Lonan froze, going as still as a startled deer. His sugar cigarette hung limply between his teeth.

"You do know those were the men's barracks, right?" She cocked a brow. "You aren't going to find any undergarments or naked ladies in there."

"There are too many beautiful specimens out there to narrow my tastes to just ladies," Lonan said with a lazy shrug. "But I wasn't snooping. I was talking with your captain."

Huh. Two things she hadn't been expecting. She crossed her arms over her chest and said, "You're a sailor. What do you know about the sky?"

He crouched down, letting Pleo jump from his arms. She shook herself off and darted off to find another quiet place to sleep.

"I'm not a navigator," he said. "But I know the night sky well enough to get my ship where it needs to be. There are four main things that everyone knows – the sun, Mene, Sin, and Aster. If you know where those are, you can navigate just fine. I know some of the constellations, too. I can't point them out right now, but it's summer, so... Let's see... The Sky Dragon, Poet's Cradle, the Bear... those should be visible. Others, too, but –"

"Back up," Ves said. She'd stopped listening after he listed the sun, two moons, and red star. His voice was annoying enough that having a conversation with him was surely shaving years off her lifespan. "Back to the moons."

"Mene and Sin," he said confidently.

Good sarding job. Want a gold star for that? She thought, annoyed.

Aloud, she said, "Yeah, yeah, Mene and Sin. Are you *sure* those are the only moons? What if there was another?"

He took a long drag of his cigarette. At least he had the courtesy to turn his head and blow the sweet smoke away from her face. Not that he could reach her face, even standing on his tiptoes.

"There are plenty of things in this world that don't make log- ical sense but exist regardless," he answered. "Giant sea serpents, kraken, merfolk... I'd even argue that some divine powers are a bit out there. I've heard of someone who's blessed to stop time. What god even gave *that* blessing? Anyway, if you told me there's three moons and I somehow can only see two, I wouldn't be surprised."

She narrowed her eyes. "Merfolk don't exist."

"Yes, they do!" cried Lonan, exasperated, like he'd had this exact conversation a dozen times before. He raked his fingers through his blond hair angrily. "That's not the sarding point. The point is, I'd believe it if there was a third moon. Why?"

Five minutes without making a lewd remark, she thought. *That must be some sort of record. Two gold stars.*

"So, you don't know anything about there being a third moon?" she asked. "A *lost* third moon?"

"Well, if it's lost, it must be *really* lost because I haven't ever heard of it," he said. "Don't tell me you're looking for it. Where would you even find something like that?"

The Salts Atoll, supposedly.

Before she could answer, Leo's voice rang out: "Lo! Come take the helm from me! This is your job, not mine!"

"That's my cue," Lonan said. "Pleasure talking with you, love. Nice to know you can have a conversation without insulting me."

She held up her middle finger. He laughed as he walked away, the sound like sandpaper in Ves's ears.

"We have a problem," Thol said flatly.

Tucked against his side was Fynch, who was still loopy and in enough pain that he could hardly keep himself upright. Illie offered to help, but her arms were twigs compared to Thol's. She'd just bring Fynch down with her.

"The problem being," Thol continued, "our ship is gone."

Illie frowned. "What? No. We docked it. Remember? How could it be gone?" She narrowed her eyes, searching instinctively for the *Serenity*'s red hull, only to remember they'd arrived in Corsa on a borrowed tea clipper.

Thol was right; the ship wasn't where they'd docked it. But...a whole ship couldn't just *disappear*.

"Maybe we're at the wrong marina?" she suggested, hopeful that maybe Thol didn't know the layout of Corsa as well as he claimed, that maybe the clipper was still docked right where they'd left it.

A couple of boys ran past them, darting down the docks toward the ships.

"No," Thol groaned. "Those were the dockhands who helped us. The ship is gone. Where would a ship even go?"

"Sard," she cursed. "We didn't leave anything important on it, did we? I have my books here." She patted the bag slung over her shoulder, heavy with her precious books.

That's when the smell of smoke hit her, filling her nostrils at once. It wasn't the savory smoke from cooking, but the acrid smell of burnt wood, faint enough that it was coming from outside the harbor, but...

Dread weighed down in her stomach like a stone. Smoke. The missing tea clipper. Doctor Isra's warnings about Ryuu Nova. She gripped the strap of her satchel tightly. Nestled beneath her books were the makeshift gloves – several pairs of thick socks that she'd pull over her hands – she needed to handle the winds.

"You don't think...?" she started.

"Nova," cursed Thol.

Fynch, half-asleep, murmured, "Can someone explain what's going on?"

"Come on," said Thol, ignoring Fynch as he started walking. "We need to lie low right now. Come up with a plan. If Isra's right and Nova does have control over Corsa, it won't be easy stealing a ship. Sard it. You should have let Ves come with us, Nox. We could use her right now."

Illie followed quietly, hoping Solveig and the others weren't getting into any trouble.

Thol led her into a secluded alley, shielded from the harsh sun and the general public. He sat down, lowering Fynch with him. Illie stood near the mouth of the alley, fingers creeping toward the gloves in her bag.

Ryuu Nova. The things Illie knew about him were limited: he was the captain of the Dragon Pirates, his ship the *Dragon King*. He came from Elluf, an independent island to the north. (It had the most delicious food Illie had ever had, second only to Natha's cooking). She'd never seen him in person before, but his bounty picture painted him as a tall, dark, and devastatingly handsome rogue. According to the poster, he had long hair, sharp eyes, a neat beard that only added to his fiendish appearance, and a dragon tattoo slithered across his muscled body. Like Illie, he had a warm, beige complexion and angular eyes, but she was all soft femininity, and he was harsh contours and jagged masculinity.

Not to mention, his bounty was more than double hers, and he was a captain while she was a meager navigator.

Their similarities ended with their most superficial features, though. In the wanted section of the newspaper, it was noted that Ryuu Nova was divine-touched but not by Poet like Illie. Instead, he was blessed by the Wanderer. The details, however, of his powers were conveniently omitted from the newspapers.

Illie really didn't want to find out what other abilities – besides fire conjuring like Leo had – the Wanderer gave out.

"Does someone want to explain what's going on?" Fynch asked, drawing Illie from her thoughts. She turned to him.

She had gotten so used to his sunken, waxen pallor, the blue sheen to his lips and the lifelessness in his eyes, that looking at him now – glowing with his proper colors, his hair messy, his green eyes narrowed – shocked her.

Thol summarized things for him, explaining how they borrowed a ship to get him to Corsa, the doctor, Isra, how he had been healed, and how, now, the ship was missing, and the whole thing smelled like Ryuu sarding Nova.

"Won't Captain and the others be coming here, though?" Fynch asked when Thol was finished. "Can't he just rescue us? Isn't our crew worth more than Nova's?"

Mentally, Illie added up their bounties: nearly one point four billion lune.

That was a lot of sarding lune.

But Nova's crew was ten times the size of theirs. There was no doubt that his top officers *alone* surpassed one point four billion lune. Just because *Solveig's* bounty was higher than *Nova's* didn't mean anything when Nova's crew was the size of an entire fleet.

"Poet's sarding teeth," she cursed. "No. We have to get a message to Sol. *Now.* The others can't come here."

Not with the tea clipper gone. Not with Nova's men crawling Corsa.

Not with Nova knowing there were intruders on his island.

Intruders that were enemy pirates. Intruders that broke the pirate code.

If a pirate steps onto another's territory not seeking refuge or sanctuary, he is there for a fight. Isn't that what Solveig quoted at Captain Philippe Rouge of the Redcoat Pirates back on Bowhead Rock?

If Solveig came to Corsa, he would not be seeking refuge or sanctuary. He would be looking for a fight – one they couldn't win. Not with their injuries still healing after the fight with the Rabbit Pirates. Not with their numbers so unevenly matched.

She looked at her hands, then at her bag where her sock gloves were. Fynch was in no shape to fight, and her powers were pathetically limited.

She returned her focus to Fynch and Thol and said, "If they come here, it will only end in slaughter."

PART TWO

INTERLUDE

The Unnamed God often wished he had been given a different epithet because his was an awkward mouthful. His crew took to calling him *Captain,* or *God,* or, simply, *Un.*

He hated all three, except maybe *Captain,* but what else was he supposed to do? Have his crew call him by his real name?

Ha. As if.

He didn't have a real name anymore. Who he was before was dead, who he was now was a mortal playing god, and as far as the navy and his crew and everyone else in the world was concerned, he was the Unnamed God, the man with the highest bounty in the world, the man whose face was hidden behind a mask – literally and figuratively – the man whose identity was so secretive people started to wonder if he truly was an unnamed god.

(He wasn't).

Regardless of whether he was or wasn't nameless or divine, he hated the nickname just as much as he hated the more menial tasks that came with being a captain. He had officers, of course. A first mate who was loud and brash and assumed the role of figurehead of the crew. A quartermaster who dealt with inventory and unruly crewmates. A bo'sun who was supposed to balance the books and make sure everyone was paid and happy, but who decided to get blackout drunk the night before, leaving the ledger to Un. A mute surgeon who offered to gouge out the eyes of everyone on the ship so Un could walk around maskless.

Sometimes, he considered that offer. The mask he wore was such a perfect fit that it often felt like a second skin. But in the heat of summer, when he sweated like a pig, it became the most inconvenient hassle ever. Sweat made the mask slick, which made it slip around his face, which made the edges dig into his cheeks and jaw and forehead, *which* led to a headache so bad he had to hole himself away in his quarters to nurse a large cup of ice water and sleep the pain off.

One such headache was approaching, made worse by the unbalanced numbers before him. Un's handwriting was ten times worse than his bo'sun's, and even he could hardly read it. Was that a six? A five? An eight? It *should* be a two, but there was no way he wrote it that badly.

He scribbled out the numbers and started over again, cramming them into the tiny bit of unmarked margin space. His mask sat face up on his desk, mocking him.

Maybe this would be easier if he wasn't half blind.

And if he didn't have some sort of ailment where numbers and words danced around the page, turning the perfectly reasonable *Checks and Balances* title on the top of the ledger's page to something more like *Chkecs anb Blanaces*.

The Unnamed God was no god. He was a man in far over his head and in too deep to back out now.

The navy doesn't know your face, he reminded himself as he set the pencil down to massage his temples. *You* can *just run away and start over. Nobody would know.*

Except, they would. His face wasn't exactly forgettable, even if he kept it covered. And if whoever saw it didn't associate *that face* with the Unnamed God, they would associate it with someone far worse.

Un couldn't escape.

But he could save payday for tomorrow when his bo'sun was no longer hungover and could make sense of the numbers that evaded him.

Shutting the ledger, Un slid out of his chair and crossed the room from his desk to his bed. He flopped down, supine, and stared at the dark ceiling. At the mural, at the three moons watching him silently. Mockingly. His hand slipped beneath the neckline of his shirt, finding the chain he always wore – the cool sliver of moonstone attached to it. He rubbed the stone between his thumb and forefinger. He needed ginger tea, or his headache would make him vomit.

Glancing at the mask with a scowl, Un dropped the necklace and stood. His quarters weren't far from the galley. He could slip in and out without being noticed.

Reaching for his gilded stopwatch, Un took off running.

Thirty seconds later, he was back in his quarters, sitting on his bed, a cup of ginger tea between his hands.

He hardly even noticed the blood dripping from his nose.

14

ILLIE HAD BEEN RIGHT. Within hours of fleeing Isra's clinic, the streets of Corsa were crawling with pirates branded as belonging to the Dragon King himself.

Good news: they didn't know who they were looking for, only that there had to be more than one and that they came from Undyne Island.

Bad news: all three of them stood out. Illie with her pink hair. Fynch with his chipped tooth. Thol with his...well, his entire presence, really. His height, his build, his tattoos – the *PUNISH-MENT* inked across his knuckles. All of it just made the target on his back that much bigger.

Not that he cared. He'd always had a target on his back. He could fight off anyone who came for him. But he had Illie and Fynch to protect – Illie, who relied too heavily on her winds to the point of overexertion and frostbite; Fynch, who had only *just* recovered from near-death two days before.

Two days.

After spending a sleepless night in the alley, Illie decided they needed shelter. She gave money to Fynch – plenty of it – and sent him to a rundown inn to book a room for a week. He was the most nondescript of the trio, the least memorable, and when he returned fifteen minutes later with a key in his hands, the beginning of a plan started to bud.

Fynch returned to the inn with a bag of groceries – all stolen, all props to make him look more normal – and went straight to the booked room. Thol and Illie watched from across the street, hidden in the shadows. Once he was inside, Thol gestured for Illie to follow, and they snuck around the back, climbing the scaffolding to slip through the window Fynch had opened.

And now, two days later, trapped in a tiny room, Thol was getting restless.

He paced the length of the room, unwrapping and rewrapping his knuckles with the bandages he'd taken from Isra's clinic. Surely, the *Serenity* was fixed by now. Surely, Solveig and the others would be headed for Corsa.

Thol needed to get a message to Solveig. *Do not come to Corsa.* It would be an ambush. A bloodbath. A devastation they couldn't afford.

It wasn't like he could just waltz into an aviary and send a missive to Solveig. It would be less risky to send a letter via the post, but he didn't trust the reliability of the post governed by Aralyth and warded by a pirate warlord. A message in a bottle had a better chance of making it to Solveig at this point, and that only frustrated Thol *more.*

No.

His best chance was to get *Isra* to send a message. Nobody would bat an eye if they visited the aviary. He just had to figure out how to sneak to Isra's clinic without getting caught.

Better me than them, he thought grimly, glancing at Illie and Fynch – the former sat on the bed, poring over a book while toying with her braid. The latter used a makeshift slingshot to knock empty bottles and discarded dishes down.

"What are you thinking about?" Illie snapped her book shut, peering over the rims of her spectacles. "You're making me dizzy with all that pacing. Sit down."

His heart ached. Meadow, his wife, used to say the same thing. Silently, he sat on the edge of the bed. Illie tucked her book and spectacles away, scooting closer to Thol.

He didn't see her as Meadow or even as a *replacement* Meadow. To Thol, Illie was a younger sister. Though, he'd never had sisters. Only brothers, and none of them by blood. He had crewmates in the past who were women, and after being married, he'd developed a bit of a soft spot. So, when she grabbed his face between her scarred hands, he didn't flinch away.

"Is it the others?" she pried.

"I need to get a message to Nox somehow," he said. "I'm thinking Isra can do it."

"The doctor?" She scowled. "They work for Nova, don't they? Why would they send a message to the enemy for you?"

He hoped his friendship with Isra ran deeper than their duty to Nova. Worst case scenario, he'd use his second favor, even though he was reluctant to waste it when there had to be other options.

Illie grabbed one of his locks and tugged on it. "I don't understand your deal with the doctor, but if you think they can help, well... They *did* help with Fynch..."

"What about me?" Fynch cocked his head to the side like a confused puppy.

Illie ignored him. "It would probably be smart to visit them at night, though. The last time any of us tried to get away with something sneaky and illegal during the day, we got caught."

Right. When she and Ves snuck into the Royal Veridin Museum of History to steal a relic and ended up with a fake. The fake led the navy – and Natha's ex-brother-in-law right to them. The fight gained them Natha, but the risk had almost not been worth it.

(Almost).

"Tonight, then," Thol said. "I'll bribe them to send a message tonight. We can only hope Nox will get it in time."

The afternoon after Isra kicked Thol out of their clinic, Thol returned, though he did not return empty handed.

"You," the doctor said flatly, a look of irritation furrowing their brow.

"*Me,*" *said Thol. "I brought you something to eat. May I come in?*"

"*No.*" *Thol squeezed through the door anyway. He set the basket he'd been carrying on an empty counter and pulled out the goods he'd brought: fried bread, skewers of meat, a bottle of date wine and two glasses, and an array of pastries.*

"*I'm not eating this,*" *droned Isra.*

"*More for me, then.*" *Thol poured two glasses of wine and sipped one. He himself didn't care for wine – especially not sweet wine – but he'd heard a rumor that Isra preferred the drink.*

Isra watched as Thol drank. Thol knew it. He made a show of grabbing a meat skewer and taking a generous bite. He didn't even have to pretend to be in bliss. The meat was so tender, so juicy that it practically melted off the skewer and onto his tongue.

"*Fine,*" *Isra said. "Only if you'll leave after.*"

"*Deal.*"

The doctor scraped their hair back, tying it in a messy bun off their face. They peeled their gloves off and sat on the counter, grabbing the glass of wine and downing it in two gulps. Then, they grabbed the bottle and poured another, drinking that, too. After their third consecutive glass, they went for the street food. Isra was built like a stick – a malnourished stick – so when they shoveled skewers and bread into their mouth, Thol could only stare.

"*What?*" *Isra asked between bites.*

"*I had five brothers,*" *Thol said, "and I live on a pirate ship. But I have never seen anyone eat like you. Where does it all go?*"

"*I assume you don't want the biological answer.*"

Thol snorted. "No, thank you. I know that answer. Five brothers and a pirate ship, remember?"

Isra took a gulp of wine. They didn't even look intoxicated. "I had the plague. It messed up my metabolism."

The plague?! Thol knew firsthand how devastating the Alkenio Plague was. Mistress Solveig, Solveig's mother, died of it a few years ago. Her insides turned to mush, and when he and Solveig rolled her into her grave, the thud she made was wet. Nobody survived the plague. Once the victim's eyes turned silver and their tongue turned black, it was too late. Their insides would liquify, and they would die a horrible death.

He looked at Isra again. They had marks on their face – he'd assumed they were moles or blemishes – like the pockmark sores plague victims got. And their eyes... They were a pale grey.

Silver.

Isra finished another meat skewer.

"Are you going to elaborate?" Thol pressed.

"No." They drank their wine. "You're not my friend."

Their cheeks flushed. Only a quarter of date wine remained in the bottle, and Thol was still on his first glass. Thol was no doctor, but he wanted to know just how bad Isra's metabolism was to allow them to drink almost an entire bottle of wine and only look a little flushed.

"I'm stubborn, Doc," Thol said with a grin. "And I'm curious. So, I'm going to make you my friend one way or another."

"Good grief," muttered Isra, hiding the twitch of their lips with their glass. "Fine, then. I won't try to stop you."

Isra paced the length of their clinic, raking their long, thin fingers through their straight, black hair over and over and over again. Healing the boy had been a mistake. Nova hadn't shown up in the twenty-four-hour period after Isra used their powers, but it had been too close. Now, the guilt of betraying their master weighed heavily on their shoulders.

Any more unnecessary weight and their spine would snap in half. That wasn't a wound they'd be able to heal.

What if Nova somehow found out? Isra knew what he did with his enemies. They'd seen the severed heads shoved onto spikes firsthand. They knew better than most not to cross the captain.

The morbid and macabre comforted Isra, but the squelching, snapping sounds of wood stabbing through cartilage and bone and squishy brains made their stomach churn. They could cut a babe from a mother's womb without flinching. They could carve open a wounded patient's chest and work around slippery organs without batting an eye.

They healed plague victims – they cleaned liquified organs from their floor. And yet – and *yet* watching Nova decapitate his enemies and skewer those heads with pikes made Isra want to puke.

Because one misstep and it would be their head on a stake.

You're worrying too much, they silently scolded. *The restoration period is up. Nova didn't catch you. He will only catch you if you continue to act suspicious.*

As they tore their hands through their hair again, the front door of their clinic swung open. Quickly smoothing their coat out and tying their hair back, Isra dashed to the foyer.

"There you are."

Dread was a three-ton stone in Isra's stomach.

It wasn't uncommon for the Dragon King himself to visit the clinic. After all, Isra could only treat patients with his permission. But seeing Ryuu Nova standing there made Isra instantly think of every bad thing they had ever done in their thirty years of life.

Ryuu Nova was a massive man in every sense of the word. He towered over Isra, each of his biceps bigger than Isra's middle. He never wore a shirt, opting instead to wear a red fur cape over his shoulders, exposing rippling muscle, scarred flesh, and a dragon tattoo that wrapped around his massive arm. Like Isra, he wore his hair long, usually tied in a topknot or in a high tail, pulled off his harsh face. His jaw was razor sharp, adorned by perfectly groomed facial hair. At his hip was a sword nearly as long as Isra was tall – *Kusanagi,* it was named (Isra didn't care about swords, but even they knew Kusanagi was the stuff of legends, right up there with the sword named Solais).

Nova's thick brows pinched together. "I won't tolerate you being slow. You're lucky I don't have an injured man with me."

It took everything in them to not flinch at the Dragon King's words. One mistake. All it would take is *one single mistake* for Isra's head to join the others on the beach.

Isra inclined their head slightly.

It was easy to act emotionless when they buried their emotions six feet under all those years ago.

"You're one of my officers," said Nova, "which means you're privy to matters such as this. I didn't drag you to the meeting with my captains, so you can listen to what I have to say now."

As doctor for the Dragon Pirates, Isra was one of the higher-ranking officers. They were below the captains of the Dragon Pirates Fleet and only held *some* power over the lower-ranking sailors on the *Dragon King*. People tended to treat Isra with respect.

They were the doctor, after all. Their lives were quite literally in Isra's hands.

Nova continued: "A shipment was supposed to come in a few days ago from Undyne. A clipper arrived at the docks, and everyone assumed it was the shipment. Until the actual ship showed up."

Damn it, Thol!

Isra swallowed their momentary bubble of rage.

"Trespassers," they said flatly.

"You know what we do to trespassers," the captain said coldly.

Isra inclined their head again. Ever since Nova took control over Servedin Island, the ports had tightened so no one could get in or out. If the harbormaster was expecting an arrival, it made sense how Thol and his colorful bunch managed to slip in.

But if Nova found them...

Anyone who defied Nova was killed – beheaded, eviscerated, torn to bloody shreds that made even the doctor shiver. But anyone who defied the rules he'd put in place – the rules he reigned over Servedin Island with – was given a *different* treatment.

For years, Isra had fought to cure the Alkenio Plague. Their medical license had been revoked because of the progress they'd made, so they worked in secret in an underground clinic where the navy's watchful eye wouldn't catch their illegal practice.

And then Ryuu Nova came along. Israfel Eliad's blood could heal, but their immunity to the plague was what allowed them to infect anyone who broke the laws of Servedin with the fatal strain.

Thol. Loath as Isra was to admit it, Thol was...regrettably...their...

Friend just wasn't the right word, yet it was the only word that fit.

"The plague," Isra said, staying as emotionless as ever.

"You didn't happen to overhear anything, did you? See the trespassers for yourself?" Nova picked up a potted plant, turning it over in his large hands. Isra watched, heart pounding. *Does he know...?*

If he did, he didn't say anything. Nova set the plant back down and walked over to one of the bookshelves, running his fingers along the spines.

"I don't leave much," they said truthfully.

Nova barked a laugh. "Sarding right, you don't. How can you be a ship's doctor if you never step foot on the ship?"

"Seasick."

A lie. They could cure seasickness as easily as they could cure the plague. They just didn't like the sun.

Among other things.

Nova pulled one of the books from the shelf and flipped through it absently, yellow eyes scanning the pages but not absorbing a single word. The captain thought Isra knew something, and he wasn't going to leave until Isra coughed up whatever information they had.

Well, two could play at that game. If there was anything Isra was good at (besides being the greatest doctor in the world), it was staying silent.

15

"You know, being a pirate is actually *really* boring," Leo said as he draped himself over the railing dramatically, both to soak up as much sunshine as possible and to get Lonan's attention.

Usually, it was the other way around. But when Lonan got engrossed in *his* work, very few things could draw him from his concentration – usually alcohol, sugar cigarettes, and scantily clad women did the trick.

Lonan turned the wheel ever so slightly. The area the *Dream-chaser* was sailing through was notorious for two things: deep currents and the breeding grounds of blue whales. It would take a skilled navigator to coast along the currents and a skilled helmsman to get out of one, but without an animal expert on board, it would be near impossible to avoid the territorial whales. Leo could only hope they were too deep to care about a single ship crossing the waters above.

Did whales even breed year-round? Was Ulamoon their breeding time? Leo didn't know.

"Didn't they just get into a fight a few days ago?" Lonan asked, his words muffled by the sugar cigarette between his teeth. "Wasn't that exciting?"

"The *Dreamchaser* didn't even get damaged. I had nothing to fix. And they didn't let us fight." Not that Leo *wanted* to fight. He was a terrible fighter, but he did have his fire abilities that would at least get the enemies to back off.

"Well, isn't that good?" Lonan asked. "Means you built a sturdy ship. One that won't break down in a tiny skirmish."

Leo held his middle finger to Lonan's back. Lonan, knowing Leo better than Leo knew himself, just laughed. He didn't even have to see the crude gesture to know it was there.

"That *tiny skirmish* isn't a good enough indicator," he argued. "A *dinghy* could've withstood that. I need the *Dreamchaser* to go through a *real* battle."

He tipped his head back, squinting against the sun's bright rays. The blobby shape of Servedin Island could be seen through a spyglass – still far away but close enough that Leo could boast that the *Dreamchaser* was one of the fastest ships in the world. She would have arrived *much* sooner if not for the run-in with the navy. Leo insisted on taking half a day to make sure the ship wasn't damaged, which put them behind schedule by an entire day.

From the corner of his eye, he saw Lonan suddenly stiffen. Lonan's shoulders rose slowly, falling even slower as he let out a long breath.

"Lo...?" Leo stood upright, concern taking shape as adrenaline pumping through his veins.

"I'm fine," murmured Lonan. "Just my heart. It's fine. Don't worry."

Leo worried regardless. He knew Lonan's heart sometimes acted up in painful but harmless ways. Still, after seeing Lonan nearly die because his heart acted up worse than normal, he had a hard time trusting the organ.

"Go sit down," Leo said. "Take a rest."

"And who's going to man the helm?"

"Lo. I built the sarding ship. *I* can handle it."

Lonan took another slow breath. Sometimes, he'd explained a while ago, when his heart stuttered and tried beating too fast and too slow at the same time, breathing slowly helped force his heart back on track. Leo had no idea how or why it worked, but if it did, he wasn't going to complain.

Well.

He *would* complain, just not as much.

Suddenly, Lonan stood up straighter. "I knew there was a reason my heart decided to act up," he said slyly. "It sensed this beauty coming."

Leo rolled his eyes so hard he practically saw the back of his head. Natha walked onto the deck, balancing a tray of drinks and snacks in one hand.

"Captain told me to tell *you*," She thrust a cup into Lonan's hands, "to take a break before you keel over. He doesn't want to infect the waters with your dead body. You're sunburnt."

She handed him a plate before going to Leo. She offered him the remaining snacks. "Lekim-ade," she explained. "Lekim juice, water, lavender tea, and plenty of sugar. And fried potato pancakes. It's a new recipe. Let me know what you think. *I* think the flour to potato shreds balance could be improved..."

Leo grabbed the circular pancake and bit into it. The outside was crispy, but the inside was soft and fluffy, perfectly savory. He finished it in two bites only to wish he'd savored it because it was *delicious.*

"Does your captain need a shipwright?" He asked, licking salt from his fingers. "Because I'd become a pirate if it meant eating more of those."

The ghost of a smile tugged on Natha's lips.

"Take over for me, Leo," Lonan called. "There's a lovely lady I need to converse with, and you're in the way."

The smile fell. "Actually, Leo, the captain wanted to talk with you. He's in the navigation room."

He gulped down the rest of his drink and handed the empty dishes to her. "Thanks. That was delicious, by the way."

He grinned, and her cheeks flushed pink.

The navigation room was located at the stern – a decent-sized office with plenty of windows, bookcases, and storage space for maps. A desk he'd carved himself was bolted to the wall, perfect for charting courses or doing whatever else it was navigators did. At Solveig's request, Leo had cut a small opening on the bottom of the door for Illie's cat, Pleo, to use as she pleased.

Leo knocked.

"It's unlocked," came the captain's voice.

He pushed the door open and stepped inside. Solveig sat at the desk, books and maps splayed open before him. Leo cleared his throat. "Natha told me you wanted to see me."

Suddenly, he felt like a child in school again, forced to face his teacher after they'd crossed out his drawings and wrote *see me after school* on his homework.

Solveig stood. Even though he was only an inch or so taller than him, Leo felt very small.

"Where do you source your wood?"

Leo blinked. *What?* Of everything he'd been expecting the captain to say, *that* didn't even make the list.

"Well," he began, "Most of the lumber is sourced from Port 3 in Undyne. But before the navy started occupying Undyne and limiting imports, I used to get some lumber from Gello. Actually, the wood I used for the *Dreamchaser* came from Gello. Well, supposedly. I don't know *where* the wood actually came from; only that it was shipped from Gello. I tried reaching out to my supplier in Gelloine, but I never got a response."

"There was another ship in history made from the same wood, wasn't there?" Solveig asked. He already knew the answer.

Leo nodded. "The *Annabel's Tears.*"

"Captain Chronos's ship," Solveig whispered. Then, he said, "How fast can this thing go? If I needed it to get from Servedin to Merdyne, how long would that take?"

Leo frowned. Why become a shipwright if everyone just assumed he was a *navigator?* He sighed and said, "I'm *not* a sarding navigator. But... She's fast. With a proper navigator, the journey could *easily* be cut in half."

"Then it's a damn good thing we have the best navigator in the Emerald," Solveig said. "We just need to get her back."

Death did not fear Isra because they were, in a sense, death incarnate. Every living thing died eventually. They never understood the urgency to keep someone alive – at least, not until old man Ginkgo. Their mother died when they were born, hemorrhaging blood from a wound they'd caused but never really felt guilty for. Ibrahim, their father, never blamed Isra for killing their mother – his wife. Was a baby even capable of murder? Ibrahim died, too, his corpse cold when Isra woke next to it. Even at seven they knew what a dead body looked like. They knew that the Alkenio Plague had snatched away their father's life, and there was nothing they could do. Crying wouldn't bring Ibrahim back.

Isra spent their entire life surrounded by death. Their ability only worked on the very cusp of it. They were the Blood Doctor, a quack who dealt with mortality and toyed with the lives of their patients like they were a god themselves.

So, even as Ryuu Nova tore pages from one of their medical books – one of old man Ginkgo's books – and let them flutter to the ground pathetically, even as they shrunk down to a tiny speck under Nova's gaze, they did not feel fear.

They felt *nothing*.

"I want to trust you, Isra," Nova said with false sincerity. The saccharine sweetness of it oozed off his words, filling Isra's mouth with the painful throb of cavities. It didn't take a genius to understand what Nova *really* meant: *I don't trust you at all, Isra, and I'm giving you this opportunity to be honest with me, or I* will *kill you.*

Emotions are a weakness. Don't feel anything. Doctors can't afford to have feelings. They repeated the words over and over again until they became true.

They lifted a dark brow, silently prompting Nova to continue.

"Don't you have to leave to get supplies?" he asked. *Interrogated.* "To eat? It must get rather boring being stuck in this sard-hole all day."

Riiiiiiip.

Another page from old man Ginkgo's book fell to the floor. Isra tracked it with their eyes, translating Nova's words silently. *I know you know something. You may claim to be a hermit, but doctors often are the best spies.*

"I like solitude," they said, ignoring Nova's underlying threats.

"Sure you do." He snapped the book shut and tossed it over his shoulder. No sign of his ability. *Yet.* They were in trouble but not in danger.

Nova grabbed another book and pried it open. Isra's heart tumbled in their throat. Their fingers flexed, but they made no effort to stop Nova, not even as he ripped out a page and crumpled it in his hand. When he unfolded his fingers, the page was gone like it had never existed at all.

Now, they were in trouble *and* in danger.

There was no situation where Isra would make it out alive. If they confessed to treating that kid, Nova would kill them. If they lied and covered Thol's tracks, Nova would figure it out and kill them – and Thol and his friends. If they continued to stay silent and play the fool, Nova would destroy old man Ginkgo's legacy, everything Isra owned, and then kill Isra out of frustration.

It was just a matter of deciding which route would lead to the quickest, most painless death.

"You're a valuable asset," Nova drawled. "Your ability rivals mine in terms of usefulness. In terms of *power.*"

Translation: tell me the truth, and I won't kill you because I need you.

Isra bit the inside of their cheek hard enough that they tasted blood.

If they confessed and sold Thol out, they would make it out alive. Nova would hunt Thol down and punish Isra, but they'd live.

If they continued to play dumb, Nova would either believe them and drop it, or he would put an end to their foolish act and kill them. They had a fifty-fifty chance of surviving.

Isra didn't like to gamble on anything that wasn't solid fact – on anything that wasn't science.

They gnashed their teeth together.

And then, they spoke.

Not for the first time since running away to fulfill her dreams of grandeur and adventure, Illie was struck with homesickness. She missed her shop, the Ink and Rose. She missed her apartment with all her plants and the murals on the ceilings. She missed walking through Carilon's streets, delivering commissioned maps, and pausing to run through the sandy beach along the Icarus Strait. She missed waking up knowing the only things she had to do that day were draw maps and deal with the shopkeeper's grandson – Elgar Quill – and his foolish antics.

She missed not living in mortal danger every moment of her life.

No, she silently scolded. *The* Serenity *is your home now. You wanted an adventure.*

And an adventure she got. She flipped the page of her book, running her fingers over the printed text absently.

She could never return to life the way it was before Nox Solveig. Not that she *wanted* to. Groaning, she shoved her hands through her loose hair. Half the stress on her shoulders would leave once Thol sent a message to Solveig and the others.

The rest of that stress would leave once they tracked down the lost moon.

But even then...

What would happen next? Would she just go back to the Ink and Rose, spending the rest of her life drawing maps? She couldn't imagine returning there, not with her face plastered on a wanted poster above a bounty of ten million lune.

For the second time in her life, she was at a crossroads.

Continue to be a pirate or return to a life of normalcy.

Live as a lady or become a mapmaker.

There was no god of destiny. No higher power that had carved out her path before she was even born. (If there *was,* she would have found them and flayed them alive for taking her sister, Mary, from her). Yet, it seemed like every little decision in her life had led to...to *this.*

To piracy. To being a navigator. To hunting down the lost moon.

She was Illie sarding Valentine. She was going to make a moving lithograph of the entire world. She was going to find the lost moon. She was –

"Can you stop *pacing?* It's making me dizzy." Fynch huffed dramatically. He'd been polishing one of his pistols ever since Thol left a while ago, clearly just as nervous as she was.

"You're rubbing the same spot you were rubbing fifteen minutes ago," she said defiantly, hands planted on her hips. Her hair swished around her ankles, free from its usual braid.

Fynch set the gun on his lap. "He's been gone a while. I'm... I'm not worried at all."

She raised a brow. "Mhm. Sure."

"I'm not!" he exclaimed, then pressed his hand against his chest, face contorted in pain.

She sat on the edge of the thin bed next to him, knees touching. "Does it still hurt?"

"I just got sliced open. What do you think?" he grumbled. "I'm fine, though. I can still shoot. I can still fight."

"I never said you couldn't."

"You were thinking it."

She shook her head. "Never. Besides, I'm *always* getting injured." She flexed her hands. The frostbite inflicted from holding her winds had never been bad enough that a bucket of hot water couldn't warm her back up, but lately...lately, she'd been toying with that certainty.

One day, she would hold on too long, and the frostbite would blacken her fingertips, and she'd surely lose her hands.

Fynch said nothing to her. He picked up his pistol and, using the hem of his shirt, polished the barrel. Illie sighed and gathered her hair over one shoulder, dividing it into three sections and twisting it into a loose braid.

"Do you think," Fynch said softly, "Thol will get the message to them in time?"

She tied her braid. "You're worried about Czardas, huh?"

"Well, and the others, too," he mumbled. "But...mostly Czar. I don't like being apart from him like this."

"Thol will get the message sent. Trust him. We'll be off this sarding island before you know it and back to the *Serenity*." She was convincing herself just as much as she was convincing him. She gnawed on her thumbnail.

Thol would be back.

He had to be.

Thol kept the message as brief as possible, just in case it was intercepted. He almost *planned* on it being caught before it could reach Solveig and the others, so he used a code only one other person in the entire world would understand.

Apple tree survivor whole.

Two and Three. No.

023Y 36s3Y.

To anyone else, it would just seem like a bunch of jumbled letters and numbers beneath strings of words that made no sense together. But to Solveig... He'd get the message.

Thol rolled the parchment into a tiny scroll and tied it with a bit of string. He handed it to Isra, who had been watching with a bored expression beneath their heavy brows.

"That it?" they asked.

"I'll count this as your second favor if you can get the fastest bird in Servedin. It needs to go to the *Serenity* in Undyne."

"Not equal enough," they murmured, snatching up the message. "Where are you staying?"

Seven words at once. Isra must be in a decent mood. Thol eyed the message as they stuck it into their pocket. "There's only one decent inn in this place. We got a room there. Hopefully, Nox will get this message and stay in Undyne. We can steal a ship and escape before Nova catches us."

"Good luck," muttered the doctor.

Thol clapped them on the shoulder. "I owe you, Isra. Really. I'll get you some good wine and some street food."

He turned to leave when Isra said, so soft he nearly missed it, "Wait."

Thol cocked a brow, waiting for them to continue.

"Don't mess with Nova," they said hesitantly, like the words were thick in their throat, impossible to choke out. "That fight isn't worth it."

He frowned. Never in his life had Thol walked away from a fight. He'd allowed himself to be dragged out of retirement just to go on one last adventure, to nosedive into the trouble and danger he'd sworn to his wife, Meadow, he'd stay far away from.

And now...now *Isra,* of all people, was telling him to stand down.

Thol had never met Ryuu Nova. He ranked just beneath the Dragon King on the most wanted list, but that hardly meant anything. Nova was older than he was, more experienced. Knight Hardy, the captain of the *Sea Wyrm,* would have stood a chance against Nova. But Thol?

There was simply no way Thol – no way Solveig and the ragtag crew he'd scraped together – would hold his own in a fight.

"The fight might not be worth it," Thol said, "but it isn't like we have much of a choice. If fighting against Nova is what it takes for our crew to be whole again, so sarding be it."

Isra clenched their hands into fists, their knuckles whitening with the intensity. They said emotionlessly, "Go away."

He nodded once and ducked out of the clinic. It was late when he left, the sky inky and full of stars. Aster, the north star, shone bright red between Mene and Sin. Mene was higher in the sky, Sin just barely cresting over the horizon, but both moons were waning gibbous, bright against an indigo backdrop.

He paused, sticking to the shadows, and watched the sky, scanning for any empty spaces where a third moon might have sat once. But nowhere amongst the constellations – clusters of stars whose silly names he could never remember but Meadow took pride in knowing – was there a spot for another moon. Just Mene and Aster and Sin and countless other pinpricks of light.

Wait.

The hairs on the back of his neck stood on end. He went statue still, every sense on high alert.

Breathing. *Breathing.*

There was someone skulking in the darkness with him.

Thol spun around, swinging his fist right where he'd heard the other person. But his fist soared through the air, not finding its target. He swung again, just to make sure, then went silent once more. Nothing. No breathing, no shuffling around, no sign that there would be anyone else with him.

Unsettled, he shook it off and started towards the inn.

You must be tired, he thought to himself. *You're hearing things. There wasn't anyone there.*

In the dark, cloaked in shadows that melded to his body like a tailored suit, Ryuu Nova grinned. *Now why,* he thought, his yellow, serpentine gaze sliding to the door that led to Isra's clinic, *would that pirate be visiting so late at night?*

16

THE ISLAND OF SERVEDIN came into view long after the sun had set and Natha finished cleaning up after dinner. Lonan had returned to the helm with Leo by his side, working on building something out of spare wood. Natha and Ves were both on the deck, talking in voices low enough Solveig couldn't hear, but were interrupted when Czardas, up in the crow's nest, shouted, *"LAND!"*

Solveig dashed to the bow, squinting to see through the darkness to spot what Czardas had seen. The kid's eyes were better than his, probably trained to spot tiny details after years of reading music. Yet... *There.* The blobby form they'd been tracking had turned into something else. Into Servedin.

Buildings speckled the landscape, tucked close together to form the capital city Corsa. Furthest from the coast was a tall building with a curved roof, grander than the rest of the buildings. Docks stretched into the sea, dotted with ships. Despite the darkness, the inky expanse of a mountain range could be seen just beyond the city. Lights reflected off the ocean, glowing orange-gold. The closer the *Dreamchaser* got, the more Solveig was able to make out the red paper lanterns hanging across the streets, the shutters on houses snapped tightly shut, the black flag that hung from every building.

A red serpentine dragon with branchlike horns and trailing whiskers, a single golden eye visible from its snarling profile.

"Wait," he called. "Lonan, circle around the marina. There should be a beach along the western side."

At least, geographically speaking, there should be. He recalled the maps in the navigation room – Illie had one of Servedin, and there was a stretch of forested land just west of Corsa that looked like it gave way to a beach. Dropping anchor there would give Solveig and his crew an advantage.

"Sure, sure," Lonan said around his sugar cigarette. He cranked the helm, forcing the brig to sharply turn.

Solveig leaned against the starboard railing, watching Corsa blur past. Unease knotted his insides. Every established pirate crew had a black flag. There were too many small fries for Solveig to know *every* colored flag out there, but he knew the important ones – the big ones, the ones the most powerful sailed under – and he knew who the flag flying from every building in Corsa belonged to.

"You know how to read, don't you?" Captain Knight Hardy crossed his arms and peered down at Solveig. Solveig sat at a desk in Hardy's office, staring at a piece of paper with crudely drawn flags on it.

"Yes," Solveig hissed, defensive. He was thirteen. What thirteen-year-old couldn't read? His wench of a mother could not have bothered to send him to school, sure, but he'd still learned, regardless.

"Then stop whining and get to work," Captain Hardy said.

"Why can't I –" Solveig started, but Hardy grabbed his ear and tugged on it.

"Because a good pirate knows his enemies," his captain said. "I'll check on you in an hour. If it's not done, you're to be on bathroom duty for a month."

Solveig gripped his wooden pencil so hard he was surprised when it didn't snap in two. Fine. If Hardy wanted him to do sarding homework, he had no choice.

There were two sections on the paper – one with the flags of the previous generation of pirates, one with the flags of the current generation. All Solveig had to do was write down who the flags belonged to and what their ship was named. It wasn't hard, *he just didn't want to do it. He'd rather be practicing his swordsmanship with Thol or watching for enemy ships in the crow's nest.*

Groaning, he leaned over the paper and got to work, scribbling in the names of different pirates. Most were easy – an hourglass belonged to Captain Chronos of the Annabel's Tears. *A red sun belonging to Captain Corona of the* Blazing Sun.

The previous generation was the name given to the navy's most wanted long before Solveig was born. They were the ones who ruled the four seas, who dominated the waters of Syrenis. The ones who inspired Solveig to become a pirate himself. They were all either dead or missing now, replaced by a new generation of pirates. A generation Solveig hoped he would one day be a part of – not as a crewmate but as a captain.

Soon, Solveig got to a flag he did not recognize. It was a wingless dragon with antlers and whiskers and curved teeth protruding from a snarling mouth. Just looking at it chilled his insides to ice.

Just then, the door opened, and Captain Hardy said, "Well, I'll be damned. You actually did your work."

Solveig looked up, then covered the paper with his arms. "It's not finished. Don't put me on bathroom duty, Captain. I'm almost done."

Hardy just nudged his arms aside. "Let me see." He skimmed the paper, then chuckled when he saw the blank spot. "You don't know this one?"

"No! I just... I forgot," Solveig said, looking away to hide his embarrassment. His ears and cheeks burned, no doubt the same crimson shade as his hair.

"You didn't forget, boy," Captain Hardy said. "That's a new captain. Might be fresh, but he's as fierce as they get. He's from Elluf and tends to stick to the eastern Emerald. Captain Ryuu Nova. Though most people just call him after his ship – the Dragon King."

Czardas still didn't understand how the bounty system worked. He knew his own bounty, eight hundred thousand lune, was...well, it was *high*. It was the lowest of Solveig's crew, but it was only fifty thousand lune less than Natha's. But he had no idea how that was determined or why the fourth most wanted, with a bounty of four hundred fifty million lune, was considered *fourth* when he, apparently, ruled over Servedin Island.

His heart thumped in his chest, a racing tempo rivaling a speeding metronome, as he watched his crew – Lonan and Leo included – jump off the *Dreamchaser* and onto the thin stretch of sandy beach below. Originally, he'd volunteered to stay behind and guard the ship, but Leo assured him that he'd built the brig with anti-theft precautions. *("Who would rob a ship with Dreamer right there?").* Then, Czardas volunteered to stay behind to watch Illie's cat, Pleo, but she was nowhere to be found, likely sleeping in some cozy nook somewhere.

He sucked in a breath and jumped over the railing. Pain exploded up his legs as he hit the sand, remembering a fraction too late to bend his knees to absorb the shock.

It wasn't that he *wanted* to stay behind. More than anyone else, he wanted to find Fynch and bring him home. But Solveig's realization that Servedin Island was under *Ryuu Nova's* control elicited a fear so strong in Czardas that he'd rather be a coward than face the Dragon King. He *knew* he was the weakest link in the crew, but...

But he'd still said the oath. He still fought with the others. He still had a bounty. He was still a pirate, and he would face the gods themselves if it meant getting Fynch back.

"SKREEEE!"

In a blur of black feathers and sharp talons, Solveig was on the ground, fighting off a winged assailant. Czardas crouched down low, knees bent, ready to attack despite the pounding protests of his heart. But no attack came – not besides the one Solveig fought off.

"Sarding bird!" Solveig cursed, grabbing the thing's wing and yanking it off.

The bird – a massive raven – puffed out its feathers and held its head high. Something was wrapped around its leg.

"It has a message!" he exclaimed.

Solveig, who'd been reaching for his cutlass, paused. Then, frowning, he reached for the bird and ripped the paper free. The bird flapped its wings and flew off in a flurry of feathers. He unfolded the paper, eyes skimming over its contents.

Then, at once, the color drained from his face.

"What is it?" Ves snatched the paper from him. "'Apple tree survivor whole. Two and Three. No. Zero two three Y, three sixes three Y.' What in the sarding hell does that mean?"

"It means," Solveig said, "that Fynch is okay, and if we come to Corsa, we are going to die. Thol is telling us to stay away."

Natha glanced at the paper. "A code..."

"We can't just *leave,*" Ves argued. Solveig took the note from her and handed it to Leo, who, wordlessly understanding, burned it.

Czardas's hand drifted toward his hip – toward the shiny new rapier, stolen right from the navy, that rested there.

Crunch.

He spun, facing the direction the sound had come from. There was someone else in the woods. The snapping branch was too loud to belong to an animal.

But just the right size to belong to a human.

He curled his fingers around the handle of his rapier, ready to pull it free at a moment's notice.

Besides music, his parents, Duke and Duchess Rossi, insisted he pick a hobby from a predetermined list. Dressage and painting had bored him, but fencing... He'd taken to fencing quite easily. A rapier was much different than the cutlasses Solveig preferred – thinner, lighter, longer – so he'd been useless in a fight with one. But now...

Footsteps!

He ripped his rapier free and shouted, "Ambush!" The word hardly had time to settle before a group of red-clad pirates tore through the trees.

He thrust his rapier defensively, immersing himself in the fight instantly. As his sword clashed against another, a grim thought crossed his mind. *Ves hadn't seen the souls coming.*

There were two reasons for that, he rationalized, his rapier sparking against a cutlass as he parried and thrust, knocking his enemy back: she hadn't been paying attention, or the enemies somehow coated themselves in Dwalenite, the strange ore that was somehow able to cancel out divine abilities.

Best not to think about that now, he thought, shoving the ideas away. He needed to focus if he wanted to get out of the fight unscathed.

Just pretend you're at a fencing tournament.

It was a lot harder to do when his opponent was a foot taller and wielded a heavy cutlass with the fury of Lady Lightbringer.

The pirate brought his sword down fast. Czardas sucked in a breath and ducked out of the way, narrowly missing the blade by a hair.

Around him, the cacophonous dissonance of metal against metal surged in a crescendo so deafening it turned his insides to liquid.

Focus, Czar! His voice of reasoning, which sounded eerily like Fynch, screamed.

He struck low, ignoring the rules of fencing, and swiped his blade along the sensitive, exposed inner knees of the pirate. The snapping of tendons fueled the orchestra of destruction, followed by the agonized scream of the pirate as he crumbled to the ground, helplessly grabbing at his destroyed legs.

Blood slicked his blade, turning the metal crimson. For a moment, Czardas paused, watching his crew as they engaged. Natha tackled a man to the ground, pinning him there as Ves stabbed him in the throat. Solveig's cutlass clashed with another, and though he grinned fervently, Czardas knew he was in pain. Leo threw a punch that would make Thol proud while Lonan spun a pilfered sword around, burying it in the gut of an oncoming assailant while taking a lazy drag of his sugar cigarette.

The crew wasn't whole, but they weren't letting that stop them. Czardas wouldn't, either.

He crouched low, brandishing his rapier, ears alert for even the slightest bit of movement. He might not have been as good at fighting as the others, but he did have one advantage over everyone else: his musically trained ears could pick up even the *slightest* sound, and in the midst of a melee, there was nothing more favorable.

Lonan dropped his spent cigarette onto the ground and crushed it under the heel of his shoe as he slashed upwards, gutting an oncoming assailant like a fish. Organs spilled onto the ground, followed by the collapsed body of the disemboweled pirate. With one hand, Lonan reached into his pocket to pull out his case of cigarettes, using his teeth to pull one free.

"Leo!" he shouted. "Give me a light!"

"I'm a bit *busy!*" Leo shouted back. He'd never been a fighter, and his amputated leg only slowed him down, causing him to lag. Still, flames enveloped his hands as he threw sloppy punches, lighting his enemies on fire.

Lonan sighed dramatically and stepped over the still-pulsing guts of his recent victim. He swung his heavy sword out with one arm, muscles flexing, and sliced Leo's opponent nearly clean in two.

"Now you're not busy. Give me a light."

Leo spun around, glowing fist grazing Lonan's face and lighting his sugar cigarette. He inhaled deeply, and when he exhaled, he shoved his sword into the belly of another pirate.

Lonan had always been good with a sword, especially a heavy longsword. They weren't as common amongst pirates since melee fighters tended to prefer shorter, curved blades. But longswords were still popular with the navy, and somehow, one of these Dragon Pirates had one with him. *Had.* All it took was a good kick to the throat to render the pirate useless so Lonan could steal the weapon. He liked the feel of the heavy hilt in his hand, the roughness of polished gold set with a chunk of amber in the pommel.

She was a beautiful sword. If she was a lady, she'd be the prettiest – all luscious curves and long lashes and ample areas for him to grab. Even though she was stolen, he decided to name the blade.

Effie, he decided, after Nefeli Catrione, the most beautiful woman in the world.

"You're a piece of steaming sard, Lo," grumbled Leo, his words slurred as exhaustion set in.

Lonan lifted his shoulders in a lazy shrug. "Nothing new there. Duck."

Leo barely ducked out of the way before Lonan charged, brandishing Effie the sword and shoving a Dragon Pirate against a pine tree with enough force to knock a considerate rain of needles down.

"You're going to tell me who you are," he said casually like he didn't have a bloodied longsword pressed against the pirate's throat. "Who sent you, what you rank, where you came from."

The pirate spat at Lonan, getting a bloody glob of saliva dangerously close to his eye.

Sighing, Lonan plucked his sugar cigarette from his teeth and ground the burning end into the pirate's cheek, right below her eye. She screamed in pain, writhing under his grip. Her thrashing pressed the longsword's edge deeper into her flesh, drawing a bead of blood.

"See," Lonan drawled, "that wasn't a request. It wasn't a suggestion. It was an order."

Beneath the snarling filth, the pirate was actually quite lovely. Soft curves, strong arms, short hair that curled around her ears... If she wasn't his enemy, he'd go for a more flirtatious approach. But...

He drilled the cigarette harder until the embers snuffed out in a puff of flesh-singed smoke.

"I'm just a grunt," she ground out. "A low-level sailor in the Dragon Pirates Fleet. I've never even *met* Captain Nova."

The Dragon Pirates Fleet. No surprise there. Plenty of big-name pirates sailed with an entire fleet. Lonan was pretty sure the only pirates who *didn't* were Solveig and the Unnamed God – but even then, he wasn't sure about the latter. With the Dragon King's flags around Corsa, it was no wonder he had hundreds of sailors beneath him.

"Are you going to kill me?" the pirate hissed.

Lonan sighed and dropped his smoldering cigarette. "Unfortunately." Then, with a quick flick of his arm, Effie the longsword slid across the pirate's throat, opening it to the bone in a spray of crimson. Blood splashed his face, slipping between his scarred lips.

He spun around, sword brandished, and grinned wickedly. With an air of casualty, he sauntered over to Natha and looped his free arm around her shoulders.

"What's a pretty lady like you getting her hands dirty fighting, eh? Captain can't protect you?" he drawled.

She elbowed him in the gut. *Hard.* "I don't need him to protect me. I can protect myself. Go be gross elsewhere."

"Ouch. You wound me." He put his hand over his heart and swooned. "How about a wager, hm? If I get more kills than you, I get to take you on a date. Just one. If you get more kills than me, I'll leave you be." He grinned.

Natha glared at him with such intensity he thought for sure she'd see his soul. She said coldly, "I try not to kill people. I'm better than you."

She lifted her leg and kicked an oncoming assailant in the chin. She delivered three more consecutive kicks, knocking the attacker down with ease.

"I'm *done* with men," she said over her shoulder. "You won't be an exception. Not now, not tomorrow, not in this lifetime, and not in the next."

He shrugged. "So, that's a no for the wager, then?"

"I don't kill people," Natha said. "But you'd be exempt from that."

Illie's pacing made Fynch dizzy, and he blamed his nausea on that. Not on the fact that he was still in pain. *Definitely* not on the fact that he was worried about Thol. Just...Illie's pacing made him dizzy.

A bellhop had brought dinner for one upstairs, and Illie divided it into thirds – pale broth for Fynch as it was all he could stomach, chicken for Thol, who needed the protein the most, potatoes and bread for Illie, who didn't want to eat anything else. Fynch barely touched the broth. He was too nauseous. It tasted like nothing. His palette was used to Natha's cooking.

Excuses, excuses, excuses.

Knock, knock, knock.

Both Fynch and Illie turned to the window. Illie moved first, darting to unlock it and let Thol tumble in. Fynch swung his legs over the side of the bed, wincing at the sharp pain in his chest. Ignoring it the best he could, he stumbled over to Thol.

"Did you send the message?" he asked.

Thol rubbed his face. "I gave it to Isra. All we can do is hope it gets there in time. Before Solveig does anything stupid."

Fynch frowned. His captain might be reckless and idiotic at times, but he wasn't *stupid*. Surely, he wouldn't do anything rash...right?

Well...

He hadn't been with the crew for long, but in that short period of time Solveig had proven himself to be stupid, reckless, and beyond incapable of making anything *but* rash decisions.

As he inhaled, sharp pain radiated from his chest, the movement pulling on his stitches. He clasped a hand over the wound, trying (failing) to ease the pain.

Sarding hell, he thought. His blasted captain better not do anything stupid because he could hardly fight in these conditions. Even just the recoil from his pistol would be agonizing.

It could be worse. He could be dead. The pain meant he was alive. The pain meant he would live long enough to see Czardas again.

Czardas...

"So, we just have to...wait here until Nova forgets about us?" Illie asked. "Because I doubt he'll just forget about us. And we can't just stay *here* forever. We have a crew to get back to. A sarding moon to find."

Fynch sat on the edge of the bed, reaching for his pistol if only to feel the comforting weight of it in his hand. *I will not die on this island,* he thought defiantly.

Thol pinched the bridge of his nose. "We're going to get off this island one way or another. If we have to steal a ship, so be it."

Fynch perked up. He'd never stolen a ship before. The riskiest theft he'd ever done was the one in Veridonia when he robbed the Royal Veridian Museum of History of that weird compass that sat safely in his pack back on the *Serenity.* But a *ship...* That would be his biggest theft yet. His grandest scheme. His fingers itched in anticipation.

He said, "I can steal a ship."

Thol and Illie turned toward him.

He grinned, giddy, and said, "I can steal a ship. I'm gonna steal a ship. Give me orders. Let me steal a ship and get us out of here."

"Fynch, you can't just...just steal an entire *boat,*" Illie said, her brow knit tightly. "Stealing a sarding ship is a lot different from pickpocketing someone. How do you even plan on doing it?"

He shrugged, his grin widening. There were two things Fynch was good at – shooting and stealing. And if he couldn't shoot because of his injury, he sure as sard could *steal.*

"You can't steal a ship," repeated Thol, shaking his head. "You're just one person. It's too dangerous. If you get caught, you'll get killed."

His grin wavered, but he held strong. "So? I'm a pirate. Don't pirates do...do *piratey* things? Like...grand theft ship? I don't know how to sail, but that's just something I'll have to deal with. What's the alternative, huh? Staying here forever? Dying on this sarding island because you're too afraid of failure to even try? What's the point in being a pirate if you don't even *try* to live freely?"

He stood, chest heaving. "You're the fifth most wanted pirate in the world," he said, pointing to Thol. Then he pointed to Illie and added, "And you're *literally* blessed by *Poet.* I'm just some nobody from the slums, some...some gutter rat who stole a chance he never should have had, and I'm the only one willing to do something. Our crew is out there. We swore an oath to them. Are you really just going to ignore that?"

Slam!

Fynch flinched, taking a step back, watching with wide eyes as Thol shook drywall from his hand. A fist-sized hole now decorated the wall.

"I am not sending you out there alone!" Thol shouted. "It's not bravery you're talking about; it's stupidity. You go out there to steal a sarding ship, you die. That's not bravery. That's not sacrifice. That's not being a martyr. That's stupidity, plain and simple. We went through all that effort to save your sorry ass, and you want to just throw it away? You're a fool, Fynch."

Illie took a step closer, putting herself between an angry Thol and a foolish Fynch. *Foolish.* Right. Because that's what he was. A foolish street urchin wearing shoes too grand for his filthy feet. He didn't deserve to be on Solveig's crew. He didn't deserve to have his life saved when he'd been the idiot to get shot in the first place.

Something hot streaked his face. He reached up, brushing his fingers against his cheek. *Tears.*

Oh. He was crying. Of course, he was. He was a pathetic, foolish child.

"Look, we'll come up with a different plan," Illie said calmly. "Okay? Thol, calm down. He's not going to do anything rash."

"*He's* standing right here!" Fynch cried, frustrated. He dug his nails deep into his palms, doing his best to ignore the tears and snot running down his face. "And *he's* not a child, no matter what you think. I'm nineteen, and I bet I've lived through worse than both of you. Stop treating me like I'm just some kid!"

"Then stop acting like one!" Thol bellowed.

Illie put her hand on Thol's chest. "Hey. That's enough. You both need to calm down. Fynch, you're not stealing a ship. We'll think of a different plan. Alright? Fynch, you need to take a deep breath. I'll go get you some water. I think we're all just hungry and tired and desperate to get back home. Let's all get some rest and come up with a plan in the –"

"*– think they're on the second floor,*" came a muffled voice from outside. "*Look, that one has a light on.*"

The three of them froze, listening as a second voice added, "*Send someone up to check.*"

"The curtains," Illie breathed.

Thol, closest to the window, grabbed the drapes and yanked them shut. Illie rushed to turn the lights off, shrouding the room in darkness.

"They know we're here," she whispered. "How do they know where we are? We need to get out of here. We need a *plan.*"

Fynch blindly checked his pistol, making sure it was fully loaded. Six shots. He'd have to make them count until he could reload.

"I'm going to clear a path," he whispered, stepping closer to the window. "They'll expect us to go out the front door, so we have to throw them off."

No matter how many heists he'd pulled off, everyone always expected Fynch to waltz out the front door when he was finished. They expected him to get cocky, but he never did.

Sucking in a breath, he pushed the window open. The streetlights did little to illuminate the dark alleyway. He'd be shooting blind.

Fine. He'd worked with worse conditions before.

Crouching down, he watched, unbreathing. Four men. Six bullets.

Bang! Bang! Bang! Bang!

He fired in rapid succession, pulling the trigger so fast he hardly had time to feel the recoil. It was too dark to see the blood, but the bodies – all four – collapsed lifelessly.

"Go!" he shouted.

Thol leaped through the window first, followed by Illie, carrying her bag slung over her shoulders. Before he could jump, something cold wrapped around Fynch's waist – Illie's wind – and dragged him down, too.

17

THE HEEL OF HER foot cracked against an enemy's jaw, shattering it with a crunch so satisfying a shiver ran down Natha's spine. He fell to the ground, screaming in agony.

Pathetic, she thought, turning to face the fight. Well, what remained of the fight. Bodies littered the ground, mulch stained red. It squelched under her feet, soggy and wet. She scanned for the survivors, making sure everyone was accounted for. Lonan, Leo, Czardas, Solveig, Ves. Ragged and bruised, but everyone was alive.

She opened her mouth, ready to suggest that they keep moving before Nova sent more goons after them, when a hand clapped over her mouth, and a sharp pain stabbed into her neck. The world blurred, colors muddling in a finger-painted swirl.

And then it went black.

Natha came to with a headache worse than any hangover she'd ever had the misfortune of experiencing and the grim realization that she was in a very dark, very confined space.

She jolted upright, half expecting to be chained to a wall. The relief that washed over her when she realized she was free faded quickly, replaced by ice-cold dread.

"Ves?" she called out. "Czardas? Solveig? Leo? Lonan?"

She was desperate enough to call out to that rat for help.

"Hey, no need to yell, Blondie, I'm right here." Ves's voice was close. Natha blinked furiously, trying to see through the dark.

Suddenly, a dim glow sparked, illuminating the cell. Leo, across the cell from her, held a burning fist out. Natha nearly cried. There was no Dwalenite here. God-blessed people could still use their abilities.

Natha, Leo, and Ves were the only ones awake by the looks of it. Solveig sat slumped in one corner, Lonan next to him. Czardas was curled up in the other corner, his chest rising and falling steadily.

"What the sard happened?" Ves cursed. "Whoever put me in *another* cell is going to regret it."

Silently, Natha scooted across the dirt floor to be closer to her. There was comfort in familiarity, and for someone whose only experience with prison came in the form of a wedding ring and a man's last name, she needed all the comfort she could get.

Her body ached, her muscles throbbing alongside her head.

"How did we end up in a jail cell if we won the fight?" Leo asked.

"Here," Natha said quietly. She tore off her outer shirt, leaving her in a thin camisole that showed off her scarred arms. She held the dirty fabric out. Leo wrapped it around his fist, visibly relaxing when his power no longer drained him, instead relying on the fabric to burn.

"My guess," Ves said, "is that we *didn't* win the fight. Those goons had people watching, waiting to strike when we were done. But they're sarding idiots! Nobody locks the Witch of the Sea in a *cell! Not again!*"

Flames danced across her face, casting an orange glow over her dark features, making her curls look like a halo of fire and her eyes liquid.

"You got out of Ivenis Justyce Penitentiary. Can't you make it out of here?" Natha asked softly, watching the fire as it reflected in Ves's eyes, her jade irises orange.

"*I* didn't get out of I. J. Pen." She thrust her thumb toward Solveig's sleeping form. "Cap did."

As if on cue, Solveig gasped and sat upright, eyes darting frantically around the dark cell. His shoulders relaxed when he saw Natha and the others, but his jaw was tense. Natha frowned. He looked right on the edge of fight or flight.

"Sinth," he whispered. "They gave us sarding Sinth."

Sinth. Natha's knowledge of the drug was limited. She knew of Sinthoxine, the depressant that they must have been injected with, and she knew of Sinthide, the steroid that made the user stronger and faster. There was a third strain, too – Sinthephane. It was navy-only, a stimulant companion to Sinthoxine.

Solveig slammed his fist against the wall. "Sarding hell, they gave us *Sinth!*"

Natha frowned. Being drugged was bad, but...they were all fine.

"Cap's last crew died drugged on Sinth," Ves whispered so only Natha could hear. "They gave it to us in I. J. Pen."

She just nodded, watching as Solveig stood up and slammed his weight against the cell bars.

"We need to get out of here," he growled. "Nova knows we're here. There's no damn point in laying low anymore."

The second Illie's feet hit the cobblestone ground, she let go of the wind she'd been holding and broke into a run, glancing back only to make sure Fynch was following.

"Where are we going?" she asked through ragged breaths, stumbling to keep up with Thol.

Without Solveig to act as a leader, Thol was the next best thing. He glanced over his shoulder, face shrouded in shadow, and said, "We go to the marina. Fynch was right; we need to steal a ship."

A grin split across her face. Straight back to piracy, then.

Her braid whipped across her back, wind blowing in her face. She stumbled after Thol, who took a sudden turn, only to crash right into his back. Cursing, she took a step back, shaking her head to rid herself of the pain that came with running into solid muscle. The iron stench of blood filled her nostrils.

"Thol...?" she asked. "What's wrong?"

Behind her, footsteps drew near – only a few blocks away by the sound of it. Reinforcements. *Sard.* Nova's men would catch up in just a few minutes, and it would be a bloodbath.

Blood.

Reaching up, she swiped a finger under her nose. Even in the dark, she could tell it came back dry. It wasn't her blood she was smelling.

She peered around Thol, and her stomach dropped all the way to her feet. Nausea flooded her throat.

There was a body on the ground, slumped against the wall, bloodied and bruised and so barely alive their chest hardly even moved. Illie was no stranger to death – she'd sarding nearly beheaded a man, for Poet's sake – but even in the dark she recognized the person slouched on the ground in a puddle of what could only be their own blood, hanging onto life by whatever means possible.

Thol crouched down, fingers blindly searching for a pulse. The footsteps drew nearer. Illie squatted and took Isra's face in her hands. They blinked wearily up at her, barely conscious. Barely alive.

"N-Nova –" They croaked. "R-run..."

"I'm not leaving you here to die," growled Thol. "I've saved your sorry ass before. I'll save it again. Who did this to you? Nova?"

Isra's grey eyes fluttered shut. They went limp, slack in Illie's hands.

"I've two bullets left," piped up Fynch. "And that sounds like a lot more than two people coming for us. We need to leave."

"They'll expect us to go to the marina," grumbled Thol. He picked up Isra, carrying the broken doctor like a bride. "We need a place to hide – at least until we can slip out of here."

"The clinic," Illie said, wiping blood off on her dress. "We can barricade ourselves in there, and there should be medical supplies to stabilize Isra."

She took off running, ignoring the thundering of her heart in her ears. She knew death, but there was a difference between the death of strangers – the death of monsters trying to kill *her* – and the death of people she knew.

Her father. Her sister, Mary.

Even though she hardly knew them, Isra had saved Fynch. Letting them die would only sour her stomach.

It took longer than expected to get to the clinic, especially with Thol taking the lead and weaving through alleys and narrow roads to throw the pirates after them off. As soon as they were down the stairs, Thol lay Isra on the counter and promptly knocked a bookcase over, dragging it to the door and shoving it in place.

"I'm going to secure the place," he said. "Illie, I'm going to trust them with you. Their blood heals. Don't let them die. *Please.*"

She swallowed the lump in her throat and nodded. Then, with shaky hands, she approached Isra.

"I-I don't know what to do..." she whispered, reaching to undo the buttons of their shirt. As they fumbled with the third button, Isra's hand shot out and grabbed her wrist.

"Do not," they growled, "touch me."

And then they passed out again.

"You're a valuable asset. Your ability rivals mine in terms of usefulness. In terms of *power*," Nova had said, the underlying threat clearer than glass. Isra had weighed their options, had debated who was more likely to come out of a fight alive – Thol or Nova – and they'd made a decision.

"Rumors," they said, skipping over the unimportant details that would make their lie more complicated, "that they are staying at the Traveler's."

Surely, Thol wouldn't be stupid enough to book a stay at the only decent inn in town, right? They'd go hide somewhere safe. Throwing Nova a false lead would buy them and Thol enough time to think of a better plan, so it had to work.

Isra didn't need friends, but they felt a strange kinship to Thol. Debts owed or not, they would show a shred of loyalty to the man who saved their life twice.

Nova snapped the book he'd been destroying shut, tossing it over his shoulder. He grinned. "I knew you were smart. Now, if you'll excuse me, I have a rat to eat."

Relief washed over Isra. It did not stay for long.

Later that night, Thol came back, message in tow. As he lingered, he mentioned staying at an inn. The Traveler's. The exact place Isra had sent Nova's men to. Dread was a block of ice in their stomach, one they forced down as Thol gave the instructions for the message and left.

Sard. Sarding sard! Their hands shook as they cleaned up the mess Nova left behind. *Idiot! Does he not know how to lie low?!*

So engrossed in their thoughts, they didn't hear the door open or the heavy footsteps that descended the stairs. They didn't realize they weren't alone until the fist collided with the back of their head, sending them sprawling to the ground.

Their nose smashed against the hard floor, sending a spark of white-hot pain bursting behind their eyes.

"I saw the most peculiar sight," drawled Nova.

Isra pushed themselves to their knees, licking their upper lip free of blood. They turned, eyes narrowed, to see Ryuu Nova standing there, arms crossed, Kusanagi glinting at his hip.

"See, I was coming back because I had the strangest feeling," he continued, smirking as he watched Isra struggle to their feet. They'd never been much of a fighter. "I saw a man leaving your clinic. Not someone *I* authorized you to treat."

He cracked his knuckles, balling his hands into fists. Isra took a step back, fear numbing their limbs. Nova wouldn't give them a quick death. If Isra wanted to go out without suffering, they'd have to use their bladed gloves to slit their throat wide open.

Nova stepped closer and said, "I recognized that man, too. Bartholomew Williams, bounty of four hundred fifteen million lune. Care to tell me what *he* was doing here?"

Isra grinded their teeth together, jaw tight. Their death was already inevitable; why give Nova what he was looking for? They took another step back, then another, until their spine collided with the bookcase.

You've survived the plague, they thought, eyes locked with Nova's. *Nothing's scarier than that.*

Unfortunately, Isra could think of at least a dozen other things that were, in fact, scarier than the Alkenio Plague, and Ryuu Nova sat right at the top of that list.

Well. Their thoughts became muddled as Nova's fist collided with their jaw, sending sparks of pain to the ends of their every nerve and black spots to their vision. *At least you did good healing that kid. At least you got to pay Thol back one debt.*

Nova grabbed their collar and slammed their head into the shelf. Sticky wetness dripped down their neck, slicking their hair. *Blood.*

"I think you know exactly why he was here," Nova spat. "In fact, I think that *you* thought I was a sarding idiot. Tell me, *Eliad,* what was Williams doing here?"

He slammed Isra against the bookshelf again. Blood – precious, healing blood – splattered on the ground in near perfect circles.

The brain was one of the most important organs a human had. There was a reason why skulls were so thick. There was a reason why children were taught at a young age to protect their heads. There was a reason why a headshot was the only way to ensure someone died. Isra's brain was more valuable than most because Isra's brain held the cure to the Alkenio Plague.

If their skull took any more damage, their brain would be at risk. And if their brain got injured...

Well, it would be death.

Weakly, foolishly they grabbed Nova's massive wrist. Their own arms lacked muscle – their wrist was closer to the size of Nova's sarding finger – but adrenaline gave them the strength they lacked, gripping Nova's arm because their very life depended on it.

"Why?!" shouted Nova. Spittle sprayed, flecking Isra's face in a fate almost worse than death.

In the split second before their head crashed into the bookshelf again, Isra debated their scant options.

There was no way Isra, who had survived the *Plague,* would die here.

They let go of Nova's wrist. Time slowed, dragging like syrup. Nova raised his fist and descended it in an arc destined for Isra's jaw. Isra raised their hand – the hand with tiny needles poking from the slits in their glove – and jammed the slivers of metal into Nova's forearm.

There was no blood in the needles but Nova didn't know that. He never cared to learn the details of Isra's ability.

Nova tore his arm away, jumping back.

Isra grabbed the bookshelf, head spinning and throbbing and bleeding, trying to steady themselves.

And then...

And then...

A glint of black metal, the shine of a broken mirror. *Kusanagi.*

With Nova's ability, the sword was at least three times the size it normally was, its double-edged curved blade blacker than pitch. There had been a mirror inlaid in the hilt once, according to legend, but it had been broken for as long as Isra knew Nova.

They had no time to dodge as the blade descended down, a grim pendulum. They saw the blood – precious, thick blood – spurt from their chest, dripping to the ground in a crimson gush before they felt the pain.

Thol, they thought weakly. Their knees gave out, and they collapsed to the ground. *I have to get to Thol...*

At once, the pain subsided, and they slipped into a blissful unconsciousness.

Ves was, by no means whatsoever, a tiny woman, but as she sat in the cell, legs pulled to her chest and hands trembling with panic – with fear – she felt very, very small. The voices around her muddled like she'd stuck her head underwater. Her body wasn't hers. She was a specter floating above it, watching omnisciently.

I can't go back, her mind raced on repeat. *I can't go back I can't go back I can't go back I can't go back I can't go back –*

Four years trapped in the darkness, and she'd *just* seen the sunlight again, and now she was right back where she started. In a cell. Trapped in the darkness. At the mercy of a man with too much power.

Pain streaked down her face; her nails dug into the flesh of her cheeks, raking down hard enough to draw blood.

" –es... Ves! Are you okay?"

She spun around, teeth bared. Natha let go of her wrist and held her scarred hands up.

"Sorry," Natha apologized. "I... Are you okay? I've been trying to get your attention for the past five minutes now."

She looked down at her hands, her breaths becoming more and more shallow. Her lips went numb, pins and needles prickling the flesh. *I can't go back I can't go back I can't go back I can't go back I can't go back.*

The dingy jail cell was nothing compared to Seven-B, the lowest, most isolated level of I. J. Pen.

But it was a cell. It was a sarding cell and she was trapped and –

Hands grabbed her wrists. Rough, but not scarred – not Natha's hands.

Solveig's.

She looked at him, tears welling in her eyes and spilling down her cheeks, stinging the scratches she'd given herself. She croaked, *"Cap."*

"What did I promise you?" he asked. "I will carry you to the ends of Syrenis and never let them forget your name. You are *not* going back to Ivenis Justyce. I've got you, Ves."

"Cap," she whispered again, her voice breaking.

He grinned. The numbness in her lips went away. He said, "As if this sarding cell could hold *you*, Witch of the Sea. We're going to get out of here. We just need your help."

Witch of the Sea. The title given to her when she'd sailed with the Ruby Pirates years and years ago. The ruthless third-in-command – the wench who slayed a (baby) kraken and sank an entire fleet. The witch who stole from Empress Nefeli's garden and courted an Amazonian warrior.

Solveig's bo'sun, his second mate, his first crew member recruited in the filthy darkness of Seven-B.

She filled her lungs with air for the first time since waking up in the cell and wiped her tears with the back of her hand.

Solveig's grin widened. "I was going to hug you, but I think that would've been *too* effective. I'm still recovering from the last time you punched me."

Despite her panic, her fear, the corners of her lips tugged upward. She said softly, "Thanks, Cap."

"Oh, are we offering hugs?" came Lonan's voice. "If so, I'll *happily* take one. From one of you ladies, that is. Nothing against you, Solveig. You just know how it is."

"Permission to punch him?" growled Ves.

"Denied," chuckled Solveig. "Unfortunately, we need him for our plan to work."

She resorted to giving him her middle finger.

"The plan," Solveig continued, "is to split up. Natha, Lonan, and I are going to find Ryuu Nova and kick his ass clear across the Emerald. Ves, you're going to lead Czardas and Leo to find Thol and the others."

Right. Without the captain or the first mate around, it was Ves's duty to lead the crew. Even if that crew was only one person and a straggler.

"Which is good," she murmured. "But that doesn't solve the big issue here. How the hell are we supposed to get out of here?"

"That's where you and Lonan come into play," he said. "You're going to figure out how many people are here and where they are. Lonan will cause a distraction and get the keys while Leo works on the *bigger* distraction – setting this place on fire."

Next to her, Natha stiffened.

Oblivious, Solveig continued: "The fire will cause the jailers to flee. Once they're gone, we can unlock the door and get out of here. The fire will keep everyone occupied while we split up and escape."

"What about our weapons?" Czardas asked.

"They can't be far," Lonan said. "We'll find them before we run."

It was a solid plan. Even though Ves didn't like the thought of splitting up, it would only be temporary. She turned to look out the bars, searching for the golden glows that were souls. There were three floating above them – the cells must be downstairs. Two were just beyond the cell, and another four were in a room adjacent to the one they were in. Nine in total. *Easy.* She could take them all out on her own if she needed to.

Luckily, she didn't need to.

"Nine," she said. "There's another room next to us and a floor above us."

"Right, then," drawled Lonan. "My turn."

He cleared his throat.

"Guards!" he shouted. "Oh, guaaaaaaaaards!"

What in the actual hell does he think he's doing?!

Leo extinguished the makeshift torch, drowning the cell in darkness. There was shuffling as they moved around – Ves watched their souls from the corner of her eye. Everyone lay down, eyes closed, as they pretended to be asleep.

"Guards!" sang Lonan. "Guards! You'd better come quick before I start causing prooooobleeeems!"

"They're coming," hissed Ves.

Sure enough, footsteps sounded and the door burst open. Three guards entered the jail – two holding lanterns and all with scowls on their faces.

"What in the name of the Wanderer do you *want?*" hissed one of the guards as she shined the lantern at Lonan.

Lonan leaned against the bars and grinned lazily, eyes half-lidded with a smolder that sent a gross shudder down Ves's spine.

"Oh, aren't you a lovely lady," Lonan *purred.* "Do you think you could help me with something? I might've had too much to drink. I've no idea where I am or why I'm in here. Lonan, by the way. What's your name? No, no, don't tell me. Let me guess. Mm... You look like a Nefeli."

He winked. The woman froze, spine stiffening. Ves wanted to gag. How depraved could that rat man get?!

"Shut up," one of the other guards snapped, kicking the bars.

Lonan held his hands up in surrender. "Apologies. Truly. Is that your wife? Quite a beauty you got there. Lucky, lucky man."

The guard's face flushed crimson. He stammered helplessly, trying to come up with an excuse. Ves bit back a smirk. The lady guard wasn't his wife, but there was some one-sided affection there.

The third guard sighed. "What do you want?"

"Well, I hardly think it's appropriate to say now that there's a lady here," Lonan said with a shrug. "Come here, I'll tell you so she can't hear. It's not like I can do anything from this side of the cell. I'm not blessed. Cross my heart and swear it on my ma's name."

"I do not have feelings for you!" the second guard helplessly defended himself, though his protests went unnoticed by the first guard.

The guard tsked but walked over, crouching down to reach Lonan's level.

"What," the guard demanded.

Lonan lowered his voice to a stage whisper. "I really, really, *really* have to take a piss. And there's ladies in here with me, so I don't want to...you know... I've no idea who these people are or if they're in some sort of relationship with each other, but I know all of them could beat me in a fight if they woke up and saw me with my...you know...out in front of their ladies."

Ves bit down on her tongue hard to keep from laughing.

"Just turn your back to them," the guard said.

"Well, I would, but my other *assets* are just as grand, you know?" Lonan slipped his arms through the bars, oozing nonchalance. "And then this place will reek of piss, and they might accuse me of pissing on their wives, and I'd still get pummeled. Still not sure why I'm even here. I had *way* too much to drink last night."

"You know I'm engaged!" the lady guard snapped. "Why do you have to be like this?! I'm going straight to *Nova* to tell him I quit at this point!"

"I don't care," the third guard said to Lonan. "Drink your piss for all I care. I'm not –"

Acrid smoke filled Ves's sinuses.

The third guard spun on the others. "Where in the sarding Wanderer's name is that smoke coming from?!"

Just beyond the cell lay the remains of Natha's shirt, engulfed in flames. Flames that spread across the wood floor.

"Fire!" the second guard shouted.

At once, Lonan was forgotten as the three guards ran up the stairs, shouting for the other six to put the fire out.

Ves sat up. Lonan lazily twirled a keyring around his finger.

"I'm hardly a thief," he said, slipping the key through the lock outside the cell.

"You know, Sugar," Ves said as she darted out of the cell. "You're tolerable sometimes."

Lonan grinned widely. "Coming from you, Miss Ves, that's the *highest* compliment a man could ever hope to have."

She rolled her eyes. "Don't get used to it. Strings, Goggles, you're with me. Let's go find Flowers."

18

How the hell am I supposed to save them if they won't let me touch them?! Illie thought, panicked, as she looked at Isra's unconscious, bleeding body. Without removing their shirt, she wasn't able to see the full extent of their injuries, but she could see enough. Bruises covered their face, and blood matted their hair from an injury to the back of their head. The wound that would be fatal if she didn't do something, though, was the one across their chest, sliced through fabric and flesh alike. With just a glance, she couldn't tell how deep it was, but the blood bubbling from the gash was so dark it was nearly black.

Her breaths became shallow. Panicked. *You can do this,* she told herself. *You can do this. Their blood heals. I have no idea how, but their blood heals, so they will be fine. You just...have to do something.*

Do what?!

Her gaze flicked to Isra's hands. They wore gloves, but sticking from the tips of each finger was a sliver of metal. Blades. *Needles.*

Maybe that *don't touch* only applied to bare flesh.

Hands trembling, she grabbed Isra's hand and plunged the needles into their neck.

"Sard!" She heard Thol curse. "There has to be a back door we can slip out. They're coming, and this won't hold."

Suddenly, Isra sat up, gasping for air as they tore their hand from their throat. They turned to face Illie, grey eyes colder than ice.

"Clever," they said. "Won't work."

"Isra!" shouted Thol. "Is there another door here? One that Nova *doesn't* know about?"

Illie watched in horror as Isra stood, blood continuing to gush from their wound. They touched their fingers to their chest briefly. Then, they turned to Illie and said, "Gauze and bandages. Now."

They pointed to a door. Swallowing her adrenaline, Illie dashed for the door. She knew nothing about medicine, but even she knew that a wound that deep needed proper treatment. Gauze and bandages would hardly do the trick. Still, she grabbed a few rolls of bandages and enough gauze to last her three months of cycles.

When she returned, Fynch had his pistol pointed at the door, and Thol stood between him and Isra.

"Can you dress a wound?" the doctor asked her without looking away from the barricaded door.

"I... I can try," she admitted.

Isra's gaze flicked to Thol briefly. He nodded and undid the buttons of Isra's shirt, exposing the bloody, shredded mess of their chest.

"Gauze," Isra said, laying on their back. They winced when their head hit the counter. "Cover the whole wound."

Illie set the bandages down and tore open the gauze. Carefully, she pressed each piece over the length of the wound. Blood seeped through it immediately, turning the white gauze a startling crimson.

"More," instructed Isra.

Shaking, she covered the rest of the wound with gauze. Blood slicked her fingers.

"Bandages," they said. "Entire torso. *Tight.*"

Bang!

She jumped, whipping her head around to face the door. The door – and its barricade – shook as something rammed into it from the other side.

"Quickly!" hissed Isra.

Illie fumbled with the bandages. The banging continued, jolting her heart with each pound.

She wrapped one roll of bandages around Isra's torso. They flinched at first but nodded for her to continue. When she finished the fourth roll of bandages, the barricade toppled over.

When she finished with the sixth, Isra stood. "This way," they said.

Fynch ran after them, followed by Illie and Thol. She glanced over her shoulder as she slipped through the other door, watching.

As the front door splintered and caved in. As pirates poured into the space they'd been in moments before.

She reached into her bag and pulled out her gloves, slipping them over her blood-stained hands.

"They're coming," she said, picking up the pace as she hurried up a set of stairs.

"We need to get outside," Thol said. "It'll be better to fight in an open space."

Illie balled her hands into awkward fists. She would be able to use her ability outside. *Survive,* she thought. *Survive, and you can go home to the* Serenity.

Cold air hit her face at once, the darkness of night stealing her vision.

She would just have to rely on her other senses. Wind slipped through her fingers. Footsteps sounded, thundering towards the pavilion where she, Thol, Isra, and Fynch waited.

"What's the plan?" she asked.

"We fight," said Thol. "And we don't die. How many bullets do you have, Fynch?"

He said grimly, "Two."

Illie stepped closer to the group, their backs together, leaving no one without cover.

Thol said, "Well, then, make them sarding count."

Following Ves's instructions, Solveig ignored the escape and instead went to the side room where, sure enough, their weapons lay discarded. He tossed the heavy broadsword to Lonan and grabbed his own cutlass. Natha quickly returned Ves's knives and Czardas's rapier to them.

"If you were Ryuu Nova," Solveig said, sliding his cutlass into his belt, "Where would you be hiding?"

Lonan snatched his pack of cigarettes and stuck one between his teeth, the end lit from the fire consuming the walls of the jail. "Probably in my palace, what with a name like the *Dragon King*. Is there even a palace here?"

Natha hacked up a dry cough. "Can we figure it out after we get out of here? Please?"

"Follow me," Solveig said.

Escaping the room he'd just been in, Solveig darted up the stairs. The upper floor had been abandoned in haste, chairs and belongings strewn about for the flames to devour. He covered his nose and mouth with his sleeve and beckoned for the others to follow. The front door had been left wide open; he ran outside, gulping in breaths of fresh air.

"There's no palace," he said, glancing back to make sure the others followed him out. "But I think I know where Nova will be."

The tall building he'd seen from the *Dreamchaser*. It was the tallest, the grandest building in Corsa. If the *Dragon King* himself would be anywhere on land, it would be there. Solveig hadn't seen Nova's ship anywhere, but that hardly meant anything. Nova likely had it tucked away somewhere safe.

Solveig slinked through the shadows, pausing at every corner to make sure no one was coming before continuing to the next block. The city was quiet. Too quiet. It unnerved him, tugging the hairs on the back of his neck taut. He brushed his hand over the pommel of his cutlass, ready to free it at a moment's notice.

The smell of smoke and the crackling of fire soon became distant, replaced instead by the soft babbling of water. The buildings became sparse, giving way to the massive structure that was, without a doubt, Nova's residence.

Built on a stone structure that rose over a sarding *pond* of all things, the building was *massive.* At least six stories tall, sprawling out to take up more space than the *Dreamchaser,* the building was a monolith of terror. Its wooden walls were stained red and black. Two golden dragons guarded the sliding front entrance, mouths wide and gilded teeth on full display.

Solveig sucked in a breath. It was now or never. He handled Bonney Reed. He handled Jonyth sarding Commodore.

He could handle Ryuu Nova, too.

"Here's the plan," he whispered. "We're going to break in and kill Nova. Neither of you are allowed to die. Got it?"

"Easy enough," murmured Lonan.

Natha scraped her hair back into a messy tail. "Let's do this."

I will pledge my final breath to your name and my first to find you again.

He said, "Follow me."

Into the dragon's den, he thought grimly. He scanned the path before darting towards the sliding screen doors. Either Nova was a fool for not putting up locks, or anyone who tried to break in was one. Solveig had long since accepted his foolishness. He slid the door open and slipped inside.

Wooden floors stretched on endlessly, the walls made up of painted screens. Despite the urgency, Solveig slowed his pace, taking in the dramatic murals. At the center of it all, surrounded by clouds and fire and an aura so intense it made the creature look divine, was a red dragon, curved fangs accentuating a snarling mouth, whiskers trailing from either side of its nose, branching antlers reaching out like bolts of lightning.

He drew his sword and slashed it across the panel, slicing the dragon's head from its serpentine shoulders.

"What are you *doing?*" hissed Natha from behind him.

"Letting Nova know I'm here to fight," he said, arcing his sword down to make a vertical slash. With the panel destroyed, he could see through to the other room.

He stepped through the torn panel. The new room was smaller, with a sliding door opposite the torn wall.

"If I were Nova," Solveig said, "I would be at the very top of this place." His heart ached at the thought of splitting up even further, but what choice did he have? There was too much ground to cover, and only three of them. Besides, they were on solid ground. It wasn't like Nova could drug them with Sinth and let them drown here... He continued, "If one of us can make it to the top, I'll consider it a win. Split up. Fight any enemies you come across. Do. Not. Sarding. Die."

Lonan tucked his hands in his pockets lazily. "Right, then. You sure we need to split up? I'd happily keep Miss Natha company."

"I'll take this floor," Natha said, ignoring Lonan completely. She popped her knuckles and ducked through the torn screen, vanishing down the long hallway.

"You take the second floor, then," Solveig said. "I'll handle the third."

He gave Lonan no time to protest, instead going out the sliding door. He stuck to the walls, crouched low, hand on his sword.

Another hallway lined with painted screen walls greeted him. Seeing *another* dragon, he scoffed. It seemed like Nova made dragons his entire personality. Dragons didn't even exist outside of myth. There were sea serpents and stories of flying beasts, but dragons?

If dragons are *real,* he thought, grinning when he found a staircase leading up, *I'll give up cinnamon rum for an entire month.*

A quick glance at the second floor and it appeared empty. He continued up to the third floor.

He paused at yet another dragon painting. This one curled around a moon, fire spewing from its jaws. Brow furrowed, he leaned closer, trying to see if there was a third moon.

Slice!

Blood trickled down his face, followed by the sting of a shallow cut right beneath his eye. He leaped back, sword drawn in a single movement.

Shoes clacked against the wood floor. Solveig spun around to face his attacker.

A woman, tall and lanky, stood in the middle of the hallway, arms crossed. She wore a slate-colored robe with wide sleeves. Her ears were full of metal. Stacks of necklaces concealed the flesh of her throat. Inked on her cheekbone was the number two.

She uncrossed her arms and flexed one of her hands. Each finger had been covered with rings. Something shiny flew into her awaiting grasp.

"I always wondered," she drawled, "if the whole *green coat* thing was real or not."

Solveig narrowed his eyes. "You're not Nova. Who in Poet's name are you?"

She grinned. Silver teeth flashed in the light. "Captain Nova's Second Division Fleet Commander. *Captain* Prim."

She flexed her hand again, and that shiny *something* tore through the air again. Solveig swung his sword up, deflecting it with a ringing *clash!*

Suddenly, she held a sword, its curved single blade wicked sharp. Then, without hesitation, she charged.

Solveig threw up his sword, blocking her blow.

"You are *nothing,*" she hissed, specks of spittle spraying Solveig's face.

"I am Nox Solveig," he countered. "You've heard of me, but I have *never* heard of you."

Sweeping his leg out, he caught her ankle, forcing her to stumble. Seizing the leverage, he slid his blade out from under hers and aimed it straight for her bare throat.

Wait.

What?

He could have sworn she had been wearing no less than a dozen necklaces just a moment ago. Was he still feeling the effects of Sinth? Of smoke inhalation?

No time to think about that now.

He drove his blade up, only for Prim to block it at the last second, her sword moving...unnaturally. Defying all laws of physics, bending in ways solid metal should not bend.

He jumped back, shoulders heaving as he panted. Adrenaline numbed his veins, taking an edge off the pain surging from his leg. His shoulder still hadn't healed completely, either, but he couldn't afford to let that weakness show. Sutures could be redone. Bones could be reset. Death was not reversible, and Nox Solveig was not going to die to this nobody fleet commander.

Prim roared and charged at him, sword held high. He noticed, nearly too late, that her sword was no longer a curved single-edged blade but a wider, heavier cutlass like his own.

She swung; he blocked. She might be faster than him, but he was, without a doubt, stronger. Her arms trembled when he put his entire weight into the block.

And then, suddenly, her sarding sword was gone, and Solveig, without the support he'd been leaning against, stumbled forward.

Prim spun around, landing a kick to his spine. Solveig sputtered, falling to the floor. His sword clattered out of his grip, skittering across the floor.

No!

He scrambled across the ground, reaching for his sword, when suddenly a metal cuff wrapped around his wrist, weighing him to the floor. He struggled, trying to get free, but the slim cuff weighed a ton and a half, keeping him stuck to the floor.

Prim was divine-touched.

"Dreamer," she said with a smirk like she had just read his mind. "Metal manipulation. As soon as you walked in here with a sword, you lost this fight."

He pulled on the cuff. Flesh tore as easily as paper, slicking his wrist with blood. Still, he reached for his cutlass.

"I don't..." he gritted, teeth clenched as his fingers brushed against the blade of his cutlass, "Lose...fights."

"There's always a first for everything," Prim said smugly.

Blood splattered against the floor. Red slicked the thin tip of the blade beneath him.

Oh, he thought, watching as the blade that was not his retracted, bringing with it a pain so unbearable he nearly lost consciousness. *I've been stabbed.*

Exhaustion set into Leo's bones, making him feel like he'd been awake for three days straight. His stamina had always been terrible – getting sick as a child took more than just his leg from him – but the mix of sleepless nights, fighting and running, and using his ability more frequently than he was used to made everything ten times worse. More than anything, he wanted to just lie down and *sleep.*

But no. This mission was his mission now.

At least it's still extraction, he thought grimly, *and not recovery.*

He stuck close to Ves, doing his best to match her pace as she wove through alleyways and darted down quiet streets like she knew the layout of Corsa by memory.

For the past ten minutes, Leo, Czardas, and Ves had traveled in silence, the former following Ves as Ves followed a trail only she could see.

Suddenly, she stopped, crouching down to brush her fingers against the cobblestone.

"Blood," she said, showing Leo and Czardas her red-slicked fingers. "It's still fresh."

Leo's stomach sank to his feet, his mind instantly going to the worst case scenario. Even with the dim light from the streetlamps, he could see that the cobblestone was covered in blood.

"Well, well, well," came an unfamiliar voice. "What do we have here? The Witch of the Sea, worth three hundred and seventy million lune, and the *famous musician* Czardas Rossi, worth only eight hundred thousand. And..."

Leo spun around to face the speaker. Three people stood there, weapons already drawn.

A woman with short, harsh hair and an even harsher expression looked Leo up and down before continuing: "And...some random guy. Who are you?"

Leo didn't get the chance to talk before Ves spoke. "Who are *you?*"

The harsh woman lifted a brow. "Noor. Second mate of the Dragon Pirates' second division. Also known as the wench who will kill you and claim that three hundred seventy mill."

Leo balled his hands into fists. Nova's men had found them first. Without a weapon of his own, he would have to rely on his fire.

It's this or death, he thought. *You can recover from exhaustion. You can't recover from death.*

Noor brandished her sword. "Cynthia, Cam, you know your orders. Take no survivors."

Ves drew her knives, the blades slipped between her knuckles like cat claws. She said, "Strings, Goggles, don't you sarding *dare* die."

And then all hell broke loose.

The woman, Cynthia, charged at Leo, her sword drawn.

She swung with deadly force. Leo threw his hands up and *ignited.* Flames met metal in a cloud of burning heat. Panic filled Cynthia's face; she changed the trajectory of her blow, just barely skimming past Leo's face.

Then, the sword *vanished.*

Smoke rose above the flames, denser than anything Leo's conjured blaze could have created.

Because, he realized with a sinking sense of dread, it wasn't smoke from his fire.

It was smoke from Cynthia's sword – from...from *Cynthia herself.*

Behind him, the smoke materialized. Heart skipping a beat, he spun around to see Cynthia standing there.

"The Wanderer," he breathed. She was blessed to turn into smoke!

Cynthia smirked. "Aye. As are you."

Leo's hands lit aflame again. He swung the fire toward her, but she dissolved to smoke where he tried to hit.

Of all the divine abilities granted by the gods, the ones from the Wanderer were always...unpredictable. They were the deity of debauchery, of sin, of everything chaotic. Their powers were a wild card, a hidden ace up the sleeve. The blessings they gave out never followed any sort of rule, not like the blessings given by Lady Lightbringer or Poet or Dreamer; their blessings weren't just a power because their blessings could change the physical form of whoever used them. Leo's body ran hotter than normal, and heat never bothered him because he had fire in his blood.

Cynthia could sarding change her physical form to *smoke.*

How was he supposed to even land a single blow if every time he made contact with her, she became incorporeal?

Think, Leo. If he couldn't hit her, he would have to *contain* her.

He glanced around the open space, looking for something – for *anything* – that would work.

There. A discarded bottle that probably was once full of cinnamon rum. If he could somehow get Cynthia to turn to smoke and funnel in there...

"You know, smoke can't exist without fire," he said, drawing his attention back to her. She manifested a sword from smoke. *Can she turn other objects into smoke?* He thought. *Or did she* make *it out of smoke?*

"A shame," she said, "That I am about to be the first."

She thrust her blade, and Leo lit up like a bonfire.

19

THERE WAS LITTLE FYNCH could not do with a gun in his hand, but taking out multiple enemies with only two bullets ranked relatively high on the list of impossibilities even he couldn't manage. The only thing he *could* do was hope one of the enemies had a gun with more ammo than his that he could steal. Because stealing a gun? That was so easy he could do it with his sarding eyes closed.

There were four of them and, in a comical twist of fates that made Fynch laugh nervously, exactly four enemies that stormed into the pavilion, weapons drawn and dragon tattoos on display.

Four enemies. Two bullets.

"Oh, we are going to die," he whispered.

"We didn't drag you all the way here to save your life just for you to die," hissed Illie. Wind whipped her braid around her shoulders.

"We still have a moon to find," added Thol, his hands balled into *PUNISHMENT* fists.

Isra said nothing. Their face still had the pale sheen of near death – a fate Fynch had only *just* escaped. A fate he would be subject to again if he didn't use his two bullets wisely.

"You damn traitor," one of the enemies, a massive man nearly as big as Thol, said. "I told Nova he kept too loose a leash on you. And look what happened. You went and joined another crew."

"Not affiliated with a crew," Isra said flatly. Then, traitorously, they pointed to each of the enemies and named them: "Markus. Anne. Sato. Brit."

Fynch ignored them all – except for Sato. There was...something about him that rubbed Fynch wrong. Something that...intrigued him.

It wasn't until Sato pulled out a sleek revolver pistol from his belt that Fynch realized *he was also a sharpshooter.*

If Fynch's revolver was a beauty, Sato's was worthy of an emperor – he could tell even at a distance that it was incredibly perfect.

He spun his own gun around his finger, grinning a chipped-toothed grin. Sato was his. That *gun* would be his.

Time slowed. Or, perhaps, adrenaline kicked in, making Fynch faster than the battle that broke out around him. He was nothing if not scrappy.

Sato raised his revolver and aimed the barrel at Fynch's head, finger teasing the trigger.

Pull it, taunted Fynch silently. *Pull it, pull it, pull it. I* dare *you.*

Life on the streets made him fast, but his revering body kicked him down a notch or ten. He couldn't dodge a bullet, but he *could* goad Sato into wasting all his ammo.

Bang!

Fynch's ears rang with the explosion. Heat scraped his arm as the bullet barely grazed him, drawing blood from the streak of torn flesh. *No time for that.*

He dove between Sato's legs, deft fingers pilfering a handful of stray bullets from his pocket. Grinning, he loaded the ammo into his own pistol and fired.

The bullet whizzed past Sato.

"You missed," he growled.

Fynch shrugged. "Grazed you, didn't I? Gave you the same wound you gave me."

Sato faltered, reaching up to touch the blood blossoming on his upper arm. Fynch hadn't missed. He'd aimed to graze Sato's arm, to give him a mirrored wound.

He'd hit exactly where he wanted to.

Fury crumpled Sato's face.

Glancing around the pavilion, Fynch took off running. There was hardly any cover. Tucking himself in an alley would only cage him in. Crates and barrels wouldn't slow a bullet. But...

There.

He hadn't noticed the statue in the center of the pavilion before, the darkness of night shrouding the dark stone in ink-thick shadows. It was hard to make out what it even was. A worm? A dragon? What even was the difference? It didn't matter. He shook those thoughts away and dove behind the thick stone, taking a moment to suck in a few greedy, albeit painful, breaths.

Slowly, he peered around the statue to see Sato running toward him.

Idiot.

Without even looking, Fynch aimed and fired – three consecutive rounds that *had* to meet their mark.

"You're a coward, huh?" came Sato's voice – from *above.*

Fynch's stomach sank. He tipped his head back to see Sato crouched atop the statue's base, gun pointed at Fynch's skull.

"Gotcha."

There was a part of Natha that wanted to peek at the kitchen before hunting down Nova – a part she begrudgingly ignored in favor of strolling the long, eerily empty hallways. She had to admit the architecture was pretty, even if the interior design was sparse at best.

She ran her fingers along the wall. No dust. Someone – or, rather, an entire staff – worked hard to keep the place clean. If there were servants, there must be special corridors for them.

Before Natha was a pirate, she came from a decent family. They weren't overly wealthy – she came into temporary wealth after marriage – but they had a single maid who helped her mother with chores. Natha and her sister were menaces as children, constantly raiding their mother's wardrobe and leaving the evidence of their crimes draped over the furniture and strewn about the hallways. Their house hadn't been anything exceptional, but there had been concealed hallways for the maid to navigate without two devious little girls chasing after.

She wondered if Nova's sprawling manor had hidden passage-ways, too.

As she turned a corner, she stopped in her tracks. Where there had just been stretching hallways before was now a room the size of the *Dreamchaser*'s deck. In the middle of the room was a low table with a steaming teapot. Sitting at the table and holding a teacup was a man.

Natha was used to being short compared to men. She was aver-age at best, and while she did have toned muscles, they tended to hide under soft curves, making her appear feminine enough that she didn't seem like a threat. There was no alternate reality where she would ever appear threatening to the man.

Even sitting, he had to be Ves's height. He was practically as wide as she was tall; the teacup looked like a thimble in his massive hands.

She took a tiny step back, mind racing with excuses. She was lost. She was drunk. She got addresses mixed up. None of them were good enough. None of them were convincing.

All it would take was one punch from that man, and she would be dead.

She took another step back.

Creeeeeeeeaaaaaaaak.

As her full weight went onto the creaky floorboard, the goliath man turned toward her. He was missing an eye, and his teeth were blacker than pitch, oily as he grinned.

Flee, desperation cried. *Run while you can! Leave him to Solveig!*

You're a pirate, bravery – stupidity – chided. *You would never let a* man *best you in anything.*

Natha scrunched her face into a grimace. "I live on a ship full of men, and even they have better hygiene than you. Don't you know what a *toothbrush* is?"

Fear coiled in her belly, liquifying her guts and turning her legs into perfectly cooked noodles. She crouched low, centering her gravity. Speed was her only advantage here; she wouldn't let that go to waste.

The goliath grunted, dropping his teacup. Ceramic shattered, creating an obstacle she would have to dodge.

She held her ground, refusing to waver. Fear turned to adrenaline, urging her to take off running when Goliath charged at her like an enraged bull.

When he was mere feet from her, Natha bolted to the side, spinning around so she was behind him. Grabbing the back of Goliath's robe, she jumped up, straddling his shoulders with powerful thighs.

Blunt, dirty fingernails scraped at her legs. Goliath stumbled back, slamming his back against the wall. Natha, sandwiched between the blow, wheezed in pain, coughing out all the air in her lungs. He slammed his back again; stars blurred her vision.

But she kept her grip.

She wished she had Ves's legs – thick and powerful and strong enough to choke Goliath out. This tactic wasn't working. *Think, Natha!*

Goliath pulled away from the wall again. An idea came to her then. In the split second before she could be crushed against the wall again, she tumbled forward. Goliath hit the wall, and Natha landed on her feet.

"Come and get me," she taunted breathlessly.

Goliath roared. The ground shook as he ran after her.

Natha jumped over the broken teacup, placing herself in the center of the room. If she got between Goliath and another wall, she was dead. But in the open, she could use her speed. She could tire Goliath out and end him before he got the chance to touch her again.

Goliath's bare feet crunched over the shattered ceramic. If the pain bothered him – if the shards even managed to slice through his thick soles – he didn't show it.

Natha tucked and rolled out of the way. Goliath didn't slow down, running right into the wall with enough force to splinter the wood.

She was behind him in a heartbeat, throwing a right hook into his massive gut. The shock went to her shoulder, but the adrenaline pumping through her veins was stronger.

Goliath spun around, shaking splinters from his hair. Natha bounced back, then ran straight for him. She jumped into the air and kicked – his gut, his chest, his sarding chin – before spinning and landing, winded.

"Come on, you sard face," she said with a grin. "Is that all you got?"

Ves could count on one hand the things that got her blood pumping with excitement: booze, powerful women, and a matched fight ranked high on the list. She was as sober as a baby, and Noor was downright ugly, but she was strong.

And Ves had been *itching* for another fight – a good fight, a bloody one – since her crew had won against the Rabbit Pirates. That little skirmish in the woods was *nothing* compared to this.

She swung her fist, knives slicing through air and flesh, splitting three parallel lines into Noor's already sard-ugly face. Blood spurted, gushing down Noor's skin with each rapid pulse of her heart. Ves licked her lips and swung again.

Noor threw up her arm, forearm clashing against Ves's before her blades could cut again.

"Witch of the Sea, huh?" drawled Noor. Blood bubbled over her lips, staining her teeth crimson. "You're still relevant?"

"You know, I *love* when people say that!" Ves said with fake cheer. Her expression stayed neutral, even as she used her free hand to throw a knife into the air, letting it stab into Noor's arm. She cried out in pain, but Ves spoke over her. "Everyone acts all high and sarding mighty because *they* spent the last four years free while I rotted in a *sarding prison cell!* You will *never* be relevant to me!

I'm going to kill you now and forget you existed in one sarding *week!*"

Noor ripped the blade free, brandishing it foolishly. The silvery light from the moons reflected against the red-stained metal. For a moment, Ves saw her reflection there, in that tiny sliver of crimson-silver.

Around her, flashes of gold danced. Four in total, ignoring Noor. She couldn't afford to be distracted by the souls. She –

Suddenly, something whizzed past her ear, severing a precious curl. If not for her hair being in the way, the *knife that sailed towards her* would have cut into her ear.

A knife that had just been in Noor's hand.

A knife that came at her from *behind.*

Ves took a step back, fists raised, knives glinting from between her knuckles.

Then, she grinned. Noor was *blessed.*

She threw another knife, then another, the blades singing as they zipped through the air. And then, just before they could bury themselves in Noor's gut, they froze.

And clattered to the ground uselessly.

Telekinesis, she thought. It had to be the Wanderer's blessing, the ability to move objects with nothing but her mind. An ability leagues above her own.

The knives flew from the ground and charged at Ves. She took off running, circling around Noor while throwing two more knives. Distracted by the ones in the air, Noor couldn't react fast enough. One blade buried itself deep in her thigh while the other soared past her head.

"Ves!" shouted Czardas, who blocked the knife with his rapier. "Careful! We're on the same side!"

"Sorry, Strings!" she called back.

Noor screamed in pain. The knives she'd been manipulating fell to the ground with a clatter. Ves dove, grabbing them from the street and throwing them again.

Noor's soul glowed bright, a golden beacon against the dark night.

But...there. Against her leg, her arm, her face... Dark spots bled through, weeping into the gold like a plague. And... It was so faint she nearly missed it – especially when she rolled out of the way and threw one of her knives again, narrowly missing the blade Noor threw back – but...right in the center of Noor's soul's chest was a faint thrum, a tiny spool of red so intangible she had to wonder if it was a trick of the light.

She blinked furiously, threw another knife, and looked again.

No. It was still there.

Somehow, through Noor's soul, Ves was able to see something she had never seen before – a person's sarding *heart*.

A weakness on perfect display, ready to be exploited. A sarding beacon pointing Ves right to the spot she needed to stab.

All she had to do was thrust a blade into it.

There was a slight wind, and the air was cool, a welcome balm against the harsh summer sun that had only just set. Despite the chill in the air, sweat beaded on Illie's forehead as her mind raced to calculate how much she could wield her power against the pirate charging toward her – Anne – before frostbite devoured her hands.

Isra had defected, abandoning the Dragon Pirates. At least, it seemed that was the case. Why would they fight Nova's crew only to return to the Dragon King's side – especially after what had been done to them? If they were on her side now, she could afford to overexert herself.

Anne swung her sword. *Not yet!* A voice inside Illie's head screamed at her. She dove to the side, narrowly missing the blow. Damn it! She needed a sarding sword!

As she stood, she glanced at her makeshift gloves – several pairs of thick socks pulled over her hands to keep her bare flesh from touching the freezing winds. She had no other sarding choice. Unless someone conveniently dropped their sword for her to take, she was weaponless.

No.

She was never weaponless.

"You're quick," quipped Anne. She pointed the tip of her sword at Illie like it was a gun. "And weaponless. What are you, a coward?"

"I'm a sarding *navigator!*" she yelled with the fury of Poet himself.

Then, despite the knowing fear that she would regret the decision in the near future, she grabbed the wind and flung it out.

It hit Anne's shins. She tumbled forward, hitting the ground with a teeth-clattering *thud!*

Illie let go of the wind instantly. The longer she held, the colder her hands got, the freeze already seeping towards her palms.

The momentary advantage didn't last long at all. In a heartbeat, Anne was on her feet again, sword drawn and a twisted mask of fury painted on her bloody face. When she grimaced, Illie noticed one of her teeth missing.

Just because she'd drawn first blood didn't mean she'd win the fight. She couldn't afford to let her guard down.

She reached for another wind when, suddenly, she was on the ground, head smashed against the cobblestone.

Anne straddled her waist, pinning her hips down.

"Pretty bad navigator if you're out *here,*" she spat, smashing the pommel of her cutlass against Illie's cheek.

She cried out in pain, the sharp ache swarming to cloud her vision. Blood filled her mouth, spraying over her lips when she gasped for air.

"The sard am I supposed to do?" she choked. "Navigate a careened ship? News flash, wench, I can do more than just look at a damn compass!"

She reached out and whipped a gale hard, blowing Anne off her, sending her crashing into a brick wall.

Carefully, she stood, ignoring the throbbing pain in her cheek. She'd be lucky if it wasn't shattered. The fact that she could still talk was a good sign, but the blood dripping from her nose wasn't. She rubbed it away with her sleeve, spitting a bloody glob of saliva onto the ground.

My name, she thought as she sank low, just like Natha had taught her, *is Illie Valentine. I am a mapmaker from Veridin. I'm a navigator who has sailed the world twice. I'm going to make a moving lithograph of Syrenis like the one of the Wandering Isle. I'm going to find the lost moon.*

A roar tore from her throat as she charged. Wind filled her hands, thick and serpentine, submitting to her. She lifted her arms above her head and threw the gust with all her might.

Czardas's heart beat in a rapid spiccato, a wicked fast metronome ticking a tempo he couldn't keep up with. His lungs sure tried. They were close to giving up now, burning in rage with each weak breath he sucked through his teeth. In through the nose. Out through the mouth. Inhale. Step. Parry. Thrust. Exhale. Repeat.

He'd never been the best at dancing. During soirees or balls or any of the other lavish parties he'd been dragged to, he always paid more attention to the music than the dancing itself. He'd left a string of heartbroken potential suitors in his wake as he drifted away from the dance floor to the sidelines where the chamber orchestras played music he knew by heart. But fighting...it was a dance, not a song. One he knew the technical steps to but lacked the skill to put them to use.

Fencing was nothing like an actual swordfight, and he had *very* quickly realized that.

Parry. Thrust. Duck. Spin. Repeat.

Repeat.

Repeat.

His arms weighed with every swing of his sword, his exhaustion evident in the sweat dripping from his face. Cam – the pirate whose sword was getting *too* close for comfort – gritted his teeth and thrust his cutlass upwards, trying to *gore* Czardas.

Lightning fast, Czardas blocked the blow before his guts could spill all over the cobblestone.

Cam slid his blade along Czardas's. He couldn't hold back the blow, not when Cam put all his weight against the unbalanced tip of Czardas's rapier.

Czardas's arms bowed under the weight. *Fast!* He thought desperate.

Mind going blank, he tucked his elbow close, pivoting his rapier just so, sliding *just* out of range of the descending cutlass.

I can't win this fight.

But he couldn't run, either. He was a pirate. A *pirate.* Not a damn coward.

And he still needed to see Fynch. To make sure he was alive. To make sure he was okay.

It was that – the thought of his best friend – that sent a surge of adrenaline through Czardas's body. When Cam raced toward him again, Czardas met him halfway. He threw his rapier up, delivering a blow before Cam could.

But it wasn't *enough*. It would never be enough. He wasn't blessed like Ves and Illie. He wasn't strong like Thol and Solveig. He didn't have natural talent like Fynch and Natha. He was just a musician, a rich, pompous future duke who decided to follow a street urchin until his very last breath – who swore an oath to a pirate that his last and first breaths would belong to him.

Even now, as his sword clashed against Cam's over and over again in a vicious, violent, vehement duet, he couldn't help but realize just how much of an impulsive fool he really was. Around him, Ves and Leo fought to win.

He fought to survive.

And now, as his stamina wore thin, he didn't know if he could do even that.

20

THOL'S KNUCKLES BURNED, WET with blood both his own and his enemy's.

When Thol homed in on Markus, the seeming leader of the group, Markus met him with a wild grin. "Oh," he'd said. "I know you. You fight barehanded." Then, instead of drawing a weapon, he swung a punch at Thol's exposed torso.

Five minutes later, both were bruised and bloodied and still refusing to give up. Beneath the burnished blood, *PUNISHMENT* peeked through, a wicked reminder of who Thol was, of what he was ready to deal out.

Markus stood in the open area of the pavilion, smartly avoiding any area where he could be backed against a wall. He swung a punch. Thol kept his elbows tucked close to his body, protecting his abdomen. He ducked, then swiftly delivered an uppercut that struck Markus in the diaphragm.

Markus choked, blood and spittle spraying from his lips as the air was stolen from his lungs.

Thol didn't hesitate. He struck again, viper fast, striking Markus's cheek twice.

Recovering quickly, Markus struck his leg out, crashing past Thol's elbows to kick him just above the navel. Thol stumbled back, pain pulsing through his body. *Sard.* He was in enough pain already. He hardly could tell if the blood soaking his shirt was his own. His nose was broken for sure, dripping rivulets of blood that clung to his mustache and beard.

If the fight lasted another five minutes, he was sure his knuckles would be broken, too.

Markus spat a glob of blood out. "That all you got?"

Jaw clenched and teeth bared, a wolfish, predatory snarl, Thol growled, "That all *you* got?"

He raised his arms, elbows tucked close, forearms guarding his aching face. Markus charged a heartbeat later, striking Thol in the stomach twice before aiming for his face.

Thol ducked again, using the momentum to swing his fist upward. It cracked against Markus's jaw *hard*. Pain ricocheted down his arm, blinding. Suddenly, his heartbeat was too loud, too overwhelming.

No, he thought, the rings around his neck humming against his chest where they rested above his heart, above the watercolor flowers inked there. *No. You can't give up. Bones will heal.*

When he punched again, bone meeting bone, the pain shot from aching to *searing,* drowning him faster than he could blink.

Lightning struck his brain, robbing him of his vision and every other feeling besides *agony*.

And still, stupidly, he reeled his arm back and swung *again*.

Crack!

Bone shattered, and he couldn't even tell *whose*.

He still had one good fist. One set of unbroken knuckles to smash into Markus's bruised face.

He struck again, a tiger going for the kill, his knuckles striking Markus in the throat. Brittle cartilage snapped with a wet, sticky crunch. When Markus inhaled, his breath was reedy, hollowed, and when he exhaled, it was all blood.

Thol grabbed a fistful of Markus's hair.

I'm sorry, Meadow, he thought as he slammed Markus's face into a brick wall. *I'm sorry. They're my family now, and I can't let anything happen to them.*

He pounded Markus's face into the wall again. Blood and teeth splattered to the ground. And still he slammed again. And again. And again and again and again and again, until it wasn't just blood and teeth but bits of skull and stringy clumps of hair and pulpy brains.

With his unbroken hand, Thol shattered the remains of Markus's skull.

That lightning strike of agony struck him in the brain again, siphoning his vision and wrenching a scream from his throat.

He let the corpse fall to the ground before looking at his knuckles – at the purple swelling that distorted his *PUNISHMENT*.

Blood ran in thick rivulets from the raw wounds. Broken. Splintered.

Useless in a sarding fight.

By the time Lonan found another person in the maze of tiny rooms and lengthy hallways, he'd burned through three sugar cigarettes. His sword, Effie, dragged behind him, and a fourth cigarette hung limply from his teeth.

On the other end of the hallway, curved sword drawn, stood a tired looking man with greasy hair scraped off his scarred face.

"Who," the man asked in a raspy hush, "are you?"

"Lonan Ryker," he said without hesitation. He took the cigarette from his mouth and exhaled a plume of sugar smoke. The saccharine sweetness clung to the backs of his teeth like a film. "Oh, and this is Effie. Named after the most beautiful lady in the world. Not that I've ever met her. I will, one day. Who are you?"

The man blinked, staring at Lonan with the keen interest one would stare at an animal at a zoo. Lonan stuck the cigarette between his teeth and let the syrupy oxygen fill his lungs. Behind his ribs, his heart palpitated, fluttering too quickly when it needed to be calm.

"Eren, first mate of the second division of the Dragon Pirates," the sleepy man said.

Ah. It clicked in Lonan's mind then. What had that pretty grunt in the forest said? The Dragon Pirates weren't just a one-ship crew. Nova had an entire fleet under his command. Finding and defeating the captain would be next to impossible with a whole fleet to filter through. He didn't have time for that. He needed to get back to the *Dreamchaser* and back to Undyne.

Back, he begrudgingly admitted, to Leo.

"I've a lot to do," drawled Lonan. "And I really don't care if you're Nova's right-hand man. I need to find the captain before my lovely lady companion does. It wouldn't be very gentlemanly of me if I let her get caught by Nova, would it?"

In a single arrhythmic heartbeat, Eren closed in on Lonan, sword held high. He swung.

With one arm, Lonan lifted Effie and blocked the blow.

He bit down on the butt of his cigarette and grabbed the sword's hilt with both hands. It took very little muscle to overwhelm Eren, forcing him back.

"It's quite embarrassing how incompetent you *Dragon Pirates* are when it comes to listening to orders," Lonan said. Deftly, he swung his sword in a crisscross, slicing an *X* across Eren's chest.

Well. It would have sliced across Eren's chest had he not dived out of the way and pressed the tip of his sword to the small of Lonan's unprotected back.

A slow, lazy grin pulled at his lips, sugar smoke seeping from between his teeth.

"I was given orders," Eren murmured. "And those orders were to kill Nova's enemies."

"How noble."

The tip of the sword punctured his back, not deep enough to wound but just enough to draw sticky, hot blood. It would be tricky to get out of the situation without getting skewered, but he had no choice.

"See, I was *also* given orders." He pulled the cigarette from his teeth and dropped it on the ground, crushing it out with the toe of his boot. "Two orders, to be exact; kill Nova and stay alive."

"Who gave you those orders?" Eren pressed the sword harder. One misstep and he'd become a Lonan Kebab.

"Well, he's not *technically* my captain. I'm just manning the helm of his ship, you know?"

His heart fluttered. Not from excitement, though he felt that pumping through his veins. He might have considered himself to be a swordsman third (helmsman first, desirable second), but he'd been *itching* for a proper fight, especially after the skirmish in the forest.

He rubbed his thumb over the pommel of Effie his sword. "But I suppose I'm sort of obligated to follow his orders right now. He's not the kind of guy you'd want to be on the bad side of."

Brace, he told himself. *This will hurt like a sarding wench, but you've had worse.*

Throwing Effie as far as he could, Lonan tucked and rolled. Eren's sword sliced through his back. He grabbed his sword and sprung to his feet, standing opposite Eren once more.

Grinning, he said, "You know Nox Solveig? Yeah, those were *his* orders."

If Isra had known they'd be getting into a fight after nearly dying – after still being close to death, their wounds still raw and bloody – they would have simply laid down and accepted the fate they'd been edging for decades now.

It wasn't too late to do just that. In fact, the temptation to just sit on the ground and let Brit slice their head off their shoulders was almost too much to ignore. Maybe then their headache would finally go away.

Despite the exhaustion and lack of a will to fight, something inside them screamed at them to keep going. It was probably old man Ginkgo's spirit scolding them. *Ugh.*

Without a weapon, they relied on the scalpels jutting from the tips of their fingers, each swipe catlike and petty.

Brit had been beneath them – *far* beneath them. Even as just a doctor, Nova had placed Isra high on the pecking order. Maybe it was because of their ability. Maybe it was because they were dangerous – the only person alive immune to the Alkenio Plague.

Whatever the reason, the roles were reversed now, with Brit holding the position of an officer and Isra being the mutinous traitor.

Brit slashed her sword. All Isra could do was jump back and gasp for air, desperate to fill their aching lungs. Their puny, pathetic scalpels wouldn't do a damn thing against a sword.

If they could just disarm Brit.

It would be easiest to dislocate the socket, the unhelpful doctor in the back of their mind piped up. *Then, with little bone in the way, you could slice between her humerus and scapula, effectively disarming her.*

Blood dripped on their polished shoes. The smell of iron thickened in their sinuses. A bloody nose. Overexertion, their injuries, using their power too much... There were at least a dozen explanations for it, but none were as important as surviving right now.

"You know," Brit said, angling her blade so the light from Mene and Sin reflected off the steel, "I never liked you."

They didn't even pretend to look hurt. Whether people liked them or not was so far down on the list of Isra's concerns that it hardly even counted.

She raised her sword, chopping through the air in a blow meant to bisect Isra vertically. There was nowhere to go. They weren't athletic in the slightest.

Clash!

The pain of being fileted didn't come. Isra took a tiny step back, trying (and failing) to ignore the pounding of their heart against their ribs.

Brit's sword hung suspended in the air, mere inches from where Isra's skull had just been, held up only by another blade.

Thol.

"How many times do I need to save your life?" he asked, grinning. The smile didn't reach his eyes. Pain did, though. All it took was a quick glance at his fist to see that his knuckles were broken. Shattered.

"Don't make a habit," Isra grumbled.

"So they *do* talk!" exclaimed Brit through gritted teeth.

They ignored her. "Hold her off."

"Make it quick," Thol panted. "This hurts like a wench."

Quick was something Isra could do. With Thol holding Brit's blade out of reach, Isra acted.

The quickest, surest way to kill someone would be to damage their brain or their heart. Damage to *any* vital organs – lungs, kidneys, intestines – would almost always kill a person, but the death would be slower, unless they were cut clean in half. If they sliced into her innards, she would almost certainly go septic, but that would be slow. Agonizing, yes, but dreadfully slow, and Isra didn't want slow.

They wanted immediate.

For that, a slash to the throat would do the trick. Any major arteries, really. The carotids would be the easiest, but so would the subclavian or femoral arteries. Their scalpels wouldn't be able to fully slit Brit's throat, but they were sharp enough to slice through her jugulars. Her arms and legs were protected with loose clothing; fabric would only get in the way. They didn't have time to saw through her trousers to cut deep enough to sever her femoral arteries.

They had to go for the throat.

On average, it took two to five minutes for a human to bleed out from an arterial wound. Medical attention needed to happen in the first minute for the injured to have a chance of survival. Isra needed to use their ability in the second before the heart stopped.

They were the only doctor around for miles – the only one who had a chance at saving someone from a mortal wound.

And so, they charged, clawed hands glinting in the moonlight before they swiped, tigerlike, and blood sprayed in a crimson gush.

You are not going to sarding die now after you survived being shot in the damn lung, Fynch told himself. Even if he wasn't back to his prime physically, he was used enough to operating under less-than-ideal conditions. On the brink of starvation. So dehydrated he couldn't see straight. Exhausted from staying awake more than twenty-four hours on end.

Vaguely aware of the fights happening around him, he raised his hands in a slow surrender.

"Drop the gun," Sato said coldly. He ran his finger sensually over the trigger of his own revolver, mocking.

"That's not fair," whined Fynch. "I worked so hard to steal this one."

Sato's sinister smile didn't reach his eyes. His bared teeth were canine, wolfish, wicked. "Not a suggestion, kid. Drop. The. Gun."

"What kind of fight is this, huh? I ain't got a weapon. That's hardly fair." His mind raced, trying to form a plan. What was he even thinking?! He *never* made plans. Impulsive was practically his middle name.

Impulsivity would have to get him out of this...

Slowly, he set his gun on the ground, careful not to scratch its precious surface.

"That's the problem," said Sato. He extended one leg and kicked Fynch's revolver out of reach. Fynch watched, stupefied, as Sato retracted his leg.

He looks like a frog...

Oblivious to Fynch's thoughts, Sato continued: "You're thinking of this as a fight when, really, it's an execution."

Sato's fingers twitched. *He's about to pull the trigger!*

And just like that, Fynch scraped together a plan so perfectly impulsive and foolish it had no choice but to work.

In the breath it took for Sato to squeeze the trigger, Fynch kicked his leg up. His toe collided with Sato's wrist, jerking the revolver a hair too high, the bullet whizzing over the top of Fynch's head. Fynch jumped to his feet.

When Sato fired again, Fynch was already gone, diving after his pistol and cranking the safety back. He fired once, then ran for the statue and fired again.

Bone cracked, blood erupted, none of it was his.

Sato cried out in pain Fynch knew all too well as the bullets hit exactly where Fynch wanted. Without his legs, Sato wouldn't be able to run after Fynch. He was bound to the statue, both shins gushing blood from two perfectly equal shots.

He raised his gun, hands trembling, and aimed at Fynch's forehead. Fynch did the same, his own grip unwavering.

"You're a sarding good shot," hissed Sato. "It's a shame I have to kill you."

"You're a good target," snapped Fynch. "It's a shame you have to die."

Bang!

Bang!

Two shots rang out. For a heartbeat, nothing happened. Fynch held his breath, biting deep into his tongue. His life flashed before his eyes in a rapid reel.

His family – his mother and father, his siblings Sparrow and Starling and Robin, the twins Dove and Wren. Learning that his father died. Meeting Czardas and being arrested over and over. Row joining the navy, Fynch trying to join but being turned away. Getting arrested for armed robbery and his mother dying two years later. Joining Solveig's crew.

He felt the pain a second later, agonizingly hot like he'd been dipped into lava, like he'd been set on fire. Blood trickled down his throat, pooling in the dip of his collarbone.

"Ha," chuckled Sato.

And he, with a hole in his chest, right where his heart was, fell over. Dead.

Fynch reached up and touched the shell of his ear. Blood slicked his fingers. The bullet had barely grazed him. An inch to the left, and he'd be dead, too.

But he was the best damn sharpshooter in the world. His shot never missed, and he aimed to kill.

With each swooping arc of fire, Leo's eyelids grew heavier, his arms leaden. Exhaustion manifested as a throbbing pulse behind his eyes.

You can sleep when you're dead.

Cynthia thrust her sword. Leo watched in amazed horror as her arm turned to smoke, following the motion of the blade to further it along.

Heart in his throat, Leo sparked a fire between his hands and swiped it through the smoke.

A party trick. One he'd learned as a kid and used at every opportunity. Blow a candle out and, while the smoke is still curling from the burnt wick, spark an ember. The smoke would catch and light the wick once more.

Something similar happened now. Cynthia's arm erupted in flames, the fire eating away at the smoke until there was nothing left. Her sword clattered to the ground, drowned out by the sound of her blood-curdling scream.

Aha!

Blood spurted from the stump of her arm. Her hand, also spewing blood, was still attached to the sword.

That's her weakness. The smoke is *her body.*

It wouldn't be long before Leo passed out from exhaustion. He had to act fast.

He took a step closer, flames sparking across his fingertips. *Wait until she turns to smoke again,* he thought, hardly catching himself as he stumbled over the flat ground.

Tamping down his tiredness, he let out a cry and ran toward Cynthia.

She reached for her sword, remembering too late that it lay abandoned, her hand still attached to it, just out of reach. Leo got close enough to see the panic in her eyes.

Leo balled his hand into a fist and swung it, aiming for her middle. And Cynthia, in her moment of panic, shifted to smoke to avoid the blow.

Which was *exactly* what Leo needed.

Putting every last bit of his strength into the blow, his fist erupted in flames. Fire caught smoke, and Cynthia became a pyre, smoldering from the inside out.

She *screamed*. The stink of burning flesh and hair clogged the air. She writhed, desperate to get the fire out of her, but it was eating her from the inside, charring her innards and turning her bones to charcoal. She crumpled to the ground, spasming in a burning death throe.

Leo collapsed, too, his knees striking the ground hard enough to bruise. "Lonan..." he croaked. Right... Lonan wasn't there. He was all alone.

His head hit the cobblestone with a *thunk* but he was already unconscious, trapped in a deep, dreamless sleep.

Goliath's fist rushed toward Natha's skull. She knew, without any doubt, that a single punch would splatter her brains against the wall.

She rather liked her brains inside her head.

Swinging her leg out, she struck Goliath's calf with her inner foot. The moment she struck true, she swung her other leg up, using the inertia to flip backward and land just out of reach. She crouched low, panting hard. Sweat splattered on the ground, slicking every inch of exposed skin on her face and neck.

"That all you got?" she taunted, wiping her upper lip with the back of her hand. Too late did she remember the rouge she'd put on that morning. Oh, well. The red smear would be sweated off soon enough.

Goliath roared.

This is going to sarding suck.

He charged again. This time, Natha held her ground, body pressed low to the floor. It shook with each thundering step Goliath took, yet she didn't move.

Not until he was mere inches from her.

She struck like a beast then, foot darting out and *up*, meeting its fleshy mark right between Goliath's massive legs.

Funny, she smirked, how men always think they're superior when it's *women* who don't have any physical weaknesses.

The color drained from Goliath's face. Natha slid between his legs and grabbed his hair, using it as rope to hoist herself up. She straddled his shoulders, thighs burning as they *squeezed*. Occupied with his precious jewels, Natha cranked his head to the side, slamming it through the wall.

Again.

And again.

And again.

Blood sprayed from his shattered nose, his screams of pain drowned out by the splintering of wood.

She let go of his hair for a moment, only to grab it again at a different angle. She yanked his head back again.

Only this time, she jumped to the ground, yanking his head with her.

When her feet touched the ground, she let go. Like a spring, his head snapped forward, crashing through the wall once more. She struck fast again, pummeling no less than a dozen punches to his kidneys before spinning, kicking him in the throat.

Goliath stumbled.

Natha kicked again, foot landing square in his chest. She kicked again. Again. *Again.*

Goliath's eyes had glazed over, yet he still stood.

She bounced on the balls of her feet. Then she charged, head down like a bull. The top of her skull hit Goliath's gelatinous gut.

And finally, he fell.

Crunch!

Landing *right* atop the shattered teacup.

Blood slicked his face, his nose torn to shreds, and splinters of wood sticking to his cheeks. His flesh was more purple than not, bruises swelling enough he looked twice his massive size.

She popped her knuckles. When Goliath didn't even flinch at the sound, she smirked, her smeared rouge making her lips a sinister slash.

Then, she turned and walked out of the destroyed wall, searching for the stairs that would take her to Solveig.

To Ryuu Nova.

The pounding in her chest didn't go away, not as she found a staircase and took it two steps at a time. Not as she made it to the next floor – the floor Lonan was supposed to clear. The distant clashing of swords was proof enough that he'd found a fight.

Natha would not be assisting him any time soon.

Instead, she shifted to the balls of her feet, tiptoeing close to the wall as she searched for another staircase. It didn't take her long to find one. She made it halfway up before collapsing, the adrenaline finally wearing off and leaving pain and exhaustion in its wake.

She lowered her head to her hands, pressing the heels of her palms against her temples to soothe the pounding headache building there. She itched for a glass of wine or a cup of poppyseed tea, anything to coax her down from the adrenaline high. Instead, she plummeted right to rock bottom. Alone, as always. She wanted Solveig, with his determination to protect her. She wanted Fynch, with his total adoration. She wanted Czardas, with his calming presence. She wanted Illie, with her storytelling abilities. She wanted Thol, with his brotherly affection. She wanted Ves, with...

She just wanted *all* of Ves. Ves wouldn't be upset right now. Ves wouldn't be shaking, blinking back tears and a throbbing headache. Ves wouldn't be aching all over from a fight that hardly lasted three minutes.

Natha sat up and scrubbed her eyes with the back of her arm. She yanked her hair into a tight braid and stood.

If she didn't get her act together, there would be no Solveig or Fynch or Czardas, no Illie or Thol or Ves to return to.

21

SOLVEIG PRESSED HIS HAND against the wound, his whole arm trembling with adrenaline, with pain, with the horrific realization that he was closer to death now than he had been when he'd kneeled on the scaffold with Jonyth Commodore's sword above his neck. Through the flashes of his life – through the panic clogged with *Anwir Helios's face* – he desperately clawed for a memory of his anatomy. Had Prim's sword sliced any vital organs? Would he go septic because the damn blade nicked one of his intestines? She'd skewered him straight through, but...

But he was Nox sarding Solveig. He wasn't going to let some nobody kill him.

That honor was reserved for someone *worthy*.

Gritting his teeth against the spots dancing in his vision, Solveig forced himself to his feet. Blood seeped through the cracks of his fingers, splattering on the floor. If Prim could manipulate metal, so sarding be it. Every ability had a weakness; he just had to find hers.

"Why won't you just keel over already?" drawled Prim. She slid off one of her rings, morphing it into a shiny dagger that would make Ves drool.

"My mother might have been a bitch," he cursed, "but I'm not."

It's very unlikely that you'll bleed out in the time it takes to end this fight, a voice that sounded too much like Captain Hardy's piped up in the back of his mind.

So sarding finish it already.

The best thing to do would be to remove all the metal from Prim's range, but that was also the hardest.

Solveig was a *pirate;* he didn't like taking the hard route. He liked taking the easiest, cheapest, most idiotic route.

So, he would simply have to overpower her.

The dagger in Prim's hand elongated into a rapier. In one fluid motion, Solveig grabbed his discarded cutlass and charged, cleaving his sword down as she sliced hers up. Metal clashed, but not for long.

Solveig twisted his wrist, pulling his sword away from hers only to swing again. She parried his thrust, but he struck again. Again. Again again again again *again.*

Sweat glistened on Prim's forehead. Her rapier became a cutlass, and when he blocked that, it became a broadsword.

Her rings were gone, the metal gone to making a sword big enough to keep up with Solveig's rapid attacks.

His muscles screamed in burning agony. The stab wound through his torso wept blood with each rapid pump of his heart. His hair fell over his eyes in sweaty clumps, but he didn't slow.

Again. Again. *Again.*

Two of her necklaces slithered away to make her broadsword a pair of curved blades.

Solveig jumped backward, nearly slipping on his own blood. He swung his sword out, slicing through a silk screen. Ignoring the sharp throb in his abdomen, he dove through the slit.

A dozen knives flew after him. Putting his pain behind him, he slashed at the knives, throwing them off course.

"You are so much worse than the stories say," growled Prim as she ducked through the slit.

Solveig slashed his sword, shattering a lamp and throwing the room into darkness.

"Stories?" He backed up, blindly feeling around for the door he'd glimpsed earlier. "What in Poet's name are the stories saying about me? That I'm the most handsome pirate to sail the four seas? That I'm a better swordsman than Jonyth Commodore could ever hope to be?"

His fingers found the slot.

"They say you're a no-good scoundrel whose glory is about to run out," she snapped. "That you're a coward."

"That hurts," he said. "I mean, I *am* a no-good scoundrel, but I'm going to milk my glory for as long as I live and then some. And I'm anything *but* a coward."

And then, like a coward, he flung the door open and escaped into the hallway.

Hand clutching his wound, he ran. Thunder filled his ears; whether it was from his footsteps or his heart, he couldn't tell. Blood, sticky and hot, slicked his hand. He reached out and smeared it against the wall before turning the corner.

Thunk, thunk, thunk!

Three of Prim's knives embedded in the wall where his head had only just been.

He stopped, turning around to face her. She had a single necklace left, her blade returned to a cutlass.

"Come on, then," he said, brow cocked and hand sliding away from his wound. "Are you going to just stand there, or are you going to fight me?"

Time seemed to slow as he channeled his adrenaline into the fight. He threw his cutlass as hard as he could, watching for a split second as it sailed past Prim's head to clatter on the floor. He struck with his fists instead, burying his knuckles into Prim's unguarded stomach.

It was all he needed. That split moment of distraction paid off. Prim's eyes went wide, and she stumbled back, coughing up spittle. Her grip on her sword loosened enough for Solveig to swing a foot up and kick it out of her hand. Before it could hit the ground, he grabbed the hilt and pointed it at her throat.

"Sur –" he started, then shook his head. "You know what? No. I'm done offering mercy."

And he ran the sword straight through her throat before she could even think of manipulating the metal in her favor.

Blood sprayed across his face when he ripped the blade free. Without her keeping its form, it crumbled back into scattered pieces of jewelry. He grabbed a handful, shoving it into his pocket, and went after his discarded sword.

He tore a strip of silk from the tattered screens and wound it around his torso tightly, trying to stop the bleeding. He could bleed out *after* he'd pummeled Nova into the ground.

Sword at his hip and pockets full of stolen jewelry, Solveig stepped over the puddles of blood and made his way up the stairs, dragging his bloody hand along the wall as he went.

There was no one on the fourth floor, nor the fifth. *Strange...* The unsettling emptiness of it all rubbed him wrong. Why would there be one person on the third floor, but the next two were empty? Where was Nova hiding during all of this?

As Solveig rounded the corner to head up the final flight of stairs to the sixth floor, he paused.

Footsteps...

His hand slid around the hilt of his sword as he slowly spun around.

"Poet!" cried Natha, hand over her heart. "You nearly scared me to death!"

At once, his shoulders slumped, and he let out the taut breath he'd been holding. Despite her disheveled hair and bruised face, she looked unharmed. Still, he couldn't help but notice the limp she walked with.

"I'm flattered you'd even compare me to Poet when we all know nothing divine runs through my veins," he said. "Did you find anything?"

"Only the biggest man I've ever seen in my life," she grumbled, limping over to him. Her crimson gaze flicked to his torso – to the blood-seeped silk bandage. "I think I killed him."

"I *know* I killed someone," he said lightly. "She got me good, though."

"Solveig..." Natha started.

He held up a hand. "Not sure how long I'll last, but I refuse to die before Nova. Let's find him before I bleed out. Have you seen Lonan?"

She cringed so hard Solveig had to laugh. She said, "Ew. No. He can suffer wherever he is. Hopefully he got lost."

"You hate him that much? I was thinking of asking him to join the crew." He held onto the wall for support as he started up the stairs. Each step sent a jolt of fresh pain from the hole in his gut to every inch of his body.

Natha put a hand on his shoulder, steadying him. "I don't *hate* him. He's just a gross flirt. I'm done with men." She dismissed the topic with a wave of her other hand. "What about *you*, hm? What's going on with you and the prince?"

Solveig's toe hit the next step so hard he wished he'd just keel over and die already. Natha's grip on his shoulder tightened. Out of the corner of his eye, he saw her lips curl into a smirk.

Anwir Helios. The sarding bane of Solveig's existence. The prince who pulled him to safety when he faced the scaffold; the prince who handed him an ancient map and half a billion lune with the orders of tracking down a god scrubbed from history.

Solveig hated the man. Hated the entire Helios line for damning him from the start.

"There's *nothing* going on with us," he growled. "I'm going to kill him when we return to Aramore."

"No need to get defensive. Just curious. I've never met anyone who addresses anyone from that bloodline so casually." Her pale brow knit together. "Are you sure this is a good idea? You can hardly hold yourself up."

Sweat dripped from his brow. He clutched his stomach, pretending the wetness seeping through his silk bandage was anything but blood.

"Nova put my crew in danger," he gritted. "He picked a fight with me when he trapped my people here. For that, I'm going to kill him."

She offered a small smile, squeezing his shoulder as she said, "I'll make you whatever you want to eat after this. You should think about finding a doctor instead of recruiting that slimy rat Lonan."

"If all goes to plan," he said, breathless by the time he reached the top of the stairs, "Thol will have found me one."

Wind tore through Illie's hair, ripping it free of its braid. It slithered around her legs, caressing her thighs like an ice-cold lover.

Beneath her makeshift gloves, her palms and fingers burned, rigid and frigid and in the throes of frostbite.

Despite being thrown into walls hard enough to shatter the foundation, despite being flung against the cobblestone with enough force to rattle the teeth from her skull, Anne did not relent.

And Illie was running out of stamina. She *knew* if she peeled off her gloves, her fingers would be ice-white and blister-thick. She knew if she kept this up, the second-degree frostbite would turn black, and she'd need the phalanges amputated. Her days of holding a pencil and charting the world would be over.

Yet she persisted.

Because it was this or death, and there was no coming back from death. Her soul would be thrust into another body when she was reborn, her memories scrubbed clean. And even though she swore an oath to find Nox Solveig again and again and again in every life, she'd have to wait until she was sarding old enough to run off on her own. She couldn't afford that. Not now, when she was *so close* to reaching all her dreams.

To finding the lost moon.

A scream ripped from her throat, raw and guttural, as she grabbed the saucy wind and split it, throwing twin whips toward Anne.

Anne ducked, slipping across the blood-slick cobblestone to narrowly avoid the attack.

No!

Poet, help me! her mind screamed. *Don't let me die weak!*

When she grabbed the wind again, she was thrust back to the fight at Bowhead Rock. The same surge of adrenaline that accosted her then – the sudden strength to nearly behead the captain of the Redcoat Pirates – accosted her now.

In her hands, the wind became *solid.*

The length of it became ice, an invisible, semi-corporeal blade of solidified *cold.*

She'd dealt with tiny breezes, with massive gales. She'd grappled slippery ropes of wind, snakelike coils of it, but *never* had it done something like...like *that.*

It had always been a whip, never a sword.

Hold, she begged the wind-sword. As she swung it with all her might. As she launched an attack no one could see and only she could feel. As the frostbite-cold of a divine-forged sword sliced through flesh and bone like butter.

As she skewered Anne with a blade of wind.

The moment the sword exited Anne's back, the wind turned slippery again, slithering away like a serpent.

She fell to her knees, cradling her hands to her chest. *You're not hot,* she desperately reminded herself, even though beneath her gloves her palms burned like she'd dipped them in boiling water. *You're not burning. It's frostbite.*

Tears slid down her cheeks, gluing her wayward hair to her face.

Get up, her mind weakly instructed. *It's not over yet. You still need to find Sol. You can't rest until Nova is dead.*

Still clutching her hands to her chest, Illie slowly stood like a newborn fawn. She could rest when Nova was dead and not a sarding minute sooner.

Knives were perfect weapons until it came to stabbing someone in the heart. Then they were just a *bit* too small. Not that Ves would use anything other than her beloved daggers. Even when she was up against someone with telekinesis.

Someone, unfortunately, more powerful than her.

As Ves swung her knife towards that smudge of red beating in time with Noor's heart, a sarding *brick* soared through the air and knocked her knife out of her grip. Before it could hit the ground, Noor grabbed it with her mind, turning Ves's own sarding weapon against her.

Viper fast, she kicked her leg up and knocked the blade off its trajectory. Metal bit into the muscled flesh of her shin, just deep enough to draw a nick of blood.

She ground her teeth together and slipped another knife free. The spool of red burned brighter. All she needed to do was sink her sarding knife into it.

"Ah!" she screamed, barely closing her eye in time to protect it from the damn knife that soared across her face, slicing open her cheekbone. "You damn *wench!*"

Noor smirked. "That's rude."

Blood trickled down Ves's cheek. The wound stung, but that was good. That meant it was shallow – that it wouldn't scar and ruin her perfect face. Her tongue darted out, catching a bead of blood before it could fall.

"You know why they call me the Witch of the Sea and not the Viper of the Sea?" She ran her tongue along the length of her blade.

She flicked her wrist, throwing her knife perfectly, aimed for the spool of red that was Noor's heart. It stopped a hairsbreadth away from its target, suspended in telekinetic air.

In one motion, she had another knife free, airborne for a split second before she buried it in Noor's chest. The red light erupted into embers, crackling and sizzling.

"Because I may be fast," she hissed, lips brushing against Noor's temple, "But my teeth aren't what I use to kill."

She twisted the knife; the fire spread, consuming every last drop of golden soul until there was nothing left, the light extinguished. Dead.

Huffing, she ripped her blade free and sheathed it. Noor's body didn't even have the chance to hit the ground before Ves started gathering up her discarded daggers, returning them to the various sheaths across her body.

Hands on her hips, she looked around, making sure the souls of the people who mattered still burned bright. Czardas was locked in a swordfight, but he was still alive. Leo...

He lay on the ground, surrounded by smoke and the acrid stink of burning flesh and hair.

Sard it.

She ran over to him, crashing to the ground and checking his pulse. Still there.

"Goggles," she hissed, shaking his shoulders. "Hey. Hey! Goggles! What the hell are you doing? Leo, wake the sard up."

He didn't so much as stir. His soul still glowed bright, alive. He was just...asleep.

She smacked the back of her hand across his cheek. "Dreamer's tits, Goggles, *wake up!*"

But he didn't. He *didn't.* And all Ves could see was Fynch's bloodied body up in the crow's nest, so weak and fragile in her arms, soul on the brink of flickering out. All she could see was Fynch stretched out in bed, so pale, so cold, so close to death.

"Leo!" she cried, panic warbling her voice. Her breaths flitted from her parted lips rapidly. Pins pricked her lips.

Deep breaths, Ves. His soul is still there. He's alive.

She inhaled deeply through her nose, and when she exhaled, she slapped him again. When he still didn't wake up, she stood, picking him up easily. His body hung limp in her arms, heavy and gangly but manageable all the same.

Czardas's sword clashed against his enemy's. Ves narrowed her eyes. *There.* That spool of red, a slim smile along the pirate's throat.

"Strings!" she called. "Aim for the neck!"

Time became an impossible vortex, freezing adrenaline to ice. Ves's vision switched, souls giving way to corporeal bodies swung in an attack neither could evade.

Czardas's enemy's sword swiped up; its range was enough to disembowel, to rip Czardas apart like a rag doll and spill his guts all over the cobblestone. His own rapier parried to the left in a horizontal arc that would slit the pirate's throat apart *if* he could somehow dodge the fatal pendulum swinging toward him.

Her entire body went tense, encased with pure fear. First Fynch and now Czardas. How many people had to die for Solveig to get what he wanted?!

Bang!

The single gunshot sucked the vortex away, leaving time impossibly fast.

The pirate's sword flew from his grip in the same breath Czardas's rapier arced across his throat in a *beautiful* spray of crimson lifeblood. The pirate's head fell back, barely hanging on to his body by nothing more than his spinal cord.

Dead.

Blood sprayed Isra's face in thick, hot arterial gushes. It flecked their cheeks, slipped between their lips, filled their nose until they could only smell iron, soaked their white coat until it was heavy and crimson.

Their scalpels tore through flesh, through cartilage, through muscle and blood vessels until Brit's throat looked more like raw, ground meat than anything else.

And still, they attacked, carving the sharp blades up and across her jaw, through her cheeks until her lips tore to make an ear-to-ear smile. They sliced through her nose, across her eyes, gouging so deep her *skull* could be seen beneath the paper-shredded skin of her face.

"Isra!" They heard someone shout.

Die, was all they thought. *Die, die, die, die, die! You deserve this! For chaining me like a dog. For underestimating me. For annihilating the one thing I cared about in this world by turning it into a sarding tool for you to use!*

"Isra, that's enough!"

A hand wrapped around their wrist. Isra spun, needle-claws bared and ready to stab. It wasn't until they saw that the hand belonged to *Thol* that they stopped. Faltered. Paused.

And looked at the desecrated body beneath them.

They were a *doctor.* They had sworn an oath to save the lives of their patients, not...not mutilate them beyond recognition.

"What..." they whispered.

"You took out your enemy," Thol said, releasing Isra's wrist. They didn't miss the flinch that flitted across his face nor the swollen knuckles he tried to hide at his side. "You did good. We need to go now, though, before they send reinforcements."

Isra wiped their face with their sleeve, smearing blood across their sharp cheek. They stood, watching hypnotized as drops of scarlet dripped from their scalpel claws like rain.

Old man Ginkgo flashed in their mind then. Their mentor. Their stand-in father when their blood father perished. Would he be disappointed in Isra or proud?

Somehow, they knew it would not be the latter.

Flicking their wrist to rid their blades of blood, Isra shrugged away from Thol.

"Go where," they grumbled.

"*You* know Nova," Thol pointed out. Isra couldn't help but stare at his very broken knuckles. "Where would he be?"

There was only one place Nova would be if he wasn't on his beloved ship, the *Dragon King.*

Servedin was not ruled by a king. Annexed by the Aralyth Empire, its only true monarch was Emperor Castros Helios. And yet, the moment Nova arrived from Elluf, he made Servedin *his.*

The massive palace built on the edge of Corsa was proof enough of that.

"Use your knuckles again, and I'll cut your hand off," they said flatly. "Come on."

22

Czardas barely watched the blood drip from his sword as he spun around. Never in his life had he been happier to hear a gunshot.

There had been a part of him that came to terms with the fact that Fynch was most likely going to die. That Fynch finally went somewhere Czardas couldn't follow. That for the first time in thirteen years, he would be alone, his best friend forever gone from his side.

And even now, as he squinted through the moonlight to make out the very much alive form of Fynch Largos, he couldn't believe it.

"F," he whispered.

That was all he could get out before Fynch flung himself at Czardas, strangling him in a full-body hug.

Czardas dropped his sword, hugging back just as fiercely. He breathed in Fynch's sent – gunpowder and sweat – and murmured, "You're alive."

Fynch pulled away and grinned his chipped-tooth grin. "A single bullet isn't going to take me out. You know me, Czar. Either I go out in a blaze of glory, or I don't go out at all."

Before Czardas could scold him for being so reckless, an unfamiliar voice called out. "Stitches."

Frowning, Czardas looked over Fynch's shoulder to see three figures running into the pavilion. Thol. Illie. And...someone else.

"Flowers! Pinkie!" Ves cried, nearly dropping Leo.

Then she *did* put him down, marching over and grabbing Fynch from Czardas's side. She hugged him so tight Czardas worried she might accidentally almost kill him. Again.

"What are you doing here?" Thol demanded. "What happened to Leo? Where are the others?"

"We're here to save your sorry asses," Ves said, peeling herself away from a near-suffocated Fynch. She picked Leo up again. "What, did you think we were going to just *abandon* you here? Plus, your little note arrived too late. I don't know where the others went. We split up after burning down the jail. I think Goggles overexerted himself."

Czardas leaned close to Fynch and whispered, "Who's the tall person covered in blood?"

It was Illie who answered. "That's Isra. They're the doctor who saved Fynch. Supposedly, they know where Nova is."

Czardas's stomach flip-flopped at the name. *Nova.* It didn't matter how many times he heard it; Nova's name would invoke a sense of fear in him.

He'd struggled against Nova's underlings. How would he *ever* be able to stand his ground against the Dragon King himself?

No, he thought. He *didn't* have to stand his ground against Ryuu Nova. He just had to fight long enough and hard enough to give the rest of his crew an opening.

"Everyone, this is Israfel Eliad. They're a doctor," Thol interrupted Czardas's thoughts. He gestured to the blood-soaked doctor, who looked like he'd much rather be literally anywhere else than here. "Isra, this is...well, almost everyone. Ves is the tall one. Leo's in her arms. Czardas is the one Fynch is clinging to."

Isra didn't even bother lifting their hand to wave.

Czardas grabbed his rapier and returned it to the sheath at his hip. "Nova's hiding in that...palace, isn't he?" He nodded toward the massive building he'd seen on the deck of the *Dreamchaser.*

He had been born to wealthy parents, groomed to fit the position of duke from a very young age. He knew wealth. He knew power. And he knew that people who had both liked to flaunt them. Someone who called himself the *Dragon King* would surely claim a grand palace as his own. He'd hide up there while sending his grunts to do the dirty work. If he was manning his ship, he would have spotted the *Dreamchaser* before it careened on the hidden beach.

Nova was in the palace. That had to be where Solveig and the others were, too.

He reached out and ruffled Fynch's hair. "I missed you, F. Don't ever do anything stupid like that again."

"Cross my heart," he swore.

"You dragged me into this mess," Czardas said, pulling Fynch along with him as he followed the others. "That means you're not allowed to leave me alone here."

Lonan tucked one hand in his pocket as he lazily swiped Effie in a seamless arc across Eren's chest. Eren parried a second too late, already cut by the time his sword clashed with Lonan's.

"Is that *really* all you've got?" Lonan drawled as he stabbed Effie three times, striking Eren's arms and chest in rapid succession. "Y'know, I was expecting more...more...*oomph*. More grandeur from Nova's pirates, but I guess size really isn't everything. Not that *I'd* know anything about that."

Twisting his wrist, he feinted an upper blow, going low instead. Eren couldn't keep up with the speed. Locks of chopped off hair fluttered to the ground, sticking to the pools of splattered blood.

He feinted again, but instead of striking, he threw Effie across the room *again.* Before the sword could clatter against the floor, Lonan struck, kicking Eren in the gut before diving to grab his precious blade. Low to the ground, he swiped the sword.

It sliced clean through the tendons on the back of Eren's feet, the leather of his boots splitting with ease.

Eren screamed in agony, falling to his knees as he was no longer able to stand.

"You're a sarding monster," he hissed, eyes full of pain and fear as Lonan stalked close.

"Ouch. I don't usually get called that. People have been calling me a rat lately. Do I look like a rat to you?" His scarred lips pulled into a sadistic grin. "Maybe I should be taking offense to that."

Eren's chest heaved rapidly. Lonan knew that he knew he was going to die. It may have been his heart sputtering in an arrhythmia, or it may have been excitement. Either way, his chest fluttered as he leaned down and lined the tip of his sword up with the lump in Eren's throat.

"Who are you?" Eren whispered. "Solveig's swordsman?"

"Oh, no." His grin widened. "I don't work for Solveig. I'm just a helmsman. I actually work selling ships in Undyne. Well, among other things. I'm not a pirate, though. My goals just so happened to line up with those of a pirate."

He leaned further, lips brushing against Eren's ear. He whispered something then, four incomprehensible words that drained the color from Eren's face.

"You –" he started, but the rest of that sentence died with a wet gurgle.

Lonan twisted his sword and pulled it free, Eren's life still clinging to the blood-soaked metal.

He stood and reached into his pocket, pulling out his case of sugar cigarettes and sticking one between his teeth. Without Leo, he had to use a lighter to spark an ember. Sweet oxygen filled his lungs in an instant, dragging him away from the adrenaline high and sending him into a sputtering bout of breathlessness.

His heart sped up, tightening his ribs and sending an ache across his chest, red hot and corset-tight.

Sard it to hell.

He shoved Effie into its sheath and dropped the cigarette, stomping it out.

"Sard," he cursed aloud, clutching his chest as though he could dig his fingers into his ribs and squeeze the pain out of his heart.

Breathe, he thought, remembering what his doctor instructed him the last time his heart acted like this. The scar splitting his upper lip burned with the memory of slicing it open on coral.

Of the silver flash and warm lips and a woman's torso stuck to the tail of a fish.

Gripping the wall with his free hand, he focused instead on his breaths.

Inhale. It's just an arrhythmia. It will go away on its own.

Exhale. Lady Lightbringer's *tits,* it hurt.

Inhale. Don't vomit. Vomiting will make it worse. His throat bobbed incessantly as he swallowed again and again and again, his mouth a pool of saliva.

Exhale. At least he would just collapse on the floor here and not risk drowning like last time.

He closed his eyes and croaked, "Leo…"

But Leo wasn't there to save him.

And there was no mermaid to coax him from the brink of a heart attack again.

Feigning strength, he grappled at the wall, the solidness of it stabilizing him long enough to stumble towards the stairs

Each step sent a dull throb of pain from Solveig's side to the rest of his body. He hadn't bled out yet; the wound couldn't be fatal. Painful, yes, but not enough to kill him.

He'd survived twenty-five years – two-and-a-half decades of piracy, of being chased down by Jonyth Commodore and the navy, of surviving on his own after his mother all but abandoned him. He was Captain Nox Solveig, cloaked in green. A tiny stab wound wouldn't take him out.

At least, it *couldn't.*

Halfway up the stairs, Natha stopped him, grabbing his arm and tugging him to a halt.

"I wish I didn't burn my shirt in that cell," she grumbled, patting herself down. When it seemed like she couldn't find whatever it was she was looking for, she groaned frustratedly.

"Don't you dare think of using my coat as a bandage," he said quickly when she eyed the hem of it.

"I wasn't," she said. "Is your shirt sentimental, too?"

When he shook his head, she grabbed it and yanked, ripping a swath off.

Forcing him to stand still, Natha got to work peeling the silk bandage off and rewrapping the shirt around his torso instead. "Gut wounds bleed a lot," she absently commented. "Especially when organs are nicked. What? Those self-defense courses taught me more than just how to kick someone's ass. I've been wondering; why is your coat so...important?"

He was grateful for the pain, then, as the wince that flashed across his face hid the look of...of grief. Of sorrow that had built up inside him, thick and unmoving like grease. Surrounded by death, Solveig *should* be used to it by now.

He'd lost his brothers. His crew. Everyone he cared about. Even now, as he counted his breaths, he recounted their names. *Kesh, Trudeau, Zayn, Prokofiev, Gael, Vern, Scorpion...*

"It," he said, "belonged to someone important to me. It...it was a gift given to me when I left to start my own crew."

Captain Hardy.

He brushed his fingers against the worn brass buttons at his breast. They'd been shinier when the coat belonged to Captain Knight Hardy. The fabric had been greener, more vibrant.

Natha just nodded and tied off the makeshift bandage. Satisfied with her work, she offered Solveig her arm, granting him balance as they continued up the stairs.

"My parents gave me something like that, too," she said after a moment, her voice hushed now. "Sort of. When I went off to culinary academy, they gave me a pair of leather gloves to cover my arms."

Solveig glanced at her exposed arms. Tough, deep burn scars mottled the flesh from her fingertips to just beneath her elbows. He'd never asked about it – it wasn't his business to pry. It wasn't like he was without scars he was ashamed of – but... "What happened?"

"I lit myself on fire," she said casually. "It's a long story. One I'll tell *after* we get through this mess."

"As your captain, I think I deserve a bit more than *that.*"

"How long were you planning on keeping that map from us?"

"Fine, then."

Suddenly, from behind, footsteps pounded against the stairs. In a heartbeat, Solveig had his sword drawn.

But the cloying, saccharine-sweet stink of sugar smoke relaxed his shoulders, if only just a fraction.

Lonan swept Natha up, leaning in to press a kiss to her cheek. "My darling Miss Divyne," he purred. "Who hurt you? I'll make sure they end up in a shallow grave."

When Natha punched him in the jaw, Solveig flinched as if *he* got hit.

"Touch me again," she growled, "And I'll cut off your hands. I won't bother with anything else because I know nothing else is worthwhile."

Pride crackled in Solveig's chest, the embers of a bonfire preparing to roil.

That pride was quickly extinguished with ice-cold guilt.

Anwir Helios promised only *one* letter of amnesty. He had six crew members whose lives were just as important as his own – if not more so.

Until he demolished the Helios reign, his crew wouldn't be safe.

At the top of the stairs was a sliding door, another dragon painted on the bamboo. Solveig gripped his sword tightly.

"This is it," he whispered. All he needed to do was kill Nova. Then he could focus on his injury. Then he could find the rest of his crew. Then he would make sure everyone was safe.

He kicked the door down and, for the first time in his life, outside of the portraits in the newspapers, he saw Ryuu Nova.

He lounged on a chaise, red fur coat hanging loosely from his shoulders. His dark hair was gathered into a tail at the nape of his muscular neck, his serpentine eyes glinting gold in the light. His claws – talons – flashed dangerously sharp.

At his side, standing with weapons drawn, were two other pirates – a woman just as muscular as Ves with a pair of curved swords and a lanky man with scars on his cheeks, giving him a permanent grin. The woman had a *2* tattooed on her cheek, while the man had a *3*.

"Shin. Sora," Nova drawled. "Kill these intruders."

A muscle in Solveig's jaw jumped. "Natha. Lonan. Don't sarding die."

When instinct took over, an adrenaline-high of strength, and Solveig charged at Nova, he realized, too late, that he had messed up.

Nova's form rippled as he stood, crimson scales flecked across his cheeks, and in an instant, Solveig knew just why Nova was so untouchable.

And why, everywhere he went, he left behind imagery of dragons.

Nox Solveig was just a man. There was no way he could win a fight against a beast able to shift from human to *monster.*

Nova did not pull free the sword at his hip. He just flexed his fingers, talons shining, and Solveig stumbled to a messy halt.

"Draw your weapon," Solveig demanded.

Nova smirked. The hair on the back of Solveig's neck stood on end. Nova said, "Why waste my energy and my sword's sharpness against an insignificant worm such as yourself?"

Fury rippled across Solveig's face.

Nova continued: "Your bounty may be higher than mine, but that's because you escaped the gallows. Because you're young and full of ambition."

Solveig bared his teeth and his fury.

"You don't think of the big picture," Nova said, serpentine pupils narrowing to tiny slits, barely visible against his gold irises. "You only think of the *now.* You only claw your way to the top to find a temporary throne. Tell me, Nox Solveig, how many allies do you have? How many people will come to your aid when you're inevitably sent to the gallows again?"

Thol. Ves. Illie, Natha, Fynch, Czardas. Maybe Lonan and Leo. The people of Carilon.

Anwir Helios.

Anwir Helios.

Everyone else was dead. Gone. Leaving him behind, ridden with survivor's guilt and a desire for grandeur so massive it outweighed everything else.

"Fight me!" he screamed.

"And gain *what?*"

Solveig was lightning, a current so strong it devoured everything in its riptide wake. He was Ves, viper-quick. He was Thol, sharklike and vicious. He was everyone who came before and everyone who would remain after. When he struck, it was to kill. When he thrust his cutlass, its only purpose was to bury itself hilt-deep in the muscles of Nova's abdomen.

When Nova drew his sword and lazily brought it up to block, it was as if he was swatting away a pest.

Crrrrrk!

Dread pooled in Solveig's gut, weighing down to his feet.

His sword. Cracked. Fissured, a fault-line schism that ran down the middle of his cutlass like a vein of weakness.

And yet.

And yet Solveig thrust anyway.

And yet Solveig leaped into the air, gravity his ally as he brought the blade down.

And yet Solveig, the thrumming pain in his gut from being sarding stabbed, shoved his blade into Nova's chest, right beneath his collarbone, and the brief glory of knowing he won was quashed so fast it gave him whiplash.

Nova's form rippled, a mirrored lake disrupted, and suddenly, the room was too small. A flash of red, of gold, of teeth and claws.

Nova stretched like taffy. Scales consumed him, horns curled from his forehead like branches, whiskers drooped from his upper lip, curled back to snarl curved fangs. His body elongated, arms and legs lengthening and curving to fit the serpentine mass that was now Ryuu Nova.

With nowhere to go, he went up. Wood splintered, bits of roof raining down. Solveig threw his arm up, shielding his eyes from the detritus. With his other arm, he grabbed one of Nova's taloned toes, holding tight as the dragon slithered through the air, finding space on the roof of his destroyed palace.

"Fine," Nova said, his voice rumbling deep and filling Solveig's head. *"You want me to fight you, I will fight you."*

He opened his mouth, a blossom of light brewing in his throat. *Sard!*

Before the fireball exploded into the sky, Solveig dove to the side, rolling uncomfortably across roof tiles, the heat licking at his back.

Well, he thought in the heartbeat it took for him to regain his footing. *I guess this means no more rum for a month.*

23

ANOTHER WAVE OF ADRENALINE surged through Natha's veins, taking away her pain and replacing it with the foolish courage to swing her leg up in an arc, boot crunching against Sora's wrist and sending her sword flying.

Sweat dripped from her lashes and onto her cheeks. She sank low, thighs burning, and lunged. Shifting her weight to her upper body, she dropped to her hands, forearms and biceps screaming as they supported her weight, allowing her to kick both feet up, legs straight as they crashed into Sora's face.

The glory didn't last long.

She springboarded in a backflip, landing just in time to feel the bite of metal against flesh. Sora's remaining sword slit through her trousers and into her thigh, deep enough to hurt, deep enough to cause her to worry that it would end up being serious.

You can worry about the severity later, she scolded herself, shaking sweat from her face and hopping from foot to foot. It was hard to find a decent opening, especially when her opponent had a sharp weapon. If she got too close, she'd get cut. But Natha's strength was close-range melee. She just had to be faster than Sora's sword.

Just then, the ground rumbled. Natha stumbled back, eyes widening when she saw the red, glistening length of a sarding *dragon* shoot into the sky, bringing the roof crashing down.

Holy Dreamer, what is that?!

The flash of silver snagged the corner of her eye. She threw her elbows up, knocking the sword descending towards her off course.

Not before it sliced into the paper-thin skin of her forearms.

She cried out in pain. Her arms were forever more sensitive, all mottled scar tissue from when she'd accidentally set herself on fire. Her family hadn't been able to afford skin grafts, leaving the flesh bubbly and uneven, painfully tight, and more susceptible to agony.

Sora's smirk grew. She jabbed her blade toward Natha's eyes.

Swallowing the sunburst of pain, she swept her leg out. Her foot met Sora's shin, forcing her to stumble, to change the trajectory of her blow so it skimmed past Natha's cheek instead of gouging her eyeball.

Her heart beat a rapid tattoo, staccato-begging her to stop. She was running on nothing but adrenaline, and adrenaline was not a sustainable fuel. It would fade soon, and she was too exhausted to keep going. Her injuries kept piling up and up and up and would continue to build before she allowed herself to rest. Her vision swam, dragging in a headache that would hurt ten times worse once the adrenaline high wore away.

Her hands trembled as she balled her fingers into fists, pretending *PUNISHMENT* was scrawled across her knuckles.

Or, maybe more fittingly, *BITCH* and *WENCH.*

In the climax of her life, everything that had ever happened to her a muddled blur of nostalgic frenzy, she gathered up all that adrenaline and pumped her legs, running at Sora.

Crashing into her.

Wrapping her arms around her tight, no matter how hard she hit Natha with the butt of her sword, with the blade, with her hand.

Using Sora as a shield to shatter the window and fall six stories down to the solid earth with her.

The sky above lit up in a river of red, a firework so massive her eyes watered at the heat.

She wasn't scared of fire. Most people would be after the accident she had, but she wasn't. And even then, plummeting to her certain death with a flailing Sora screaming and clawing and bleeding all over her, a smile tugged at Natha's lips. It was dangerous. Wicked.

Beautiful.

She slid her elbow around Sora's throat, squeezing her bicep. Soon, Sora stopped flailing. Stopped moving but didn't stop bleeding. Dead. Unconscious. It didn't really matter anymore.

Because Natha hit the ground.

Maybe Leo (and his doctor) was right – Lonan needed to lay off the sugar cigarettes. And the alcohol. And the excessive salt. And whatever other horrible restrictions they *recommended* he abide by.

Nausea roiled in his gullet, his head spun, each pulse of his heart hurt more than the last, and as he swished Effie the sword through the air, crashing into Shin's blade with enough force to draw sparks, his arms and legs became cooked noodles, ready to collapse at any given moment.

He owed Solveig nothing, yet here he was, fighting for him like he was one of his pirates.

Gripping Effie with both hands, Lonan thrusted, only for Shin to parry the blow.

Many things had happened in the span of a single painful, ir-regular heartbeat: Natha and Sora crashed through the window, Nova became a serpentine dragon, and Solveig hitched a ride with the beast to the roof.

Leaving Lonan and Shin alone.

Teeth gritted, Lonan feinted left. With Shin momentarily dis-tracted, Lonan swung his leg out, hitting Shin in the side.

"I was given two very specific orders," he said as nonchalantly as he could, swooshing Effie into a downward slice. "Don't sail outside Undyne's borders, and don't die. Unfortunately, I already disobeyed one of those orders, so it would look *really* bad in front of the beautiful specimens in Solveig's crew if I disobeyed the other."

Even though Lonan was half convinced he couldn't die (he *did* technically die once, so now, clearly, he had to be immortal), the risk was still there. A risk he continued to take as Shin knocked Effie off course with a parry and thrust of his own, feinting right and jabbing left instead. Lonan only barely managed to jump out of the way, weakened heart protesting the entire time.

"You're good with a sword," Lonan said, wishing he had a sugar cigarette between his teeth. "Not good *enough,* but still good."

He threw Effie into the air.

Shin, of course, lowered his own sword and looked up in a precious moment of confused hesitation.

Lonan seized that moment. He struck his leg out, kicking Shin in the gut twice.

Ba-bu-dum.

He reached out for Effie, but when his heart beat painfully, reminding him that he was seconds from a heart attack, he recoiled, clutching his chest instead.

Shin recovered first, kicking the broadsword out of the way, leaving Lonan hurting and weaponless. In a single breath, his sword rested against Lonan's cheek.

"You're good with a sword," he drawled, copying Lonan's earlier words. He smirked, scarred cheeks making the expression ten times more unnerving.

Lonan dug the heel of his palm into his ribs, trying – failing – to soothe the pain of his heart.

"Not good enough, but still good," said Shin.

He flicked his wrist, sword slashing.

But Lonan moved first.

He collapsed to the ground, Shin's sword barely nicking his cheek, legs folding, and back hitting the floor.

His heart could hurt later. He didn't have the sarding time for a heart attack right now.

Grasping blindly at his sword, Lonan sprung back, hands supporting his weight as he planted both feet on Shin's chest and *kicked.*

Springing onto his feet, Lonan jabbed Effie, the blade sheathing itself in Shin's gut.

"Like I said," he growled, twisting the blade. Blood spurted, dribbled from Shin's mouth as he gaped helplessly, a fish out of water. He ripped the sword free in a geyser of more iron-thick blood. "You're not good enough. There's a reason you're the Dragon King's *third* and not the king himself."

"Did you read the newspaper this morning? They're finally executing the last great pirate."

It usually took a few days for the news to reach the tiny nameless village at the base of Mount Kiva in Elluf since the couriers in the capital, Arbyn, rarely prioritized making the journey, but with news as big as this, there could be no delay.

But Ryuu Nova wished there had been.

At sixteen, he was too old to live in an orphanage, and nobody in the village had any pity for him. His parents, as the rumors claimed, were pirates. Ones who were gunned down by the navy many years ago, leaving their only son behind. Too far inland, escaping to the sea to become a sailor was nearly impossible. But that didn't stop him from idolizing the big names.

Most of the top pirates had been killed years prior, leaving only one behind. The most wanted. Alexander Chronos.

Three years ago, Ryuu's divine ability manifested, though he kept it a secret. The other village kids tormented him enough as is for being without parents, for being the child of pirates. They didn't need to know that anything he imagined could become real.

Kneeling in the field, Ryuu dug his hands into the dirt, clawing a hole to drop a handful of seeds into. The other village kids his age sat in the grass, avoiding their duties in favor of poring over the newspaper. Alexander Chronos was to be executed that day, clear across the Emerald Sea in Aramore, Aralyth.

"Will you shut up and get back to work?" Ryuu snapped, glaring over his shoulder at the others.

One of the girls snickered. "Aw. Ryuu's upset that they're killing that dirty pirate."

His cheeks burned with embarrassment. "I am not!"

One of the boys smirked. "You are! You totally are! I'd show you the newspaper, but can you even read?"

He could. Just...not well. While Aralythian was the global standard for speaking and writing, Ryuu's parents prioritized the old language of Elluf at home. Ryuu had taught himself Aralythian, but he still struggled with reading it at times. It didn't help that education in the village only catered to kids up to ten since most of them were expected to either become farmers or parents.

Not Ryuu. He would rather die than stay in this village for the rest of his life. His parents saw the world. They brought him trinkets from the different continents – dried flowers from Merdyne, a bottle of white sand from Veridin, a little dragon figurine from Servedin Island... One day, he would sail the world, too.

He still had that little dragon figurine, tucked safely in his pocket. Of all the treasures, that was his favorite. Dragons bowed to no one. He wanted, more than almost anything, to be as fierce as one.

He tightened his fist, crushing the seeds inside. "I can read!" he snapped. Dropping the crushed seeds, he stood, snatching the newspaper.

The kids laughed at the joke that was Ryuu Nova. He ignored them the best he could as he skimmed the headline. Beneath the bold words was the wanted poster for Alexander Chronos, including his bounty. Two and a half billion lune, the highest bounty to ever be recorded. In his picture, Chronos was grinning. His dark hair was pulled back, a few pieces hanging over his face. Stubble lined his jaw, making him look both younger and ageless at the same time.

The paper crinkled under his grip. What did this mean for piracy? Would pirates continue to sail the seas in search of freedom with Chronos gone? Or was the fear of the navy's admiral, Wilhelm Edward Commodore, too much?

"Ryuu's gonna cry!" the girl sang. "Look, he's so upset!"

Without thinking, he crumpled the paper into a ball and imagined it was a solid rock. When he threw it, the girl didn't bother ducking. Why would she expect it to be anything but paper?

But when the rock cracked against her skull hard enough to lodge in the bone, forcing her to topple back with a spray of too much blood, the kids stopped laughing.

"You sarding monster!" one of them screamed, voice hardly audible over the girl's bloodcurdling cries.

Ryuu just stood there, unmoving.

Wanderer, he thought, eyes wide. What am I supposed to do now?

There was truly only one thing he could do, and that was flee.

Turning on his heel, he dashed over the uneven soil, going straight to the tiny hut he called his own. It would be only minutes before the village adults came looking for him; he had to move fast. Grabbing a single rucksack, he shoved everything that mattered inside. Then, slinging it over his shoulder, Ryuu Nova ran.

And not once did he look back.

When Thol – and later Captain Hardy – taught Solveig how to fight, they drilled one lesson into him: *don't be afraid to run away when you know you can't win.*

Solveig knew he could not win in a fight against a literal dragon, but if he ran, he would be damning everyone he cared about.

Nova rose higher into the sky, flashes of his red scales illuminated by the moonlight as he slithered through the air. In his talons was a sword – the same sword he'd been wearing earlier, only a hundred times bigger now. A single swipe from that would cut Solveig clean in half.

Swallowing hard, he took a tiny step back. The tiles beneath his feet slid, reminding him just how high up he was. If Nova didn't kill him first, gravity would.

"Not so eager to fight now, are you?" Nova growled in Solveig's head.

His stomach flopped helplessly. It was nothing short of a miracle that he hadn't thrown up all over the place yet.

Nova's sword rippled, reality melding as it welded itself to his reptilian arm, making his flesh razor sharp.

Fire bubbled in his throat, glowing beneath the scales.

Sard, sard, sard, sard, sard!

When Nova opened his jaws again, Solveig dove, though not for cover this time. Fire licked at his heels. He jumped, grabbing hold of the thick scales on Nova's underbelly. He'd have an easier time chipping away at solid basalt than he would trying to pierce Nova's scales with his toothpick cutlass.

Nova roared, body writhing as he tried to shake Solveig free.

But Solveig, stubborn as ever, clung tight. His nails bent under the strain, blood pooling where they peeled away from their beds. The lightning zaps of pain were nothing. Adrenaline numbed most of it, anyway, and the sound of Nova's roaring deafened the sticky crunching sound.

Tightening his core, Solveig climbed over Nova so he was straddling his back. He grabbed fistfuls of the billowing red fur running down Nova's spine like reins.

Nova let out another fiery roar, neck twisted back as he snapped his jaws at Solveig. He rose higher, winglessly flying through the air. Solveig pressed his body against Nova's back, trying to ignore the pain pulsing in his abdomen.

Die later, he told himself. *Defeat Nova first. Make sure your crew is safe.*

Glancing down, he saw his crew. They were nothing more than tiny dots, but even then, he could make out familiar features.

A flash of pink hair. The glint of daggers. Ves had found the others.

They were *safe.*

Nova rose higher and higher, smudging Solveig's crew until he couldn't see them at all. His ears popped, his sinuses straining under the pressure as Nova went for the clouds. At once, the temperature dropped until he felt like he'd been wrapped in one of Illie's winds.

Beneath him was nothing.

And then...*stars.*

Mene and Sin, the twin moons, hung on opposite ends of the sky, the red star Aster between them, glowing dimly amongst the diamond-pricks of the other stars.

His stomach flip-flopped.

And he was a kid again, laying on his back in the apple orchard, stomach burning from the rum-juice concoction he'd downed hours earlier, watching the stars with the only family he'd ever truly cared about. Family that was all (but one) buried near that apple orchard, forever stuck in the hell only Solveig had managed to escape.

I will pledge my final breath to your name and my first to find you again.

Teeth gritted, Solveig pulled his gaze away from the stars and grabbed his cutlass. Then, with everything in him, he jammed the blade between Nova's scales, burying the blade to the hilt before –

Crack!

His sword broke clean in two, the blade still buried in Nova's writhing body and the useless hilt in his hands.

And then Nova, roaring loud enough to shake the sky, plunged straight toward the ground.

Air flooded Natha's lungs all at once. A dizzying rush, the realization that she was...*alive.* She gasped, grabbed at her body, sat up, only to fall the remaining few inches to the ground.

"Sorry! I couldn't hold it!"

Illie.

Without wasting a second more, Natha scrambled to her feet and smothered Illie in a hug so tight her own arms ached. Even though they had only known each other for a few weeks, Natha's bond with the other women, Illie and Ves, was unbreakable.

She pulled away first, tears burning her eyes when she looked over Illie's shoulder. Thol and Ves. Leo, unconscious. Czardas. A bloodied person she didn't recognize. *Fynch.*

The little thief had been a thorn in Natha's side for a long time, but all those hardships vanished the moment she swallowed him in a hug.

She whispered, "You're alive."

"Not for long if you crush me," he choked out.

Natha let go with a rushed apology.

Above them, a roar shook the clouds. Natha's legs went limp. *Solveig...* There just wasn't enough time.

Quickly, she caught the others up, explaining how she and Lonan fought Nova's uppermost officers, how Solveig somehow got himself stabbed, how Nova revealed his ability by shifting into a literal dragon, taking Solveig with him to the roof of the palace. As she explained, she ushered the others inside, leading them upstairs to the fight she'd just fallen from.

Lonan sat atop the bloodied body of what once was Shin, a sugar cigarette hanging from his lips and his hands pressed to his chest.

"Ew, the rat lives," said Ves without hesitation.

"Leo." The cigarette fell from Lonan's teeth as he stood, ignoring Ves's jab to see the body in Thol's arms.

"Alive," Thol said, and Natha felt a strange weight being lifted from her shoulders. "I'll make introductions quick. Everyone, this is Israfel Eliad. They're a doctor. Isra, those two are Nathalia and Lonan."

"Oh, good, a doctor," said Lonan. "I think I'm going to have a heart attack."

Natha scanned the room, heart pounding hard. Solveig needed them. Which meant she needed to get to the roof.

Ignoring the chain of command, she said, "Who here isn't injured? Our captain is on the roof fighting against a literal sarding dragon. He needs our help."

Lonan and Leo were both out, the latter sitting slumped against the former on the floor. Fynch was out, too, whether he wanted to be or not. And if he was out, Czardas would be out. She could tell, with just a single glance, that Thol's knuckles were broken, but would that stop him from fighting? Would Illie's undoubtable frostbite stop her? She knew nothing about Isra – they were soaked with blood but moved unhindered, leading her to believe the blood wasn't theirs.

"I'm fighting," said Ves.

"As am I," said Thol.

"Me too," chimed Illie.

"I..." Czardas glanced at Fynch. "I'll fight, too."

Something fluttered in her chest. *Hope.*

"Fine," grumbled Isra, their voice flat. She waited for them to elaborate, but they never did.

Scraping her hair back and tying it in a tight tail, she turned to look at the gaping hole in the ceiling. She'd killed two people so far that night, a feat she had never accomplished before. Her hands felt dirty as if she'd dunked them in a vat of grease and let it dry. The classes she took with the navy were for self-defense, something she took just in case her ex-husband ever decided verbal abuse wasn't enough. Murder wasn't self-defense. Except...she hadn't killed Goliath and Sora in cold blood. She'd done it because she had to, because she had a promise – an *oath* – to keep.

What was a dragon added to that tally?

"Thol," she said, glancing at the window she'd fallen from only minutes before, "Are your hands okay enough for you to climb?"

"They will be," he said, ignoring Isra's obvious glare.

"Then, I think we should climb the side of the palace to get to the roof," she said.

Ves popped her knuckles, grin stretching wide enough to put her dimples on display. Something tumbled in Natha's stomach then. She glanced away, barely hearing Ves as she said, "Well! Let's sarding do this. I've always wanted to slay a dragon."

24

"WHAT ARE YOU THINKING about, Captain?"

Solveig turned to see his first mate and close friend, Scorpion, approach him. Leaning against the bow of his ship, he had the best view of the melting sunset over the Emerald Sea. Late Zylfmoon left the weather freezing, but the skies clear, the cold only amplifying the golds and reds as the sun set beyond the horizon, making way for the moons Mene and Sin.

He was thinking about death, though it wasn't something he'd confess to. He thought about death a lot. It followed him like a plague. Four brothers, one wench of a mother, countless others felled simply for existing within his presence.

At twenty, he was filled with more existential dread and nihilism than anyone else his age. He was a pirate captain; he ought to be thinking about cinnamon rum and wenches and gold.

"Nothing important," he sighed.

Scorpion frowned. "That clearly means you're thinking about something important. Come on. Spill." He leaned against the railing, back to the sunset, and crossed his bare arms over his bare chest. It was the dead of winter, and still, he refused to wear anything on his top half.

Even though they were close friends and had been sailing together for years, Scorpion didn't know the extent of Solveig's past. He knew his captain came from a tiny town and that he'd escaped after his mother died from the plague, but that was about it.

"What're we talking about?" Tiny and fierce Kesh swooped in. She was the smallest of the three yet somehow took up the most space. She reached her arms above her head, stretching like a cat in the last rays of sunlight.

"Captain's keeping secrets," said Scorpion.

"Am not!" Solveig argued.

He ran his hand over his face, scrubbing at the stubble along his jaw. He could still taste the tang of blood on his tongue from the fight earlier that day, even though he'd washed his mouth twice and spent half an hour in the shower, attacking himself with soap until his skin was red and raw and no longer bloody.

It had been eight years since his first kill, and even though he no longer had nightmares about the people whose lives he ended, it still felt...wrong.

Eventually, he would surpass the threshold of caring and no longer be bothered by the meaningless deaths despite the fact that he always offered mercy first.

But for now...

Kesh took a deep swig of her cinnamon rum, the spicy scent infiltrating his senses.

Sighing, he looked to the sky. The sun had vanished, the first stars just barely peeking through the indigo swath of dusk. And there, like always, situated between Mene and Sin, was the red north star. Aster.

Maybe it was because he was getting older, but the star seemed dimmer than it had ten years ago.

"Captain, you're not even listening," Kesh suddenly loudly accused.

"I am," he lied, only to instantly regret it when Kesh asked him what she'd just said.

She groaned at his panicked face. "I was saying, we should go below deck because it's colder than Lightbringer's ass out here. If it wasn't such a clear night, I'd bet my left hand it would snow."

Scorpion ignored her, like usual, and said, "I won't pry if you don't want me to, but I can tell something's bothering you."

Something was bothering him.

Aster.

That damn star.

Kesh nudged him with the bottle of cinnamon rum. Sighing, Solveig took it, allowing himself a deep drink. The burn slithered down his throat and settled hotly in his belly. It took some of the anxiety from his shoulders, loosening his muscles until his limbs were slack enough to let him lean against the railing. He draped his arms over, the bottle hanging precariously over the frigid water.

"I lost some people I really, really cared about," he finally said, the alcohol working overtime to relax his tongue. "And I wonder why I was the only one to survive. I mean, Thol – you know him – survived, but...we aren't blood related. Unless I figure out who my father is, I'm the only one of my blood left. The last Solveig. I'm glad Ma is dead. I hope her next life is awful. But... Why me?"

"I don't think I'm sober enough to unpack this right now," murmured Kesh, who hopped up and down as she tried to get warm.

Scorpion ran a hand over his bald head. "Family isn't just blood," he said. "You should know that better than anyone else. What happened happened a long time ago. Don't you deserve to build something new now?"

He did not.

He didn't say that, though. He just touched the rings on each of his fingers – moonstone, amethyst, ruby, emerald, sapphire – and sighed gently. Then, taking a deep gulp of cinnamon rum, he said, "If I don't find them again in this life, I'll find them in the next. In the meantime..."

He turned around to face his friends. "Nobody else is allowed to die."

Convincing his father that shadowing Jonyth Commodore would be more beneficial to the kingdom than if he hid away in the palace had been easier than anticipated, yet Anwir almost wished it had not been. All he'd had to do was tell his father, *"How can I rule*

the world if I've never seen it all?" and just like that, Castros Helios allowed him to board Jonyth's ship and follow him on his pirate hunt.

Really, his reasoning was that he wanted to follow Nox Solveig.

The task he'd given the pirate seemed impossible, and Anwir wanted to see it through. (Or so he told himself).

But now, weeks later, standing in the captain's quarters of the *Mary Jolyne,* war raging around him, Anwir had his regrets.

Anwir could handle a sword and command a ship, but he'd expected to go after *Nox Solveig.*

Not the sarding Unnamed God.

Bang!

Cannon fire left his ears ringing, even though he was nowhere near the explosions. Disoriented, he clapped his hands over his ears and stumbled to the window, peering out the thin sliver of glass to see the carnage. He had no idea how Jonyth managed to track down the Unnamed Pirates, and if it weren't for the masked figure striking Jonyth's sword again and again, he wouldn't believe that they'd found them.

Reaching down, he gripped the hilt of his own cutlass, ready to pull it free at a moment's notice. His heart pounded in his throat.

Another explosion rocked the boat. Anwir let go of his sword, grabbing the wall instead. His face smushed against the glass as he tried to regain his balance.

Outside, Jonyth swung his sword faster than Anwir could track, and yet...

And yet somehow the Unnamed God was *faster,* striking harder, quicker, deadlier, each of Jonyth's thrusts and swings blocked by parries so rapid it became nothing but a silver blur.

The Unnamed God was *fast.* Every time Anwir blinked, every time he slid away from the window, the Unnamed God seemed to be in a different position, dancing across the deck with grace.

The *Mary Jolyne* rocked precariously, struck by another cannon that sounded too close for Anwir's comfort. He'd been instructed to stay put and stay hidden; if anything were to happen to him, his sister, Iori, would be the one to take the throne.

Anarchy would be better than the hell she would make Aralyth.

The Unnamed God zipped across the deck in a heartbeat, sword angled to stab right between Jonyth's ribs. Anwir tensed.

Lady Lightbringer, Jonyth is going to sarding lose.

And then Jonyth struck. Before the Unnamed God had a chance to react, he was on the ground, Jonyth's hand at his throat.

Anwir should have felt relief, yet the lead-heavy feeling that washed over him like an angry tide was anything but.

Meanwhile, Un hit the ground hard enough to knock the air clean from his lungs. He choked, gasping desperately behind the shield that was his mask.

Despite being pinned down, one good squeeze away from death, Un smirked. Blood oozed from his nose and crusted over his lips, his vision swimming from overexertion, but his gaze was fixed on Jonyth's face.

On the mangled scar cutting across his cheek and nose.

Un had heard rumors that the pirate Nox Solveig gave Jonyth that nasty scar, something that made his chest warm with pride.

"Go ahead," he said, his accent thick and recognizable if one knew where it came from.

Jonyth stiffened. He knew where it came from.

In that hair of distraction, Un reached out and grasped the golden stopwatch, slamming his thumb onto the crown and slithering from Jonyth's grip.

But his power had drained him.

And by the time he grabbed his sword and held it high to execute Jonyth the way Jonyth executed pirates, a sharp jab pricked Un in the neck.

"Got you," hissed Jonyth.

Un dropped his sword, reaching up to touch the syringe still stuck to his throat.

The ground beneath him swayed, not just from the rocking of the ship as his cannonballs struck hard and fast, and the Unnamed God collapsed, defeated.

Wind whipped through Solveig's hair, forcing his coat to billow out behind him like smoke. He gripped Nova's fur tighter, knuckles white with the desperation to stay seated. His heart leaped to his throat; his stomach sank to his feet.

Then, before Nova could crash into the solid ground, he pulled up, shooting straight into the sky.

Poet's sarding breath...

Nova spun in a barrel roll, twisting and writhing as he flew higher and higher, trying to buck Solveig off his back.

The remains of Solveig's sword flew from his grasp.

"Just die, you pathetic worm!" Nova's voice filled Solveig's skull.

Solveig scoffed. Really? Of all the insults, he had to be called a *worm?* If he wasn't clinging to Nova for his life, he would have been more offended.

Nova dove again, body snapping violently. Solveig squeezed his thighs, muscles burning with exertion.

Heart pounding, a terrible plan formed.

When Nova swooped close to the roof, Solveig let go, tumbling off the dragon's back. He hit the roof hard, rolled to protect his bones.

"What in Dreamer's name is that?!"

Solveig clambered to his feet, legs unsteady, torso throbbing with pain, and turned to see his crew.

Well, most of it.

Ves, with her hands on her hips, repeated the question. Ignoring her, Solveig looked to Thol, to Illie, to Czardas, to Natha, to the unfamiliar figure drenched in blood.

"I got your message," he said to Thol.

"Too late, apparently," Thol grumbled. "You were supposed to stay away."

"And miss all the fun?" He grimaced, pressing his hand against his wound. When he glanced down, his palm was slicked red.

"*Ahem!*" Ves loudly cleared her throat. "That. What the actual sard is that?!"

"That," Solveig said grimly, "is Ryuu Nova. Does anyone have a sword I could borrow?"

Illie's face scrunched up in concentration. Moments later, a cold breeze swished around Solveig's ankles as she pulled a sword up from the room below with her winds.

He grabbed it, tested its weight against his hands. Light and curved, thinner than the cutlass he was used to but sharp enough to get the job done. Not that he truly expected to be able to stab Nova while he was a dragon, but what else could he do?

Another roar shook the sky.

"Brace," Solveig warned his crew.

Nova tore through the clouds, jaw unfurled, fire brewing like a captured star in his throat. He stopped just before he could crash into the palace.

"*Run!*" Solveig shouted.

The word hardly had time to settle before fire erupted from Nova's jaws.

Solveig dove for cover, but the scalding heat from the fire never reached him.

"Someone do something!" Illie screamed. "I can't hold this forever!"

Standing in the middle of the roof, dress and pink braid billowing around her like a tempest, hands covered with socks acting as gloves, was Illie.

And in her hands, the only thing holding the fire back, was a zephyr.

His heart thundered against his ribs; he saw her standing on Bowhead Rock, sword in hand, bloody from the pirate she'd almost decapitated. He saw her in Veridonia, he saw her against the navy and the Rabbit Pirates, always pushing herself to her limit and beyond, hands always blistered and raw and frostbitten after every fight she won.

She had given them an opening. He would not let that go to waste.

"ATTACK!" he cried.

Smoke curled from Nova's nostrils, his serpentine eyes narrowing as he realized not a single person had been scorched in his blaze.

But instead, they raced to attack.

Solveig held his sword high.

Next to him, Thol raced, broken knuckles curled into fists of *PUNISHMENT.*

Next to him, Ves brandished her knives, the blades slipped between her fingers like panther claws, a wicked grin on her face.

Next to him, Czardas held his rapier and ran like he'd never been surer of anything in his life.

Next to him, Natha charged, her face bloody and her smile feral, her scarred arms flexing under the moonlight.

Next to him, the doctor quickened their pace, knives glinting from their fingertips and blood rushing to soak their glove.

I will pledge my final breath to your name and my first to find you again.

If he was going to die tonight, he would make it sarding count.

The old man simply could not be taller than five feet, and that was all Isra could think about. He shuffled around the room, collecting various jars he hardly paused to read the labels of, and Isra worried he might trip on a loose floorboard and simply vanish into thin air.

Well, maybe old man Ginkgo wasn't that short, but Isra, even at their gangly height, wasn't used to being taller than their elders.

They sat on a stool, shoulders hunched and dark hair hanging over their face, grey eyes tracking old man Ginkgo's every move.

"Are you just going to sit there, or are you going to get off your ass and help?" the old man finally asked.

Isra startled, looking up quickly to meet the man's gaze behind his thick spectacles. His gold hair stuck up in every direction, reminding Isra of a leafy tree.

Old man Ginkgo used his cane to point at a shelf. "Grab the tarragon from up there, will you?"

Isra unfurled their limbs and stood, standing on their toes to grab the jar. They handed it to the old man, who just gestured to the copious jars in his arms. Sighing, they set it on the counter and went to sit on their perch again.

"That's it?" the old man scoffed. "You grab one jar for me and you're done for the day? If you want to be a doctor, you need to know how to mix medicines. Grab the tarragon and follow me. These old hands can't handle a pestle like they used to."

They rolled their eyes, grabbing the jar as they followed old man Ginkgo into the back room.

Sconces lined the walls, but the drapes around the windows had been pulled tightly shut. Glass shelves displayed wet and dry specimens – everything from tiny frogs to coiled black-furred creatures that looked like a mix between a cat and a serpent – as well as medical tools. On a counter, next to a mortar and pestle and several empty jars, old man Ginkgo set his herbs down.

"You know the recipe," the old man said, much to Isra's dismay.

They did know the recipe. Didn't mean they wanted to mix medicine. When they said they wanted to be a doctor, they meant they wanted to cure the Alkenio plague and perform surgeries and deal with guts and gore. Not measure out precise scoops of tarragon and willow bark to make some fever medicine.

Sighing through their nose, they pushed up their sleeves and got to work.

First came tarragon, the king of all herbs. They crushed that into a fine powder.

Then ginger, which took longer to grind up thanks to its large size.

Finally, cardamom, just a pinch. Isra mixed the herbs together, making sure the ratios were all correct. The aroma of the crushed herbs filled their nose, bringing a lull of calmness that made their eyelids heavy.

Their father had died three years ago, when Isra was eight, and it had barely been a year since old man Ginkgo took them in. Hardly enough time for them to become a proper doctor. Mixing herbs was boring when they knew Ginkgo was out there performing surgeries and preparing bodies for funerals.

They weren't jealous. Nope. Not one bit.

The pestle nearly slipped out of their iron-tight grip.

Sighing, they grabbed the bottle of clear liquid. It looked like water, but it was actually an alcohol so refined a single sip would make even the most severe alcoholics swear off booze for good. They added a few drops and mixed the herbs into a paste.

"Done," Isra said flatly.

After waking up next to their father's corpse and being forced into an orphanage, they'd just...stopped talking completely. For months after their father died, every time Isra closed their eyes, they saw him.

They had caught the plague, too, but somehow survived, making them the only survivor of the otherwise fatal disease. The only proof they ever had it was their grey eyes and the black scars spotted along their face and body, appearing like beauty marks from a distance.

Old man Ginkgo worked overtime to get Isra to open up, and after over twelve months of trying, he finally got Isra to say no more than ten syllables at a time.

The doctor walked over with a handful of empty jars. Isra wordlessly measured the medicinal paste into each, pushing them aside so old man Ginkgo could write the labels. His handwriting was better than Isra's – and Isra, eleven, still struggled with spelling some long words.

Suddenly, Ginkgo reached out to ruffle Isra's hair. They bristled, shrinking away from the touch. When old man Ginkgo laughed, their ears flushed red, and they turned away. What was so funny about that?

"You didn't try to sever my hand from my arm that time," he said.

Isra faltered. Was that...it? Ever since they woke up next to the bloated corpse of their father, dead from the Alkenio plague, they loathed touch.

All bodies were the same. All bodies would die and decay, and the fat, waxy limbs would touch Isra and infect them both literally and metaphorically and –

They grabbed the labeled jars, forcing their hands to be busy lest they relieve Ginkgo of his.

When he reached out to ruffle Isra's hair again, they shrugged him away and strode across the room to put the medicine away. There was no logical explanation as to why their heart skipped a beat. Arrhythmias were natural – they happened to everyone at one point or another.

"Come here," old man Ginkgo said suddenly. Isra nearly dropped the jar of medicine they were holding. Quickly, they put it away and hurried back to the doctor.

Ginkgo reached into the pocket of his coat – on his short frame, the hem nearly brushed against the floor – and pulled out a pair of gloves.

"A gift," he said, "for you. You're going to make an excellent doctor one day, Isra. Or should I call you Doctor Eliad?"

Doctor Eliad...

They liked the sound of that.

Taking the gloves, Isra carefully slipped them on. No longer were their fingers exposed to the world, to the germs polluting the air, to the memory of dead flesh. The cheap leather gloves became their shield, their weapon.

They curled their hands into fists.

"Doctor Eliad," they said. Then, adding two more syllables to make seven – almost the most they'd ever said at once – they said, softly, "Thank you."

The scream that ripped from Illie's throat was pure carnage, raw and undiluted, and it scraped her nerves exposed. Her hands had gone numb long ago, the tingling ache of frostbite settling in gone.

Nova's fire dissipated, and with it, she lost her grip on the wind.

She collapsed to her knees, cradling her hands to her chest. *Would it be stupid to stick my hands in the path of his fire next time?* She thought, teeth gritted as she breathed through the numbness.

Get up. They need you. You can't tap out now.

Sucking in a breath through her teeth, Illie stood. Her hair had long since fallen from its braid, the pink strands whipping around her shoulders.

My name, she thought, *is Illie Valentine. I am blessed by Poet. I have a power that makes me extremely valuable. I have a power that can defeat Ryuu sarding Nova.*

Time slowed. She watched as her crew – her *family* – attacked the dragon keeping them chained to this island.

"Natha!" she called, spotting the other woman quickly.

Natha swung a kick into Nova's arm, flipping through the air before running to Illie's side.

"Your hands…" she started.

Illie shook her head. "No time. I need you to rip the hem of my dress. Bind my hands with it. I'm not giving up yet."

Concern filled Natha's ruby eyes, but she nodded. Swiftly, she grabbed hold of Illie's skirt and *yanked*. Fabric ripped, the sound practically drowned out by the fight around them. Natha quickly wrapped the strips of fabric around Illie's hands, adding another layer of protection. Anything to stave the frostbite a moment longer.

"Duck," she said.

Illie reached out, feeling the winds slither around her hands. Then, she grabbed one. Just like before, it solidified in her grasp, forming a wind-spear.

Poet, help me.

She reared her arm back. Inhaled.

Exhaled.

Threw the wind-spear as hard as she could.

It whistled through the air, flying faster than anything she'd ever seen before.

She tensed, holding her breath. The wind pierced right between Nova's scales. Even at the distance she was at, she could see the sudden spray of blood.

Nova's roar shook the roof.

Natha grabbed at Illie, steadying her as a tremor wracked the ground. Nova writhed, clawing at a projectile that wasn't there – the wind had already returned to the skies, leaving Nova injured and Illie with a surge of power.

"Did you see that?!" She turned to Natha, eyes wide. She knew she had to look ridiculous, hair flying around her, dress torn to shreds, hands covered with socks and strips of fabric.

But Natha grinned wide enough her eyes squinted shut. "When did you learn how to do *that?* Can you do it again?"

Illie looked at her hands. Could she? She knew the frostbite was settling in bad, but with Isra on their side now, maybe she could get proper treatment. It didn't really matter, anyway. What use were her hands if she was fried to a crisp?

"I just need an opening." *And a particularly cooperative gale.*

Another tremor shook the roof. Nova's roar was deafening. Someone else must have gotten a good hit on him.

Natha nodded. "I'll get you an opening, then. Make sure you survive this. I have some good gossip I need to tell you over drinks later."

And she was off, running toward the dragon with stamina Illie wished she had. She hadn't even been running, and yet her lungs ached with exertion. If she survived to see tomorrow, she already knew she'd be aching in places she didn't even know *could* ache.

She closed her eyes, inhaling sharply through her nose. *You're a pirate, Illie. What, did you think you'd just sit in the sun and draw maps all day? You don't need to be the best; you just need to be good enough to give Sol and the others an opening.*

"HEY!" She shouted at the top of her aching lungs. *"OVER-SIZED LIZARD! LOOK OVER HERE!"*

Nova turned his massive head, yellow eyes narrowed as they homed in on her.

"Gotcha," she whispered.

She grabbed another wind, swallowing a scream of pain as the blisters on her palms erupted, and forged it into another spear.

Illie reared her arm back and threw with all her might. The wind took off, racing toward its target. Illie stumbled, falling back.

Not once did her eyes leave the wind-spear.

She smirked when it hit its target, burying itself deep in Nova's eye. His roar wasn't enough to keep her awake, though.

Exhaustion settled over her, crashing into her all at once like one of Thol's *PUNISHMENT* punches, and she fell onto her back, the world going dark.

25

Blood splattered on the ground in thick, hot drops. Solveig narrowly avoided getting hit in the head with a glob of dragon blood.

"Nox!" called Thol, drawing Solveig's attention away from the blood rain. Thol pointed behind Solveig; he turned to see Illie lying supine on the ground, hair fanned around her like a pastel pink aura.

Dead?

He cursed, abandoning the fight long enough to get close, to see that her chest still rose and fell with steady breaths.

Unconscious.

"You pathetic child!" Nova's voice roared in Solveig's head. *"Give up now. You cannot best me in a fight. Reality is whatever I want it to be. Surender now, and I will make your death quick."*

He tightened his grip on his sword.

"Then get used to the reality where I will never surrender," he shouted, "Because I will either live to see you defeated or die trying!"

He adjusted his grip on his sword.

The world tunneled around him, loud and then quiet, all at once. His heart pounded with exertion, lungs trying to keep up with his screaming muscles.

Nova swung a clawed paw in a viciously sharp arc aimed directly at Solveig. Ignoring the pain burning in his torso, Solveig jumped, lodging his sword into the fleshy bit of exposed wrist. His abs clenched; he pulled himself up, caged in Nova's talons.

Solveig ripped his sword free only to bury it deep in Nova's palm. The dragon roared, the blade slicing through the unprotected flesh with ease. Nova's body rippled, writhing as he tried to shake Solveig off.

Another burst of fire glowed in Nova's throat. Solveig cursed aloud. With Illie down…

Solveig tore out his sword and pushed through Nova's claws, jumping to the ground.

"Hey!" he shouted.

Nova's serpentine gaze homed in on him. A shiver struck him like a bullet, freezing his insides to permafrost. Solveig took a step back, his grip on his cutlass never once wavering.

Wind whipped his coat around his ankles.

Captain Nox Solveig, cloaked in green, set out to conquer the Emerald Sea. One day he'll go down to the drink. How many navy ships will he sink?

If Ryuu Nova was to strike him down on this rooftop, so sarding be it.

He was doing this not just for himself but for his crews – the one he left behind when he set off to be a captain of his own, the one he let die at Jonyth Commodore's hands, and the one he scraped together with the first intent of betraying and the new intent of saving.

For Thol, his brother, the only family he had left, who wanted to be the strongest pirate in the world so he would never lose another brother again.

For Illie, who wanted to create an impossible moving map of the world and find the lost third moon.

For Ves, the Witch of the Sea who spent four years locked away in prison, forgotten by the world, the Witch of the Sea who wanted the world to remember who she was.

For Natha, broken and betrayed one too many times, hungry for family and adventure, who wanted to visit every island in the world.

For Czardas, the quiet musician whose talent had exploded in the past few days, who, despite claiming his hands were for music, fought with a sword like he'd been born to hold one, who wanted to learn the origins of the symphony he loved.

For Fynch, the little thief who only just got his nearly-stolen life back, who wanted to be the best sharpshooter Syrenis had ever seen.

For Lonan and Leo, barely more than strangers, two men with zero purpose to be here but two men who fought like they were one of Solveig's.

For the two empty graves by the old apple orchard and for the two graves that held bodies long since turned to dust.

Nox Solveig's death would not be selfish if it meant saving them.

But before Nova could spew the fire that would burn him alive, a blur of blonde hair whizzed across the sky, pummeling into the side of Nova's head.

Natha knew what she had to do.

Exhaustion ate away at her, decomposing her muscles and bones until only a shell too tired to function remained. *Everything* hurt. Even her sarding eyelashes, her bloody fingernails, all of it.

Illie was out – Thol dragged her sleeping form behind a stack of rubble to shield her from the attacks – and each minute the fight dragged on, the remaining crew got closer to defeat.

Among the five remaining, only Natha, Ves, and the odd doctor – Isra, they'd briefly introduced themselves as – were *mostly* uninjured.

Mostly.

She glanced at her bare arms – arms she'd kept hidden for most of her life, afraid that others would find the puckered scars disgusting. Her ex-husband had. Even after all those years, Natha did not fear fire. It had been a mistake – she was too young to be using the stove unsupervised.

As Nova spewed fire, engulfing the city of Corsa with his draconian blaze, Natha still did not fear fire. But Solveig... He stood right in the path, stabbed and bleeding and moments from getting fried.

And so, she knew what she had to do.

Sucking in a breath between her teeth, she took off running, legs pumping with strength she simply did not have. Her thigh burned, blood making her skin sticky.

Grabbing onto Nova's scales, biceps screaming, Natha climbed onto the dragon's shoulder. He was too focused on Solveig to even notice the pesky gnat that was Nathalia Divyne atop him.

Her smeared-red lips curled into a smirk. *Good.*

With every last bit of her energy, Natha raced across Nova. She leaped into the air, legs outstretched.

Her feet cracked against Nova's face. She was not a light woman by any means; the force of her blow, of all her weight slamming against Nova, snapped his head to the side.

"Natha!" someone screamed.

Heat flooded her body, followed by a strange, burning tightness.

Her back cracked against the ground, forcing the air from her lungs and blood to spill over her lips. Her stomach tightened even more; she reached down to touch it.

Squelch.

If there had been any color left in her pallid face, it would have drained when her blurred vision focused on the red slick coating her hands.

No.

No, no, no, no, no.

She couldn't die. Not like this.

Unable to move, she pressed her trembling hands against the wounds. Without looking, without even feeling what had happened, she couldn't tell what her gut looked like.

Blood dripped from Nova's talons onto her face. *Her* blood.

He'd clawed her open.

Gasping for breath, she tried to fight off the black spots creeping into her vision like soot. Blood – or tears – rushed down her cheeks.

I saved Solveig, though, her mind weakly thought.

A numb heat exploded from her stomach outwards, engulfing her wholly.

The world went black moments later.

And then something sharp pricked her skin, and she felt *everything.*

Ves's screams tore through the air, louder than Nova's roars. She wasn't fast enough – she could never be fast enough to outrun a dragon. All she could do was watch in frozen horror as Nova reached a clawed paw up and swiped Natha across the stomach.

All she could do was watch as Natha, in a cloud of blood, fell through the sky.

No, no, no, no, no, no!

How many people were going to get injured? How many people were going to die before Solveig got what he wanted? She switched to her other sight, keeping an eye on the dim gold glow of Natha's soul as she raced across the battlefield. Natha fell faster, hitting the ground hard.

Ves skidded to a stop, nausea clenching her belly like a vise.

"Ves!" Solveig shouted.

She whipped her head around, locking eyes on her captain. Solveig clutched his side with one hand, the other holding his sword weakly. Nova's soul burned bright, jaws unfurled as he swooped in close.

Footsteps sounded, rushing to Natha's side. Ves swallowed the lump in her throat.

Natha would be fine. She had to be. Ves returned her focus to Nova and –

There.

A red coil, a weak spot, right where his heart surely was. And... There, attached to his arm, a void spot – something not living.

Something that could be sliced off.

Dreamer, keep Natha safe.

She took off running.

She was the Witch of the Sea – the ruthless pirate who slew a (baby) kraken and sunk an entire navy fleet. She could sarding take out a dragon.

Flipping her knives in the air and catching them by the points, she reeled her arms back and, one after another, threw the blades with all her strength.

Each blade hit its mark – Nova's eye. The dragon roared, clawing at his eyes as he tried to pry the blades free.

But Ves was already moving again, racing across the rooftop. A half-formed plan solidified in her mind; scooping up a discarded rope, she called, "Flowers!" and tossed one end to Thol.

"Follow my lead," she shouted.

Heart pounding, lungs aching, muscles screaming for a pause, Ves ran, springboarding off a broken bit of roof to catch the rope against Nova's other arm. Thol mimicked her, and soon, the rope was wrapped just under his scaly shoulder.

"What's the plan?" Thol asked through clenched teeth.

"Tie the rope to something. *Tight.*" She yanked on her end – Nova clawed at his eye, ripping the blades free – and glanced around. Teeth gritted, she pulled on the rope and tied it to one of the curved eaves as tightly as she could

This isn't going to work, she thought grimly.

Nova slammed his other paw onto the roof, blood sluicing down his face. His eye was bloodshot, weeping red tears from the deep tears to his retina.

"PULL!" Ves screeched.

She grabbed the rope with both hands and *yanked.*

Crrrrrrrack!

Sweat beaded down her face, sticking her hair to her cheeks and forehead. Blisters bit into her palms, but she pulled harder, harder, *harder.*

And then, all at once, she fell back, head hitting the ground hard enough to send stars across her vision.

Too dizzy to see, she could only hear the wet, meaty *schlap* as Ryuu Nova's arm crashed into the ground.

"Cap!" she cried out weakly, struggling to get up. A wave of nausea crashed over her; she turned and vomited everything in her stomach and then some, acrid bile scraping against her throat.

You are not about to pass out in a pile of your own vomit again.

Weak, arms trembling, Ves pulled herself away from her puddle of sick only to collapse prone against the roof.

Czardas watched in horror as, one by one, his crew began collapsing.

First Illie, who was breathing steadily but unconscious.

Then Natha, her guts all but spilling from the rips in her belly. The doctor Isra rushed to her side, but Czardas couldn't linger to see if she was all right.

Then Ves, curled up in a fetal position, the back of her head glistening with sticky blood.

He gripped his rapier tightly, trying to hide the trembling in his hands.

There was a sarding dragon leg on the roof, spurting blood from the amputated stump.

And next to it was a sword.

Ryuu Nova was down an eye and down a leg, but what were those two things to a man who could quite literally turn into a *dragon?*

Because it was just Czardas, Solveig, Thol, and Isra left. Two of the strongest fighters had tapped out – Ves and Natha – and Illie, with her divine blessing, was the only one who could stop Nova's fire.

Not for the first time since joining the others on the roof, Czardas wished he'd stayed with Fynch, Leo, and Lonan.

Nova turned his attention to Solveig and Thol, stumbling as he tried to balance on his remaining limbs. Blood oozed from the stump left behind, a crimson waterfall Czardas would have to dive through to get to that discarded sword.

"Nox Solveig," Nova's voice ricocheted through Czardas's head, causing him to stop. Somehow, the man-turned-dragon was able to speak without moving his massive mouth. *"You will pay for this."*

"It's sarding pronounced *Sol-vay!"* Solveig shouted, racing blindly into the fray.

Czardas's stomach turned.

No.

No!

Nova was purposely goading him, trying to get him to rush in impulsively. Nova reared his head back like a cobra about to strike.

He didn't think; he just ran, feet slipping against the hot blood. It soaked him through, sliding between his lips, into his ears, slicking his tongue, and pulling bile into his gullet.

"Captain!" He didn't pause to care about the blood flooding his mouth, sour and metallic and hot. His hand wrapped around the hilt of the sword – *Dreamer*, it was *heavy*. *"CATCH!"*

Czardas threw the blade as hard as he could.

Snap!

Pain shot up his body, bringing with it a wave of nausea and tears that burned his eyes like acid. Glancing at his arm, dread filled his belly. It hung lower than normal, his shoulder protruding like the peak of a mountain.

It's not broken, a little voice said in the back of his mind. He knew what a broken arm felt like, and this...this was not that.

He still had one good arm left.

Most instruments he played – including his beloved violin – required both hands, but he favored one arm when it came to fencing. The arm that currently hung limp at his side, yanked from the socket when he'd thrown that blade.

It felt backward, wrong, to grab his sword with his left hand. This wasn't a fencing match. This was an actual battle, one where if he messed up, he would die.

For good.

Nova raised his remaining front leg, claws poised for the attack that would inevitably cut him, Solveig, and Thol in half.

A scream erupted from the pits of his stomach; Czardas thrust the blade up, skewering the fleshy, unarmored palm of Nova's palm.

It slid all the way to the hilt before it struck bone.

Clutching his shoulder, Czardas ducked out of the way before Nova's paw could come crashing down. His knees hit the ground with a wet thud. Tears slid down his cheeks, burning clear paths through the blood painted there.

What had once been ten against one was now three against one very bloody, very pissed-off dragon.

The gods themselves could be on their side, and Czardas knew his crew had no chance of surviving.

26

THERE WERE TWO SWORDS worthy enough of having legendary names and a place in Solveig's mind.

Solais, the blade of light belonging to the pirate Alexander Chronos, lost when his ship was sunk and his head was taken from his shoulders.

And Kusanagi, the unbreakable blade that Solveig thought was nothing more than a myth until he felt the weight of it in his blood-slicked hand.

It wasn't shaped like the cutlasses he was used to – it had more of a curve to its long, thin blade, and it wasn't nearly as heavy. Even without the delicately intricate script along the base of the blade spelling out its name, Solveig *knew* this was Kusanagi.

Nova would have to sarding pry it from his cold, dead hands if he wanted a sword this beautiful back.

The unbreakable blade. It could slice through Nova's thick scales.

This would be the sword to kill the dragon.

"Nox," Thol said at his side, voice barely audible over the dragon's screaming roars. A sword stuck out from the middle of his paw like a thorn. Thol continued: "I'll do what I can to help you, but I don't think we're winning this fight. It's just you and me now. My knuckles are broken, and *you* were stabbed – which you *still* need to explain."

Right. In the heat of the moment, explaining how he'd been stabbed clean through slipped his mind. He pressed his hand against the wound.

"I'm not backing down," he hissed through his teeth.

"I wish you weren't so sarding stubborn all the time."

Before Solveig could reply, Nova's dragon form rippled, stretching and compressing, and soon, he was a man again.

Well, more man than he'd been before. He still stood well over nine feet tall, scales glistening across his body and a whiplike tail curling from the small of his back. Horns branched from the top of his head, and tusk-like teeth pulled his lips back.

One arm was missing, gushing blood, and one eye was oozing goopy liquid. His remaining hand had a sword stuck through it; he grabbed the hilt with his teeth and ripped the rapier – Czardas's rapier – free.

Solveig took a tiny step back. To Thol, he whispered, "If I die, bury me with the others. You can't miss it – all the graves are by the orchard."

Thol nodded. "If I die, I want to be buried by Meadow and Evangeline."

Without looking away from Nova, the two shook hands.

Solveig pivoted, sinking low to the ground, and charged, Kusanagi held high.

Nova flipped the rapier in the air. When he caught it by the hilt, it had changed, forming a broadsword so massive it had to have been at *least* half of Solveig's height, if not double that.

He swung it down; Solveig threw Kusanagi up. The blades clashed hard. Solveig's muscles screamed as he fought to keep Nova's force from snapping his sword in half, but Nova didn't even break a sweat as he shoved all his strength into the attack.

"Kind of hard to fight with one arm, huh?" Solveig smirked.

"And yet you're the one struggling," growled Nova.

His smirk twitched, flickering into a scowl. He slid his blade against Nova's, swinging it into an upward arc that Nova blocked with ease.

The moment his side was exposed, Thol struck, slamming a rapid succession of *PUNISHMENT* into Nova's kidney.

Using that moment to strike, Solveig swung Kusanagi across Nova's belly.

But Nova didn't pay any attention to Solveig, nor did he even register that he'd just been sliced. He tossed his sword into the air and spun, smashing his fist into Thol's face with a wet, sticky *crunch!*

Thol stumbled back, eyes watering, nose gushing blood. Broken without a doubt.

Nova caught his sword, placing the hilt between his teeth. He grabbed Thol's locks, yanking on them *hard*.

His foot met Thol's middle, sending him flying across the roof.

"THOL!" Solveig screamed. *No.* He couldn't lose another brother, not like this. That was *Thol.* He *had* to be okay.

Solveig's vision went red.

Nova spat his sword into his awaiting bloody hand. "Just you and me now, kid."

"I'll sarding kill you," Solveig seethed.

And he attacked.

The world funneled into a tunnel of nothingness, of rage and fury and focus on no one but Ryuu Nova – the gods damned Dragon King. Adrenaline blocked out the pain from his stab wound, from the other minuscule injuries he'd received battling his way to this rooftop war.

In a blur of silver, he rained blow after blow after blow, each strike met with Nova's sword in a clash of sparks and steel.

A lifetime stretched and molded to fit in the breath of a split second.

He was fast.

But Nova...

Nova was *faster.*

The still-healing gunshot wound beneath Solveig's shoulder tore open, muscle shredding as Nova's sword sliced straight through his arm, sinking into the fleshy bit right beneath his shoulder.

He twisted the blade with a sickening *crunch* before yanking it free. Nova smashed the pommel of his sword against the side of Solveig's head, splitting flesh and sending a slurry of stars to accost his vision.

Solveig stumbled, knees crashing against the ground hard. Blood sluiced down his face, staining his flesh the same color as his soaked hair. Each throb of his heart was amplified in his wounds – his torso, his arm, his head.

It was getting hard to breathe.

Solveig pressed his hand against his ribs, fighting the sour nausea the barrage of pain brought with it.

Was this how his brothers felt moments before their deaths?

Nova struck again, the toe of his boot slamming into Solveig's chin, sending him flying. Solveig hit the ground hard, bloody spittle spraying from his lips. He choked, coughing as he tried – failed – to fill his lungs with air again.

Get up. It doesn't matter how much it hurts, just get up!

Teeth gritted against the pain, Solveig stabbed Kusanagi into the ground, using it for balance as he rose to his feet.

In a blur of red and gold, Nova flew across the roof. He grabbed a fistful of Solveig's hair, yanking his head back. Solveig cried out in pain, but he was on the ground again before he could raise his stolen sword to fight back.

"You couldn't just give up," growled Nova. He stomped his foot onto Solveig's chest, heel digging into the tender flesh of his wounds.

Solveig choked, gasping for air. Blood-thick spit coated his teeth like paint.

"You came into *my* territory," Nova roared, "and picked fights with *my* men. You used what belonged to me. You deserve this. I gave you a chance for mercy, but you squandered it. Now, you will die."

Nova kicked Solveig in the side, once, twice, three times, bringing tears to his eyes each time his kidneys were struck.

He tightened his grip on Kusanagi, but any chances of striking Nova with the sword were lost. Nova pinned Solveig to the ground, feet braced on either side of him.

He only had one fist, but that didn't stop Nova from pummeling Solveig. Knuckles met his face, his stomach, everywhere – and Solveig, crushed under the weight of a ten-foot-tall man, couldn't move to protect himself.

Soon, he couldn't even feel the pain as each punch landed, flesh too swollen and bruised to differentiate what was already blackened and hurt and what was new.

I'm sorry, he thought to Thol, whom he dragged out of quiet retirement for one last fleeting chance at adventure.

I'm sorry, he thought to Ves, who never would get the chance to remake her name after four years of solitude.

I'm sorry, he thought to Illie, who had given up the perfect life she'd known to follow an ancient map to nowhere.

I'm sorry, he thought to Natha, who'd just wanted a taste of adventure but got a whole fistful of destruction instead.

I'm sorry, he thought to Fynch, who nearly died for Solveig's cause and was as good as dead again now that Solveig couldn't protect him.

I'm sorry, he thought to Czardas, who had everything he could ever want but gave it up to stay by Fynch and now would pay for that choice with his life.

I'm sorry, he thought to Lonan and Leo, who just wanted to take the ship they'd made on her maiden voyage but ended up in the middle of this mess.

Once again, Nox Solveig faced death, and the only faces that crossed his mind were the brothers he'd once had and would meet once again the moment the pain vanished, his mortal body too destroyed to hold him up.

Solveig closed his eyes – they were already mostly swollen shut – and –

Get up.

That voice was not his. It was the voice of a sad little poet with amethyst eyes and a perpetual frown.

Get up.

It was the voice of an angry little boy with ruby eyes and a permanent scowl.

Get up.

It was the voice of a patient little boy with moonstone eyes and a heart so pure it couldn't belong to a mortal.

Get up!

It was the voice of a furious little boy with sapphire eyes and freckles across his nose and –

Solveig's fingers twitched, curling around Kusanagi's hilt.

Nova crushed his foot against Solveig's hand. Bones crunched, wet, and sharp. A mangled cry escaped his throat, the agony *blinding*.

You have an advantage, he thought weakly over the thumping pain from every sarding injury. *You have* two *arms. He only has one.*

He just needed to get the sword into his other hand.

Nova stood, barely giving Solveig any time to switch hands before he brought his foot down *hard*, slamming it into Solveig's gut.

Bile surged into his gullet; he turned his head to the side and emptied his stomach onto the ground. Tears welled in his eyes, nose aching as acid burned his sinuses. Globs of saliva clung to his lips like glue, refusing to leave no matter how many times he tried spitting it away, mixing with tears and blood.

He needed a miracle.

He needed something – *anything* – to get Nova on the ground.

Starbursts exploded throughout his body at once. Solveig flew across the roof, hitting the solid ground with a *crack* before he even realized what had happened.

Pressure flooded his head, an agonizing tension that built and built and built until Solveig was sure his skull would explode.

Sure every bone in his body was broken, Solveig slowly pushed himself to his feet, gripping Kusanagi in his (mostly) uninjured hand.

Broken and bloody and running on adrenaline alone, Nox Solveig stared Ryuu Nova down. Unflinching, unafraid, unprepared to go against a man blessed by a deity to manipulate reality to his will.

He had no choice but to fight.

In spite of his missing arm and blinded eye, Nova raced across the roof faster than a bolt of lightning. He swung his arm out, fingers lengthening and curving into knife-like talons.

Solveig swung Kusanagi up. The curved edge of his sword met Nova's talons.

Roaring his fury, the fury of those who came before him, of those who lay scattered about the building injured because of Nova, Solveig shoved every bit of his strength into the blow, willing himself to overpower the monster of a man.

Nova swished his arm away, yanking Kusanagi with it. Solveig stumbled with the blade, distracted for a perfect second. Nova struck, slamming his fist into Solveig's side.

Bloody spittle sprayed from his lips. Coughing, Solveig tripped over his own feet, falling to the ground.

Nova's lips curled into a twisted, sadistic grin. "Finally," he growled. "You've stopped squirming."

His talons glinted in the moonlight. Solveig braced, praying to whichever god cared to listen that it would be over before he could feel the pain.

But the pain never came.

Slowly, cautiously, he peeled open one eye.

Nova stood frozen, blood dribbling over his bottom lip. His remaining eye had been a serpentine gold only a moment ago. But now...

Now, it was silver.

27

The day Isra's father's eyes turned silver, they knew, even at six years old, that he would die. Most of their neighbors had caught the Alkenio Plague; it was only a matter of time until Isra and their father caught it, too.

They lived in a hovel so small it could hardly be called that. Squished in an alley in the poorest sector of Corsa, the two were lucky they had only spiders and bugs for roommates. Most people in the district lived five or six to a house minimum. Isra's mother would have lived there, too, but Isra came into the world bloody and screaming, nearly tearing their mother in half. She died before she could even hold her child, leaving her husband behind to care for a newborn.

The hovel only had one room – there was no kitchen, for they cooked everything over the fireplace. There was no washroom, for they had to use the communal bathhouse to clean and relieve themselves – so

Isra's father, Ibrahim Eliad, couldn't properly quarantine himself. He was sick. Contagious. Isra had no protection from the disease.

The Alkenio Plague had a one hundred percent fatality rate. Once it was caught – once the spots appeared on its victim's skin and their eyes turned silver – the victim was as good as dead, as the plague's final stage of infection turned their internal organs to liquid.

For two years, Ibrahim suffered under the plague's grasp.

And for two years, Isra waited dreadfully for the day they, too, would get sick.

And then, by some sort of miracle, Ibrahim seemed to get better. His eyes remained silver, but the rashes and spots on his skin faded, as did his cough and fever. He was no longer stricken to his bed. Soon, it was as if he'd never been sick at all. The fireplace roared as he cooked for seven-year-old Isra, he accompanied his child to the bathhouse, everything that had gone wrong had been erased, replaced with the sense of normalcy that poor Isra clung to.

Maybe the Alkenio Plague didn't have a one hundred percent fatality rate. Maybe it just had a ninety-nine percent death rate.

Or so Isra thought.

That hope was stolen from them when they awoke one morning, the bed they shared with their father cold and damp.

Isra rolled over and was, for the first time in their very short life, glad their stomach was empty.

Sickness rising up their throat, their chest heaving as their body tried and failed to vomit, Isra scrambled off the bed, backing up until they were flush against the wall.

Their father had died sometime in the night, his body long cold and bloated, stiff with rigor mortis. Thick liquid oozed from his orifices, seeping into the thin mattress. Into Isra's clothes.

Heart in their throat, Isra yanked their clothes off, desperate to get the sticky film of their father's liquified organs off their body.

They collapsed to their knees, tears streaming down their face as they dry heaved over and over again, stomach aching and head spinning. Finally, they crumpled, curled into a fetal position as they sobbed and sobbed and sobbed.

They weren't sure how long they lay on the ground, but eventually, the door opened, and one of their neighbors came inside.

"Israfel," the stout woman who lived two doors down said in a gentle tone. She looked from the dead body atop the bed to Isra, curled up and naked and trembling as they clawed at their flesh, trying to get the clinging death gone.

She sighed and walked over to them. Her eyes were silver and had been for a few weeks now. The Alkenio Plague's gestation was anywhere from half a year to two years. Her death sentence had been signed, but she wouldn't perish for some time still.

"He's gone," she said, not unkindly. "You need to get up, Israfel. You're not infected yet, so let's get you cleaned up. You can't stay here."

They couldn't, but where else could they go?

That night, Isra fled the orphanage their neighbor had brought them to. They made it clear across Corsa, nearly into the richer sector, before they were caught and dragged back. They were locked in a broom closet as punishment, their only company an old mop and a dusty mirror they could just barely see with a sliver of light.

There wasn't a mirror in their hovel, but there was one at the bathhouse, and Isra knew their skin didn't have any blemishes and that their eyes were brown.

There weren't supposed to be marks on their cheekbones.

Their eyes weren't supposed to be grey.

Israfel Eliad, unknowingly, had caught the Alkenio Plague and somehow, in the cruelest, most vicious twist of fate, managed to survive.

Many, many years – and one old mentor, one unauthorized medical license, and one illegal practice – later, Isra discovered how to bring that one hundred percent (ninety-nine, now that they had survived it) mortality rate down to zero.

It was a shame the Aralyth Empire found out about it and took away Isra's research and medical license.

It was a shame a reality-bending dictator found them before anyone else could, harnessing their knowledge and power for selfish destruction instead of selfless healing.

Israfel Eliad carried the plague in a jar. It was a pure concentrate, a deadly poison vital for the cure, something Ryuu Nova discovered and had Isra use on his enemies. He kept all the bottles safe in his palace, locked away where only he could get to them.

Or so he thought.

His biggest mistake was underestimating the Blood Doctor. Because Isra stole a bottle. Because Isra continued to make cures in secret.

Because Isra, the only person alive immune to the plague, poured the virus onto their arm, letting it slither into the syringes at the tips of their fingers.

Ryuu Nova stood posed over Nox Solveig, moments away from gutting him the way he'd gutted the blonde woman earlier. They were lucky their power reset, lucky they'd made it to her side just as her heart stopped. The stitches they put in her belly were sloppy, but field work always was. She'd live.

But Nova wouldn't.

Isra flexed their fingers.

And just before Nova could strike Solveig down, they shoved the plague-filled needles deep into Nova's back. In just a few heartbeats – or less; Nova's heart was pumping hard, fast, by the way the blood gushed from his severed arm – he would be infected.

They ripped the needles free, taking a few steps back before Nova could whirl around and pummel them.

For years, they served under him.

For years, they feared him.

For years, they weren't allowed to practice the medicine old man Ginkgo taught them, the medicine that brought them out of their shell and gave them something to love again.

But Nox Solveig – that sarding pirate – came and...and just *ruined* everything.

(Or fixed it all).

Isra *hated* pirates, but...Solveig...

Thol trusted Solveig, and Isra, regretfully, trusted Thol. As they collapsed to the ground, exhausted and dizzy and in desperate need of a bottle of wine or seven, their mind had been made up.

It was finally time to leave Corsa.

The sarding *plague.* Nova stood before Solveig, infected with the Poet-damned *plague.*

Just who was Thol's Blood Doctor?

A grin split across Solveig's face, barely masking his pain. Nova's movements had become sluggish. Solveig swung Kusanagi down; Nova couldn't move fast enough to block.

"I have the cure!" shouted an unfamiliar voice. *The doctor...*

The...cure to the plague? Solveig faltered. Such a thing didn't exist, right?

He had to chance it.

The tip of his sword ripped through flesh, cutting Nova diagonally from shoulder to hip. Blood sprayed, hot and thick and infected.

Solveig struck again, slashing Kusanagi horizontally before pivoting and thrusting. Nova defended himself weakly, claws hardly strong enough against the unbreakable blade. His form rippled, but he wouldn't – couldn't – shift.

He stumbled, choking on a mouthful of blood.

Serves you right, you scaly bastard, Solveig thought, his own pain dulled only by the adrenaline pumping through his veins like Sinth.

"I'm not going to ask you to surrender," Solveig said coldly. "You hurt my crew. You hurt innocent people. You hurt those who are very important to me."

He gripped Kusanagi with both hands, sinking low.

"My name is Captain Nox Solveig," he roared for everyone to hear. "Remember it well, for it's the name of the man who slayed the Dragon King."

And then he shoved his unbreakable sword, the legendary Kusanagi from lore, straight through Ryuu Nova's chest, piercing his heart and shoving until the blade came out through his back.

Nova's eyes went wide. He opened his mouth, but no sound came out.

Solveig twisted the sword, then ripped it free with a deadly arc spray of blood.

Before Nova could fall, Solveig jumped into the air, swinging Kusanagi like he'd been born to wield the sword.

It sliced through flesh and muscle and bone.

When Solveig fell to the ground, crumpled like paper, Ryuu Nova's head fell, too.

It rolled across the ground before coming to a stop at the Blood Doctor's foot.

Nox Solveig didn't wait for Nova's body to collapse before the sweet release of unconsciousness swept over him.

Part Three

28

WHEN SOLVEIG OPENED HIS eyes, he half expected to be dead. He also half expected to be in a hospital or back on the *Dreamchaser*.

The last thing he expected was to be sprawled out on the floor of Nova's palace. Moonlight streamed down from the hole in the ceiling, pale and dusty as dawn slowly approached.

Unable to move the rest of his body, he turned his head to the side.

And nearly died when he came face-to-face with the severed, pale head of Ryuu Nova.

"Son of a –" he cursed, turning his head to look the other way.

Next to him, sprawled out in the same manner, was Thol, his eyes still closed and his chest rising and falling slowly.

Nova was dead. His crew was safe. *For now.*

Solveig closed his eyes again.

"What do you think happens when you die?" Solveig, eleven, tossed an apple in the air absently, catching it like it was a ball. Dirt clung to his nailbeds, thick as tar and just as stubborn.

"You're reincarnated," Thol, sixteen, said. He was older, stronger, and there was no dirt beneath his nails because he'd been the one to dig the graves, not cover them back up.

That was Solveig's responsibility.

In the span of a single day, he had gone from being the once-again youngest to being the only one left. He hadn't been born into the world an only child, yet he would die one now.

There were once five Solveig boys, the devil spawn of Mistress Silje Solveig – the little terrors who ruled the apple orchard atop the hill like they were kings.

And now there was only one Solveig boy left – Nox.

He tossed the apple up again but didn't bother catching it when it came falling down. It hit his head and bounced across the mulchy ground, rolling to a stop when it hit the roots of another tree.

"How long does reincarnation take?" he asked, eyes unfocused, turning the apple into a blob of red.

Thol hesitated. "Probably more than a day…"

Would his brothers even remember him when they were inevitably reborn? They wouldn't be his brothers anymore – not by blood. His wench mother was too sick to leave the house, and he didn't know who his father was. Silje Solveig always claimed that two of her sons shared a father, but that was the only thing she ever said about the men who managed to knock her up.

Not that it was very hard, but what did an eleven-year-old know?

Many years ago, the Solveig Boys had sworn an oath – I will pledge my final breath to your name and my first to find you again. Silly words coined by a want-to-be-poet, but words they all swore by regardless.

Loyal to each other until the end, loyal to each other in the next life.

He pulled his knees to his chest, trying – failing – to stay strong, to keep the tears back.

He couldn't even wrap his brothers in blankets before dropping them in their graves. All he could do was tear the makeshift flag they'd all made together in half, placing each piece around each brother. He couldn't bury his oldest brother with his quill and note-book; he couldn't bury his slightly older brother with his drawings because their wench mother was sick and quarantined in the house, infecting everything inside.

Tears streamed down Solveig's dirty cheeks, splashing unceremoniously on the ground. He wished the earth would open its gaping maw and swallow him whole so he wouldn't be alone anymore.

"Nox," Thol said softly. "They'll find us again. All of them will. They're my brothers, too."

Solveig wouldn't realize until much, much later, that Thol blamed himself for the deaths of three out of four of the Solveig Boys. He'd promised to protect them all, and yet two of them lay in fresh graves, their bodies still warm, and one would never return to the orchard again, his body lost somewhere uncharted.

But Thol didn't cry – he didn't cry when Solveig ran to him in tears, sobbing that the navy had come, that his brothers were dead. *He didn't cry when his shovel hit the earth, digging through dirt and rocks to create holes deep enough for a twelve- and thirteen-year-old. He didn't cry when Solveig covered their bodies, still wet with blood, and placed stones atop the graves.*

And he didn't cry now, not as he pulled the last Solveig Boy close, arms nearly suffocating as he hugged him tight.

"You're not alone," Thol whispered. "You still have one brother left. I might not be a Solveig, but I drank with you all, and I swore the same oath."

Solveig sobbed into his shoulder, surprising himself with how many tears he had left.

"I hate the navy," he whispered, voice thick with tears. "I hate them. I hate them. I hate them so much. I want to kill every last one of them. I want to make them suffer, too."

"You need to become a proper pirate first," murmured Thol, not once discouraging the idea. Because he, too, wanted to see the navy suffer. He, too, wanted vengeance for the innocent blood that had been spilled.

"That man..." Solveig broke free from the hug, rubbing his eyes with his dirty, tattered sleeve. Cold hatred seeped into his emerald eyes.

He would never forget the face of the man who pulled the trigger, shooting his brothers dead. It would be many years before he learned his name, but that face... Solveig burned it into his memory.

With cruel determination, he said, "I'm going to kill him one day. He will never take anything away from me again."

Czardas dreamed of cake. Delicious, tiered cake with thick layers of ganache and buttercream and fluffy sponge. Cake with slices of strawberries, with coffee cream, with edible flowers. Cake with sweet jam, with chocolate chips, with a dusting of powdered sugar. Chocolate cake, vanilla cake, strawberry cake, lemon cake... There wasn't a single type of cake he would not drool over, and he dreamed of plates of perfect slices all laid out for him to indulge in. He would eat cake for every meal if he could and never once get sick of it.

He didn't remember falling asleep, but he knew he must have passed out, not from exhaustion but from pain.

He'd watched as Solveig was pummeled, as Solveig killed Nova. Unable to move, he couldn't do anything but watch when Solveig crumpled to the ground, bleeding and surely on the verge of death.

The strange doctor, Isra, approached him, bloody and eyes gleaming silver, and said, "One good arm. You will help me."

And so, Czardas found himself dragging the bodies of his crew over to the gaping hole in the ground. Below, Lonan and Leo were unconscious, but Fynch was awake. The three of them – Fynch,

Czardas, and Isra – worked together; Fynch dragged cushions under the hole, and Czardas and Isra rolled the unconscious bodies of the crew down.

Before Czardas could join them, Isra put a hand on his shoulder – his uninjured one.

"May I?" they asked.

Czardas didn't get a chance to reply before Isra grabbed his arm and shoved it right back into the socket.

And then, the next thing he knew, he was dreaming of cake.

Delicious, fluffy, sweet cake…

His eyes shot open, and reality hit him all at once.

"F –" His eyes darted around the room.

"I'm right here, Czar." Fynch reached out, playfully tugging on one of Czardas's curls. "If almost dying gets people to care this much about me, maybe I should do it more often."

"I'll kill you myself if you ever say anything like that again," promised Czardas.

He sat up, wincing at the residual pain that sparked down his arm.

"The others –"

"All fine," Fynch interrupted. "Captain woke up once but is asleep again. Doctor Isra has been taking care of everyone."

He wore a bandage around his head, the fabric stained red by his ear. Noticing Czardas's stare, he reached up to touch it and said, "I got grazed by a bullet. Twice. I'm fine. Doctor Isra came back with medical supplies from their office. They've been treating everyone."

Czardas touched his tender shoulder gently, hissing in a breath through his teeth when he learned just how sore it still was. "Do you know what happened to everyone?"

Fynch just shrugged. "Dunno. It's barely been two hours since everything happened. I know Leo is just asleep because he over-worked himself, and Lonan apparently has heart problems. I think Miss Natha got the worst injury 'cause Doctor Isra had to use their ability on her, too. They're with her now."

He pointed to a corner of the room where Isra crouched hunched over Natha, a pile of bloodied rags next to them.

"Too?" he asked.

"It's a long story and one I don't really know," Fynch said flip-pantly. "Ask the doctor. Or Thol or Illie, 'cause they were there, too. I was just unconscious the whole time."

Czardas rubbed his face, trying to piece everything together. Had it really been two hours since the fight? It felt like a lifetime ago. But his pain was still fresh, his arms still sore from fighting enemies far stronger than he.

With a groan, he lay back down, staring up at the sliver of sky visible from the hole in the ceiling.

"We got a new ship," he said after a pause.

"Hm? Is the *Serenity* not fixed?"

"Captain sunk her. She was too damaged. So, we got a new one. The *Dreamchaser.* Don't worry, I moved your secret stash to a new hiding place. I'm sure you'll find it." His lips curled into the whisper of a smile. He knew Fynch too well for the thief to hide anything from him.

"Wow…" murmured Fynch. "What's the new ship look like?"

"She's…big. But faster than any ship I've ever seen. Her sails are black, too."

"Like a real pirate ship…"

"She's green, just like Solveig's coat. And she has tons of cannons – oh, we saw Sparrow."

Fynch grimaced. "What was my *brother* doing there?"

Czardas quickly explained how they ran in with the navy and fought Sparrow Largos, only for Sparrow to retreat before any real damage could be done.

"I wonder if he'll go back to Veridonia to tell the others," Fynch mumbled, clearly irritated at the fact that his brother was still around. Czardas knew there was some tension there, but it wasn't his place to say anything.

Even if he wanted to tell Fynch that Sparrow was a no-good coward and didn't deserve a brother as strong and talented as Fynch.

"He'll probably go to Aramore to tell the emperor that he fought bravely against the infamous Nox Solveig," Czardas grumbled.

"And lost."

"And ran away."

Fynch smirked. "Good riddance."

Czardas turned his head to face Fynch. "I'm glad you're okay. You're not allowed to get shot again."

Fynch turned away, gaze landing on Isra and Natha. For a while, he said nothing. Not for the first time, Czardas wished he could peer into Fynch's mind to see just what, exactly, he was thinking about.

Then, he said, "Do you regret running off with me and becoming a pirate?"

Czardas blinked. He must still be asleep because what sort of nonsense was *that?*

"F, what are you talking about?" he started, but Fynch, once again, interrupted.

"I took you away from your fancy life with your music and your family and all of that. And we've done nothing but get in fights and nearly die. You hurt your arm. Can you even hold your violin?" Fynch's shoulders shook, and at once, Czardas knew why he'd turned away.

He was crying.

"F, I told you I'd follow you anywhere." Czardas sat up. "Remember when I broke my arm when I was a kid? I couldn't play my violin, but I could still make music. I don't regret following you. I would do it again. There's nowhere you can go that I won't follow. You know this. Besides..."

He placed his hand on Fynch's shoulder, a silent reminder that he was there, that he wouldn't leave. He continued: "I want to figure out the origin of the *Eldoria Symphony,* remember? I can't do that if I'm trapped in my fancy life."

"You got hurt because you followed me," Fynch whispered.

"I got hurt because I threw a sword that weighed more than it looked."

Through his tears, Fynch snorted. "That's why I stick to guns. They're never heavy."

Czardas lay back down, an easy smile on his face. Changing the subject, hoping to get Fynch to stop crying, he said, "When Natha wakes up and recovers, I think I'll ask her to make us a cake. I'll show you where the galley is on the new ship if you promise to bring me a piece before Ves gets it all."

Fynch turned around, wiping his eyes, a lopsided grin plastered on his face. "Deal."

Lonan opened his eyes to find Leo slumped across his lap and a note tucked into the collar of his shirt. Frowning, he pulled the scrap of paper free and read the messy scrawl written across it.

STOP. SMOKING.

He clicked his tongue, crumpling the paper up and deciding that whoever wrote it was an idiot. Stop smoking? It wasn't like sugar cigarettes were actually harmful. They just filled his lungs with sweet oxygen and gave his teeth something to chew on. He could stop if he truly wanted to, but he didn't.

Reaching into his pocket, careful not to disturb Leo, he paused. His box of sugar cigarettes was gone; in their place was another slip of paper, one that read:

TOO MUCH OXYGEN MAKES YOUR HEART ACT UP.

He crumpled up that paper, too, tossing it as far as he could without waking Leo. Frustrated and unable to move or smoke, he looked around the room, taking in the destruction. He wasn't sure how much time had passed since his heart decided to try and kill him, but it seemed like someone let a cannon loose, taking down everything and everyone in its path.

Fynch and Czardas lay near each other, both awake, both talking softly. Lonan could hardly believe how the blond kid recovered so fast. Back in Port 16, he'd looked a day away from death, but he had a flush to his cheeks now, color that hadn't been there before.

Nox Solveig lay supine, body wrapped in bandages to keep him from moving around. Lonan's lips quirked at the sight; the infamous captain looked like a mummy, like a swaddled newborn. If not for the sword at his side and the severed head watching over him, he would have assumed Solveig was completely harmless.

Next to him was Thol, hands bandaged tightly. Cold cloths had been draped over his forehead, keeping the swelling bruises at bay – though they weren't doing a good job. Lonan could see the bruises from clear across the room.

Illie was tucked under a pile of blankets, hands wrapped in so many layers they looked like giant paws. Her pink hair fanned out around her. What had happened to her? It was the dead of summer; a clammy layer of sweat glued Lonan's shirt to his back, and he'd barely done anything to exert himself. Why was she bundled up like she was about to face Frys in the middle of winter?

On the other end of the room was Ves. Her head had been bandaged, hair sloppily braided to stay out of the way. A slight smile graced her deliciously full lips. Good. Lonan hated to see a pretty lady in pain. He hoped whatever she dreamt of was kinder than the hell she'd faced only a few hours ago.

And then there was Natha. Beautiful, exquisite, wonderful Miss Nathalia Divyne. The bloody doctor from before hunched over her, dabbing at her forehead and checking her pulse. Then, Lonan saw the pile of bloodied rags. Swallowing hard, his mind jumped to the obvious, terrible conclusion that she had been mortally wounded.

"Is she okay?" he asked, careful not to be too loud.

The doctor glanced over their shoulder. "She will be."

They offered no elaboration. Lonan frowned, but the doctor turned back to their work before he could say anything else.

The doctor must have been the bastard to take away his sugar cigarettes. Teeth grinding together, he said, "What happened?"

The doctor didn't look up this time. "Evisceration," was all they offered.

Oh, that bastard...

Leo stirred, and Lonan faltered. Sighing, he raked his hand through his hair and tipped his head back, staying as still as possible so Leo didn't wake.

"Can I have my sugar cigarettes back?" he asked, gaze fixed to the ceiling.

"No."

Leo held his middle finger up to the doctor's back.

"Fine. We didn't get properly introduced earlier. I'm Lonan Ryker, best helmsman in the Emerald."

He didn't expect the doctor to reply, but they did. "Isra. Doctor."

"Wow. So much information packed into those two words." He rolled his eyes. "Want to give me a bit more? How should I refer to you? As a gentleman? As a lady? Neither? Both?"

"Gender does not apply to me."

Well, there was something.

To his surprise, Isra continued: "I'd prefer it if you did not refer to me at all."

"And I'd prefer to have my sugar cigarettes back."

Leo stirred again. Lonan froze, biting the inside of his cheek to stay quiet so as to not wake him. Isra went right back to work without even hinting where they'd hidden the precious sugar cigarettes.

Oh, well. He'd just have to buy more come morning.

With a sigh, he reached down and rolled up Leo's pants, exposing the wooden leg he'd made for himself. Carefully, Lonan unclasped it, prying it off with ease. He knew the thing was uncomfortable if worn for long periods and that if Leo slept with it on, he'd wake up sore and cranky and usually took all of that out on Lonan (as if Leo forgetting to take his leg off was somehow Lonan's fault. It probably was). He propped the prosthetic against the wall and closed his eyes. His mind was too loud to sleep, but Leo was a human radiator, warming him more than any blanket ever could, and it was enough to lull him into a calm, not-asleep-not-fully-awake state.

Illie had been awake for some time, but her body ached too much for her to even think about moving. At least she knew she wasn't dead...

As much as she wanted to get up and get on the *Serenity* to resume the journey to find the lost moon, absolutely nothing could drag her up. Not even the sun spilling across her face, turning the pile of blankets atop her into an oven.

Eyes closed – even her sarding *eyelids* were sore, it seemed – she just listened to the conversations whispering around her.

Fynch and Czardas were both awake, currently whisper-arguing about the best flavor of ice cream (Czardas defended vanilla while Fynch claimed raspberry was the best. Illie liked both of those, but her favorite was black sesame).

Lonan rambled on about some lady he'd had three one-night stands with while Isra did their best to ignore him. Illie did, too.

Leo was still asleep, lying across Lonan's lap. Solveig, Thol, and Ves hadn't moved either, and Isra was still busy with Natha. It would be a while before they could return to the *Serenity*.

Sighing softly, she closed her eyes, mind drifting. Was her cat, Pleo, okay? Somehow, she'd managed to keep her books safe throughout the fighting. She hoped the plan was still to go to Merdyne and the Salts Atoll. She could use a week in the tropics, surrounded by warm water and white sand and more fruit trees than she knew what to do with.

It had been a long, long time since she'd last been to the Merdyne Empire. She'd sailed the world twice with her teacher, Henry Elgar, to work on charting the globe.

Fynch and Czardas's conversation shifted to whether caramel or chocolate went better with ice cream, and Illie's stomach grumbled. She already committed murder, treason, and a plethora of other crimes, yet she'd commit more for a gooey scoop of sweet ice cream smothered in chocolate sauce.

Burrowing deeper into her oven of blankets, hands tingling when she moved them ever so slightly, she began daydreaming of everything she'd beg Natha to cook once they were all back on the ship. Fried buns stuffed full of juicy meat, soup with noodles and crunchy vegetables, chewy cookies still hot from the oven...

"...Illie reading to me, I think."

She perked up when she heard her name, turning her head toward Fynch and Czardas.

Fynch continued: "It kept me from fading, I think. Even if the books were so boring, I'd rather die."

A smile tugged on her lips; she couldn't help but say, "Sorry I didn't think to pack adventure novels when you decided to start dying."

Both boys turned to face her. Then, without even speaking, they both scooted across the floor to be closer to her.

"How are your hands?" Czardas asked.

"I can feel them, so it can't be that bad," Illie said, shrugging as best as she could under the mountain of blankets. "What happened to you?"

His arm lay flat against his chest, held in place by a fabric sling.

"He threw a sword and dislocated his shoulder," Fynch answered, already back to his talkative self. He reached up and touched the bandage around his head before Illie could comment on it. She *had* been curious and was going to ask before he said, "I got shot again."

She stiffened, panic gripping her heart. Had he been shot *again* after his fight in the pavilion?

"A bullet grazed him," Czardas groaned.

Fynch ignored the comment. "What happened to *you?* I saw you throw your wind earlier. How did you do that?" His eyes sparkled like polished bits of jade.

"I don't know," she said truthfully. "It just...happened. I've had enough frostbite this year. I don't need any more."

And enough battles. Poet's breath, she felt like she'd been hit by a steam train that decided to back up and hit her again for good measure. If she never saw another dragon, it would be far too soon.

Czardas said, "Pleo is fine, by the way. She's adjusting well. She really likes the navigator room."

Illie frowned. Adjusting? To what?

Fynch, interrupting her thoughts, explained, "Captain Solveig sank the *Serenity,* and we have a new ship now. Apparently, it's way cooler and way better."

"What...?" she whispered.

"The *Serenity* was too damaged," Czardas explained. "But we have the *Dreamchaser* now. Leo made it. It's... I think everyone will like it. She's big, but she's fast. Faster than any other ship, probably."

She closed her eyes. It had only been a few weeks, but Illie felt a strong connection to the *Serenity*. Knowing it was gone... It felt like a piece of her had been sunk, too.

The *Serenity* would never make it to the lost moon.

But maybe, just maybe, the *Dreamchaser* would.

The headache tearing through Ves's skull was worse than any hangover she'd ever had. At least a hangover meant she'd had fun the night before. Not this. This was just pain, pain, and more pain that throbbed behind her eyes and made even her sarding teeth hurt.

Groaning softly, she pressed the heel of her hand to her forehead, trying to massage some of the tension away. What she needed was a barrel of cinnamon rum and enough ginger to make her sick. A film of acrid residue clung to her mouth, drying her tongue and leaving the vile aftertaste of vomit in her throat.

She rolled over, head throbbing as she sat up, blinking against the light.

Light.

Sunlight poured in from the hole in the ceiling, bathing the desecrated room in a warm wash of gold. Her heart jumped to her throat. *Natha.*

The last time she'd seen Natha, she'd been cut down – quite literally – by Nova, blood and guts spilling as she crumpled to the ground.

There. Next to a pile of bloodied rags lay Natha. Ignoring her headache, Ves scrambled across the floor.

"Alive," came a monotone voice.

Ves spun around – too fast. *Sard.* Everything blurred in a colorful frenzy, bleeding black at the edges. She swallowed a wave of nausea. Crouched next to Solveig was the doctor Isra. They barely looked up before resuming their work, stitching a wound on Solveig's scalp.

"For how long?" Ves asked, glancing at Natha. Her torso had been wrapped in bandages splotched with rust-colored stains. Her scarred arms lay by her sides, her blonde hair fanned around her head like a halo.

"Until she faces death again," answered the doctor. There wasn't even a lick of emotion in their voice, much to Ves's irritation.

She brushed a piece of hair from Natha's forehead. Then, carefully, she licked the pad of her thumb and wiped away the smudged lipstick across her chin.

"How's Cap?" she murmured.

"Stupid," grumbled the doctor. "But alive."

Ves sat back on her heels, trying to remember what had happened. The last thing she remembered was Natha falling, Nova's arm being sliced off, and that was it. Czardas, Solveig, Thol, and Isra had still been in the fight when she tapped out. How long had the battle drawn out after that?

"You're blessed by Dreamer, too, aren't you?" She turned around, still close to Natha but facing Isra now.

"Yes."

Her eyebrow twitched. Would it kill them to say more than one word at a damn time?

"What's your ability? I can see souls. And their weak spots now, apparently," she added, thinking of the dark spots that manifested in her last opponents.

"Blood heals," they explained poorly. "I can bring people back from the brink of death."

That must have been how they healed Fynch. And...*Natha.*

She swallowed hard. "A handy ability for a doctor. Did you become one before you learned about your ability or after?"

"My license was revoked."

She blinked. "Oh."

"But..." They looked up from their work. "Before. Survived the plague."

"What?!"

Isra flinched, eyes wide at her outburst. The others who were awake – Lonan (disgusting, she wished he was still unconscious), Illie, Czardas, and Fynch – all turned toward her.

But Isra went right back to work, trimming the stitches and wrapping a tight bandage around Solveig's head. Only then did Ves realize he'd been wrapped up like a mummy, bandages tight to keep him immobile.

They said calmly, "I'm immune. He is, too." They nodded toward Solveig.

Like that was a good enough answer.

They didn't elaborate, moving away from Solveig to look over Thol. Sighing, Ves lay down next to Natha, hoping the ebbing headache pounding relentlessly against her skull would fade soon.

29

WHEN THOL OPENED HIS eyes, three things hit him: the sharp ache in his hand, the gnawing hunger in his stomach, and just how dark it was.

Sard. Solveig –

He sat up, only to be met with a rush of pain from the back of his head, dizzying and confusing and –

And he wasn't on the roof anymore. There was no sound of battle. Just... Quiet chatter and soft snoring. Brow furrowed, he looked around to see that he was in the throne room just beneath the roof where the battle had commenced. Though sprawled out somewhat, the others took up only a small portion of the room.

Illie, Czardas, Fynch, Natha, Lonan, Ves, and Isra sat on one end of the room, Leo stretched across the floor by Lonan's side, and Natha lain out by Ves.

Solveig was next to Thol, wrapped up tight, a sword on one side of his supine body and a sarding decapitated head on the other.

Ryuu Nova's head.

Well, there went any appetite Thol might have had…

His fingers – the unbroken ones – twitched; he reached out to grab a strand of Solveig's red hair, tugging on it.

Solveig didn't stir.

Thol swallowed his worry. Isra was there; if anything happened to Solveig, they'd fix it. Thol still had one more debt to cash in, so Isra couldn't exactly refuse.

Asleep or not, Thol was just glad to have his brother back.

He tugged on Solveig's hair again, this time causing Solveig to stir.

Then, softly, Thol said, "Remember when we snooped through Mistress Solveig's jewelry box and gave the shiniest pieces to the crows in your orchard? I don't even remember why we did that, but I remember how furious she got. I think her face was as red as your hair. I was sure she was going to kill us. That was the most scared I'd ever been in my life."

"She burned one of Tuo's journals," Solveig croaked, voice barely even audible. "It was justified."

A grin split across Thol's face. "Welcome back, dragon slayer."

"Technically," Solveig murmured, voice thickly laced with pain, "He wasn't a dragon when I slew him."

"And technically, nobody knows but you."

The ghost of a smile graced Solveig's lips. It faded quickly, replaced by a grimace.

"Do you need Isra?" Thol asked, concerned. He knew Solveig was in pain; there was a reason Isra had tied him up to keep him from moving, even if Thol himself didn't know the extent of Solveig's injuries.

"The others are more important." He paused, then added, "But if you want to untie me, I'd like that."

"Not a chance."

Solveig huffed a sigh. "Then can you move this head? It's creeping me out."

That, Thol could do. He clambered to his feet, ignoring the throb in his skull, and grabbed Ryuu Nova's head by the hair. Just to annoy him, Thol set the head by Lonan with a smirk before returning to Solveig's side.

"I have something to tell you," Solveig whispered.

Thol turned his head toward him, silently prompting him to elaborate.

Solveig took a breath. Then, quietly, he said, "I sank the *Serenity.*"

Thol choked. Surely, he hadn't heard Solveig right...*right?* Maybe he just meant he left the *Serenity* behind in Port 16 and used a borrowed ship to get to Corsa. That seemed far more likely...

The room had gone quiet, though Thol didn't notice. Everyone seemed on edge as they listened to what Solveig said next. "I had to. Her keel was cracked. Unfixable. I'm sorry. I didn't want to, but...but there was no fixing her. I wanted to wait, but...I messed up. I know I did. We have a new ship now, but I know it's not the same."

Thol stared at the ceiling, unblinking. He barely even heard the rest of Solveig's words.

The *Serenity* was gone.

The ship he and his wife Meadow sailed on. The ship he'd worked to maintain even after he retired, the ship that he let Solveig sail...

Gone.

Part of him wanted to reach over and throttle Solveig for being such a selfish idiot, for sinking the ship without the whole crew present, but...

But he glanced over and saw the pain on Solveig's face – the way his brow creased, the way his eyes narrowed as he held back tears – and he let out a soft sigh.

It had been Solveig's ship, too. Solveig had been the one to make the impossible decision to retire the *Serenity* – a decision he'd made *alone.*

"I guess it's payback for sinking the *Sea Wyrm* alone," Thol finally said. "Tell me about this new ship, then."

Natha stood on her toes, barely reaching the top of the stove even when she stood on a stool. She wasn't allowed to be in the kitchen alone, especially not in front of the stove. If her parents found out that she'd turned the burner on and set a pot of water atop it, she'd be in enough trouble that any dreams of cooking ever again would be squandered.

She had to be extra careful and extra quiet.

She pretended to go to sleep that night, but after her parents retired to their room, she snuck out of hers and went straight to the kitchen to get to work, her nightgown trailing behind her as she went. Hopefully, the surprise meal would be enough to get her out of trouble when her mother and father inevitably figured out what she'd done.

Sticking her tongue out, she peered at the recipe book for the next step. Frowning, she leaned closer, trying to get a better look at the words.

As she lowered herself just a bit, spoon in hand, she thought that the stove seemed hotter than normal.

That's when she saw the orange lick of flames not safely contained beneath her pot but on the gauzy sleeves of her nightgown.

Natha screamed, falling off the stool as she waved her arms like a bird, desperate to get the fire gone. But the air only made the fire burn hotter, brighter, and she could hardly feel the tears that raced down her cheeks as the searing agony consumed her arms.

Footsteps thundered; the door swung open.

"Nathalia!" her mother cried.

A blur of things happened next, but she was too stricken with tears, with screaming, with trying to get the fire off even though it had settled deep in her bones, to notice.

The next thing she recalled was waking up in a very uncomfortable bed with bright lights around her and a sharp needle stuck in the back of her tightly bandaged little hand.

Natha groaned softly. It still felt like she was holding her arms in a pool of lava, but she couldn't move.

At once, arms wrapped around her, nearly crushing her.

"Oh, Nathalia," her mother murmured into her hair. "What were you thinking?!"

Tears welled in her eyes. "I-I wanted to surprise you..."

Her mother choked on a sob and just hugged her tighter, whispering over and over and over again how happy she was that Natha was still alive.

Natha stayed in the hospital for two weeks while her burns healed. The doctor quietly told her mother she would be lucky if she ever held a pen again.

She dreamed.

She dreamed of that moment, that precipice where she had the whole world beneath her and how it had crumbled to nothing in less than a heartbeat.

She dreamed of her organs outside of her abdomen, slick and sticky.

She dreamed of her arms, of how her ex-husband was so disgusted by them that he required her to wear long gloves all the time.

She dreamed of fire and claws and inescapable death.

She dreamed of the burning flash that accosted her at once, the heat that had been inside her now outside as talons gutted her like a fish, dooming her to a fate that should have been fatal.

(But wasn't).

Natha dreamed because she was still, against all sarding odds, *alive.*

Throughout the day, the pirates woke and slept. Isra checked on each of them, assessing their injuries one by one. Solveig and Natha were in the worst shape – the captain had been stabbed twice and suffered a concussion that could be dangerous without close monitoring, while Natha had been eviscerated. It was nothing short of a miracle that their power had reset, that they made it across the roof in time just before her heart stopped completely. She would recover; Isra would make sure of it.

It surprised Isra just how resilient the pirates were. The only ones who had yet to open their eyes were Natha and Leo – who was so exhausted Isra could not blame him.

Despite their injuries – rather, in spite of them – the pirates seemed to have just as much energy now as they did when Isra first met them. Crouched by Natha, they watched as the pirates huddled close, talking about nothing. Occasionally, one would lay down to rest, and the others would speak softer, careful not to disturb their companion. Part of Isra wanted to scold them – between the seven conscious pirates, there were three concussions, two stab wounds, one broken hand, one dislocated shoulder, one severe case of frostbite, and one still-healing gunshot wound – but...it wasn't like they were getting up and moving around. They stayed contained to one area of the room, hardly moving, never once complaining about how much pain they were surely in.

Had Ryuu Nova or any of his crew suffered even a *fraction* of the injuries Solveig's crew had, Isra's clinic would be overbooked and full of sobbing men.

They peeled back Natha's bandages, checking the wounds that sliced across her abdomen. Pleased with how the sutures looked, they rewrapped the bandages, listening to the snippets of conversation behind them.

"It has *so many* cannons. Ves could probably sink another fleet with them." That came from the musician, Czardas. He'd sustained a dislocated shoulder but would recover quickly if he limited his usage of the arm.

"'Course it's the best ship out there," bragged Lonan, the one who had quite nearly had a heart attack and a horrible sugar cigarette addiction. "Leo built it."

"And you did nothing, Sugar," said Ves, one of the many who suffered a concussion.

"Ooh, pet names, I like it," said Lonan, and even Isra shuddered.

"Not a pet name. I'm just calling you what you smell like," shot back Ves.

Isra glanced over their shoulder to make sure they weren't fighting. Their gaze drifted involuntarily to the decapitated head sitting on the throne Ryuu Nova once called his.

They pressed their fingers against Natha's neck, checking her pulse. Satisfied, they turned toward the pirates.

"Nova put the heads of his enemies on pikes," they said plainly. Something Nova threatened Isra with.

Something that instilled fear in anyone who came to Servedin Island.

Something that would, without a doubt, prove to everyone that Nova no longer ruled Corsa.

Whether the others realized it or not, Ryuu Nova had been dead for over a day. The only reason his head hadn't started to smell was because Isra took care of it with supplies they brought from their clinic. The sun rose and set and rose again, and for the first time in years, Isra was free to practice medicine as they wished.

Sort of.

Their medical license didn't magically get *un*revoked the moment Nova died, but it was a step, and that was all that truly mattered.

Pushing to their feet, Isra tugged off their gloves and put them in the pocket of their stiff once-white-now-rust-brown coat. A ghost of a smile tugged on the corner of their lips, there for a fraction and gone in a heartbeat.

They stepped out of the room, making it only a few steps before a hand touched their shoulder. Spinning around, they raised their hand, ready to attack, only to falter when it was just Thol.

"You need to rest," they said stiffly.

"I've had worse, as you know."

And then Thol's arms were around Isra, their body pulled close against his in a constricting hug that made them feel like a fish trapped in an octopus's tentacled grasp.

"Unhand me," they hissed, writhing like a worm as they tried – and failed – to get free.

His grip only tightened, and for a moment, Isra worried they were going to pop, that this was some sort of attempt on their life for siding with Nova and double-crossing Thol and his friends.

But before Isra could burst, Thol pulled away, the smile across his face barely masking the pain beneath.

"Go rest," they said, straightening their coat and pushing their long hair off their shoulders.

"Nox told me what you did," he said instead of obeying and going back to rest. That stubborn meathead of a man... "Plaguing Nova. Literally. You saved all of us. *I* owe *you* now."

They raised their brow. All of this because...they'd infected Nova with a plague concentrate so deadly its effects were instant? Because they, too, wanted Nova gone and resorted to biological warfare to weaken him?

Pirates were such strange people.

Shaking their head, they said, "The plague is awful. Shouldn't have resorted to that."

Thol lifted his shoulders in a lazy shrug. "Doesn't matter. You did it regardless, and it saved all our asses. And you saved Fynch and Natha, so... Thank you."

Isra looked away. *What is this strange feeling...?* they wondered, brow furrowed at the odd fluttering in their chest. They said, "I'll be back. Go rest."

They could hear the grin in Thol's voice: "Whatever you say, Doctor. But *you* need to rest, too."

They could rest later. They still had patients to take care of.

Isra returned later with more bandages and food from a nearby café. As hungry as he was, Solveig was still, unfortunately, tied up, so he could only watch as his crew scurried over and began passing things out. The smell of buttery bread and cooked meat made his stomach grumble.

Lonan said something to Isra, then walked over, crouching next to Solveig and using a dagger to cut the bandages away. "Doc said you can be free, but you can't move too much."

He grabbed a bowl and handed it to Solveig, who took it gratefully. Inside was a mix of chicken, rice, and pineapple. It could have been inedible slop for all he cared, too hungry to even notice the flavors as he shoveled it into his mouth.

Lonan stretched his legs out with a sigh. He eyed the sword that hadn't once left Solveig's side. "That piece there... It's cracked."

Solveig paused mid-bite, looking down at Kusanagi. He hadn't noticed it before, but sure enough, the mirrored glass set in the center of the handguard was fissured. He lowered his fork, brow furrowed, and reached into his pocket. His fingers met the smooth surface of what he was looking for.

It felt like a lifetime had gone by since he'd bought the small disc of glass, way back when his crew was just two people. He ran his thumb over the surface. He'd got it to use as a signaling device, to reflect the sun and shine messages in case he was separated from his crew again. But... It was the exact size and shape as the broken mirror.

Using his fork, Solveig wiggled the mirror free. He slid the glass disc in.

It fit perfectly.

Lonan popped a piece of pineapple into his mouth. "That's one of those legendary swords, huh?"

"Kusanagi," answered Solveig. He tore his gaze from the sword, snatching his bowl away from Lonan before he could pilfer another piece of fruit. "The unbreakable blade. Legend says it can cut through anything."

"Cut through a dragon nicely." Lonan glanced at the severed head. "And Nova."

And Nova...

"You know, I was starting to think that head of yours was incapable of thinking," Lonan said flippantly. "But you look lost in thought. Kase for your thoughts, Cap'n?"

Illie had killed the captain of the Redcoat Pirates on Bowhead Rock. Solveig held power over Carilon and the Icarus Strait.

But Solveig killed Nova. And now...

He shoved his bowl into Lonan's hands and stood, ignoring the shockwave of pain that engulfed his body. It was a temporary ache. He had to do this now before anyone else claimed what was his.

Kusanagi slid into his belt, and he grabbed Nova's head, fisting his hair and trying not to gag.

"Nox, where are you going?" Thol asked.

"Cap?" Ves frowned.

Solveig ignored them all, focusing instead on taking one step, then another, then another, pain reverberating up and down his spine with each calculated movement.

One step at a time.

Just one step at a time.

For them – for all of them.

Sun washed over Solveig the moment he stepped outside, warm and welcoming. A group had gathered outside the palace, though their chatter died the moment they saw Solveig.

Captain Nox Solveig, cloaked in green, set out to conquer the Emerald Sea. One day he'll go down to the drink. How many navy ships will he sink?

In the daylight, he got a better look at the palace. Sharpened stalks of bamboo lined the pathway, the ends stained a rusty brown. *Perfect.*

"My name is Captain Nox Solveig!" he shouted.

His words smothered the crowd in a thick blanket.

A wicked grin split across his face. He held Nova's head high. "And I killed Ryuu Nova. Tell everyone the Dragon King is dead and that *I* killed him. That Servedin Island belongs to *me* now."

The crowd exploded. And Solveig just *grinned.*

He slammed Nova's head onto one of the spikes. In one fluid motion, he drew Kusanagi. The newly embedded piece of glass glinted in the light. He pointed the tip of the blade at the crowd.

"You make sure this gets all the way back to Helios," his voice boomed. "You make sure he knows that I, Captain Solveig of the *Dreamchaser,* am the new king of Servedin."

30

NATHA HAD NOT SLEPT in a proper bed since she left her flat in Veridonia, so when she opened her eyes and realized she wasn't in a hammock but atop a mattress the size of her old flat's bedroom – one swathed in red silk sheets embroidered with serpentine dragons – she thought for sure she was dead.

And then three very distinct things hit her at once, proving that she was not dead.

Hunger gnawed her insides.

Pain blossomed from her belly, hot and burning and making it impossible for her to breathe.

A fullness in her bladder overwhelmed the former two, and that alone was what made her realize she was (unfortunately) still alive.

Because why in Poet's name would she have to *piss* if she was dead?

Pressing a hand to her belly, she sat up and looked around the room that was most definitely not a room on the *Dreamchaser*.

I'm still in the palace, she thought, glaring at a painting of a dragon. Nova's ego was even bigger than her ex-husband's...

Nova.

Her eyes went wide. The last thing she remembered was kicking the dragon and a flash of claws...

Heart in her throat, Natha tore at the bandages wrapped around her middle. There, stretching across her torso in three jagged lines, were rows of stitches, reaching from her ribs to her hips. The longest one curved across her belly, and she knew... Gods, she knew that was the one that her organs had spilled out of.

She lay back down, lungs heaving. Sweat sluiced down her face, soaking into her cracked, dry lips.

She should be dead. She'd been sarding *eviscerated.*

How in Dreamer's name was she still breathing?

She must have said that aloud because Vesperine sarding Genevieve said, "The same way Birdie's still breathing. Doc saved your life. Fixed you up real good."

The chair she'd been sitting on creaked as Ves stood. She tossed something that Natha weakly caught. A shirt – one of Ves's.

"How long...?" she whispered, gripping the fabric tightly.

"Two days." The bed dipped as Ves sat down. "Give or take."

Natha's gaze drifted down, landing on the bunched fabric in her hands. The smell of Ves's mango soap accosted her senses. *Two days...*

Were the others okay? Had...had Nova been defeated?

As if reading her mind, Ves said, "Cap killed Nova. Cut his head right off and stuck it on a stick outside. Declared himself king of Servedin. Doc is pretty pissed at him 'cause of how hurt he got, but everyone's fine. The only one who hasn't woken up yet is Goggles, but Doc said he's fine. Just exhausted."

Natha pulled the shirt over her head, wincing when the stitches along her belly tugged. The fabric settled loosely over her body, several sizes too big but soft and familiar, if slightly too sweet smelling.

Ves continued, "You got the worst injuries of us all. Well, Cap was hurt pretty bad. Stabbed twice, apparently. But Doc had to use their ability on you. They're blessed by Dreamer, too. The others will want to know that you're awake."

She stood, ready to leave, but Natha reached out and grabbed her wrist. Ves paused, then wordlessly sat back down. Natha didn't let go.

"You know, I think out of everyone else," she mused, "The one most eager for you to wake up is Birdie. I think Cap's about ready to tie him up because he keeps coming in here."

Fynch...

Natha and Fynch hadn't gotten off on the right foot. He was crew, and she would catch a bullet for him, but...the little thief drove her to the brink of her sanity more often than not. Their paths had crossed when he stole from her kitchen back in Veridonia, and even now, she found him stealing from the galley often enough that she started making extra just for him to pilfer.

As much as she wanted to believe his concern stemmed straight from his never-ending stomach, Natha knew better.

She looked up through her lashes, meeting Ves's jade gaze. "What about you?"

With her free hand, Ves pushed a stray curl off her forehead. "We were all worried," she said, nonchalant.

Natha peeled her eyes away, gaze flitting around the room as she took it in fully for the first time. It looked to be some sort of guest suite – large but not massive enough for a king. It was decorated simply, the repeating motifs of dragons everywhere. It was the same way she'd decorated the guest rooms in the house she shared with Adrian – bland, monochromatic, themed. While she used themes of seashells and nautical ephemera, Nova clearly preferred dragons. They decorated the walls, the lampshades, there was even a tiny jade dragon carving with a ring around its neck on the table next to the bed – almost hidden amongst the plates and cups and piled dishes that looked so out of place they had to be new.

A tiny smile tugged on her lips.

She could act as nonchalant as she wanted, but Natha knew the truth; Fynch had come and gone, visiting Natha frequently, but Ves...

She'd never left.

It was evening when Natha finally felt strong enough to leave the plush bed. The jade dragon carving tucked in her pocket, she stood with the help of Ves. Her belly throbbed, aching with each tiny step she took, but Ves... Ves wrapped her arm around Natha's middle, steadying her without ever touching the tender stitches there.

"I'm sorry," Natha whispered, sweat dripping down her face as she concentrated on taking another step, another, another. Each footfall sent a nauseating wave of intense agony from gut to fingertips.

"For what?" Ves scoffed. "You're hurt because that dragon douche attacked you. I mean, unless you're apologizing for being possibly the only person in history to survive being gutted by a dragon – and even *then,* I have no idea why you would – there's nothing to be sorry for."

Warmth flooded Natha's cheeks. She shook her head. "Because it's taken us ten minutes to walk fifteen feet."

"I *am* a foot taller than you," said Ves pointedly. "Half of the reason why we're going slow is because I have to walk at a right sarding angle."

Natha snorted – and instantly regretted it, the pain sending white spots to invade her vision.

"You don't *have* to bend down so much," she said, stifling a laugh that she knew would pull her stitches free. "And I'm only *eleven* inches shorter than you."

"Psh. Details." Ves grinned, her lip ring glinting in the light. "It's not like the others will leave without us. We're too important."

That wasn't what Natha was worried about. An hour ago, Solveig came into the room to let her and Ves know that they were going to head back to the *Dreamchaser* and that he'd arrange to have a carriage waiting so Natha didn't have to make the trek through the forest again. She knew Solveig wouldn't leave without the two, and she knew the rest of the crew was probably already well into their cups, savoring the booze they'd been gifted by the people of Corsa.

Isra had left after checking her wounds once more, presumably returning to their clinic to accept new patients. They'd left her with a list of instructions on how to care for the sutures, the notes tucked in her pocket alongside the dragon carving.

No, what worried Natha was Ves.

"You don't have to do this," she said, guilt eating away at her just as much as the hurt was. "You could be with the others. I can walk on my own."

"You could," Ves said, "But I want to help you. We're crew, Blondie. We stick together. I know Doc said you need to walk –" that was one of the instructions Isra wrote down, claiming that if Natha didn't move around she could risk getting blood clots in her legs "– but they can stick it where the sun doesn't shine if you'd rather I carried you."

A month ago, Natha would have pummeled Ves for even suggesting such a thing, stitches be damned. She would have assumed the kindness was a mockery, a cruel jibe meant to insinuate she was weak.

Natha was not weak. Ves was right; how many people in the history of Syrenis had been gutted by a literal *dragon* and *lived?* If that made her weak, what did that make Solveig, an un-blessed man who severed the head of a dragon alone?

As if the world would call *him* weak.

She shook her head. "I'm fine. I'll manage.

Ves beamed. "You always do, Blondie. You always do. Come on; we have a lost moon to find."

Solveig was three glasses of cinnamon rum deep when he heard the familiar voice of his third calling from the gangplank.

"Oh, Cap!" Ves cried in a singsong voice. "I'd ask if you missed us, but of course you did. The more important question is, did you leave any liquor for us?"

Two hours ago, Solveig and the others said their goodbyes to Isra and left Natha and Ves at the palace to return at their own pace. Thol had told Solveig to stay as well, but he insisted. By the time they made it back to the careened *Dreamchaser,* his face had gone pale, and he needed to sit. The others worked to get the ship back in the water and around to the marina.

It felt strangely empty with Nova's fleet gone. The liberated people of Corsa were quick to sink any ships bearing the flag of the Dragon King.

And then came the gifts. The people of Corsa came in a parade, bringing barrels of rum and rice wine, crates of food, and chests full of what Solveig could only assume were riches from Nova's treasury. He accepted most of those, telling the people to keep the rest. At first, they resisted, but when Solveig reminded them that he was the king and he could simply order the citizens to keep their riches, they relented.

(Though he did hear a few murmurs that the treasure would go right back to the treasury for Solveig to take later).

He set his glass down and made it across the deck in just a few strides.

"I swear to Dreamer if you're using anything from *my* kitchen..." Natha threatened. Despite her easy smile, Solveig knew she was being serious.

"Only a few dishes that Lonan already volunteered to wash," he said with a shrug.

"Did not!" shouted Lonan from across the deck. "Oh, lovely Miss Natha! How is the loveliest lady in the Emerald Sea faring?"

By the way she held up her middle finger, Solveig could tell she was faring just fine.

All things considered, at least.

"The people of Corsa gave us gifts. Monetary *and* edible," Solveig added. "You can add everything to the inventory later. Right now, we're celebrating."

Celebrating the death of Ryuu Nova.

Celebrating Solveig's newfound title as pirate king of Servedin Island.

Celebrating the reunion with Illie, Thol, and Fynch.

Tomorrow, they would resume their journey to Merdyne and the Salts Atoll to find the lost moon and Anwir's dead god.

Tonight, they would revel in their freedom.

If Nox Solveig was only meant to be a king for a day, he would make it count.

Illie came by with a handful of mugs. She passed them out – cinnamon rum for Solveig and Ves, water for Natha – with a grin. At her ankles was Pleo the tabby cat, purring up a storm.

Despite her initial qualms with the new ship, Illie had adjusted quickly. Solveig refused to step foot in the ladies' barracks, but he could hear her squealing with joy on the other side of the door as she found her hammock and books. She didn't stay in there long, throwing open the door and racing to find the navigation room. Solveig *did* follow her in there, leaning against the doorframe with a wide smile as he watched her figure out where her maps and tools were. The moving lithograph of the Wandering Isle sat on display right where she could see it. He'd given her Anwir's map to copy down – he refused to part with the original, just in case – and she quickly pinned that to the wall above her desk.

Fynch had been just as excited, practically drooling when he saw all the cannons and the ammo stored in the hull below. He only allowed himself to be dragged away from the armory of pistols and swords and endless bullets when Czardas whispered something in his ear, and they took off running like children.

He'd been the most worried about Thol, nervous to see how his closest friend would react.

Thol had stood in the middle of the deck, head tipped back to watch the black flag rippling in the gentle breeze. He'd said nothing for a long time.

Then, turning to Solveig, he simply stated, "They'd be proud."

And then he went off in search of a drink.

Illie held the fourth glass in her bandaged hands. "I always thought it was, like, illegal to have Dreamer as a figurehead on a ship. Isn't this so cool? You should sit down, Natha. I can have Lonan bring some chairs out..."

Natha shook her head. "I've sat on my ass long enough. I'll be fine."

Solveig brought his glass to his lips, downing the spicy rum in just a few gulps. It settled in his belly like magma, taking away some of the pain and replacing it with a familiar, warm buzz.

With a swing of his arm, he turned to face his crew. "It won't be long before Jonyth Commodore hears about what we've done here. Servedin Island may be ours, but that sarding man doesn't know how to say *no*. So, drink! Eat! Celebrate, because tomorrow we weigh anchor and head for Merdyne!"

Leo's eyes shot open as panic flooded his system.

He forgot to take his leg off before going to sleep.

It wasn't like he'd spontaneously combust if he left it on overnight, and he was sure his illness wouldn't come back, but he'd done it before, and it was always a miserable experience. His stump and prosthetic became slick with sweat, and his leg ended up being sore, both from a rash and from the limited circulation and mobility sleeping with a chunk of wood strapped to his body brought.

He reached for his leg only to find nothing there.

Not the first time he'd woken up to find his leg surprisingly missing...

"Cool it, legless."

He whipped his head around to see Lonan slouched in a chair, tucking something into his pocket. Leo's leg rested against the wall next to him.

"About time you finally woke up." He took out his box of sugar cigarettes – no, not his box, a new one. Leo didn't recognize this brand – and stuck one between his teeth. "I might just start calling you Princess Sundown."

Princess Sundown was the name of a fairy tale protagonist who, after kissing a tigress's mate, ended up cursed to sleep for a hundred and one years. Eventually, the hero of the story, Mage Anatole, slew the tigress enchantress and her mate, breaking Princess Sundown's curse. Lonan's sisters loved the story, so Leo heard it a million times whenever he was at the Ryker house.

Leo frowned. "What's that supposed to mean?"

Lonan, to his surprise, didn't ask Leo to light his cigarette. He flicked open a lighter and held it over the sugar cigarette until a sweet string of smoke filled the air. He said, "You were asleep for over two days. I was starting to wonder if I had to go slay a couple of tigers for you to wake up."

Two days...

Leo flopped onto the stiff bed, memories coming back to him in dreamlike fragments.

Then he sat up again, blurting, "Wait, where the hell are we?"

Lonan snorted. "You don't recognize your own ship, Sundown? We're on the *Dreamchaser*. Captain's quarters. Which, apparently, aren't being used for any captain. They've turned this place into a meeting area slash recovery room."

Bleary, Leo glanced around the room. The familiarity of his ship came back to him. How could he forget?

You overexerted yourself, piped up the helpful voice in the back of his head. *You're exhausted. And hungry. Because you were asleep for two days like some sort of fairy tale princess.*

Lonan explained the situation, though Leo barely listened. After his fight with Cynthia, Leo had been taken to the palace where the battle against Nova took place. Solveig eventually won, beheading Nova, and declared himself pirate king of Servedin Island. The pirates celebrated well into the night, and now, several hours later, Leo was awake.

"Which means I have to get to work," finished Lonan with a sigh. He puffed out a cloud of smoke. "And get this baby ready to sail first thing in the morning. We're heading to Merdyne next. You think we'll see Nefeli? Gods, I hope so. I bet the pictures of her don't do her any justice."

We...

"I hope for Nefeli's sake we *don't* meet her," Leo murmured. "If you're not going to do anything important, you can at least get me something to eat. I'm hungry."

"I was recounting our adventure, Mister Impatient," Lonan said flippantly. He waved his cigarette through the air, leaving a trail of saccharine sugar smoke in its wake. "Which is rather important, if you ask me."

"I'm not asking you."

"There are these things on your face, you know, called *eyes.* If you used them, you'd see that I grabbed you something to eat before everyone else could hoard it all." He pointed at a tray on the floor with the butt of his cigarette.

Groaning, Leo reached down and grabbed the tray. It wasn't the most decadent of feasts, more of an amalgamation of things that he wouldn't normally pair together – rice balls, roasted vegetables, a whole stack of pineapple rings, fried fish coated in a crispy batter – but he was hungry enough that he wolfed it down.

He licked his fingers clean and said, "Give me my leg."

Lonan grabbed the prosthetic and handed it over. Leo pushed up his pant leg and got to work fastening the prosthetic to his stump. He flexed it a few times, making sure it fit just right. Then, he swung both legs over the side of the bed and stood.

"Come on. I have to make sure these pirates didn't wreck my ship like they did with the last one," he said.

31

MORNING CAME WITH A pounding headache, a dose of regret, and a newspaper Solveig did not want to read until he was far, far, *far* away from Corsa.

Lonan and Leo – who had awoken sometime in the middle of the night, apparently – prepared the *Dreamchaser* for a hasty departure, hauling the anchor up and dropping the sails. As she sipped on her tea, Illie grabbed a flighty little gale and threw it into the black sails, giving the *Dreamchaser* a boost as she tore out of the marina and into the open ocean.

Late last night, after drinking and eating until he felt like he'd explode, Solveig pulled his crew onto the deck and cast a vote. The answer had been unanimous, but Solveig had yet to act on it.

Standing at the bow, he watched the horizon, knowing Servedin was becoming nothing more than a speck behind him. With a sigh, he opened the newspaper, flipping to the most wanted pages.

His heart leaped to his throat and stuck there.

Fifth most wanted: *vacant.*

Fourth: Vesperine Genevieve, three hundred seventy million lune.

Third: Bartholomew Williams, four hundred fifteen million lune.

Second: Ellery Anor, four hundred ninety-nine million lune.

First: Nox Solveig, five hundred million lune.

And beneath his wanted poster was a new list: a list of titles and a list of names.

Nox Solveig, Captain of the Dreamchaser Pirates, Warlord of the Icarus Strait, Pirate King of Servedin Island. The Dreamchaser Pirates include Bartholomew Williams, Vesperine Genevieve, Illie Valentine, Nathalia Divyne, Czardas Rossi, Fynch Largos, Lonan Ryker, and Galileo Genovese.

It wasn't the fact that *two* of his crew – of the so-called Dreamchaser Pirates – made the top five. It wasn't the fact that the fifth most wanted space was left vacant. It wasn't even that his crew had been given a formal name or that Lonan and Leo were, apparently, considered Dreamchasers.

It was the fact that he had made the first most-wanted spot – a spot that always belonged to the Unnamed God.

The Unnamed God's wanted poster was missing completely, as though he'd been wiped clean off the planet.

Solveig flipped hurriedly through the pages, trying to find some-thing – *anything* – that hinted at the Unnamed God's fate, but...

Nothing.

Crumpling the paper in his fist, he turned toward his crew.

Illie, who sat beneath the sails, sipping tea and flipping through a book, her cat Pleo curled up on her lap. She wore bandages around her hands, but frostbite was easy to heal compared to other injuries.

Natha, who walked up and down the stairs to and from the quarterdeck, hand clasped over her middle, her face contorted in pain. Still, she didn't stop, determined to get back to normal. She had given him an amethyst ring she claimed to have found on a dragon. It fit perfectly on his ring finger next to his moonstone ring.

Ves, who sat on the ground, a crate beside her and her orange ledger balanced on her knees. Her concussion was healing nicely, and she went right to busying herself with the inventory.

Czardas, who followed Fynch around, singing some song Solveig had never heard before. His arm rested across his chest, held in place by a sling. It would be a while before he could play the violin again, but he seemed just fine with singing.

Fynch, who inspected each cannon before standing near the railing, aiming his pistol and firing, only to start laughing as if whatever he'd shot was the funniest thing ever. He didn't have the same energy as he did before getting shot, but his cheeks were flushed, and he smiled his chipped-toothed smile.

Thol, who sat near the helm, tinted spectacles over his eyes, ice wrapped in cheesecloth balanced on his broken knuckles. It wasn't the first time he'd shattered his fingers, nor would it be the last.

Lonan and Leo – who weren't officially crew but were apparently recognized as it – at the helm, steering the *Dreamchaser* toward the Ruby Sea.

He took a breath and walked up the stairs to the helm. One by one, as if sensing what he was about to do, the rest of his crew followed him until all nine were huddled around the wheel.

"This isn't creepy one bit..." murmured Lonan. He leaned on the wheel, taking a slow drag of his sugar cigarette.

"The navy made up a name for us," Solveig said, brandishing the crumpled newspaper. "They're calling us the Dreamchaser Pirates. *Us.* That includes you two."

Lonan perked up. Leo's eyes went wide.

Solveig continued before either of them could speak: "So, I'm formally inviting you to join as helmsman and shipwright. There's an oath I'll have you swear, should you choose to join. If not, that's fine. You can sail us around until we get our treasure and return back to Port 16. It's up to –"

"What's the oath?" blurted Leo.

Solveig recited the words.

Chest puffed out, Leo said, "I will pledge my final breath to your name, and my first to find you again. There. Am I a pirate now?"

Solveig grinned. "Welcome aboard, shipwright."

Lonan pulled his cigarette from his teeth and repeated the words. "I will pledge my final breath to your name, and my first to find you again."

But before Solveig could say anything, before he could properly welcome his helmsman, a third voice spoke up.

"I will pledge my final breath to your name, and my first to find you again."

Nine heads spun around to see, standing at the base of the stairs, none other than Israfel Eliad, wearing their white coat, sleeves rolled up to expose a bloody bandage on their wrist.

They cocked a brow. "You need a doctor."

Solveig grinned wildly. "Doctor, helmsman, and shipwright! Well, Dreamchasers, how does it feel to sail under the most wanted pirate in the world?"

Solveig stood at the bow of the *Dreamchaser,* watching the gentle lapping of waves against the ship's green hull three days later, the sun sitting low in the sky as it threatened to sink beneath the horizon when Fynch's shrill voice cut through the peace.

"Man overboard!"

At once, Solveig pushed away from the railing, spinning around to do a desperate headcount. Nine. There were nine people in his crew, and all nine were on the deck.

Heart racing, Solveig ran to the starboard railing to see what had caught Fynch's attention.

A piece of wood floated gently in the waves. At first, Solveig thought it was nothing more than a piece of flotsam with netting and cloth atop it.

But he caught a flash of flesh and grabbed a rope.

"Oh, sard..." breathed Illie, who joined them.

Looking up, Solveig saw what caught her attention.

A broken mast stuck out of the waves, barrels, and wood floating around it. A sarding *shipwreck.* Acrid smoke filled the air, tainted with the stink of brine. The fire had gone out days ago, leaving only smoldering charcoal behind.

Illie moved before Solveig could, grabbing a wind and whipping it down, hauling the shipwrecked survivor up. She dropped him on the deck, turning away quickly – not before Solveig caught a glimpse of tears in her eyes and the way she cradled her hands against her chest.

The person was a man, no older than Solveig by the looks of it. He wore a form-fitting sleeveless top that showed off his toned arms. One of them had a scar on it – three crescents stacked atop each other. *Where had he seen that before...?*

"Move," demanded Isra, shoving through the crowd. They dropped to their knees and checked the stranger's pulse. "Alive. Barely."

They pressed their hands to the stranger's chest and began compressions. Solveig held his breath – they all did.

Then, the stranger rolled onto his side, vomiting up seawater. Isra pulled back, never once flinching, not as the stranger heaved and choked, spitting out salt.

He rolled onto his back, chest heaving, staring into the sky.

"Wh-where...?" he croaked.

That accent!

Solveig crouched down. "You're on the *Dreamchaser.* I am Captain Nox Solveig."

"N-Nox Solveig..." his eyes went wide before rolling back into his skull. Unconscious.

There were two things Solveig noticed in that fifteen-second span of the stranger being awake.

The first: he said his name wrong. *Sol-vig,* not *Sol-vay.*

The second: he had a scar more impressive than the one on his arm. It stretched from his left temple, splitting through his eye and beneath his nose, bisecting his lips, his chin, and curving across his jaw and neck. One eye was milky and opaque, blinded by whatever gave him the scar.

The other was sapphire blue.

EPILOGUE

Sparrow Largos stared at a spot on the wall just past Admiral Jonyth Commodore's head, trying – failing – not to flinch.

"What in Lady Lightbringer's name do you mean you *let them get away?!*" Jonyth shouted. He slammed his fist against the wall, causing the entire cabin aboard the *Mary Jolyne* to shake.

Row had no excuse. He said as much.

Jonyth tore his hands through his hair, spitting a whole slew of curses loud enough to wake the dead. "You incompetent son of a sarding wench! You had *one job! One!* And you let Solveig get away!"

He turned slowly. Row took a step back, legs feeling like cooked noodles. He'd made a mistake, sure, but... But Jonyth hadn't been there. And Row was just one man, barely even an officer. He wouldn't stand up against *Nox Solveig!* Not without Sinth, which he *didn't have.*

Jonyth spoke slowly, his voice void of any emotion, and Row knew he was well and truly sarded. "Your brother is a Dreamchaser Pirate, is he not? Did you perhaps spare Solveig because of your brother?"

Fynch!

If Row had a kase for every time Fynch utterly ruined his life, he'd be the richest man in Syrenis.

"No!" Row blurted. "Fynch wasn't even on the ship. I swear, Admiral, I –"

He was on the ground before he even realized what had happened, before the pain in his cheek even registered. Jonyth shook his fist out, unamused.

He was right. Row was a coward. He'd boarded that ship and goaded Solveig, fought dirty, but...in the end, he'd retreated like the pathetic coward he was. Maybe it was a good thing Fynch hadn't been there to see him.

He spat out a glob of blood; his teeth must have bitten into his cheek. He'd feel that pain later, surely, once the pain from getting punched in the sarding face went away.

"Is that necessary?" That came from Prince Anwir Helios, who sat perched on the desk like some sort of exotic cat. Not a single indigo curl was out of place, and his black eyes shone wickedly.

Row gritted his teeth together. The only thing keeping him from attacking Anwir Helios was the fact that Jonyth Commodore would, without hesitation, kill him for committing treason.

Anwir was the epitome of everything Row hated: rich, gluttonous, born with a silver spoon in his pretty mouth. Not Row. Never Row. The Largos family would never amount to anything, and Anwir held the world in his hand only because his parents were at the top of the food chain.

Luck had never been on Row's side.

"Watch it, Highness," snapped Jonyth. "You're starting to sound like a pirate sympathizer."

Anwir's face scrunched up. He gnawed on his inner cheek but said nothing.

Row slowly pushed himself to his feet. "I'll prove it," he said. "Let me go after them again. I'll prove my brother means nothing to me. He killed my mother. I hate him."

"I say do it," mused Anwir. "Besides, you just killed the Unnamed God. Shouldn't we head back to Aramore to tell my father the news?"

Jonyth's jaw twitched. "Fine," he relented. "Sparrow Largos, you will get *one* more chance. Either bring me back Solveig's head, or you will be stripped of your duties and sent right back to the slums you came from. You can join Captain Zimmer's crew for this mission."

Row flinched, not because of Jonyth's cold tone but because he knew the Admiral meant it. It wasn't the slums that bothered him, either. He'd spent most of his life there, anyway. It was facing his siblings for the first time in years. Starling, Robin, Wren, Dove...

Would they welcome him back?

No. He couldn't take any risks.

He raised his hand in a stiff salute. "Yes, Admiral. I won't disappoint you."

"You better not," growled Jonyth. "Because I know you have siblings back in Veridonia. It would be a shame, would it not, if something were to happen to them because of your incompetence?"

Row swallowed hard. It felt like a lie when he spoke. "I'll bring back Solveig's head. I swear it on my mother's name."

Jonyth pointed to the door. "Good. Now, go. Time isn't on your side."

As he left, Row glanced over his shoulder.

Anwir Helios glared at him, his scowl colder than the bottom of the ocean.

Deep, deep, deep, leagues beneath a sea that simply should not exist, the faint trail of blood filled *her* senses.

At once, the waters began to churn, a tempest brewing at the bottom of the world.

Her eye snapped open.

She found him.

The last one alive.

The last of her kin.

Slowly, slowly, slowly, she unfurled, limbs stretching out after decades of being curled up.

All she had to do now was track him down and kill him.

And then everything would set itself right again.

To be continued...

ACKNOWLEDGEMENT

GODS ABOVE I'VE FINISHED another one.

There was a point in my life where I never expected to write anything ever again, yet here I am, five (!!!) books under my belt. That's insane.

Thank you to my mum, of course. You've always been my biggest cheerleader. Am I surprised you actually read the first book? Perchance... But thank you for reading my books, for telling me your theories, for, well, just for being the best mama ever.

Thank you to my dad, too, even though you still haven't read any of my books. You never hesitate to be my own personal Google and you've always encouraged my storytelling.

Thank you to my sisters, Penny and Fiona. Piss Boy and Gorbit Supremacy.

Thank you to my cats, Lysandra and Mephisolou, who did nothing to help, but you are cute so who cares? Lysandra is laying on my lap as I write this.

Thank you again to Aster for the COVER. Did I cry when I saw it? Yes of course. Who wouldn't? It's absolutely beautiful.

Thank you to my author friends over on Instagram and Threads! You've really helped me come out of my shell over the years. I love you all so much.

Dani and Sal — I miss you both every day. I love you.

To everyone else who I am definitely forgetting but will randomly remember three months after this is published: THANK YOU. I love you. I haven't forgotten about you. Hugs and kisses.

To the librarians, the booksellers, the readers who thought, "hey, pirates sound cool!" and picked these books up, THANK YOU!!!!!!! Nothing I do would be possible without any of you.

And to the little seven-year-old Emma who was told over and over again to just give up, to find a more realistic dream job, to stop reading and writing so much — this is for you, kiddo. I hope I've made you proud.

The search for the lost moon continues in

THE DREAM CHASERS

About the Author

Emma T. Shannon has been writing since before knowing how to actually write. On the rare occasions where they are not writing, Emma can be found hunched over a drawing, circling the same shelf at the local bookstore, obsessing over 2D men, and singing loud enough to annoy the neighbors.

Emma lives in the dreary PNW with their tiny house tigers Lysandra and Mephisolou, their tiny house dragon Andarna, two cursed dolls, and more tarot cards than they know what to do with.

Instagram @goth.witch.writes

Threads @artem.mxrtis

ko-fi.com/artemmxrtis